Frozen Assets

ANITA R. MILLER

This is a work of fiction. Names, characters, places, brands, media and incidents are either the product of the author's imagination or are used fictitiously. Any resemblance to factual persons, living or dead, business establishments, events or locales is entirely coincidental.

Copyright © 2018 Anita R. Miller
All rights reserved.
Ebook - ASIN: B07DGM5M2F
ISBN-13: 9781983055157

DEDICATION

Dedicated to my good friend Dawn Holbrook, who said to me, "I see a frozen man, staked to the floor in a cabin." That's all I had to go on. The rest is history.

Prologue
Rand Dubois, Investigator

Some say Montana is a God-forsaken country. Others believe it is where heaven meets hell. Certainly, the wide expansive plains give way to calling this state The Big Sky Country. But as one travels the state to the northwest, across the expansive walls of the Rocky Mountains, the majestic beauty will mesmerize and astound. As you look to the chiseled peaks of Glacier Park, the sight can steal one's breath with the beautiful sculpted rock cliffs and limpid pools. However, visitor and residents alike must take warning as winter may appear at any given moment and the sting of the devil's hand may freeze one's last breath. This is truly the land of higher beings playing tug-of-war with those of us who forget who is in control. It's not a place for the hoity toity or faint of heart.

For some of us, Montana is an addiction. To move away would be to live a long and empty life. I'm among one of the addicted. I love and respect this country, but I hate what it can do to the innocent. I lost my lovely wife, Caroline, in a simple car accident. I say simple because her car merely slid off an icy road into a deep snowbank, blocking her ability to open her door. She froze to death. I only hope it was quick. The loss of my wife has been unbearable, yet the thought of leaving is just as insufferable.

Despite my tragic loss, I've chosen to remain a public servant protecting and serving this place I call home. That was precisely what brought me to the house on Bull Lake, surrounded by the relentless cold and snow. I stood before the renowned philanthropist, and very dead, Ira Goodman. He was frozen solid.

Chapter 1 – Rand Dubois

My breath froze with each exhalation, and hung in mid-air like miniature clouds. Someone, possibly the killer, had turned the thermostat off leaving the temperature inside Ira Goodman's living room the same as the great outdoors. An arctic blast had unexpectedly dipped down from Canada during the night, plunging temperatures into the minus twenties and dumping two feet of snow across Northern Montana.

While I waited to speak to the medical examiner, I stood at the dead man's feet observing the crime scene. Ira Goodman appeared to be in his early fifties, six three or four, with advanced male pattern baldness. He was stark naked, no clothing within visual range. Frost crystals covered the white down body hairs and sparkled in the glow of the examiner's lighting. The eyelids were partially opened, and the dead eyes stared at nothing. His penis was limp, yet frozen between his legs.

The body was stretched in the middle of a pentagram, splayed like Leonardo da Vinci's Vitruvian Man, with a fireplace poker protruding from his chest. His hands and feet were tied and nailed to the floor like Jesus to the cross. The binds were tight, and cut off circulation, leaving his toes bunched together like a cluster of purple grapes.

I bent down to examine the body closer. The man's wrists and ankles had been wrapped in electrical cords and affixed to the floor with ten penny nails. The pentagram encircling his body was made up of a powdery substance, gray in color. I wet the tip of my finger and went in for a sample, then back up for a tongue test. Salty. And a hint of smoky ash from the cold fireplace ten feet from Ira Goodman's head.

I did a quick visual inspection of the living room, and I pondered the fact that everything seemed in its place. This didn't appear to be a burglary. Nothing was obviously out of order except for several table lamps that were overturned, their cords unattached. I assumed they were the cords that bound Goodman's arms and legs. There were no open closets or drawers.

The protruding rod from the body cavity was an ornate brass-handled fireplace poker that had missed the sternum. But I was reasonably sure, noting the angle of the rod, the heart wasn't as lucky.

I shifted my weight to the other knee to get a better look. I observed no noticeable scars on his body, just normal freckled areas from too much sun, and brown spots dotted his hands and face. There was a circular bruised area on the palm of his right hand, but no blood. I pondered that a moment, but I had no answer for what caused this.

"Rand Dubois! I am so glad to see you."

"And you as well, Sheriff Gregory Bishop." I replied, as I struggled to my feet. We hugged as if we were brothers. When you have walked the trail of death together as we have, we can certainly call ourselves brothers.

"Hey, Rocco. Come here," Bishop said, flagging over a man who was paying more attention to the svelte medical examiner's breasts than he was the information she was relaying. Cindy Colter was new to the Lincoln County staff of employees. She was easy on the eyes. No man could resist a second glance, and Rocco was clearly no exception. She snapped her fingers in front of his eyes and snorted, "Eyes up here, Rocco. You're being summoned," she said, pointing in our direction.

Rocco turned and made an annoyed production of walking toward us. He was wearing a long black coat over a power suit. He reluctantly gave a half-hearted handshake. His long, dark hair was pulled back in a slick ponytail that flopped to the side as he tipped his head and narrowed his eyes. He was the only one not dressed for the severe cold that still engulfed the house. He had several spiked diamond studs in the cartilage of his right ear that glinted blinding colors under the halogen lights. He smelled of pipe smoke and Armani cologne, a nauseating combination.

"I want to introduce you to a good friend of mine. I hired him to investigate this murder. Rocco Basham, this is Rand Dubois," Bishop said, as he placed a supportive hand on my shoulder. "Dubois used to work as a muckymuck Canadian Mounty but now's got his own investigation firm, works mostly for the state. We've sure had our share of cases together."

"Hmm, am I supposed to be impressed?" Rocco asked, looking skeptical.

"He's got credentials the length of my arm," said Bishop, bobbing his head. "Can't get a better man for the job."

"Bishop has employed me to investigate this murder because of my depth of experience in solving these—well, shall we say—bizarre cases. These investigations are my specialty," I explained.

"Huh, that so," said Rocco. "Make the investigation quick so I don't have to listen to tax payers bitch about sleazy PIs pissing away their money." With a sneer and a final flip of his ponytail, he shot a leering look towards the medical examiner and swaggered out the front door.

"Charming. Who is he?" I asked.

"The new D.A.," Bishop answered between clenched teeth. "He thinks he needs to be involved with every friggin' thing. Can't leave us alone to do our jobs—just wish he'd do his."

"But hey, how were the roads from Kalispell?" asked Bishop, changing the subject. Did you come through Thompson Falls?"

"Nah, I came through Libby," I answered. Libby is a slightly longer trip to Angel Island from Kalispell with scores of road challenges. Thus, the quizzical look from Bishop.

"They get up earlier to plow the roads," I reassured, and that brought a smile to his lips. He believes his sleepy little town is the "Triple A" of communities. It's certainly not a bad little town, but I couldn't bring myself to travel the roads past Thompson Falls since that is the stretch of highway that took away my beloved wife.

"What a shame this is," Bishop clucked, as he turned his attention toward the body. "Hard to believe something like this can happen in such a fine house."

I followed his eyes as he scoped the enormous floor-to-ceiling rock fireplace. You could host a dinner party within its confines, I admired. "Death doesn't know the difference between light and dark, let alone unsightliness and beauty, Bishop. It will come to visit you wherever you are. It only seems to know the price of lunch."

"Yeah, take-out orders," he snickered.

Bishop gave a low whistle. "Look at this house, gotta be at least four stories high." We took a few steps back to take in the whole of the open floor to ceiling foyer, dodging the homicide crew scurrying by talking of fingerprints, pupil dilation, morbidity and the likes—just doing their jobs.

"Indeed," I said.

A uniformed deputy tugged on my arm. "Ah, sir, that guy says he's with you?" He pointed at the floor where a long-legged, stick of a man laid. His long, bright-red hair spread on the floor like an immense fan.

"Good God," I murmured. To my horror, the young man was lying beside the deceased in mirror image of the body, holding Goodman's hand. At least he had his rubber gloves on.

"What's he doing?" mumbled Bishop.

"He's, ah . . . sensitive."

"Ah yeah. So is Deputy Mallory's son. Perhaps we should introduce him to—"

"Not sensitive in that way!"

"Oh, sorry, I didn't mean to imply—," Bishop's voice trailed.

Embarrassed but feeling the need to explain, I said, "He is sensitive to life energy, as he calls it." Bishop shot me a quizzical look.

"Alan, please be careful," I began, but before I could say more, the lad rolled to his knees, straddled over the body—head to head, face to face. He pressed his face then his ear to within inches of the deceased's lips.

"He's your assistant then?" quizzed Bishop as he made his way over to him. Alan pulled himself up to his full height, towering over Bishop, and began shaking his hand.

Red-faced, I began the introductions. "Sheriff," I emphasized for Alan's benefit, "Gregory Bishop, I'd like you to meet my son, Alan Dubois."

"Pleasure to meet you," greeted Bishop, while Alan vigorously pumped his hand. I nudged him to the side before the lad could break off the poor man's arm.

"Alan, get some pictures of the body while the Sheriff and I talk, eh?" The boy obviously needed something to do.

"Sure, Dad," he replied.

"So, he's your son? Doesn't look a bit like you," offered Bishop. looking a bit confused.

"My adopted son. He's the only child of my late wife. I adopted him when he was three, that was twenty-two years ago," I reflected.

"Anxious one, he is," commented Bishop.

"Yes, he is. He's young and unsure of where life is taking him. Remember those days. Bishop?"

"All too well," he nodded in agreement.

"He's a talented photographer and artist. Says that maybe he'd like to be a detective like me. I feel he's just not cut out for this business, eh? He seems a little too, I don't know, fragile. So, I thought I'd introduce him to my world—you know, maybe change his mind—talk him into to being a doctor, or an accountant. Something less…"

"Exciting?" Bishop winked.

"The word that comes to my mind is gruesome. He's always been a bright spark in my life and I don't want a job like this to change him," I said to Bishop, as he nodded. The boy has always been excitable and a bit careless. He reminds me of a puppy I once had—called him Sparky. He was most always happy and looking forward to the next moment with wagging tail clearing off any surface in its wake. The dog, too, was innocent and unaware of his surroundings, bounding through life, crushing every flower in its path.

"Dad, look at this!" Alan wiggled as if he'd just won the lottery. He held a drawing tablet and wagged a pencil between his fingers. I peeked over his shoulder at his creation. Although the sketch was quite good, it revealed a roaring fire with demons poised to devour our Mr. Goodman.

I laid a hand on the lad's shoulder to explain, "First, the deceased is frozen solid, not engulfed in flames. Second, I doubt demons wear Nikes. Alan, this is not what I see. We need to see reality. We need facts, not ghostly images from beyond. May I suggest you use the CAMERA!" Somewhat wounded, he reluctantly pulled his Nikon from his bag and began to shoot.

"I gotta say, this murder is God damn disturbing," commented Bishop. "Remember the Mary Bell murder about fifteen years ago, remember that one, Dubois? I still have nightmares. Her body was found in the same position as Goodman's, and stabbed just like this poor bastard, except she wasn't frozen."

"If I remember right, hadn't Bell joined some cult

group?" I questioned as I tried to recall the specifics of that case. "What was the name of that—Chosen something."

"Yeah, yeah. I'll never forget that shit piece of work," sniffed Bishop, hiking up his pants. "Called themselves the Chosen Trojan Children, the CTC, mainly a white supremacy group. Found out later they were also dabbling in the occult, saying they were the sons and daughters of Satan, or some damn thing. I broke up those crazy bastards' little group after the Mary Bell murder, but it could be some knuckleheads trying to roust it up again."

Pulling out a mini notebook, I asked, "What do we know so far, eh? Is there a Mrs. Goodman? Is she here?"

"Na, she's in Greece soaking up the sun. Doesn't like Montana winters. I'm with her on that," said Bishop and shivered. "She's on her way back."

"Hmm, good alibi," I retorted, skeptically. It's been my experience that spouses are usually the first ones to suspect. Being out of the country seems too convenient and usually includes an accomplice.

"How about kids? Do they have kids?" I asked.

"Yeah, three boys. We're still trying to track them down. Although, one of my deputies says a neighbor told him that she overheard an argument. It seems Goodman and his youngest son, Seth, got into some brouhaha. The boy took off, and no one's seen him since," reported Bishop.

"When was that?" I questioned.

"Couple nights ago."

I jotted down the neighbor's name and added it to my list of other notes. Looking up from my pad, I said.

"Guess I'll look around, have Alan take some more pictures of the house, some of the rooms—if you don't mind, eh?" I observed Alan wiggling a finger deep into his ear. Where were his manners?

"Not at all, make yourself at home," he invited, and grinned sheepishly. "Well, you know what I mean. Wish it was mine." He reached out to shake my hand but was suddenly distracted.

"Oh, Cripes!" Bishop groaned.

"What, what's wrong?" I asked

"No, not cripes, I mean Carol Cripes, the reporter. Has she been standing behind us the whole time we've been talking?"

I shrugged.

"She's our Loco News Hag."

"Sheriff!" called Ms. Cripes. "Do you think this murder is related to all the local animal disappearances and bizarre mutilations?"

Bishop flagged over a deputy. "Go after her and don't let her print anything stupid. We've got to keep this thing under wraps if we can. We can't have this community thinking there are some crazies out there and panicking the masses. Next thing you know, she'll be telling people there's a 10 p.m. curfew or some dumb thing. Now go get her!"

The deputy ran after her. Ms. Cripes waved a feathery pen to Bishop and slid on out the door.

"Mutilations, eh?" I asked Bishop.

"Oh, damn that woman," said Bishop, clenching his fists. "Yeah, people have been finding their pets and other animals torn to bits. The carcasses have been found in one general area, a campsite just outside of town.

We've had a watch on it. The findings were reported in the paper. So now the whole damn community is calling me and asking how I'm going to protect their Fluffy, Max or Sweet Pea. But now I got a goddamn murder to solve."

"Hey, Bishop," hollered a man clicking a tape measure. "Legs and arms don't fit. How are we supposed to get this seven foot, four-hundred-pound frozen corpse through that 32 x 80-inch door?"

Bishop and I turned to look at the body, frozen arms and legs spread in each direction. Bishop scratched his head and began to move away, shouting orders and mumbling under his breath—something about doing despicable things to Carol Cripes's tongue and offering it to the CTC.

"Dad, what was that about mutilations?"

"Nothing, son, just some goofy lady, eh? Listen, we need to discuss a few things. First, this is business here. You are my assistant so don't call me 'Dad.' You will address me as 'Sir,' eh?"

"Cool, just like real detectives, eh?" Alan nodded and winked.

I gave him a warning look, to which he replied, "Yeah, okay, Dad—Sir."

"Ah, yeah. Also, please don't touch the body. Do your best to not move, touch, or so much as breathe on anything that could be evidence. We've talked about this. And furthermore, keep your fingers out of your ears."

After Bishop moved on to conduct his public relations duties, Alan and I ducked out. I needed to think, and Alan needed to keep busy with the photos.

We climbed the stairs and wandered from room-to-room, our shoes lightly crunching on frozen carpets. Bedrooms were immaculate if not sterile, lacking personal effects. There was a large bath and sauna room. Water was frozen in the toilet.

I continued to look for rooms that may have been ransacked. I was looking for drawers that were emptied, open safes, signs of disrespect, but nothing seemed out of order. Instead, I found large, beautiful rooms containing sculpted woodwork, woodsy paintings, and many glass prisms. Nothing broken or disturbed. The basement contained a theater room filled with tapes and DVDs.

Returning to the second floor, I entered a large room, perhaps used as an entertainment and game room. It contained a wet bar with fully stocked shelves of alcohol for any libation preference. A pool table, a couple of small card tables and a plasma TV seemed to provide enough entertainment possibilities to keep the inhabitants engrossed throughout the long Montana winters. Halogen-lit display shelves lined the other wall and exhibited thousands of small glass figurines. They sparkled like diamonds, reflecting prisms in the dark corners of the room.

My brain reeled with questions claiming no answers. What would drive someone to murder in this fashion? Was it merely a random attack by the CTC? The last group trashed the cabin that Mary Bell was in. Nothing here seemed out of order. Were they interrupted before they could finish? Was Goodman involved with the CTC in some way? Was his wife having an affair and wanted this to look like a satanic act? Were

Goodman's boys involved with the CTC? That's not a stretch, rich kids looking for cheap thrills.

My mind zoned out, contemplating such speculations. I vaguely listened to voices coming from outside the house. Hammers banged and saws buzzed—the homicide team at work.

"Whoa dude!" said Alan, startling me out of my reverie—with camera poised, shooting pictures from the window.

Peering out the back of the house, I saw several men hanging on to Goodman's body as it dangled from the upper deck. They had taken the body out through a set of French doors off the dining room. From the back, the deck was a good story high but they couldn't get the hearse all the way over in that direction. The body swung, suspended from ropes tied to each limb, guided by a makeshift pulley, swinging from side to side. Goodman's stiff, naked body looked like a chandelier bare of candles attached to appendages. Men were lowering the body as gently as possible while others below wait with a blanketed platform.

The body began swinging back-and-forth. There was an audible SNAP, then shouts. People began to scatter like mice, running, jumping, and diving into snow banks.

"Oh shiiiiit!"

"Oh man!"

"Crap...Crap!"

The corpse began spinning cartwheels through the air. Spinning, spinning, spinning. It made a final landing with a flump in the freshly fallen snow.

The body lay face up with eyes wide-open, head

cocked to the side in an unnatural pose resembling a deformed snow angel.

"Oh man, that's just wrong," came another shout.

All the while Alan clicked off pictures.

"No more, son," I said, placing a hand on his shoulder. "Leave the man his dignity." From above, he snapped a final shot of stunned faces and gaping jaws.

I bowed my head and said a silent prayer for the deceased to have a safer passage to the next world—and another prayer for the men who now had the challenge of getting the splayed frozen corpse into the coroner's hearse, all 400 pounds of him.

Chapter 2 - Rand Dubois

Like witnessing a train wreck, unable to tear our eyes away from the scene, Alan and I stood watching men scratching their heads and scrambling about Goodman's naked body, which lay in a heap. I was thankful that no family members had seen the fall. I could only imagine how ghastly it would have been for them. I felt a pang of guilt and helplessness.

"This is awkward," said Alan, voicing my feelings. "Should I go help them?"

"No, they'll have it taken care of soon," I speculated, and we continued to watch.

There were several failed attempts to get the body into the hearse—the frozen statue, it's arms and legs stretched too far to maneuver properly. Four men were finally able to wrap the body in a blue tarp and load him into the back of a pick-up truck. The truck was parked on a slope at an odd angle, and before they could secure the body it slipped from the bed. Once again Goodman's body was on the move. The tarp fell away. As if a clown in a circus act, Goodman's body did several cartwheels, pirouetted on one heel, and then made its final bow with a face plant in the snow. Shouts came once again, some cursing and some laughing.

"Though the cartwheel was excellent, the pirouette was a little wobbly. I'll give him a 9.5 on that," quipped one man.

"And I'll give you a pink-slip if you don't zip it," crowed another.

The final act was to load him back into the truck bed. Once again, the blue tarp was wrapped around him, this time secured by bright red tie-downs that wrapped around legs and arms were anchored to a silver-rimmed spare tire. Packaged in this manner, the corpse resembled an ornamental star—albeit a fallen star. The task was complete.

"Dad, look over there, there's a boy watching. See?"

"Oh my," I groaned. "I'll go talk to him. Where is he?"

"Over by that outhouse or shed, or whatever it is. See him? He's wearing blue shorts and a red t-shirt."

"What, in this weather? He'll freeze." I craned my head around and scanned the area. "I don't see him, Alan. Did he leave?"

"He's right there!" Alan pointed to the shed. He raised his camera and clicked off a picture. He tabbed the arrow on his digital camera to display the photo, then handed the camera to me. "Here, see?"

I peered into the display screen, cupping my hands to filter out the light, but could only see the shed. "No, there's nobody there, Alan."

"Yeah, see?" Alan grabbed the camera. Peering at the camera screen, he looked confused. He looked to the window, then back to the camera.

"He probably got cold and went home. Kids are always curious."

"But I see—I was just—he's so..." Alan stammered and grew pale, looking once again out the window,

"Small."

I peered out the window again but saw nothing. "I'm sure he went home. It's much too cold. I bet he got an eye-full though."

Alan looked quite concerned, so I asked, "Do you want to look for him to be sure he's okay?"

He was out the door before I could say another word.

Focusing on task once again, I returned to the room with the glass figurines. At first glance, it looked like a mass of beautiful glass and prisms. But, as I drew closer and focused, I saw they were of thousands of carefully sculpted people. They all were basically the same size, yet each was as different and unique as two people can be. Some were of nude women, some were young with long, flowing hair, some old and delicately portrayed the lines of age. There were some with detailed faces, yet some were without heads at all. The few male figurines within the collection were slightly taller than the females, less defined, and all placed in the case backwards, or face to face with the women. Some were holding women in loving embraces, while others were wielding hatchets, knives or hammers over their heads. One was even holding the head of a woman.

I believe we all have reasons for our actions. At face value, these first glimpses may not seem logical, perhaps even disturbing. But one must look closer to see the true meaning. For example, I collect historic weapons: tomahawks, guns, and knives—that sort of thing, but my favorite is arrowheads. I choose to do so because I feel it brings me closer to my native roots. I am French Canadian and Indian. My father, God rest his soul, was an Indian Chief and my mum a beautiful French heiress. My Indian heritage surrounds the Pacific Northwest, and every time I purchase something new, I see the past and I feel a connection that gives me a certain peace, a knowing that the entire world is in its place, and it is my turn to lead my ancestry into the future. Also, to preserve the past, be it good or bad, learning to build a better world from both. But, if someone were to stumble upon my collection, what might they think? That I'm obsessed with war, destruction and death, given my history and career? I try to keep an open mind to one's possessions. Therefore, I refused to pass judgment on Goodman's collection.

Lost in speculation I was startled when Alan appeared by my side. I jumped.

"Oh, sorry, Dad," he said.

"No worries, eh. I was just theorizing about this collection. Did you find the boy?"

He shook his head.

"He probably went on home."

He shrugged.

"Are you all right, son?" I asked. Alan's face seemed paler than before.

He shrugged once more.

"Well, perhaps it wasn't a boy, maybe a dog or a strange reflection. It happens, especially if one is under stress," I tried to assure him. "You've had a very long day so far. This is your first case. This can't be easy for you."

He puffed out his cheeks and blew out slowly.

"How do you do this, Dad? How do you do this day after day?" he asked.

"I'm sorry, son, maybe I shouldn't have brought you with me."

"No, I'm glad you did. This is just one day for me and it's depressing. You have tracked killers most of your life. You live and breathe this stuff. Doesn't it turn you inside out? Don't you have nightmares?" he questioned.

"Yes, I've had my share of nightmares. But, what comes of it is bringing about the justice that is deserved for the dead. I do it so that I might bring peace to the families by letting them know that someone cares enough to dig for the truth," I tried to console. I put a reassuring hand on his shoulder. "And what has kept me sane all these years is coming home to your mother and you, the sunshine of my life."

"What makes you think you're sane, old man?" he teased, with grin.

"Touché," I answered.

"But, can't you see the darkness, feel the pain of death, smell the stench of evil? Don't the voices haunt you, Dad?" asked Alan.

"Wow, when you put it that way, my job is pretty depressing," I confessed. "I've learned not to fear these things. It's not the dead that can hurt me, it's the living that makes me weary. Listen, son, I know that you have a higher level of sensitivity than I do. That is just one of the things I truly admire about you. However, I must admit, it took a while for me to learn how to put those things in a safe place so that they didn't haunt me. Part of the trick is to face what you fear the most. Don't let it rule you. You must stand up to it. Then suddenly it doesn't seem so frightening and horrid." I looked at him to see if he understood what I was saying. His too-big t-shirt hung from the bottom of his parka. His long, red hair was disheveled and sported a tattered old ski hat, his baggy pant legs were piled around his ankles leaving only the very tips of his boots peeking through. Focused on me, his eyes held pained inquisition. He looked so much the little boy I raised, my vulnerable son.

"One day I realized that I was good at what I do," I continued. "I know how to get the answers people need. People need to know the "why" of things gone wrong. I answer the why. I learned how to keep those things in perspective. I can deal with the voices, and I can give them a peaceful silence."

He nodded.

He looked around and studied the figurines for a moment. "So, what do you make of these?" he wondered.

"That was the source of my reverie when you startled me. I'm not sure yet, the jury's still out. What do you make of them, Alan?"

He thought for a moment and sighed. "I think, if I had a dog, he would bite Goodman."

"What?" I asked, unsure if I had heard correctly. Sometimes I have a hard time following the boy's thought process. I hoped bringing him wasn't a mistake. I hoped he was going to be okay.

"Yeah," he said. "Dogs are sensitive. They can tell if someone's nice or not. I just read in Cosmopolitan that if you bring your dog on a date and your dog doesn't like your date, your date's probably not a very nice person."

"And?" I prompted.

"And so, if I had a dog and I brought him to visit

Goodman, I think he'd bite him—in the ass no doubt. Dad, I don't think Goodman was a very nice person."

"Huh," was all I could say to that. "And to think all that money I spent on school books went to waste. Who would have thought Cosmopolitan could be such a font of information? And since when did you start buying girl magazines?" I inquired.

"Oh, I read it while I was standing in line at the grocery store. It's the issue with Heidi Klum on the cover—wearing nothing but a scarf," he added, wiggling his eyebrows all googley-eyed. "Can we go get a hamburger? I'm starved."

I needn't have worried. The boy was going to be fine.

Chapter 3
Ira Goodman Murdered
Cult or Clan?

By: Carol Cripes, Staff Reporter

The body of philanthropist and property tycoon Ira Goodman was found, late Thursday afternoon, at his home on Angel Island at Bull-Lake, located west of Libby, Montana.

Cause of death is not yet disclosed. However, per county medical examiner, Cindy Colter, Goodman's nude body was found in the middle of a pentagram, with his hands and feet tied and nailed to the floor with a fireplace poker driven through his chest.

"It is one of the most disturbing and chilling murders since the Mary Bell murder of '82," stated Lincoln County Sheriff, Gregory Bishop.

Bell was the victim of a brutal murder after she allegedly joined a White Supremacist group known as the Chosen Trojan Children (CTC). The group was also known to dabble in the occult, touting to be sons and daughters of Satan.

"...I got rid of that no-good cult after the Mary Bell murder, but it could be some knuckleheads trying to roust it up again," claimed Sheriff Bishop.

Bishop pleaded no comment when asked if the

murder could be linked to the bizarre animal disappearances and mutilations that have been reported lately.

Sources say Seth Goodman, Ira's youngest son, has disappeared after several heated arguments with his father. It is believed that he is the last person to be seen with his father late Wednesday afternoon. He remains a person of interest in this case.

Sheriff Bishop has employed Rand Dubois, private investigator, to assist him in solving this murder. "...Dubois is an expert. If anyone can get to the bottom of this, he can...We need to get this matter under control as quickly as possible," said Bishop.

Dubois worked as a Canadian Mounty for twenty-five years before retiring from the force into his now private investigation business. He is well-known for his success in solving the Nightingale murders, the death of Mary Bell, and apprehending the Reeking Red Bandit, to name a few of the more publicized cases. Dubois first gained notoriety while assisting with the famous China Hat murders.

Ira Goodman was well-known for his compassionate support of the Friends of St. Paul, a group that builds and remodels homes for the disadvantaged. He was the Chairman of the Board for the Holly Foundation for Abused Children, sat on the board of directors for the local Community Action Team, was Chairman of the Board for the Kootenai Partners Federal Credit Union, and sponsored several youth programs as well as donated money for yearly scholarships, and was active with the Boy Scouts.

He is survived by his wife of twenty-five years,

Mora Goodman, and sons Ira Jr., from Sandpoint, Idaho, Jake, who attends college at Montana State University, in Missoula Montana, and Seth, a senior at Libby Senior High School.

Due to the unknown elements of this case, a ten-p.m. curfew has been set in force for all teens. People are warned to keep their doors locked and are asked to report any unusual or suspicious activity to Sheriff Bishop or Rand Dubois by calling the Sheriff's office at 406-293-5555. More information to follow further investigation.

Chapter 4 - Olivia Hope

I looked out the window, wondering if there was more snow to shovel before I ventured out to get the newspaper. There was. But, thankfully, I could still walk without employing a shovel. It was colder than a witch's tit in January, as my father used to say. I've always wondered what he knew about a witch's tit.

It had been a beautiful Indian summer; however, without warning, the storm of the century had changed all that with three feet of snow. Temperatures dropping to thirty degrees below zero and still falling. School had been cancelled since Thursday, not because of the snow, but because the cold had snapped power lines. Just as well they cancelled because attendance would be low, and I'd have to review the same lesson plans again as soon as I had a full house. Oh well, I had health papers to grade and exercise plans to develop for my high school PE and nutrition classes. I hoped by Monday the weather would improve and things would be back to normal. I was getting cabin fever, and the thought of another week of this miserable crap would drive me completely insane.

I contemplated getting dressed, but then decided I'd probably be just as warm with my long johns and flannel pajamas—I planned to go back to sleep after reading the newspaper anyway—and the thought of taking off perfectly warm clothes to put on cold ones didn't even register on the "reasonable" scale. And, it was six-thirty in the morning Who in their right mind would be out this time of morning on a Saturday to see me in my PJ's? I slipped into my parka, donned my boots and gloves, and opened the door to hell's freezer.

With my nose hairs freezing and nostrils sticking together as I inhaled, I walked the hundred feet or so down the hill to get the morning newspaper.

"Top of the morn' to you Olivia, darlin'," said a voice with an Irish accent out of the cold and dark.

Startled, I almost slipped and fell. Flailing arms to regain my balance, I gasped, "Hey, Frenchie." So, tell me, how does an Irishman get a name like Frenchie? "Out looking for the ice queen of snow birds? Or, did hell freeze your favorite cockroach?" I'd never seen a cockroach in Montana, but I knew they were prevalent in tropical areas, which is where I wanted to be.

"Aye, everyone knows cock-a-roaches could survive a nuclear bomb, and sub-zero temps simply make the whole world their refrigerator."

"Yeah, I should have guessed that, Frenchie."

"I'm lookin' for me rabbit gone missin'."

"Oh, sorry. Hope you find him," I said. Although a nice old man, he was always raising some exotic kind of insect, foul, fish, animal, or whatever. I looked in the newspaper bin and, alas, no paper.

"I hope he didn't hop away with my newspaper," I hollered.

"Nah, he only reads the Wall Street Journal," he quipped, with a tip of his hat, and pulled down his facemask with his thickly gloved hand and turned to trudge farther up the road.

Feeling less intelligent than a rabbit, I made my way back up the hill to build a nice warm fire in the fireplace and go back to sleep—to blissfully dream of white sandy beaches and warm, green tropical water.

I heard the distant sound of beating drums as I swam up from a deep sleep. The beautiful, sun-filled beach began to fade the closer I came to the surface.

"Olivia! Olivia!" shouted Mrs. Bixby as she rapped on my door.

Groggily stumbling to the door, I thought, what does that gossip monger want now? I swung it open to see my neighbor red-faced and eyes bulging with rage.

"That damn dog of yours is at it again," whined Mrs. Bixby. "Every time I turn around, that damn thing is stealing from me!"

Behind Mrs. Bixby a big black Labrador was jumping, wrestling and rolling with something blue in the deep snow. I swallowed back a laugh that leaped to my throat so as not to offend my angry neighbor. If only I could enjoy snow that much, I thought as I watched the dog frolicking like a child.

"You do something about that mutt of yours, or I'm going to turn you into the humane society and call the cops, too. I'll get you for stealing! They'll throw your ass in jail. What do you think about that?"

"Mrs. Bixby, how many times do I have to tell you, that is not my dog!" I said. But Mrs. Bixby wasn't having any of it. She continued to rage so I settled back to listen to the blah, blah, blah and watched the dog enjoying his romp.

For several weeks, the dog had been lying on my doorstep when I'd go out to get the morning paper. I'd shoo him away, but he'd be back the next day, or sooner. I had no idea where he came from, but he seemed to be a good dog, and he kept Mrs. Bixby's cat off my car. As the days went by, he became skinnier and skinnier so I began feeding him. After the first day of feeding, I returned home from work to find him nestled in a tattered old blue blanket lying on my porch. I didn't have the heart to shoo him away. I ran a lost-and-found ad in the classifieds, but got no replies. I thought I'd have to take him to the pound eventually. In the meantime, I got an evil pleasure out of watching him rile Mrs. Bixby. He seemed to have a fixation for all things blue, and that's what I began to call him.

Blue, finally tiring of his game, bounded out of the deep snow. He popped up behind Mrs. Bixby, goosed her butt with his nose sending a surprised "yip" from her, and then deposited a snow clumped object at my feet. Snow flew and covered both of us as he shook himself. Mrs. Bixby had silenced her verbal rant for only a moment as her blazing eyes rolled toward the dog. Looking quite pleased with himself, tail wagging, he nosed the object closer to her as if to say, "Here, you can have it back," and maybe expecting a treat from Mrs. Bixby for returning her possession.

Mrs. Bixby slowly bent to pick up the present. She held it up and shook off the snow. I recognized it as a throw rug that was a twin to one I found on my porch earlier in the week. To my horror, Mrs. Bixby raised the frozen mass and smacked the dog hard on the nose, gaining a return "yip" from the dog. Shocked, my hand flew to cover my mouth.

And then I heard a low, angry growl breaking the

stunned silence. I feared the dog was posturing to bite, but then realized the noise was coming from Mrs. Bixby! Her face was even redder than before, and I saw a frightful fury in her eyes. Then I feared Mrs. Bixby might bite. I stepped between the woman and the dog. The dog shyly peeked up at us from around my legs.

I was steamed and could not hold back my fury. "Don't you ever touch that dog again. If you so much as try to pet him, I will take that broom you love to swing and maybe I'll bop you on the nose with it. Do you understand me, Mrs. BIXBY?"

"Are you threatening me?" Mrs. Bixby's voice was high and shrill. "That's it! I'm calling the cops. And I'm telling them that you and your dog are thieves!"

"You do that, Mrs. Bixby." I reached inside the door and pulled out the twin to the rug Mrs. Bixby held, and threw it to her. "Be sure to tell them I took that one, too!" I opened the door wider and invited the dog in, then slammed the door in Mrs. Bixby's face—he deserved a great, big treat.

Inside, satisfied with his treat and affectionate pats, the dog found the warm fireplace and laid down. Steam soon began to roll off his fur from the melting snow and puffed like a locomotive in unison with his snores.

I fixed a pot of coffee and sat at the kitchen table with my thick winter robe bunched around me, grinding my pink, fluffy slippers together in rhythm to my jaws as I munched on granola. I held my cup of coffee in both, hands trying to thaw my cold fingers. I was still stewing over what had just happened. How dare Mrs. Bixby hit that dog! What did he ever do to her? Except, well, steal her rugs. And why in the hell would she have those ugly things where he could get to them in the first place?

There was another knock at the door. What the hell does she want now, I thought.

"Haven't we had enough for one day?" I hollered, as I pulled open the door.

"Nice to see you, too!" said Idaho, pulling off her coat and throwing it over the back of a kitchen chair. "You look like crap."

I tucked my long blonde, bed-head hair behind my ears and glared at Idaho. "I thought we were friends," I complained, and went to pour a cup of coffee for her.

"Hey, if your best friend can't be honest with you, then who can? Oh, by the way, here's your paper." Idaho threw a newspaper on the table. "Since when do you have a dog?"

"It's not my dog..." I started to say. Seeing the front-page headlines, I froze in mid-sentence. I barely noticed when Idaho took the cup out of my hand. I slowly picked up the paper and began to read. I only got through the first couple of sentences before the shock set in. The room began to swim. I tried to focus but I could only make out snippets: "Ira Goodman . . . murdered . . . body . . . Goodman . . . found . . . Cause of death . . . Thursday afternoon . . . Angel Island . . . Lake. . . death." Every word for death began to pop into my head like rain on a roof. He's dead, dead, dead, dead. . . he bought the farm, kicked the bucket, he's dead, as in gone, departed, deceased, non-existent, caput . . . This has got to be a joke, I thought.

I stood in shock. This can't be happening, I kept telling myself. Bile rose to my throat, making me want to lose what breakfast I had eaten. It felt like ice surged through my veins. The claws of fear began to sink deep into my heart. I had to get a grip. I could feel Idaho staring at me. What could I say to my friends? Goodman dead. Be strong, be cool, take control, make a plan.

Who was I kidding. This was entirely my fault. I was the one who handed Goodman all my friends' money. It was my idea to go see him at the lake house, and I was the one who nailed him to the floor.

Chapter 5 - Olivia Hope

I forced myself to breathe calmly. I desperately needed to center myself. I needed to change my perspective on this ugly matter of murder. I changed it, but only succeeded to replace fear with anger. I slapped the newspaper on the table and growled, "That son-of-a-bitch."

"Wow! Not the reaction I was expecting," claimed Idaho. "I thought by your surly mood you'd already heard the news—I'm guessing not."

I began to pace the floor. "That son-of-a-bitch did it to us again."

"What do you mean? The man is dead, in case you didn't catch that part."

"Oh, I got it, and that's what I mean. He screws us out of our money and now he's dead—that slimy bastard." Be strong, be cool, take control, make a plan—the thought was becoming a mantra.

"You make it sound like he died just to spite us!" Idaho followed me to the couch by the fireplace and slumped down.

"Maybe he did," I grumbled.

"No, he'd give us lead boots and a free trip off the Swinging Bridge directly to the bottom of the Kootenai River before he'd do something like that," said Idaho.

"Yeah, and then erase our identities as if we'd never existed, like the nobodies he thought we were," I pouted.

I grabbed a pillow and hugged it tightly to my chest as I plopped down beside her. I stared into the fire. "Damn that man. We gave him our money to invest and he loses every red cent of it. What were we supposed to do?"

"Ah, well, killing him may have been a little over the top," Idaho pointed out. She flicked her shoulder length, auburn hair back with a shaky hand. She cleared her throat, "Olivia what are we going to do?"

I wished there was an answer I could've pulled out of my ass. "I don't know just yet. I'm letting it sink in," I said, as I took a deep breath, "Be strong, be cool, take control, make a plan." The mantra had taken to voice and Idaho looked at me as if I was off my rocker. I shrugged.

Several years before, five of us single or divorced women discovered—during one of our men-bashing discussions—that each of us had a little nest egg we had secretly stashed away during our failing relationships. Consciously or subconsciously, each of us determined we might one day need a safety net. I observed that living in our very different worlds we had all come to the same conclusion—stash cash. I figured perhaps, it was an innate notion that was born out of survival.

At the time, I had invested some of my stash in an IRA and dabbled in the stock market with the rest. Since I had blazed the trail with some success the others wanted to invest their stash, too. Oh yeah, I was all about helping women get ahead in a man's world, so the idea of helping these women was a no-brainer for me. That was the beginning of the Women's Investment Club Association (WICA)—like wiccans. We thought it fitting since each of us had been called a witch at some point by our past significant others.

We played around with stocks and bonds, which was okay for a while. Gained and lost some during the housing dip, but soon the markets had gone flat. Despite that, our nest eggs had come a long way from their fledgling little nests. Knowing we could do even better in another arena, it had been my bright idea to take our investments to the next level.

Ira Goodman was always looking for investors to help fund short-term, high-interest loans, unconventional loans that were usually not funded by financial institutions. He found people with money, who were looking to invest, and loan it out to property development groups or perhaps someone who was looking to start a business. Usually these loans turned over relatively quickly. We made a good chunk on several of those loans. We earned as much as thirteen to fifteen percent interest, so the more we invested, the more we earned. Because of the previous loan successes, I had talked the group into investing a healthy portion— several millions between us. We were helping to implement a development plan to renovate downtown Libby. It promised to build up existing business, bring in new industry and business, increase tourist trade, and generate jobs for the locals, all directed by Goodman. We saw the blueprints, we saw the plan, and we saw a wonderful future. Not only for the community, but for our pocketbooks, too. Then we saw Goodman take our money and run.

A few days after signing the papers, I ran into a friend who worked for the city. I was thrilled about the city project and bubbled with excitement as we chatted.

But confusion furrowed my friend's brow. Cringing, I had to ask, "Why the funny face?"

"Are you sure it was for the city project?" my friend asked.

My stomach dropped. "Yeah, you know, new restaurants, parks, swimming pool, shopping center, complete with the new civic center," I suddenly realized I was practically shouting. Sure that my voice was beginning to rise in panic, I added, "We've invested about a million to see it complete!"

"Oh, honey, if that's the case, you better get your money back. We're not planning to start on the project for another couple of years or so." She must have seen the panic in my eyes, because she gently patted my hand and said—as if to console me, "Don't worry, I'm sure Goodman will clarify it for you. He knows all about the project. In fact, he's the project manager if we should ever start it. I think you must have misunderstood him, and your investment has gone to another one of his many projects. He's a very clever man you know."

I tried to contact Goodman but message after message revealed that he was "unavailable." I knew nothing of what was happening with our money.

I replayed the scene from several nights before in my mind. I had called a special WICA meeting. When I tried to reach Goodman on the telephone to come join us, I was told once again, "unavailable," that he was out of town. And that's when I suggested to see if he was at his lake house.

"Road trip!" hollered Pamela, and off we went in her Suburban to Angel Island on Bull Lake.

We were in luck. Goodman was there. He didn't

want to talk and kept his girth against the door. As he started to shut the door on us for a final time, Lily dropped her purse, flashing a mountainous cleavage as she bent to pick it up. I saw Goodman's eyes widen. I shouldered the door, and we were in.

We followed him to his living room. The room was largely lit by a fire burning in an oversized fireplace. It was toasty warm, certainly more inviting than Goodman's attitude.

"Goodman, I talked to the city. They say they aren't starting the project for another two years. What's happening with our money?" I asked as civilly as possible.

He said nothing.

I tried again. "Hey, come on. We've tried to contact you, but you're never in. Just tell us, tell us—please tell us you invested our money in another project."

Still he gave no answer. He seemed to be pretending that we weren't even there, as if we were invisible. I grabbed his arm, and felt a lot like Glen Close in the movie Fatal Attraction as I growled, "We will not be ignored."

He swung toward me, almost knocking me down as he spat, "Don't touch me, you piece of trailer trash." Then he shrugged and added, "You think you lost a lot of money? Fuck you, I lost some, too. It's just money."

I heard gasps from the women behind me. Shocked by his revelation, I asked hesitantly, "Wha-what are you talking about? What losses?"

He couldn't even look me in the eye, "The money was signed over to a construction company. They filed bankruptcy shortly after the deal was signed. No one is getting their money. Everything is frozen." Then he yawned. For Christ sake, he yawned! "Oh well, so you lost a few dollars." He picked up a newspaper and began silently reading.

It wasn't the way he scorned me or the apathetic look in his eye. It was more his I-don't-give-a-shit attitude, and complete lack of remorse that I might have expected. Even if he lost more than us, he should have been sympathetic, not hostile! Suddenly, I realized he was lying—duh, right? That's when my blood really began to boil.

I rolled this over in my mind. I felt incredibly responsible for having lost all our money, and now we were probably facing murder charges because of my getting them involved. Staring into the fire I asked, a little dispirited, "Oh God, Idaho, if we had this to do over again, what would we change about this situation? Would we confront him like we did?"

"Hell, yes!" Idaho blurted. "I am not about to let a scumbag like that walk away with my money. I've been through too much to see my money disappear into a black hole without any explanation!"

Idaho had been in a bad relationship with a man her father was expecting her to marry. He was a farmer, and he figured farmers made good money. It was never about what was right for Idaho. For her father, it was always about the money. She told me he probably would have pimped her out if there had been more men in town instead of women. She added that thankfully, considering his intentions, he felt strongly against homosexuality. One day she won a sizable amount of money in the lottery. She never told her father about it. She just packed her bags and moved to Libby. She didn't want to cast suspicion on her sizeable winnings in the event her father came looking for her. Therefore, she took a job with the city—digging graves.

Idaho was finished with her rant. "What an arrogant son-of-a-bitch. He called us 'silly little women'. And then tells us," Idaho lowered her voice a few notches to mimic Goodman's drawl and said, 'Shut up and take your lumps like a man, your aaassets are frozen. Deeeeal with it!'"

Her voice depicted a perfect performance of Goodman's deep timbre, and it struck me funny. I began to giggle and added, "And then Pamela says, 'I'll show you frozen assets,' and pulls out a gun!"

That made both of us begin to howl with laugher and snorts.

Pamela had reached behind her back to pull out a gun she had tucked in the waistband of her pants. It slipped from her right hand but she caught it with her left before it hit the floor—from between her legs—then pulled it up right between Goodman's eyes. It was a bumbled act, but I thought it was a slick move.

Idaho, hiccupping to get her breath said, "Then—then Goodman starts screaming like a little school girl. 'Oh, oh, did you just pull a gun out of your aaass?" Drawing out the word ass, she said it again, this time in the high-pitched voice Goodman used, "Your aaass?"

He-haw laughter engulfed the both of us again. I gulped for air and held my ribs. I finally squeaked out, "I can't believe he couldn't tell it was a squirt gun!" That started another round of laughter.

Pamela told us that she grabbed a squirt gun from one of the kids who had used it on her. She didn't give it back. Instead, she used it to keep her kids in line. Her two young boys are aggressive and competitive, always wrestling and scrimmaging, a volatile combination, so it sometimes calls for "interactive redirection" as she calls it.

Panting and wiping her eyes, Idaho tried to speak and sputtered in between gulps of air, "Plastic, plas—tic squirt gun. Her son's—and, and she, and she pulled it out of her aaass." And we began the regalia of laughter again. Stress can make one act in seemingly inappropriate ways, like a grieved one laughing at a funeral while trying to present the eulogy. It is a valuable human way to relieve tension. I guess it worked for us as I felt the tension in my shoulders release. But, in my mind, I was replaying what happened next at the lake house.

I could no longer stand the drivel spewing from Goodman's mouth. I did the only thing I could think of in the moment to invoke humiliation and maybe shut him up. While Pamela trained the gun on him, I ordered, "Take off your clothes and throw them in the fire." I gave another shout for someone to find some nails and duct tape. Another shout for someone to tape his mouth shut. Maggie must have read my mind because by the time it took me to grab an end-table lamp from beside the couch and rip out the cord, Maggie appeared with the duct tape, a couple of large ten penny nails and a hammer from Goodman's garage. I told Goodman to lie on the floor, but he just stood glaring at Pamela and the gun. He didn't go down easy. Idaho helped Maggie wrestle him to the ground. I wrapped the cord tight and tied his wrists to gargoyle-like bronzed statues imbedded into the tile floor on each side of the fireplace. The other women had pulled a few more lamp cords and the telephone cord, too.

Maggie was busy binding Goodman's feet when I began to pound the nails into the hardwood floor, to which Lily screamed, "No, no, no, you can't pound nails into that beautiful wood floor!"

"Need I remind you," explained Idaho, "we have more than paid for this floor."

An evil smile spread across Lily's face and with that, she grabbed the hammer from me and began pounding in the nails herself.

I found the thermostats and turned them off. The fire was still burning but at least if the rest of the house cooled off, he might be a little more miserable. He was being cold hearted. I wanted him to feel that coldness in equal measure.

With our work done, we stood back and looked at Goodman lying naked before us. I remembered feeling a sense of gratification, but not total satisfaction. The money was still gone.

I watched as Idaho tried to gain a modicum of control, wiping away tears of laughter and catching her breath. I got up from the couch to pour myself another cup of coffee, but realized I had to brew another pot. Pulling the coffee out of the cupboard I found a bottle of brandy and thought it might be a good idea to add some of the liquid courage to our cups. While I waited for the coffee pot, I picked up the newspaper again and returned to the article.

"Wait, wait, wait a minute!" Hope soared in my chest as I turned to Idaho.

Idaho, her laughter still fading and wiping at her cheeks, joined me at the table and asked, "What are you talking about?"

"Here, look at this. It says that there was a pentagram drawn around the body and a fire poker in Goodman's chest."

Idaho let out a low whistle. She reached over and grabbed the brandy. She took a long swig from the bottle as she read over my shoulder.

"I thought you read the paper?" I accused.

"No, you did. I heard he was dead listening to the radio, and they didn't say anything about fire pokers. Chocolate! I need chocolate!!"

"I was so shocked, I couldn't get beyond the first few sentences the first time," I mumbled. I threw the newspaper down once again and started down the hall toward the bathroom for a shower. I hollered over my shoulder to Idaho, "Call the WICAs for an emergency meeting. Here! Pronto! There's money in my purse, go get some doughnuts, something chocolate and really gooey." My heart pumped with the faintest of hope. I turned to look at Idaho and chortled, "Oh, by the way, just in case you missed it, someone was there after us. We didn't kill Goodman!"

Idaho brightened. Waving the bottle of brandy at me and saluting its contents pronounced, "I'll drink to that," and took another long swig.

I replayed the final moments with Goodman as I

undressed. This man who tried too hard to portray a lady's man, lay before us in the most humiliating position I could think of. He was totally naked, legs and arms spread and tied, mouth taped, the bald part of his head reflecting firelight, dripping sweaty black hair die from what hair circled his bulbous head, beady eyes glaring, belly bulging, blubber sprawled, and sporting a limp dick in front of five beautiful women. Oh sure, there was the stress of the circumstances to account for the limp dick. But it has been my experience, most men who scored as high as Goodman did on the Slease-O'Meter—especially in front of hovering women— would have proudly waved the American flag from the end of his manhood.

As we stood back looking at Goodman, the first to speak was Maggie. "Don't think this is the last you've seen of us." She laughed and bent down to poke at his blubber. "We will have the law-dogs of Libby on your ass before you can say lend me the liposuction."

Pamela knelt beside him and held up the butt of the gun and in a condescending, mocking giggle, simply said, "Plastic," and smiled sweetly. "Oh, and by the way, the name is Pamela Phuchet," she added, accenting the pronunciation of her last name as (Fooshay). "Not 'Fuckit', dick head." Unfortunately, the mispronunciation of her name was a common mistake made by many, but I supposed that Pamela took a greater offense when it came from Goodman.

Lily, who was a fund raiser and the social coordinator for many organizations—the latest being a promotional fund raiser for the Boy Scouts of which Goodman was the recipient, put her hands on her hips to anchor back luscious fur coat tails, bent low to plant her face in front of Goodman's scowling brows. She cocked her head to the side and said, "My, my, my. Aren't you just the Boy Scout poster boy. I wish they could see how good their leader looks in bondage. I bet they could teach us some knot tricks to keep those slimy mitts of yours from working out of those cords." She swiveled over and tightened one of the cords. Goodman's eyes rolled around to stare at her cleavage. She stood. And then planted and turned a spike heal in the palm of his hand as she walked away. Goodman cried out pained obscenities behind the tape.

I thought it curious that he should don an erection at that moment. Was it Lily's cleavage? Perhaps he envisioned an audience with her seductive closeness, or was it a dose of S&M that excited the man's libido? Perhaps it was fear.

Idaho leaned over to look at the surprisingly small penis and crowed, "Holy crap. Is that all you got?" and promptly delivered a steel-toed cowboy boot kick to his ass.

With that, Goodman struggled and began screaming muffled expletives from behind duct-taped lips. Things like, lawyer, lawsuit, bitches—which sounded more like "pishes" and "phik yr money"—and with eyes bulging from their sockets he complained a little clearer, "Yr gonna die."

By this time, I was pissed as hell. "Oh, yeah? Bring it on, Goodman. I've dealt with higher profile scumbags bigger than you. I'm so tired of the bullshit. Goodman, you are an outright liar. We handed over our money in good faith, and you won't even tell us where it is or where it's going, or what our inherited collateral is. I also understand that you have no idea how hard we've individually worked for our money. So, you might want to know that we are not taking this lightly. I'm telling you, if we don't get some answers from you soon, we will have your ass in a legal sling before the day is over. You will be charged with fraud and grand theft."

He snorted at that, but didn't blink an eye.

That made me nervous. I quickly tried to think of something that he'd respond to. "I don't think we're the only ones coming after you, Goodman," I started. "I'm quite confident that you are an expert at fraud, and I'm going to find out who those people are and we are all bringing you down."

He only glared back at me.

"You may not give a squat about what I do or who I contact," I continued. "But maybe you'll think twice about having to answer to a few newscasters and the IRS when they start auditing your books. In fact, we have downloaded your computer files." I reached into my coat pocket, pulled out a small, dark breath mint dispenser, turned it sideways and palmed it in such a way to make it appear to be a thumb drive. I hoped his eyesight wasn't very good from a distance. "Something tells me that you can't afford to lose your shiny image." I wiggled the object for emphasis.

That got a rise out of him. He finally seemed outraged. So, he does have something to hide, I thought. Perhaps he's afraid of the IRS after all.

Before stepping into the shower, I finished pinning up my hair. Looking in the mirror, I pushed a lock of loose hair back behind my ear and fingered dark circles under my eyes. Dark circles that looked like storm clouds settling in on my face—clouds filled with fear, anger and something like shame—or was it guilt? I clearly remembered my parting words to Goodman that night. High on adrenalin, so full of myself, so cocky and smug. I, the queen of revenge said, "Never underestimate five women scorned, Mr. Goodman. You'll live to regret this."

But he hadn't.

Shame and guilt, like ghostly fingers, began to take a stronger hold on me as buried secrets began to fly in my face, threatening to haunt me once again. I looked down at my shaking hands with open palms, looking for blood that had been washed away so long ago. How was I going to keep my demons buried now?

"Dear God! Demetri and now Goodman—dead," I whispered.

Chapter 6 - Olivia Hope

"...Yeah, so there's Gabe, he's just in his underwear and coat, with bare legs and cowboy boots — in this weather—and he follows Parker out to the barn," I heard Pamela talking from the living room as I finished with my shower. The women were already starting to arrive, and I listened to voices chattering down the hall.

"So, I follow them to see what the heck's going on, right," recounted Pamela. "Parker's already in the barn with no parka on, cowboy boots and his Spiderman underwear hanging below his scrawny little butt, legs spread, penis in hand, PEEING ON THE GOAT'S HEAD!"

"Ugh. Gross!" cried Lily. There were other comments but I couldn't quite make out what was said. I heard Idaho slur something like, "He seriously did that?"

Boys are so disgusting I thought, but couldn't contain my own chuckles as I pictured the blond, blue-eyed boys, Parker, seven, and Gabe, five—bare legs and cowboy boots—up to their shenanigans. Pamela had her hands full with those two. They were always up to something. Last summer, Parker was double-dog-dared to jump from the second story of the farm house on to an old mattress below the window. Pamela said she walked into the boys' bedroom to see Parker wearing a cape, helmet, and knee pads singing, "Here I come to save the day," standing on the edge of the windowsill. I hoped they lived to see age ten.

"Did you make them bathe the goat?" I heard Maggie ask.

"Damn straight I did. I made them both get dressed then hose and suds that goat. You should have seen the excitement when they tried to blow dry the poor thing," Pamela added. "I stopped the boys there, before they were kicked into next week. The goat got a nip in the rump of Parker's jeans in the process."

"You've got your hands full, woman," I said, joining the women.

"Tell me about it," Pamela groaned. "So, it turns out that I was in the bathroom, and Parker said he had to pee 'like a race horse.'" He told Gabe he was going outside. So, the 'race horse' thing must have given Gabe the idea. He told Parker he'd pay him ten bucks. I can't believe that stupid, damn goat stood for it. After all that, we're walking back into the house, and I hear Parker ask Gabe, 'Where's my ten bucks, dude?' and Gabe says, 'I don't have ten bucks. Go ask mom.' Can you believe it?"

"Too bad we didn't think to do that to old goat, Goodman," mumbled Idaho, still holding the brandy bottle. Laughter rang, but things grew quieter after that. I assumed it was the mention of Goodman's name.

"I brought my potato casserole," announced Maggie, jumping up to uncover the dish.

"I brought cinnamon rolls," added Lily. "They're a couple days old but you can nuke them."

"Oh, we let your dog out, Olivia, I hope you don't mind," said Lily.

"Yeah, we couldn't take the farting any longer,"

reported Maggie, wrinkling her nose. "What do you feed that thing?"

"That's not my dog," I insisted. "I gave him some eggs and leftover hotdogs with chili."

"No wonder. Not such a good combination," Maggie gagged.

Looking towards the counter, I noticed the potato casserole, a bowl of spaghetti, chips and dip, chocolate cake and cookies, among other assorted food items. "Where did all this food come from?" I asked.

"Well, when trouble hits, there's nothing like a little comfort food to get you through," said Maggie.

"Yeah, nothing says lovin' like somethin' from the witch's coven," hiccupped Idaho.

"Hey, that was a good one, Idaho," roared Maggie with a mouth full of chips. There was more laughter, but not from me. How could these women laugh, when the threat of incarceration hovered over us like the sword of Damocles?

"I called you all here to talk about Good—" I started.

"Let's eat," said Lily, totally ignoring me.

Eating's good, too, I thought, although I really didn't feel hungry. I really wanted to get the conversation started. I was strung tighter than a guitar string.

We gathered around the table, filled our plates and ate in silence. I thought it best to finish eating before I continued with the meeting. Maybe I needed a few moments of silence to get my thoughts in order. My hope was to talk these women into not going to the police—at least not right away. I knew that if we were the slightest bit suspect, we would be the center of the news media. I was going to do my damnedest to not let that happen. I was almost paralyzed with fear that we wouldn't get a fair break. Each of us had too much at stake to end up in prison for a murder we didn't commit. I would do an investigation of my own, and by god, I would find the killer if it was the last thing I ever did—which it might very well be, I thought.

We were good, honest and hard-working women. Each one would want to do the right thing. But really, what was the right thing to do? One thing was for sure, if we went to the police, we'd be the number one suspects. If it wasn't out right murder, we'd probably go to prison for manslaughter. After all, we left a man tacked to the floor in a winter storm—although to be fair, we didn't know a freak storm would move in. If we kept quiet, and we were found out later, it would only be worse for us. But if I could find the killer, and come forth with the evidence, we'd still be in trouble for our part in the whole affair. It was a double-edged sword. But could five women keep their mouth shut? Could they do it just long enough for me to ferret out the truth? It was a lot to ask of them. I considered each one of my friends as we quietly ate.

Pamela and Lily sat at my small kitchen table; Idaho perched on the arm of the couch. Maggie sat on the couch and I sat cross-legged on the floor by the fireplace. Each woman was bright and attractive in her own way.

I eyed Lily, the most beautiful of us all. Lily White, was anything but lily white. At age thirty-two she was all woman, and made sure every man knew it. She has quite possibly slept with every man in Lincoln County. She had long, red, curly hair, a creamy white complexion, pert pink lips, naturally long eyelashes, and long shapely legs. No man could resist the crook of her red acrylic-nailed finger pointed in his direction. She was all about fashion. She dressed to the nines just to go to the post office. That day she wore a black Dior pantsuit with white pearls draped around her neck, and tan Louis Vuitton boots that accented the curve of her legs. A matching fur parka draped over the back of the kitchen chair. She loves her furs. I wondered if she'd ever bedded an animal activist—yeah, stupid question. She had been married to an accountant. He was short, fat and bald with a bland personality. He had high blood pressure and cholesterol issues. Rumor had it that she killed him—with salt. She is looking to find another rich fool. Lily doesn't work much these days except to do volunteer gigs and fundraising for different charities—when she does, she's paid well. It's not the charities that have her interest, it's the shameless flirting she gets to do that floats her boat, and boy can she bring in the money with that. Somehow, I talked her into joining our club, so she could become her own source of income. Lily said she'd never stop looking for Mr. Goldbar but exclaimed, "Oh, why not? You can never have too much money." I expected she could never have too much of anything. I figured Lily wouldn't have a problem keeping her mouth shut about our escapade to Goodman's house. She loved keeping secrets, especially from men.

I trained my thoughts in the direction of Maggie Burns. She was thirty-one years old, five foot ten, maybe one hundred twenty-five pounds of which at least fifteen must be boobs. Her short, dark brown hair, was cast in a whimsical pixy cut. She was a famous childhood actress, staring in sitcom's like House Made of Kids, Daddy's Girl, and a few movies too, those were just the first ones that came to mind. She pretty much was living off her royalties. She got tired of the Hollywood life and wanted to make her life real, so she loaded up her car one day and drove north. She told me she spent the night in Libby, intending to settle in Canada somewhere the next day. That night she happened to attend a high school play, Annie Get Your Gun. It was such a horrible production that she couldn't bear to leave until she could give them some pointers. She's been in Libby ever since. She got her teaching degree and was now the English and Drama teacher. The high school drama group has since won awards for their productions. She has started a summer theater, too. Several students have gone on to successful acting careers in Hollywood—much to her chagrin. She has had a few failed relationships, but has one guy who seems to be enamored with her lately. He is a fishing and hunting guide. He has not seen even one of her movies, and Maggie thinks that is pretty darn cool—he doesn't even own a TV. She loves her new life. She wears weird outfits, like the one she had on—short denim skirt with orange and black striped tights, a tie-dyed t-shirt and thigh-high fur-lined black boots. She wears her body piercings only on the weekends because she can't wear them to school. Not so much that day though. I figured maybe the metal might freeze her nostrils together permanently in the frost. I first met her at the high school, and we had quickly become good friends. I figured there'd be no problem with her not talking because she hated any kind of personal publicity, and she was a damn good actress to boot.

I turned to Pamela Phuchet. She was wearing her typical sweat pants outfit from the gym. Pamela's skinny build at 5'7" almost made her look too thin. Her hair was long and silky-black. She had a streak of premature gray adding an exotic flair—it was most assuredly acquired from her boys. Says she wouldn't trade even one strand of silver for a moment of their insane lives. She wears those streaks like a badge of honor. At thirty-four she's a single parent and widow. Her husband died in a logging accident, and she inherited their acreage. She turned it into a Christmas tree farm that supplies most of the Pacific Northwest. The business is doing well, but she prefers her job as a personal trainer at the athletic center. She and Lily are best friends, but it's unknown if Pamela knows that Lily had also slept with her husband. I thought of how much Pamela loved her children and would do anything to protect them. If their mother was a murder suspect, she couldn't keep that news from the boys. If she were in prison, how could she cope without them? Would that be enough for her to keep silent?

Then there was my dear friend, Idaho. Her birth name is Ida Crenshaw. But she was married to William Hoe for about five minutes. Bill turned out to be a drunk. She rid herself of the man but kept his last name. She stands about five foot four and one hundred thirty pounds, mostly muscle from digging graves. Her brown hair was usually cropped short like a man's but lately she was growing it out and it hung to her shoulders. She had a pretty face but hid it most of the time under a baseball cap. She's the youngest of our group at age twenty-five. She's into the black gothic look but wears a lot of bib overalls, too. In the summer, it's cutoff overalls. That day she wore a black skull and cross-bone t-shirt with earrings that matched and faded black jeans. Her t-shirt sleeves were rolled up exposing solid brown biceps. She was born and raised in Bonners Ferry, Idaho. She's a tough woman, a hard worker, and has a great sense of humor. Most people think she's a lesbian, and Idaho is just fine with that, but I expect she's not. Outwardly, she has no interest in men, but I once found her stash of romance novels, and Idaho swore me to secrecy. She lives on her labored income, although she could be comfortable on her lottery winnings. It's her lottery winnings that I talked her into investing and are now lost. This thought pained me greatly. Several years ago, Idaho and I met when I was remodeling my little house. She lived only a block away and came every evening and weekends to help me finish before winter set in. I wasn't worried about convincing Idaho to keep quiet. She'd probably take any opportunity to challenge the system as she's pretty much a rebel.

I scanned my friends' solemn faces as they ate. I had grown to love these women. They had become my personal Salvation, my confidants, my support system, my lifeline. All, who because of me, were about to be subject to the legal system. I could no longer bear the silence. I needed to talk.

Chapter 7 - Rand Dubois

"Rand Dubois, how may I help you?" I answered the telephone for the umpteenth time. Sheriff Bishop assigned the phone to me in a phone booth-like office, which was a changing room for officers. How they squeezed a desk in it remained a mystery—my chair was a small, built-in bench. The four surrounding walls were already wall-papered with notes, pictures, old newspaper articles, and a few of Alan's photos of the crime scene. The full-length mirror was covered in yellow, orange and blue sticky notes.

The voice was that of Mrs. Haugen—another curious caller wanting to find out more about the Goodman case. No new information from her of course. It was frustrating, but I had to remind myself that people were scared and wanted to know we were doing something. It was Saturday, and the autopsy reports wouldn't be back until Monday. I focused on finding out who were Goodman's friends and business acquaintances, and tracking down information about the Chosen Trojan Children, the cult group that we all hoped hadn't made an unwanted entrance back into this community.

As I talked to Mrs. Haugen, I watched Alan, on the other side of the desk, doodle on some scratch paper and sporadically waggle his pencil, giving it the illusion that it was made of rubber. "Yes, Mrs. Haugen, we are interviewing people from Troy, Eureka, Thompson Falls and Noxon, as needed . . . Yes, Kalispell, too, if we need to. . . We do indeed keep our eyes open for suspicious characters . . . Yeah, yeah . . . Yes, I know . . . Mrs. Haugen. Just because Marlow Jenkins has a ratty ponytail and no teeth does not make him a suspect. No, Mrs. Haugen, we don't interrogate people unless there is a reason to . . . Mrs. Haugen . . . should we have reason to interrogate you?"

I was sporting a massive headache. I pinched the bridge of my nose for relief, to no avail. "Yes, huh," the conversation continued. "Well then, did you kill Ira Goodman? . . . That's what I thought . . . Yes ma'am, I'm sure the quilting women could verify your whereabouts at the time of the murder . . . No, Mrs. Haugen, we don't need another casserole, and the cookies were much appreciated . . . Yes, Mrs. Haugen . . . Okay, let us know if you hear anything, eh. Thanks for calling, goodbye."

Alan looked up as I hung up the phone and gave me a conspiratorial wink. "Life is a bowl of cherries and then you die, amigo," he said and went back to doodling—if life were only that simple.

Bishop poked his head in the door. "Mora Goodman is here," he announced. "Are you ready?"

"More than," I answered. "Come on, Alan. I think you should be there, too."

"Cool," was his reply, and off we went into one of those interrogation rooms with the depressing, green florescent lighting, dark mirrors and bad coffee. I left Alan to observe from a room with microphones and mirrored glass. I didn't want Mrs. Goodman to feel ganged up on, but I felt it important for Alan to witness. If there was one thing I was learning about him it was that he has a keen sense about the living as well as the dead.

Mrs. Goodman winced looking up toward that green plasma-like illumination. "Can we tone down these god-awful lights?" she complained. She pulled off her white parka and hung it neatly on the back of the chair.

"Lights gotta stay, Mrs. Goodman," growled Sherriff Bishop as he set up the tape recorder and tested the tape. While we waited, I took discreet inventory of the deceased's spouse. She looked to be in her late forties. Her ash blonde hair was coifed in a fifties style—Lauren Bacall silky waves that rolled over her shoulders. She wore a pink sweater and pink stretch pants that were right out of the sixties. Her gray boots matched the piping on her white parka and wrapped snuggly around shapely legs. She was maybe 5'6". She was slender with a slightly expanded waistline, which was maybe due to the aging process. Her tanned face showed a fair number of wrinkles, maybe age, maybe sun, but could be due to smoking. An expression of anger was pasted on her face, but who could blame her, it's one of the stages of grief. All in all, she was a handsome woman.

"This coffee is crap," she grumbled. "Don't you have a latte, something besides this cowboy shit?" She wasn't used to common amenities, to be sure.

"I'd like a latte myself, Mora," I piped. "May I call you Mora?"

"Why not, that's my name."

"Good then, Mora. I'll just have someone make a coffee run for us."

"Get some donuts too, while you're at it," mumbled Bishop from under the table where he messed with a tangle of long cords.

"Jesus, don't you people prepare for this shit, or what," Mora continued her grumbling as she watched Bishop under the table—shamelessly flashing a plumber's butt crack. "Here, let me help you with that thing," she said reaching for the end of one cord.

"Frank," hollered Bishop, "Come fix this damn thing, will ya?" Frank rolled into the room with the power of a steam engine. A giant man, with thick fingers. But he can work magic in the technical department. Mora gasped and backed away like a frightened little girl. Bishop smiled at that, and I headed to the door to order the lattes.

With lattes in hand and donuts powdering the table, the interview was finally in session. After the preliminaries of legal verification of who was in the room, date and time, and the reason for the interview, Mora asked, "How long's this gonna take 'cause I have a nail appointment."

Bishop shot me a look that hinted I better take the good cop role because he might have to strangle her.

"Just a few questions, Mora, and you can be on your way. I realize this must be very difficult for you," I sympathized.

"Okay, look," she began. "I'm gonna be right up front with you guys. I was going to divorce my husband as soon as Seth graduated. He's graduating this spring, you know. I'm really not as heartbroken as you might think I should be, I'll admit to that." And she didn't look heartbroken either. Bishop's expression didn't change.

"There were problems?" I asked, turning her information into questions to garner more information.

"Damn right there were. He's an ass. Sorry, was an ass."

"How long were you married?"

"Twenty-six years this next June." She smiled a little, "We had a June wedding with all the trimmings. Everything was good, fun, and exciting at the time. Damn was I naïve. I was happy though! Yeah—for about two weeks," she scoffed. "After the honeymoon, I only saw him on occasion, if that, and we had sex even less."

"I bet that was hard for a newlywed, to have your husband gone so much," I prodded.

"Yeah, I felt abandoned. You know, like a love-sick puppy. Not that he was a good lover. I've had better."

"Did he have other lovers?"

"Probably, I figured he did 'cause he wasn't into me, that's for sure."

"Why didn't you leave him?"

"Got pregnant on our honeymoon."

Bishop gave a condescending grunt.

"What! It can happen," a defiant Mora said as she sat up straight and bent toward Bishop. He didn't flinch. "Happens all the time," she added as she slumped back in her chair.

"Oh, geez," said Bishop. "Twenty-six years is a long time to wait for a divorce Mrs. Goodman."

"I thought maybe my pregnancy was a good thing."

She shot Bishop a glare. "I thought maybe he'd pay more attention to me. He did, too, for a while. And when Ira, Jr., was born, he was excited and stayed home a little more; until he got tired of night feedings and shitty diapers. Not that he'd help or anything."

"You had the baby, and things still didn't improve. Didn't look like things were gonna change, Mrs. Goodman—twenty-six years," bellowed the Sheriff.

"I said you can call me Mora, that's my name," she spat. She looked to be near tears.

"No, I prefer to call you Mrs. Goodman. Because I don't like the fact that you didn't like your husband and now he's dead," argued Bishop.

Mora shrank back and lowered her head as she said, "Don't get me wrong. Things weren't always so bad. He made a lot of money. He was good looking back then, real eye candy in an Alec Baldwin sort of way. There were lots of parties, and all the women were envious of me. And he was good to the boys. All I had to do was to find something to keep me occupied. But then one day…"

"One day what, Mrs. Goodman? You got tired of playing house with hubby, and Jack Crack walks in the door and the two of you decide you can take his money and start a new fucking life once baby number three is out the door? I don't like it. And why did you portray your husband's death to look like Satanism?"

Mora's mouth hung open with genuine shock, mouth gaping lips working to form words. The room was silent. Then she finally spoke, "Who is Jack Crack?"

Bishop threw up his hands.

"Things weren't going well with your husband," I reiterated. "Did you have a lover, Mora?"

She began to squirm in her seat, and tears began to flow. "From time-to-time," she said finally.

"Do you have a lover now?" I pressed.

"I wish!" she blurted with a half laugh, blowing snot bubbles from her nose. She quickly covered her face and sobbed, "Sorry, sorry," she whispered into her palms.

I handed her a Libby Café napkin, and she blew her nose.

"Mrs. Goodman," Bishop continued, "You stayed in the marriage long enough to have two more sons. I want to know what kept you there for twenty-six years!"

"I told you, he treated the boys good. He made good money. We didn't fight over money or anything like that. He did his thing, and I did mine. But I wanted a real life, maybe a husband who would treat me better. I deserved that! But the boys needed a sense of a normal life, too. That's why I was gonna wait till Seth graduated."

"So, what finally brought you and your lover to kill your husband?" demanded Bishop.

"I didn't kill my husband," Mora said, sounding tired. "Are you married Sheriff?"

"We are talking about you. Answer my question."

Mora stared at him. "Of course, you're married. I know that. It's not like I don't know who you are. I even know who your wife is, don't recall her name though. She's a nice person—unlike you. She's a buyer for some fancy clothing department store in Kalispell, isn't she?" Mora didn't wait for an answer. "I'll bet that she works some long hours. And commuting ninety miles from Libby to Kalispell is a bitch, you can't deny that. And how about those long buying trips she needs to make. Gone, what, several weeks during a month sometimes? Don't see her much, do ya, Sheriff? So, how lonely do you get, how frustrated do you get? How hard is it to get someone to watch the kids when she's not around? How low do you feel when she tells you about her exciting buying trips and about all the boring men that she's had to have dinner with? And how pissed off do you get when she says she won't be home for dinner AGAIN!! Has she taken a lover, Sheriff? Have you taken a lover, MR. BISHOP?"

A pulse bulged in Bishop's neck.

"Mora, what do you know about the CTC?" I asked, redirecting the conversation.

"The what-what-what?"

"The Chosen Trojan Children."

"Oh! That's that sicko group that stirred up so much trouble a few years ago." Her eyes started to widen. "You don't think—," her breath caught in her throat.

"Did your husband have any dealings with them?"

"FUCK if I know! He had dealings with lots of people. For all I know he could have been having regular meetings with fucking Charles Manson!" She took another deep breath and said, "You don't think he was killed by those weirdos, do you? They were in my house? That's just creepy!"

"Do ya really care?" came the sarcastic question from Bishop.

She ignored his comment.

"Do your sons have any connections with the

CTC?"

She shook her head and thought for a moment. "No, no, I really don't think so. Ira, Jr., has a good engineering job and a wife, for Christ sake. Jake is at college. He's in Bozeman. Why would he come all this way to belong to something like that? And he wouldn't kill the father he adores!" Her tone softened a little. "And Seth . . . He's a sweet boy. I . . . just can't. But he and his father . . . they didn't get along. Well, at first they did."

"What do you mean at first they did?" I asked noticing her hesitation as she nervously licked her lips.

"Well, at first, Seth loved his father the most of all our boys, I think. He idolized him. He wanted to be like his dad. He's too sweet though. I always knew that. They spent a lot of time together. He even went on some of Ira's business trips if school schedules allowed. Ira was adamant about a good education and the boys not missing school."

"What happened? Why did Seth stop going with him?"

"I don't know. I guess Seth was about eleven or twelve. He said he was bored and didn't want to spend so much time on the road. He said he wanted to spend more time with his friends. Good God, he was becoming a teenager, I couldn't blame him for that! His dad said they were starting to fight all the time and he thought it best for Seth not to travel with him as much, said that he was worried about his mental health. And sure enough, Seth grew depressed, anxious sometimes. I couldn't get him to talk to me anymore either. And he didn't have many friends." Mora reached for a drink of her latte. She sipped slowly and gently set it down. "I figured he had spent so much time with his dad that he never had the opportunity to make friends."

"Where is he, Mora?" I asked. "Has he contacted you?"

Her head hung as she shook it. She pulled her head up and grabbed my hand. "He's a good boy, Mr. Dubois. A good boy. A gentle boy. A loving boy. I wish I knew where he was."

"Can you tell me about your husband's business dealings?"

She withdrew her hand from mine. "Are you off your rocker? The only business dealings I saw were in the newspapers. If you want to know about his business dealings, consult Cabinet Mountain News, The Libby Cornicle, The Daily Inter Lake or The Spokesman Review! Maybe even USA Today. YOU probably know more than I do about his fucking business deals!"

"When did you last see your husband, Mora?"

"Right before I left for Greece. That was about three weeks ago."

"Did you argue? Was he acting differently?"

"No, we didn't argue. He's always glad to get rid of me this time of year. But now that you mention it, he was acting kind of weird," she looked thoughtfully at her latte.

"How so?" I asked

"I don't know. Little things, like he had dark circles under his eyes. I thought it was from lack of sleep. And he started stuttering when he talked sometimes. I've never heard him stutter before. And he developed a twitch in his right eye. I remember having a fleeting thought that maybe he was headed for a stroke or heart attack."

"That would have been convenient wouldn't it have, Mrs. Goodman?" accused Bishop.

"I never gave it another thought, Sheriff. I was thinking more about my trip."

"Did you go by yourself?" I asked.

"I go without Ira. There is a group of about six of us that meet. You can talk to each of them if you wish. I have nothing to hide."

"We already did, Mrs. Goodman. They said you disappeared about the time your husband was killed. Did you fly home, meet your lover, knock off your husband, and then sneak back to paradise?" Bishop was relentless.

"I had taken a side trip to Italy. I love Italy in the fall. You can check my travel records. And why are you so sure that I have a lover? If I were going to kill my husband, I really don't think that I'd need any help!"

Changing the subject, I asked, "Can you tell us anything about the glass figurines that your husband had collected?"

"Why? What's that got to do with his murder?"

"I'm curious. I have to say that some of the figurines are rather odd."

"Yeah well, he is odd—was odd. That was another sore spot with me. He's got thousands of dollars into those stupid things." Mora wrung her hands. "I don't pay much attention to them 'cause I think they're creepy."

"What kind of a childhood did your husband have?"

"And you need to know this why? My husband was murdered he's not the murderer," she quipped.

"I realize that, Mora, but sometimes people act out

things relating to their childhood, like collecting things that have a secret meaning. Maybe he had trauma that was never dealt with. By the sounds of it, he didn't like women much and it showed through his disrespect. We all have baggage, Mora. We're looking for anything that may connect him to why he was murdered."

Mora sat back and groaned. She cranked her head in a circle and massaged the back of her neck before she answered. "I guess he had an okay childhood. He didn't get along with his mother so much. She was a bitch. His dad treated him okay. His dad was a salesman, and he took Ira with him occasionally like Ira took Seth on some of his business trips. He said that they had some good times. His dad died when Ira was eleven. I think that was hard on him. His mom took off after that, and he's only seen her once or twice since then. He lived with his uncle Henry, who died several years back. He was a strange nut bag."

"Strange, like how?" I prodded.

"Kind of sleazy. He was all about tits and ass, always degrading women that way. His belief about women was the old 'find 'em, fuck 'em, and forget 'em' philosophy." Mora laughed dryly, "I guess Ira took that to heart."

"Where did your husband buy those figurines? Was there a certain art gallery he'd frequent?"

"No, he always bought that junk on the road. He's collected them ever since I met him. And then he found this guy in one of those glass-blowing tents at a flea market. We were out shopping, and Ira bought some of the nicer stuff from him then. More started appearing on the shelves at home after that. I thought they were kind of pretty at first. But then they started getting bizarre, and I was sick of cleaning the damn things. I told Ira he had to get them out of the house. He took them out to the lake house. That's where they started to multiply. There were a couple new ones every time I went out there."

"Do you know this artist's name?" I asked.

She threw her head back and laughed. "Yeah, I know his name. It's funny because of what he does with his art. It's Brent Glasser, you know like, bent glass? Get it?"

"Yes, that's funny," I humored, and it kind of was. But, Bishop didn't crack a smile. "Do you know how we can contact him?" I asked.

"Na, I have no idea. I think he lives in Sandpoint or Spokane. You might find him at some Christmas bazaar or someplace. 'Tis the Christmas season." She shrugged.

"Are you sure that you don't know this artist better than you think?" asked Bishop.

"No, I don't know him, I don't know where he lives, I don't know where he works. I don't know what he eats. I don't know how many times he wipes his ass. I don't like him! I am not having an affair with him! I don't care if he eats shit and dies! Now I'm wondering, do I need to lawyer up?"

"That is certainly your right, Mora," I said. "Again, I know how hard this can be. But we do have a job to do, and we really need your help, eh. There is someone out there killing in the name of Satan. Who knows, you or your sons may be next. We'd like to get him or her off the streets before that can happen." I reached over and gently squeezed her hand. "Mora, we really need your help. Will you help us?"

"Fine," she suddenly blurted. "Are you French?"

"Why yes, I am," I said, "French Canadian to be exact, eh."

"Well, you're so damn cute I can't resist you. Love the mustache, and that little accent, but if you don't mind, I need to pee. Can I pee by myself, SHERIFF, or do I need you to hold my hand?"

"We can take a break," I said, and showed her to the restroom.

"What do you think? Think Mora did it?" I asked Bishop as we stood waiting for her in the hall by the interrogation room.

"You're the one who's so damn cute. Do you know?"

I know from experience that the good-cop-bad-cop can be difficult at times, but something else was bugging Bishop. I'd address that later.

"At this point, I don't think so. But we don't have a lot of information yet. What do you think?" I repeated.

"I don't know, maybe yes, maybe no. I'd like to probe the lover thing though. I know she's gotta be lying there."

"Why is that, eh?"

"No way a good lookin' woman like that is gonna spend twenty-six years without sex. Know what I mean? No way she'd stay in a marriage like that. And I know damn well that it took at least two people to kill Goodman." Bishop seemed agitated. "Oh hell, I just don't like her."

"Why do you say you don't like her?"

"Just a feeling. Well shit, who is she to say what my marriage is like, 'Your wife got a lover, Mr. Bishop?'

she says. My wife is a damn good woman." Bishop moved from agitation to downright anger.

"Let me know if I'm out of line here, but is everything okay on the home front, Bishop?"

Mora appeared from the restroom before he could answer, but I had a feeling that I wouldn't have gotten one anyway.

The interview started again. Bishop and I continued with more questions and asking some of the same ones in a different way. She seemed to give us the same answers. However, she became surlier by the minute. The only new thing we uncovered was the fact that she had seen a group of five women meet with her husband from time-to-time. She had no doubt that at least one, if not all, was having sex with him. When asked why she thought that, she proclaimed, "Because at least every man in town has slept with that Lily White. And probably those other witchy women, too. They're thick as thieves."

Bishop made a notation on his notepad—Lily White. "And affairs are certainly things you know about, don't you, Mrs. Goodman?"

"Huh?" Mora questioned as her head swiveled to look at him.

Bishop was impatient, "You see, it had to take a couple of people to do what they did to your poor husband. It had to take at least two people, one to hold him down and another to tie him up. Then you turned off the furnace and left him there to freeze to death. Then when you came back, he still wasn't dead and in an angry rage you stabbed him with the fire poker." Mora was shaking her head, and tears began to spill down her cheeks as he continued. "Was that when you decided to make it look like a cult did it? He was already splayed out, so, was it you or your boyfriend who drew the pentagram around his body? Was that when you left him to finally die, Mrs. Goodman?"

Mora covered her mouth with a shaky hand and drew in a gusty breath, "Dear God," she gasped, hearing the gruesome details of her husband's death for the first time.

"Did you kill your husband, Mrs. Goodman?" Bishop bellowed.

"NO! I! DID! NOT! KILL! MY HUSBAND!" Mora shouted. She dropped her head and covered her face again, sobbing quietly for a moment. Pulling her head up and rolling red teary eyes to look directly at Bishop, she whispered, "But God knows, sometimes I wish I had."

Chapter 8 - Olivia Hope

"Are we ready to talk about the elephant in the room?" I blurted.

No one commented. It remained silent, except for forks clinking on plates while we continued to eat.

Lily reached over and grabbed the newspaper. Examining it for a moment, she asked, "Who's the weirdo with his finger in his ear?" pointing to the accompanying photo pertaining to the article about Goodman's death.

Idaho moved over for a closer look saying, "I think he's kinda cute."

"Yeah, but you're looking at him through brandy bottom glasses," teased Maggie. "Look at all that curly hair."

"Rand Dubois," hummed Lily. "Now there's a real man. Look at that handlebar mustache. I can't even get a nice curl like that in my hair."

I rolled my eyes. Exasperated, I said, "Can we please talk about this? What are we going to do? Focus, people!"

"Wow, I still can't believe Goodman is dead," said Maggie continuing to stare at the photo. She finally sat down and said, "I wondered why we hadn't heard from him. I mean I knew he was angry. Snow storm or not, I thought we'd be in a lawsuit by now."

I had been thinking the same thing. We visited his

lake house on Monday night. The storm moved in early the next day. He was found on Friday. I'd been busy with classes, and then the storm shut everything down. It was the week before the Thanksgiving break and I, too, felt it was odd we had not seen or heard from Goodman during that time. His death certainly explained his absence.

Plates were set aside. Rubbing our overstuffed bellies, we started the discussion. It began with how we'd learned of the death. Most heard it on the TV or the radio. Locally, Goodman's murder was the top story. It was big news in Kalispell and Spokane as well. So, no matter what channel you were watching or listening to, you couldn't miss it.

"I am so sorry I got you all into this," I started. "I've called this meeting to find out how you want me to handle this situation."

"What do mean you handle this?" complained Lily. "We're in this together. We will all figure out how to handle this." There were nods and murmurs of agreement.

"I'm the one who talked you guys into handing over your money! I'll take responsibility."

"Shzip it, Blondie," scolded Idaho. I realized the bottle of brandy was almost empty. "You don't need to be a martyr." Considering the amount of alcohol Idaho had consumed, I let the comment slide.

"Besides," interrupted Maggie, "our fingerprints are probably all over the house. I didn't wear gloves. Did anyone else?"

Shit! I hadn't thought of that! We hadn't been there to kill the man. He was alive when we left. There had been no need to wipe down fingerprints. I began to think out loud, "Okay, someone was there after us. Whoever it was, stabbed him, maybe they didn't want their fingerprints found. Maybe they wiped everything down."

"One could hope, I suppose," said Lily.

"Let's take this step-by-step and think if there are any other details we need to worry about," offered Maggie. We began by rehashing the night we visited Goodman.

"Oh, my god, Pamela, you are my hero," said Idaho. "You made Goodman squeal like a little pig on roashting day. Only thing we're misshing iz the apple in hiz mouth."

"Leave it to Idaho to paint that visual," laughed Pamela.

As it happens so many times when us women get together, we invariably find ourselves in fits of laughter—even something as serious as this, we find humor.

"I was thinking more of a skewer up his butt," mumbled Pamela.

"Harsh, but fitting, if you know what I mean," giggled Lily. "Only I'm sure he'd have liked it. At least a little. Did you see his erection after I snubbed the heel of my pump into his palm? I just bet he was into S&M or some dominatrix shit."

"Yuck, maybe we played right into one of his sexual fantasies," moaned Pamela.

"Why is it that men like Goodman feel the need to belittle women?" asked Maggie. "I mean, calling us 'silly little women' like we're these bobble heads that bounce in favor of his every whim."

"I was so mad at him that night," fumed Pamela. "Just think, if he could drive five women to take him down, what do you think he did to someone who put the final blows to him? It's his own damn fault as far as I'm concerned. There is a part of me that feels like he got exactly what he deserved." Pamela sat up straight with a look of revelation and added, "Wow, I guess that really does make me a witch!"

"Sorry, honey, that only makes you a witch with a 'b', said Maggie.

"I had to work with the man sometimes," said Lily. "I think I knew him better than any of you. I'm gonna say it right out. I am not sorry the bastard is dead."

"Here, here!" went a round of cheers.

"You know what's the froshting on the cake?" slurred Idaho. "I get to dig hish grave. I'm gonna make sure he's at least six feet deep, or deeper."

Another round of "here, here" ensued.

"Okay, on the assumption that we didn't kill him," Pamela said. "Nothing is for sure yet. We don't know how he died. That part does scare me. Should we go to the police and tell them our side of the story? Tell them what we did?"

Thoughtful silence hung in the air. I knew the answer. I had my own idea about what to do, but for the moment, kept quiet.

"Yeah right, we could do that. Oh, wait," Maggie scoffed, "Goodman died by the hands of a satanic cult and our little WICA club is not a suspect? Come on ladies, do you know how many times I've had to defend that we are not a bunch of crazed witches? And that's on a good day."

"I have to agree," nodded Lily. "I had a practicing white witch at the bank ask me if she could join our meetings."

I had something similar happen to me at school. A first-year teacher claimed to be a white witch, and wanted to know if the WICA group had any good spells she could borrow. Pamela's question still hung heavy in the air. What should we do?

"Hell, I work in a grave yard. I deal with dead people all day. I'd probably be the first one they'd suspect," hiccupped Idaho.

"How so?" asked Maggie.

"Well, it might be my fault actually. When we started our WICA meetings, people asked if it was a witch's cult, and I'd just wink."

"You turd, that's not what we're about," squealed Pamela and threw a pillow at her.

"Oh, come on, a little fear never hurt nobody. I get a lot of mileage out of it. And besides, the assholes left me alone after that." Idaho grinned, "It'z kind of fun. Sometimes, I get bored and shout chants, and cast spells. I see the guys lean in a little further to me. It keeps all that male shitosterone at a manageable level."

"Spells? Like what?" Pamela asked, "And have ya got any that will help control the boys?"

Everyone laughed.

Idaho continued, "One time thish freaky guy named Ben I worked with was," she paused to burp, "bugging me —I called him Ben because he looked like a rat. Anyway, I told him to leave me alone but he kept it up. So, I was ready. I'd caught some bees in a little jar, cause there iz a shit load of 'em in the cemetery, because of the flowers people leave. So, I got these big-ass gloves on and I grab the jar that nicely hides in my gloved hands. I loosen the lid and hold the jar upzide down and turn sideways slightly. I make sure he's looking at me. I start mumbling shtupid shit. I make sure he's listening and then I zay his name real loud. 'Ben!' I sez. And start to cough while I pull the lid off, and it looksh like bees are flying out of my mouth every time I cough. And I'll be damned if those bees didn't start swarming him. I laughed my ass off watching him run the full length of that cemetery."

"Sweet!" squealed Pamela.

"Did he leave you alone after that?" I asked.

"Yeah, but I figure he talked to the mayor 'cause that's who our boss is now cause of all the budget cuts. Zo the mayor comes out. I'm diggin' away. Zo he asks me, do you belong to the WICA? Sure, I tell him and smile real big. Zee I know he's thinkin' I'm this witch now. Zo I'm standing over thish grave I'm diggin' and I kinda make the sign of the cross over the grave and shay to him, 'There's zome newt eyeballs in that can over there, throw a couple of them in the hole.' Course they're jush marbles I've been collecting from the flower pots. I had another can that I threw some leaves in last fall and they turned all skeleton-like. Zo I zaid, 'And while you're over there, taste one of those dried bat wings. If they crunch, they're ready!' He grimaced like a kid being asked to eat his broccoli. 'Tastes like chicken' I say." We laughed hysterically.

Idaho had her audience, "Zo about that time old man Zooker—you know, that nasty old Fuller Brush salesman they arrested last fall for pooping in people's yards?"

Idaho was referring to a man the cops arrested for defecating in yards, or on porches, of "mean nasty bitches." It was his revenge for their rude, snooty remarks, and disrespectful treatment he'd endured over the years, by those old biddies. One night, he was caught by a startled twelve-year-old girl walking by about the time he'd humped over to assume the position. She thought he was a bear, and out of reflex, she smacked him hard with a big stick. Knocked him out cold. When the police arrived, he had his pants down around his ankles. He had a hard time convincing authorities he wasn't a flasher. That's when he confessed to the towns "Pooper Scandal."

Nodding their understanding of Zooker's arrest, the women laughed uncontrollably.

Idaho continued, "So, while the mayor's there, Zooker comesh all limping in to the graveyard sporting a cane, 'cause he's got some big leg disease, or something. Zo, I sez to the mayor, 'Crazy bastard. Told him not to drink the testicles rhino potion. He can't stand straight now. Knees bruise his scrotum—hasn't walked the same since.' Zo I turn around and there's Hiz Honor, all white-faced holding my water bottle. I look all scared-like, and I zay, 'Duuude, don't drink that.' He puts it down real gentle and backs away wiping his hands on his shirt."

The women were gasping with laughter.

"Damn I missh that man," Idaho lamented. "Hashn't been back since."

"Who," choked Maggie, "Zooker or the mayor?" The laughter continued.

When the conversation came back around to the seriousness of the meeting, Lily made a good observation, "I'm thinking that if we go to the inspector now, we will be the focus of the murder. I think in the end they'd hang their hats on us and we'll be in jail. We know how quickly they bury the sordid cases around this town."

"Do you really think the CTC is behind this?" asked Pamela. "I mean, that's just too creepy to think about. How would Goodman be involved with something like that?"

"That's the kind of things I'd like to investigate," I said. "If I can poke around for a couple of days, we could hold off talking to inspector Dubois. If I don't come up with anything, then we'll need to come forward."

"There you go with the 'you' thing again," argued Lily. "We have some culpability too, you know." All women emphatically agreed.

And so, the plan began to take shape. We each had someone we could talk to about the Goodman family or the CTC. It's a small town and Goodman was an important part of the community. The murder would surely be the town buzz. Since we lost mega money to Goodman, it seemed reasonable that we'd want to know more. And too, we were sure most people would love to add their two cents to the gossip mill.

Once we discussed who was going to research what, and talk to whom, we agreed to meet again on Monday night.

This "plan" included me finally accepting a date with Rocco Basham, the district attorney. I had avoided his advances for months, but the women agreed that I might be able to find out tidbits of information from him. My stomach turned at the thought, but I guess it was a small price to pay.

The discussion turned to thoughts on recouping our money. We added more research and interviews to our to-do-lists.

"Damn, there went the dream of owning my own fitness center," sighed Pamela, turning the conversation to a more somber reflection of what she had planned to do with her lost money. "I was hoping that when the boys were off to Harvard, or some other Ivey League college, I could get rid of that damn tree farm. I pictured myself standing on the veranda of a big white house admiring my garden tended by a hunky gardener who doubles as my cabana boy and loves to massage my feet." She smiled wryly. "And I envisioned myself eating off of fine china and drinking out of Waterford glasses instead of Lighthouse dressing jars. Oh, and there are beautifully colored pillows on my new white couch!"

"Wow, white couch, you dream big," said Maggie. "But, I know what you mean. I've had such high hopes for this little town to come out of its slump."

Libby has been undergoing a superfund cleanup by the EPA after they shut down the W.R. Grace Zonolite Mine. The mine closed in 1990. Still, Libby residents were at high risk for contracting asbestos–related diseases and mesothelioma. Then to make matters worse, the sawmill shut down. Those were the only two major industries in town. Because of that, the once booming Libby dwindled to almost a ghost town.

"Libby is just as quaint and beautiful as Big Fork, or Whitefish," continued Maggie. "The EPA is coming to an end with the cleanup sites, and it's time to breathe some life into this community. Clean it up, build up tourist trade. I envisioned a community playhouse to rival what Big Fork has. I want to make it more than just a playhouse. I want a dinner theater where I can serve caviar, duck a l'orange, chicken Kiev and venison tartar."

"Eww! Gross!" piped Pamela. "Make it mac and cheese and the boys and I'll be there."

"Throw in some Dom Perignon champagne and I'll stay awhile," purred Lily.

"So, what were you saving for Lily," asked Maggie.

"It's simple. I want money, lots of money."

"Oh, come on," argued Pamela. "You've got money. And what you don't have you can get from any man. Which, by the way, you can get any man you want. What more is there?"

"Oh, all right. If you must know, I was hoping to build a teen center. Somewhere where the kids in this god forsaken town can go and have some good clean fun." All heads whipped around to stare at Lily.

"Get outta here," said Maggie.

"Whoa! I didn't see that one coming!" choked Idaho.

"Oh pull-eeze," countered Lily. "Do you think I became a cold, money-grubbing, man-eating beyotch by being a nice girl? No, my parents were raving alcoholics who never wondered, or even cared, about where I was. I spent my time with boys to get the love and attention I wasn't getting from my parents. That's no big secret.

Maybe if there was somewhere that kids felt safe and part of a better community, there might be a few less girls becoming like me." All eyes were still staring and mouths gaped.

"Who are you and what have you done with Lily?" teased Maggie.

Lily waved her off. "Besides," she continued. "It will leave me with less competition from the younger generation."

"Whew," said Idaho, making an exaggerated effort to wipe her brow with the back of her hand. "We thought we lost you there for a minute. Good to have you back, Lily."

"And just what are your frightful dreams, Ms. Cemetery Queen? Do we see some new graveyard plots ala Stephen King style in your future?" chided Lily.

Idaho grinned fiendishly. "How did you ever guess? Maybe I'll add The Room of Terror to Lily's teen center."

"No, I think the kids got enough terror after playing in the Zonolite bins and the asbestos laden piles down by the ball park," said Pamela.

"Seriously, though," continued Idaho. "I'd like to buy a farm. Make it a community garden, something like that. All organic, everything done in a green way, you know? Frankly, I have found I like digging in the dirt, but I'd rather plant vegetables than dead bodies."

"You've been awfully quite Blondie," noted Idaho, as she turned her head toward me.

I had good reason to be quiet. Every one of these women had a noble dream to give back to the community in a positive way. Guilt plagued me, not only because I was the reason they lost their dreams, but my dreams were strictly selfish in nature. All I thought of was getting out of this cold dead-end town and see some sunshine. I hesitated but thought maybe I could lighten the mood, so I blurted, "Boob job."

They all looked at me in surprise.

"That's right! Cut these babies down to size," I said as I hefted a breast in each hand.

"Don't be stupid," crowed Lily. "Do you know how much money women spend to look like you?"

"My god, Olivia!" said Maggie. "You are the Jessica Rabbit of every man's wet dream. You are not touching those things."

"Your money is spent better elsewhere, I have to agree," added Pamela. "So, what else were you going to do with your money?"

"Okay, how about you all come visit me on the Florida Keys beach at Olivia's Tiki Bar and Grill—in the middle of January!"

"Now you're talking Girlfriend!" There were high fives and laughter all around—until the blue and red police lights began flashing just outside of my living-room window.

Chapter 9 - Olivia Hope

The flashing police lights in my living room momentarily paralyzed all five of us. I took a deep breath and parted the curtains to look out. When I turned back around, I stared into four very pale faces. Maggie smiled then, and calmly said, "Well folks, it's show time."

"There's only one policeman, let me talk to him," I said, walking toward the door. I was assaulted with a blast of arctic air as the door swung open. I hugged myself, and jammed my hands into my arm pits for warmth. I recognized the older man. He was the officer who covered the high school if there were disturbance issues. "Hey Dan, what brings you out on such a fine afternoon as this?" I schmoozed.

Dan McKenzie tipped his hat back and smiled. He was portly, with thick graying hair. He had a nice smile, and was a good man who the kids respected like a grandpa. He climbed the steps and reached out a gloved hand to greet me. This is good I thought. He doesn't seem to be apprehensive, like he's expecting trouble. No guns blazing.

"Damn cold, isn't it?" he hailed.

"I can do without it," I answered. "What can I do for you?"

"I hear you and your dog have been into some mischief."

"Oh, that," I sighed, laughing with sheer relief. "So, Mrs. Bixby did call the police, huh?"

"Yeah, you and your dog stole her rugs." He grinned wide now.

"It's not my dog."

Dan nodded toward the corner of the porch where the black Labrador lay on a large, fluffy dog bed with a tattered blue blanket—all snuggled in a makeshift cardboard box for a dog house. "Want to tell that to him?" he asked.

I glanced over my shoulder to see eight wide eyes and four noses pressed against the window. I looked back to the dog. "He's a guest."

"Apparently a naughty one," Dan suggested. The dog lifted his head, yawned, passed gas and tucked his nose back into the blanket.

"Why don't you come on in for a cup of coffee while we talk," I offered.

"Sounds good," Dan said as he followed me inside.

As I passed through the door, all four bodies turned as one mass unit and centered themselves in the middle of the kitchen, eyes still wide. I tried to discreetly wave them off, and mouthed, "It's okay, turn around."

Dan walked over to the fireplace and took off his hat. He nodded hello to the women. The women nodded in unison. Behind Dan, I tried to wave for the women to turn around and sit down, still with no success. They seemed to be frozen in place, with eyes even wider. I cleared my throat, "Maggie, could you get Officer McKenzie a cup of coffee?" Maggie didn't move. I called her name again. She jumped, snapping to attention.

"Yes, yes of course," she answered.

"Cream too, please," Dan called after her.

"So, you're wondering about the altercation with Mrs. Bixby," I said, hoping the women heard and quit their paranoia. Maggie returned with the coffee.

"Mighty obliged, ma'am," said Dan taking the coffee cup.

I heard murmurs from the women, ". . . Mrs. Bixby? . . . What's the deal? . . ." Then silence, and stares once more. When I gave them a warning look, they quickly turned and began quietly whispering among themselves.

"How about you tell me what happened? Why did you steal Mrs. Bixby's rugs?" quizzed Dan.

"First, I need to tell you the dog on the porch out there, which is not my dog, is obsessed with the color blue. He runs around the neighborhood pilfering blue items. I've got a garage filled with blue mittens, a blue coat, a blue Frisbee, a blue boot, a blue book, a blue bat, a blue ball, a blue bra and blue jump rope. So, can you guess what I call him?"

"I don't know, Packy?" guessed Dan grinning.

"Blue, Dan. I call him Blue. Try to keep up."

"I thought dogs were color blind."

"I don't know, maybe you should ask him," I whined. "All I know is that I have a garage full of blue trinkets. Anyway, Mrs. Bixby must have been out shoveling snow this morning and I guess Blue wanted to play. He chased her around the yard and then she began chasing him with a broom. She had an ugly, old rug hanging on her fence, only it was frozen stiff. Blue probably thought it was a Frisbee and wanted her to play fetch, only he wouldn't let go of the rug. Instead he decided to play tug-of-war. But, Mrs. Bixby was a party pooper."

I heard giggles from the kitchen as Idaho slurred, "Ha, she shaid 'pooper'. Wonder if Bixby's related to Zooker," this was followed by more giggles, then shushes.

"When Mrs. Bixby banged on my door," I continued, "he was cavorting in the snow with the rug in his mouth. I didn't know what it was at first, not until he placed it at Mrs. Bixby's feet."

"Rugs," said the officer. "Plural, as in more than one rug. That's only one."

"I'm getting to that," I acknowledged. "Blue's all excited see, because he wants her to play with him, that's all. So, Mrs. Bixby is just standing there doing nothing, and Blue gives her a little nudge. She takes offense and proceeds to pick up the rug, which I recognize as the twin to the one I found earlier in the week. Only I didn't know where it came from, so I just threw it on the chair over by the door, where it sat until this morning."

"Ah, rugs," said the officer.

"I wonder what's the sentence for stealing rugs these days," I heard Idaho whisper, and then more shushes.

"Yes, I had her rug in my possession. But do you

know what Mrs. Bixby did?"

"Asked to have it back?" guessed the officer.

"NO, she took that frozen old rug and whacked the dog."

"Whoa, whack a dog. Just like 'whack a mole,'" chortled Idaho. Lily reached out and clamped a hand over Idaho's mouth.

The officer flipped a thumb over his shoulder toward Idaho and asked, "Ah, she's not driving anywhere, is she?"

"No, she's drinking, Dan, not driving," I said exasperated. "Look, Dan, I didn't steal her rugs, and Blue doesn't know any better. He's a dog!"

"Mrs. Bixby said you threatened her. Is that true?"

"Only after she smacked Blue. I told her if she ever laid a hand on him again, I'd smack her with that broom she rides." I was clearly worked up now and I felt indignant that I was being questioned for such a stupid dispute. "Maybe I should file an animal abuse complaint against Mrs. Bixby. Can I do that?"

"Okay, okay," Dan said holding up a hand. "Look, I think this has gone far enough. What I'd like you to do is come with me right now, and let's get this straightened out with the two of you. Are you willing to do that?"

"Oh, fine," I said giving in. I glanced over at the women where Idaho still struggled to free Lily's hand from her mouth. "I'll be right back, ladies," I called to the women. To Dan, I said, "Let me get my coat."

I had time to cool off before Dan and I reached Mrs. Bixby's house. I realized that this whole thing was pretty darn silly in comparison to what my friends and I were facing with Goodman's death. I needed to be as congenial as possible. And so, I was.

Dan was gracious enough not to ask me to apologize to Mrs. Bixby like some insolent child, but I did. And, when Mrs. Bixby told the officer that I was bad news for the whole neighborhood, I bit my tongue until it bled. I willed myself to breathe deeply while making the effort to let it go as we parted by shaking hands and agreeing to be better neighbors to each other.

Dan walked with me back to the house. "Thank you, Olivia, you were very cooperative," he said. "I know it's hard when you've got a neighbor like her, who wants to be in everyone's business. But you were the bigger person. I thank you for that, too."

"Yeah, well thank you for acknowledging Mrs. Busybody for what she is," I replied.

Dan turned to me again as he was getting into his car and said, "You might want to think about some training for your dog. There are several good dog trainers I could recommend. Oh, and you should probably get him licensed."

"Yeah, thanks for the info," I said, and waved goodbye. "I'd certainly do that if it was my dog," I grumbled to myself.

When I returned to the women, they were full of questions. I recounted the story of Blue and Mrs. Bixby. "I didn't think she'd really call the police though," I griped. "What timing, for Officer McKenzie to show up when we're already nervous as hell. But why were you all so paralyzed when I brought him in? You looked darn silly staring at us like we were a car accident or something. I told you it was okay and tried to get you to turn around."

Pamela mumbled something.

"What did you say?" I asked.

Maggie cleared her throat and said, "Well, ah...the way you were flapping your hands and doing the shoving motion thing, we didn't quite understand what you were asking us to do."

"What do you mean asking you to do, all I wanted was for you to sit down."

"We thought you said put him down," Lily answered.

"Why on earth would I say 'put him down' for crying out loud? Put him down as in 'whack a man' knock him out, like that?" I fumed. The women sheepishly shrugged in unison.

"See why we were confused?" explained Lily.

"There's communication for you," noted Pamela. "It's pretty funny, when you think about it."

"Okay," I said, "Obviously, we've got murder on the brain. Are we up for this? I mean, if we panic like this just because a cop walks in the door, how are we going to deal with a real questioning on the subject of Goodman?"

"Actually," said Maggie. "I think this was a good dry run. I've been thinking about it. I'm sure we can carry on with our current plans."

"I agree," said Pamela. "Seeing a policeman standing in your living room kind of made Goodman's death a little more real. I'm more ready than ever to see justice is done. And to make sure my kids don't become orphans."

Snores were emanating from Olivia's couch. Idaho was passed out cold. Lily took the bottle of brandy from

Idaho's loving embrace, tipped it up and polished off the contents.

"Count me in," chirped Lily waving the empty bottle.

Taking their to-do-lists, the women said goodbye and suddenly the house was quiet. Except for the sound of Idaho's rattled breathing. I draped a blanket over her. And then I decided I had one more thing to do before the day ended—before I could talk myself out of it. I googled phone numbers on my phone, then dialed the number for Rocco Basham.

Chapter 10 - Rand Dubois

"You heard what Mrs. Goodman said, right?" asked Alan. The sheriff, Alan and I were at the interrogation table to debrief the interview with Mora Goodman. Alan seemed excited to add to the discussion. I was pleased he was taking a serious interest in the case.

"What's that, son?" I encouraged.

"She suggested that Mr. Goodman may have been sleeping with Lily White," reminded Alan. "Witches is what she called the group of five women with whom Goodman had met. Maybe they are a real coven."

"Witches, hmm, I remember that, yes," I noted.

"Okay, it got me to thinking. While you were finishing up the interview, I got on the internet. I searched for rituals and pentagrams. You said you suspect that this may have been a Satanic act. It's true, the pentagram is used by Satanists, witches and black and white magicians to invoke or banish demons."

"You say banish demons?" Bishop inquired, "Why would a Satanist banish a demon. Don't they want to call the demons to do whatever it is they're supposed to do?"

"Good point," replied Alan. "However, it seems in the Satanic world, if the pentagram is inverted, meaning that the point is facing down, it usually means casting evil. It wasn't until about the late 1960's that the pentagram became a symbol as a common neo-pagan and Wiccan symbol, usually used to banish demons and evil spirits."

"Hmm, we found Goodman in the right side up pentagram—if you will, which you say is more indicative of the Wiccan or witches," said Bishop.

"That certainly fits," I observed. "Again, I'll refer to the Mary Bell case. The pentagram found there was inverted, which looked like a goat's head. And it was most definitely a Satanic murder."

"Wait, there's more," Alan explained. "The Wiccan sometimes use the inverted pentagram with one point down signifying 'spirit subservient to matter, of man subservient to his carnal desires'."

"I'm not following you," I said. "That last bit of information seems irrelevant. We found Goodman in the right side up pentagram."

"Maybe they just ain't too smart," offered Bishop.

"And are you saying that there may be a sexual connotation to this murder?" I asked.

"Mrs. Goodman said that she figured one or all those witches might be sleeping with her husband," Alan pointed out. "The murder could have been sexual in nature. Women scorned, that sort of thing."

"There's a motive for you," said Bishop. "But Goodman was found in an up-right position in the pentagram."

Alan shrugged. "Maybe not," he said. "Perhaps it's all a matter of perspective. We observed the body while we faced the fireplace. Perhaps the CTC, or witches, drew the pentagram facing Goodman with their back to the fireplace."

"Shit, double whammy—body upside-down in an

inverted pentagram," quipped Bishop. "Now that's a bad day."

Alan continued, "The normal tools of a ritual usually consist of a dagger, a chalice, candles and pentagrams. Were there any of those other items besides the pentagram found with the body?"

I'll be damned. The boy was asking the same questions I might have asked given a few moments to think. Bishop and I began searching through the evidence folders for those answers, but with no success. "No, I don't see anything like that listed here. Except the fire poker could represent the dagger I suppose," I said. "However, it does say the pentagram was drawn with smudges of ash."

Alan looked over my shoulder and said, "Yes, using ashes fits with the Satanic ritual."

"Perhaps there had been a fire in the fireplace. That could have taken the place of candles," I suggested.

Bishop pointed to the list and said, "Here it says there was a belt buckle found in the ashes of the fireplace. It looks as if they burned his clothing. Still, the thing that bothers me is that the pentagram was drawn after the body was nailed to the floor." He pulled out a photo and pointed to the open lines on the pentagram where the drawer of the pentagram had skipped over a leg and an arm. "It wasn't drawn none too straight either. To me that screams of someone coming in after the fact and making it look like Satanism."

He let the file folder fall to the table. "I don't know," grumbled Bishop, "I don't believe all this hocus-pocus shit. That's just too complicated for me. I believe in the Occam's Razor theory. When things get too complicated, the simpler answer is usually the better."

"Well, it's definitely interesting that there are five points to a pentagram and five women meeting with Goodman. And those five women were called witches by Mora. I was going to question Ms. White, but let's check out the rest of them. I'll get Ms. White's address, and we'll pay her a visit. I'm sure she can help us with the rest of the names."

Alan grabbed my arm and said in a whisper, "Dad, I have a really strong feeling that these women have something to do with this."

I nodded, because I had the same feeling. However, I told him, "We need to be careful not to jump to conclusions, son. We need to stick to our facts, and we will get this resolved."

"Let's get back to the little Mrs.," said Bishop. He wasn't convinced that Mora was not guilty. "Maybe she didn't kill her husband, but that doesn't mean someone else she knows and loves didn't help her," Bishop was saying. "Maybe those women helped her. Maybe she hired her son to do it. If you ask me, she seemed awful protective of her son, who had just happened to disappear at the same time we found his dead father."

"That's certainly a possibility, Sheriff, and I will not dismiss those facts," I said, "But I'm inclined to think she didn't kill him. First, at the time of the murder she was in Italy, not Montana. We've proven that. Second, as she said, they lived separate lives. She could come and go when and where she wanted with no financial worries. Third, to me, she seemed genuinely concerned about her son Seth's disappearance. Fourth, and pardon me for saying this, I don't think she's bright enough to pull off something like this to the degree of complexity that it took to kill Goodman."

It was late afternoon, when Bishop had sandwiches brought in. We sat munching burgers and fries as we continued to review the Goodman file.

I turned to Bishop. "I see that Jennifer Stephens found Mr. Goodman?"

"Yeah, she was a neighbor walking by," he answered. "She saw his car door open. He had wine in the front, said it was frozen. She walked up the steps, knocked on the door to let him know. When there was no answer she looked through a side window. She saw Goodman lying on the floor not moving. She knocked again, took another peek, and realized not only was he down, but was naked and tied to the floor. She ran home to call 911.

"Can I have some of that ketchup over there?" Bishop pointed in Alan's direction.

Alan picked up a couple packets and tossed them over to Bishop. One landed in a coffee cup spraying dark liquid across the paperwork on the table. "Hoorah! Two points for the dude. Good pass, son. And you have just succeeded in officially breaking in the case by leaving coffee stains to show we're doin' our homework. You sure you've never worked homicide before?" Alan snorted and beamed with delight.

"What kind of a neighbor was this woman? Did she have any vendettas or any reason she might want to kill Goodman?" I asked.

"Well, I know she didn't like the man. She told one of my deputies he got after a neighbor's dog earlier this year for snooping around his property. I guess there was a property dispute between the two, which made for uncomfortable relations to begin with. He claims the dog nipped him in the butt when he tried to shoo it away. I guess he told her neighbor to take care of her dog or he would."

Alan's eyes almost popped out of his head. With a cheek wad of hamburger, he managed to muffle, "He freatened to kill the dog? Shee, Dad, I told you dogsh would bite him in the assh." He turned to Bishop, swallowed the contents in his mouth and said, "He wasn't a nice guy."

"Alan," I explained, shaking my head, "just because dogs don't like him doesn't mean he wasn't a nice guy. And it's not enough for her to want to kill the man."

"Are ya sure about that, Dad?" Alan retorted. "Better not jump to conclusions." Bishop's smile and glance in my direction was much too smug.

Bishop reached over and pulled out a faxed page from a clipboard and pointed. "Here's some information I had my secretary Google." He raised an eyebrow, winked at Alan and said, "Gotta love that internet. Seems Goodman was quite the philanthropist. He's most known for his financial support to the Friends of St. Paul, a group that builds and remodels homes for the disadvantaged. He was the Chairman of the Board for the Holly Foundation for abused children. The man was heavily involved with Boy Scouts of America. He sat on the board of directors for the local Community Action Team. Became chairman of the board for the Kootenai Partners Federal Credit Union last year. And sponsored several youth programs. Through those programs, he set yearly top dollar scholarships. He put lots of his own money into those scholarships, from what I understand.

"Oh, here's something else," said Bishop. He wiped away some crumbs from his chin and chest. "He's an investor who gets others to invest and loan money to different projects at high interest rates. I always knew he was a big-money man."

"Hmm, sounds like a model citizen, eh? Could there be some bad loans? Perceived loan sharking going on?" I asked, thinking aloud.

Bishop frowned. "Yeah, well, so anyway the town's people will be pretty upset to have their funds cut off like this. I know he's been the sole support for some of our agencies since the mill shut down."

"Yes," I said. "I understand that the two major employers in Libby, W.R. Grace Mining Company and Stimson Lumber Mill, shut down. It must have left behind a crippled community to say nothing of the economy. I'm quite sure that any money to help support this town was very welcomed."

Bishop shook his head and said, "I tell ya, I sure hope it's something as simple as loan sharking and not some damn cult group again." He stood up and gathered the garbage from our lunch and tossed it in the waste basket. "I better get back into my office and answer some phone calls and emails. You kids have fun." He waved and was gone, leaving behind the smell of French fries wafting in the air and coffee stained papers lining the table.

"Come on, Alan," I said jamming papers back into the file, "Let's go talk to Lily White. That might be fun!"

We drove over the bridge on Highway 35 out of

Libby. Then took the first left after the bridge and another left following a dirt road. When we reached the end, an old Victorian mansion overlooked the Kootenai River and most of the small town of Libby. Prime real estate for sure. There was a white picket fence that surrounded a large yard and garden area. This place shouted upscale affluence. Lily White was just getting out of her vehicle when we arrived. When she saw us, she graced us with a smile and warm handshake as if we were long-lost friends.

"Well, if it isn't Mr. Dubois," Lily greeted.

I was taken aback. The woman was stunning with her long red hair and shapely figure—and very stylish, which seemed out of place in a town like Libby. "Have we met, Ms. White?" I asked, trying to reclaim my hand and reel my tongue back into my mouth.

"Not formally, but we have now," she cooed and nodded with a sexy look that engulfed both Alan and me. "I certainly know who you are," she winked.

I introduced Alan as my associate, but then wondered if I should have introduced him as my under-aged son. But I guess, at twenty-six, the lad is pretty much on his own.

"Why don't you come on in a while? I can put some coffee on," she purred.

Alan and I helped her with her grocery bags. Then we found our way to the living room. She went to the kitchen to get sodas, since I told her we were past the coffee hour and wine wasn't an option since we were on duty.

"Look at this house," whispered Alan gawking around the room. "She must be rich!"

It was a large two-story home with exquisite hand-carved, crown moldings in every visible room. Her home was warm and inviting despite its size. The living room was tastefully done in light browns with brighter floral accents that were not overpowering but still caught the Victorian flavor. A staircase wound up to the second floor where, at the top of the stairs, I could see a large portrait of Lily in a dazzling evening gown clasping the hand of—I had to look closer, but I was quite certain it was—Bill Clinton. I craned my neck to get a clearer view.

"Would you like to get a better look?" hummed Lily in my ear, handing me a drink.

Startled and guilty as charged for intrusion, I stammered, "Is . . . is that Bill Clinton?"

"Yes, at a fundraiser," she sighed and brushed a lovely manicured hand across my shoulders, sending goosebumps clear down to my crotch. "But that damn Monica Lewinski got to him first."

Lily handed Alan his drink. He was perusing the many other photos that adorned her sofa table and grand piano top. "Just more fund-raisers I'm afraid," she nodded to the grouping.

"You've really met all these people?" Alan questioned pointing to pictures of Lily at a golf tournament with Tiger Woods. Another of Lily at the beach in a sexy bikini on the arm of Mel Gibson, on stage with U2, and playing chess with Sting. Those were just a few of the ones I saw at a glance.

"It's not as glamorous as it all seems," she said. "Many of them are grouchy, dirty old men. But if I want the funds, I need to play with the guns, as they say. But

I'm sure you aren't here to give me money, or are you? Perhaps you're looking for help to fund the policeman's ball?"

"No, Ms. White, unfortunately, it's not that," I said trying to connect with my professional voice as the conversation was becoming too easy and the couch too comfortable. "You may have heard that Ira Goodman has been murdered."

"Oh yes, I saw your picture in the paper this morning," she replied. "Murdered—huh? Too bad. He had lots of money to give to this community. But what has that to do with me?"

I sat up a little straighter. I said, "There is a rumor that you and he were having an affair."

Her eyes widened and blinked twice. Suddenly, she began to laugh.

Allowing her time, I finally questioned, "May I ask what's so funny, Ms. White?" I wondered if I'd missed a joke or something else.

"I'm sorry," she said, wiping her eyes. "I guess my reputation precedes me."

"So, you were having an affair."

"With the little dick that man had?" she tossed her head, and laughed again.

I waited a moment and continued, "Well? Were you?"

"No," she said, shaking her head, still laughing. She must have sensed that I wasn't convinced because she added, "Oh, I guess you're wondering then, just how I know he was dickless." And she began the laughter again.

I waited.

"Oh, all right," she said. "I nailed him once. Well, I tried. However, he couldn't finish the deed. But it was a long time ago, a time when he was good-looking, and I was less particular. A long time ago," she emphasized. "It was at a fund-raiser and we were in the back of an old bank building in the vault, if you can imagine that." She began laughing again. "He was tugging at my panties when the vault door swung shut and —"

I held up both palms. "I don't need the details, please!" I said cutting her off.

"Too bad, it's a pretty funny story. Did you know, he screams like a little girl when he's scared?" and then in a whisper, she said, "He's afraid of the dark. Well he was. I wonder if he's screaming now?"

"Please, Ms. White."

"Well, suffice it to say, I had way too much to drink that night. It was never reenacted, no second chances for him."

"Do you know of anyone else who may have been having an affair with him?" I asked.

"Don't know, don't care."

"You were seen with Goodman and four other women having dinner about a month ago. Were any of those women having an affair with him?"

Lily gave me a confused look, "Mr. Dubois, I know lots of women, and men of course. I've no idea what you're talking about. I've had many dinners with lots of people in the last month. Can you be more specific?"

"Are you a Wiccan?" Alan chimed in.

Leave it to Alan to be so blunt. I had been toiling with how to broach the subject myself. It's been my experience that one should be subtle with a delicate question such as this. Take a moment to gather some facts. Put the implications on a board and scramble the possibilities, shuffle the outcome and then reshuffle. Lay it out on the board again, and then run over it with a Mac truck. But there it was, out in the open, with no thought and only four words. That's my boy.

Lily's head craned slowly to the side to look at him directly. "What kind of a question is that?" she grouched. Alan stared back coolly, the corners of his lips turning up into an innocent smile, and shrugged. No fear in the face of a riled barracuda. I liked that. He was taking to this job.

"Alan," she answered, "Yes, I am a witch. At least once a month. Or, if I don't get my way. But I do not cast spells. I believe people make their own karma by voodooing themselves."

"I'm sorry, Ms. White." I said coming to Alan's aid. "But you must understand that we're investigating an abnormal murder here. There are Satanic and Wiccan implications, and we cannot leave any stone unturned. We need to ask these questions, eh?"

"Well, let me help you out then and cut to the chase," said Lily. "The only time I can recall that I was in public with a group of women was when we were meeting with Goodman to close a financial deal. That was about three weeks ago. I'm sure you know by now that he was an investor, among the many other things he had his sicky fingers in." I nodded, and she continued. "Well, we had the misfortune of investing with the pig. We invested a lot of hard-earned dollars with him, and we just found out that the construction company he gave the money to filed bankruptcy. Now, Mr. Dubois, you can imagine how upset we were to read in the paper this morning that our only link to our money had just been 'offed'."

"Did you and your friends confront Goodman?" I asked, trying to keep accusations out of my voice.

"We tried, but he kept giving us the slip. Conveniently out of town, that sort of thing. There are probably a few more people out there that got stiffed as well. All I can say is that someone got to him before we could get our hands on him. It was probably for the best, because I'm thinking that his chest is not where the fire poker would have been found." She stole a side glance at Alan and apologized, "Sorry kid, just close your eyes to that visual."

"So, you were all mad enough to kill him?" Alan asked.

"Actually, no. Killing would have been too good for the scumbag. We would have tortured him," she glowered with narrowed eyes.

"Who are the other women?" I inquired. "And I'll need their phone numbers and addresses as well."

"Sure, no problem, I'll get that for you."

After Lily gave me the addresses and phone numbers, Alan and I were on the road again.

"You were right, Dad," Alan said. "That was fun! And what a fox." He wiggled his eyebrows.

"You can say that again. A lying, sly, little fox." I said.

Alan bobbed his head, "Yep, I get it."

"Yeah, well the fun's not over, Son. You better tighten that scarf around your skinny, little neck. We need to get to those other wily foxes before they begin to pack and circle in on us."

"Yeah, God knows I don't want a fire poker up my a—"

"Alan," I interrupted. "Keep your eye out for the turn to Pipe Creek Road."

Chapter 11 - Rand Dubois

I called and left a message for Sheriff Bishop to let him know that Alan and I were going to follow up the lead on the other four women. Catching people off guard has always been one of my investigative techniques.

Pamela Phuchet lived nearby so she was first on my list. Several miles down the road I found the cutoff connecting us to Pipe Creek Road. I drove a quarter of a mile and came to a dead halt at the Red Dog Saloon and Pizza. The Red Dog is a Saloon that was constructed out in the middle of nowhere ten miles from town. It was first built as a small grocery store to cater to the hunters and the few folks who lived in the area. They expanded to a restaurant and then started serving pizzas. The skiers returning from Turner Mountain ski resort took full advantage of that. The only food at the resort was candy bars, soda pop and beef jerky served out of an old yurt. Over the years, the Red Dog's pizza has gained a reputation of being the best this side of the Rockies, and now people come from all over—Canada included—if not for the pizza, for the experience of it all. I should know, I've spent plenty of time there myself.

It's a rustic, old, log building with warped floors, where you can shoot pool, gamble the slots, swill beer, and throw your peanut shells on the floor. This evening proved to be a busy night, and we waited in a line of cars to pass. A big party was taking their time to give handshakes and hugs, and say their good-byes in the middle of the road while they crossed to the other side—completely oblivious to the waiting traffic. Even though Ms. Phuchet was only three miles away, it took us at least twenty minutes to get there.

Ms. Phuchet lived in an old farmhouse that looked like it needed a good handyman, if not a total makeover. A barn stood in the background with a sign advertising the Moosehead Tree Farm. A big moose head was displayed over the sign. Flood lights in the background lit up a forest of rowed trees ready for the U-cut customers, and potted trees for those who prefer live ones. There were several rows of tied-up Christmas trees lying in the yard that looked as if they were being prepared for shipment. Alan and I wound our way to the door in a makeshift path. The porch light blazed as we set foot before the door. After ringing the doorbell, the door cracked open as far as the door chain would allow, and two sets of small eyes peered up at us through the opening.

"Well, hello, young man," I greeted. "May I speak to your mother?" I said to a small boy on the other side of the door.

"Mooooom!" called the small boy. "There's a man and a woman out here and they want to talk to you!" I heard a woman's voice from a distance ask who it was.

The older boy hollered, "I don't know but the woman has a beard." The younger boy snickered and sang out, "Yeah, a weirdo with a beardo!" In surprise, I looked at Alan with his long red hair and noted that indeed he was due for a good lather and razor.

"I love kids," Alan breathed through clenched teeth. We began to laugh.

"Parker and Gabe, stop that!" I heard a woman say. "Get back away from the door." The door closed, I heard the latch slide, and the door opened. A tall, thin woman in her early to mid-thirties smiled sweetly and invited us in. She had gray streaks intermingled in long dark hair. Unlike the fashionable Lily, Ms. Phuchet was dressed in sweats. The two young boys took refuge behind their mother's legs and peered up at us. They stood ready with weapons to take on the strangers that invaded their mother's doorstep. The two boys were wearing only superhero underwear One was Superman, the other Avengers. They sported no shirts, and their feet were shoved into oversized cowboy boots. Each one had a red towel used as a makeshift cape clipped at the neck with a clothes pin. Both wore large-rimmed swimming goggles. The older boy pointed a toy laser gun at me, and the other a toilet plunger.

"You know, I've been a detective for a very long time. I don't believe I've ever had a welcome such as this," I humored. "Your mother is in good hands with the two of you protecting her." The boys began to make mock shooting sounds.

"Ms. Phuchet, I'm Inspector Dubois, and this is my son, Alan Dubois."

"I am sooo sorry," she said as the shooting continued. "Parker, Gabe! Stop that!"

"Mom, can we have our ice cream now?" asked the older boy.

"Yeah, you thaid we could have thome after we washed the pee off Baker'th head," lisped the younger boy.

Ms. Phuchet blushed and said to us, "Baker's the goat." She shrugged and said, "It's a long story."

"I'm sure it is," I nodded.

"Please come in. I'm sorry about this. I'm trying to get an order of Christmas trees out before morning. Sorry about the mess, too," she explained.

Unlike the outside of the tattered house, the inside was homey, and well-decorated for the holiday season. Except for the children's toys scattered about and a few newspapers on chairs, the house was tidy. The smell of cookies baking filled the living room. My stomach growled. The younger boy looked at me with his goggled eyes and pointed his toilet plunger at my stomach. "You got aliens in there, Mithtr?"

"Guys, to the kitchen! NOW!" demanded Ms. Phuchet. She said it with such authority that all four of us stood at attention and marched to the kitchen, Gabe and Parker leading the way.

"I'm so sorry, Mr. Dubois," said the thin woman. "As you can see, I've got my hands full. Oh, and by the way, thanks for pronouncing Phuchet correctly. I sure get tired of 'Fucket'. But please call me Pamela. I'm more comfortable with that anyway."

"All right then, Pamela it is. And, thank you for not calling me 'Mr. Doboyz'. Please call me Rand."

"Iiiiice cream noooow, Paaamela!!" came a sing-song call from one of the boys already sitting at the table.

"You, Mr. Superman, will call me mom! And you will get it when I am ready to give it!" She turned to us and asked, "Rand, Alan, would you like some cookies and ice cream, or milk?" We gladly accepted. I tried to remember the last time I had chocolate chip cookies with a glass of milk. I was starting to like this woman, who did indeed have her hands full.

When Alan bit into his warm, fudgy cookie, his eyes rolled to the back of his head. With milk mustache and smacking lips, he whispered, "She's another sly temptress," and then he bit into another lure of decadence.

"Alan," I said, "could you stay in the kitchen and entertain the boys while Pamela and I talk a moment?" He gave me the evil stink eye, but plunked down at the table beside the boys.

Pamela and I moved to the living room. "Don't let them talk you into giving them any Mountain Dew, Alan," she hollered over her shoulder. To me she said, "I know you're here to talk about Goodman."

"You do?" I questioned

"Yeah, Lily called and gave me the low-down," confessed Pamela. "All points bulletin to all of us women actually."

"All women?" I feigned ignorance.

To which she replied, "Seriously? Please, don't play dumb with me. You know, us women in the investment club?"

I nodded, and she continued. "You really scared her. She said you accused us of being witches? Is that right?"

"As I told Ms. White, this is a rather peculiar kind of murder. We need to ask a lot of hard and sometimes odd questions. I'd like to hear how you answer it."

She sighed and her shoulders sagged, "I am not a

witch. We women are not witches. I don't even like that sort of stuff talked about in front of my kids. There is enough scary stuff in this world without living the Blair Witch Project. The CTC is who I've got my money on."

"You've read the news article," I nodded toward the end table, where the newspaper laid folded so that mine and Alan's photo was face up. "The CTC are only a suspicion. There are facts that I'm not allowed to discuss with you that suggest it may not be them."

"Lily also told you that we lost a lot of money to Goodman," she said. "We were angry but we did not kill him. We couldn't even get close enough to talk to him!"

"So, I understand," I said. "But maybe you found him tied to the floor and even though he may not have been in a mood to talk, maybe you were angry enough to plant a fire poker in his chest."

"Was that the actual cause of death?"

"You tell me, Pamela."

"Wow! You must think I'm a real psycho."

"Are you?"

"I've got two high-strung, imaginative, and very curious boys who love to experiment with anything they can get their hands on. Of course, I am! At least a little bit, but don't tell them that. They think I'm just a mean drill sergeant."

I couldn't help but smile at that. "I'm curious, too. What is the significance of urine on a goat's head, eh?" I inquired.

"Wow, you're really stuck on that witch thing, aren't you?" Pamela snorted.

"Pretty much," I shrugged.

"The significance is a dare made by a six-year-old

boy for his little brother to pee on a poor, defenseless goat. Rand, it is not some witch's sacrament, and it damn well better not become a weekly ritual or some little butts will be very red. Don't read so much into those innocent bits of detail."

"I have to—" I started but she cut me off.

"You have to ask, I know. But let me tell you this, I have a house to fix up before it caves in around my ears. I have a business that almost failed because I lost a couple of Christmas tree crops to a forest fire last summer. I've two boys I need to raise and put through college. And I'm still trying to pay off some of the debts left by my late husband. I lost every ounce of my savings to that asshole Goodman. And by god, I'll tell you right now, nothing is going to stop me from finding out where that money went. If anything, I'm pissed as hell that he died before I got some answers from him. And who knows, if I had talked to him and hadn't got satisfactory answers, then maybe your visit today would not be in vain."

I could only nod. I admired her spirit. She and I both looked toward the kitchen where we heard giggles escalating. Alan and the boys were playing Rock, Paper, Scissors, where the prize for the winner was a sip from a liter bottle of Mountain Dew. Alan quite possibly was giggling the loudest.

"Damn, not the Mountain Dew," she moaned. "They'll never get to sleep tonight." And then to me she said, "Oh, by the way. I was not sleeping with Mr. Dickless either."

It was me who snorted this time, "I see your friend, Ms. White, was very thorough with her account of our conversation." I smiled even though I was pissed as hell not to have gotten to the women before Lily had. "I am sorry for taking up so much of your time and," I tipped my head toward the kitchen, "the Mountain Dew, too."

Pamela smiled and said, "Well you and Alan can make it up to me by helping me get the last of those bailed trees out front onto the truck. It'll save me at least two hours of work."

And so, we did.

Chapter 12 - Rand Dubois

"Cute kids, eh?" I said, as Alan and I were on our way to Maggie Berns's house.

Alan nodded.

"Lots of energy. Did they ever figure out you were a man?"

Alan shrugged.

"You seemed to be having lots of fun with them, giggling and all."

Alan shrugged again.

"Alan, what were you thinking, giving those boys Mountain Dew after she asked you not to?"

He shrugged once more but smiled mischievously. "Pay backs a bitch," he said.

At the end of Pipe Creek Road heading back towards town, I turned right onto Highway 37 and then right onto River View Road. Maggie Berns had a large contemporary home built on a knoll that also looked over the Kootenai River. I rang the doorbell, then heard loud thuds and banging on the other side. Just then the door opened. A St. Bernard bounded out, planting his front paws squarely on Alan's chest, knocking him ass-over-teakettle. Alan sprang up as if nothing had happened, although covered in slobber. I was glad the dog had chosen Alan, as I'm sure a tumble like that for me would have ended my evening in the emergency ward with a bad back. Dog spittle flew and covered both of us. The dog began licking Alan with its big tongue completely covering his face in one swipe, probably getting the scent of cookies and milk.

"Baby! Come here. Down, boy!" cried a buxom woman in a clinging silk green robe. She was quite lovely with her brown hair a little mussed and flying around her face. The silk outlined every curve highlighting that she had nothing on underneath. "Sorry," she called to us and tried to retrieve the dog. "Baby is still a puppy, and he kisses those he likes. He's harmless. Please go on in."

Alan, wiping dog drool from his face and clothing, asked, "Does Baby like Mountain Dew?"

"No, why do you ask?" Ms. Berns quizzed, giving him a look that seemed to question his sanity.

"Just wondered is all," he stood wiping more drool from his clothes. She looked at him as if he was very odd, but I thought him quite clever.

"Ms. Berns, I'm Detective Dubois, and this is my son Alan. We'd like to speak with you for a moment."

"Okay, let me get Baby calmed down," she said. "Go on in the house, and I'll put him into his kennel over there," she pointed to a cement slab with an enormous two-story dog house—a replica of the main house, complete with curtains in the windows, and I could see an insulated doggy door. Steam rolled up around the edges of the dry cement suggesting the concrete slab was heated.

"In my next life, I want to be her dog," announced Alan.

We stepped inside to a large foyer. To our left was a living room and to the right was an open door to a den with a full office setup. We stepped aside as Ms. Berns came in the front entrance and closed the door to the den. "Okay, I got him settled. He really likes you, Alan. Do you have a dog?" she asked.

Alan shook his head.

"He normally cowers when people come. He doesn't take to strangers like that," she whispered. Alan shrugged. Then she turned to me and said in a whisper, "What can I help you with, Mr. Dubois?"

"Ms. Berns, I'm investigating the death of Ira Goodman. I understand that you had some investments with the man."

"Wait a minute," Alan speculated. "Are you the Maggie Berns from House Made of Kids and Daddy's Girl?"

"Yes," she whispered. "But I think you're a little young to remember that."

Alan was bubbling with delight. "No, no. I watch all your shows on Nick at Night." He turned to me, "This is Maggie Berns!"

I cleared my throat. "Yes, I know. And isn't it interesting that you, Ms. Berns, have invested your money with Ira Goodman, who is now deceased."

"Dad, she is sooo funny!" Alan insisted.

"Yes, and isn't it funny that Ms. Berns has invested money with a dead man, Alan," I said trying to redirect the conversation.

Alan began a hee-haw. "Oh yeah, remember the episode where you had to do summer school? You were outside terrorizing the cat with a hose and didn't want to do your homework and your mom said, 'Oh, yes, you are because I'm the Wicked Witch of the West,' and you said, 'Oh yeah? Well, I've got a hose, and I'm not afraid to use it.'" Alan seemed quite amused by that. He turned to look at me when I didn't laugh and explained, "You know, the wicked witch from the land of Oz?" When I still didn't respond, he continued, "You know, a little water on her and she melts into a pile of . . .?"

"Alan," I warned, "I've seen the Wizard of OZ. Let's find out what Ms. Berns has to say."

"Yes, those were the fun times all right," she whispered. She turned to me. "So, that's what Lily was babbling about on my voice mail. I guess I didn't realize I'd get a visit directly from you, Mr. Dubois. Yes, we did invest money. But what does it have to do with his death?"

"Well, Ms. Berns, most murders happen due to love, hate, greed, money, and/or avarice."

"Ah, avarice?" she chuckled.

To my surprise, Alan answered, "Greedy insatiable desire." He licked his lips and waggled his eyebrows.

"Ah, yes indeed," I confirmed. "I think your investment with Goodman is a good place to start. And why are we whispering?"

"Oh, I've got company," she smiled wanly and tipped her head toward a door that I assumed to be a bedroom. "We were kind of interrupted, but I'm sure he's asleep by now. He's had a hard day, and I don't want to disturb him. But to answer your question, yes, we all invested money. However, we aren't the only ones. You may want to talk to Fred Barlow, Arnold Grey, Alex Martin and whoever else invested with him. Several of them are on the city council and have done business with Goodman for a lot longer than we have."

I wrote down the names. "Are any of them involved in witchery, Satanism, or perhaps the CTC, that you know of?"

"Of course, I wouldn't know something like that. I hardly think that would be common knowledge, except for those who believe in such nonsense. But I see where you are going with this. I read the article. Do you suspect that the CTC is back?"

"It's either them or another group. I need to ask if you and your friends are practicing witches."

"What?" she tried to hold back a laugh. "Like brooms and spells and bump in the night kind of shit?"

I shrugged.

"Heavens, no," she scoffed. "Although, I did play a witch in the Wizard of Oz one time, does that count? Quite a superb performance, if I say so myself." Then she winked at Alan, and he beamed like a school boy as he rifled through his pockets for something.

"How well did you know Goodman," I asked. "Were you having an affair with the man?" She had been taking a drink of something as I asked the question and almost snorted it out her nose. She covered her face and began to laugh.

"Sorry, I thought you asked if I was having an affair with Goodman," she said, dabbing up her fluids with a napkin.

"Yes, I did say that," I replied bluntly.

"For as good an actress as I am, I swear, I couldn't even act the part of having an affair with that horn dog. Why would you ask such a thing?"

"You were seen having lunch with him. My source says that someone from the "women's group" you hang with said that one or all of you were sleeping with him."

"You are crazy!" she accused. "Even if your source used a camera in my bedroom, they would definitely understand that I don't swing towards that species."

"Species?" I inquired.

"Yeah, I don't do jack-asses."

With that, Alan's eyes almost popped out of their sockets. He smiled wide and presented a pen and a piece of crumpled paper to her, "Could I have your autograph?" She cupped one hand around his face as if he were a child, smiled and signed the paper. Handing back the paper, she asked, "Is that all?"

"Thank you, Ms. Berns. You must understand that I need to ask."

"Okay, you asked. Is there anything else, or do I need to get my attorney?"

"Not yet," I surmised. "We'll be on our way. Thank you for your time Ms. Berns."

We began to walk out when she called after us, "Wait! Watch out for the flying monkeys!" I looked at her in surprise. Her sly smile was aimed at Alan. "Just a little witch humor," she winked.

Alan began to laugh hysterically, "See Dad? She is so funny."

Exhaustion overcame me when I realized that we had two more stops to make. Idaho was next on the list. That was the only name I had—not sure if it was a first name or last—but I had the address. We traveled over the bridge into town and down Mineral Avenue to make a turn on Hwy 2 West. I followed my GPS out past ShopKo. I turned right onto a road that led toward the river on the opposite side from Lily, Pamela, and Maggie's places. I pulled up to a small house that couldn't have been more than a few hundred square feet. No lights were on and, when I knocked, there was only a mew from a cat beyond the door. Alan went around the back, looking in windows, and when he returned, he reported no one was in the house.

I drove on to the home of Olivia Hope, only two blocks down. The blocks were longer than city blocks and less populated—at least for now. It looked as if development was about to explode if the town were to recover from the economic demise. We passed a large, old Victorian home. It was stunning, with the Christmas lights illuminating the entire street and shimmering like diamonds on the snow and river water—an ideal Hallmark card for sure. I paused to take in the Norman Rockwell moment. Alan asked, "Is this Ms. Hope's house?"

I looked at the mail box planted in front of the house which said it belonged to Mr. & Mrs. Bixby. I looked at my GPS and shook my head. "No, I think hers is the next house down."

We moved slowly, still ogling the incredibly lit street. We pulled up in front of a small log house with a dimly lit porch higher up on a hill. The cabin looked as if it may have been an original from the early 1900's. A woman stood on the porch steps calling out something. Her long blond hair floated like wings in the puffs of wind that swirled around her. She was dressed in blue jeans, a thin white t-shirt that accented firm, full breasts and a brown plaid flannel shirt with shirttails flapping lazily around her shapely hips. I heard her calling, "Blue,

Blue."

I was taken aback at how beautiful she was. She looked like an angel. And I must have said as much because Alan sighed dreamily, "Yeah, Victoria Secret meets Eddie Bauer."

I took a moment to gather myself, and I finally took a firm hold of my badge and trudged forward with bold manhood. I realized—when my senses returned to me—that this goddess was calling to a dog. I could see under the streetlights a big black dog running after a boy pulling a saucer sled—dog, head down, on a dead run, growling wildly. I suddenly feared that the dog might bite the child. I found myself shouting to the woman, "Does your dog bite?"

"No, no," she shouted back.

Just then, the big black dog chomped a hold on the boy's saucer, the boy fell to the ground. The three of us quickly ran to the boy. When we reached him, he was giggling uncontrollably. The dog was licking him and intermittently pulling on the rope of the sled in a gesture of play.

Perplexed, I asked the woman, "I thought you said your dog didn't bite?"

"It's not my dog," she shrugged.

We looked at each other a moment, then began to laugh at the same time. Feeling duped into one of the oldest jokes, I said, "Pink Panther."

"Pink Panther Strikes Again," she said more specifically. We smiled at each other for an eternity, or perhaps only a couple of seconds. I needed to get a grip.

I held out my hand. "Hello, Ms. Hope, I'm Mr. Dubois."

"Yeah, I know," she said shaking my hand. "Please call me Olivia. If you call me Ms. Hope, I'll think you're talking to my mother. Anyway, Maggie called and said you were probably on your way. Idaho is with me so I knew you wouldn't be long. That's why I was on the porch. My house is easy to miss next to the Bixby Mansion," she mused as she pointed to all the lights. "Then I saw the dog running after Brandon. You see, Blue is what I call that dog. He's adopted me and he likes all things blue, hence the blue saucer that he just confiscated from poor Brandon."

"I thought dogs were color blind?"

"Seriously, does anyone really know?" She had a point.

I could see by the Bixby Christmas glow that the dog had indeed succeeded. However, the saucer was not taken with force, but by play. The boy, laughing heartily, was so enamored with the dog's licking, rolling, tumbling, that he may surely have given up his life savings to that lapping, loving hound, if the canine had desired such things.

"Blue, you give that back right now," reprimanded Olivia. "Drop it." The dog hung his head but held on to the saucer, "I said drop it." The dog obediently dropped it at her feet, where she picked it up and handed it back to Brandon. "Sorry Brandon, he just likes blue things." The dog sulked back to Olivia's porch. He huffed and slumped down on a pile of blue blankets inside a cardboard box, used as a dog house.

"Can I come over and play with him tomorrow?" asked Brandon.

"Sure, anytime," Oliva laughed as she bent to pick

up his stocking cap. She tousled the boy's hair, then she slipped his hat back on his head. "But don't wear or come with anything blue if you don't want to lose it."

The boy giggled and waved to the dog.

Then she turned to me and said, "Come on in. Let's go talk about Goodman's affairs, lost money—and my favorite topic, 'witches.'" She smiled sweetly.

"Lily strikes again," I lamented. "Why do I even bother?"

"Because you have a job to do," she said matter of fact, and patted my arm as we walked back to her little log cabin.

Olivia's house was much smaller than her friends' but no less striking in a cozy, rustic style. We stepped into an open room with vaulted ceilings. To the left was a small living room with a fireplace, where a dark-haired woman was draped over a plush dark green couch, apparently sound asleep. A matching chair and table completed an L-shape that divided the room from a bright, cheery kitchen. Although the kitchen was small, it seemed functional. A small mobile island made good use of counter space. Quite cleverly, a small picnic-type table folded out from a wall cupboard that could have easily seated five for dinner and then folded back neatly into the wall to allow for more room. A stairway went up to a loft above the kitchen area. A short hallway led to rooms beyond. The modern house seemed bigger on the inside. It could have been a stunning model for Better Homes and Gardens.

"What a cleverly designed home," I commented.

"Thank you," she beamed. She told me she had bought this rundown log cabin on the banks of the

Kootenai River when it was little more than a shed. She got it for "dirt cheap" and did the design herself. Then she and her friend Idaho worked together to finish the inside. Around the back was a trail down to the river with a dock and a bench to sit and fish from. That's where she spent most of her time in the summer, fishing and reading. The up-coming summer project was to build stairs all the way down to the dock. It was very impressive.

She was impressive—maybe too impressive. She presented herself in a friendly manner and spoke easily about her work on the house. But when I thought back on the conversation, she seemed somewhat guarded and fidgety when the conversation returned to Goodman. My instincts sent warning bells off in my head. That had brought me back to my reason for the visit. That, and the fact that Alan was standing over Idaho examining her as if she were in a fishbowl.

"I'm sure that Mr. Goodman was impressed with your efforts," I offered, gesturing to the work on the house. "How long were the two of you having an affair?"

She turned and glared at me. "I said we'd talk about Goodman's affairs, not having an affair with him. Mr. Dubois, I don't know of anyone who could stand to have an affair with that warthog. Our relationship with him was purely for investment purposes."

"So, none of your friends were involved with him?" I inquired, wondering if Lily had revealed to the rest of the women that she had sex with him.

"Absolutely not!"

She said it with such surprise I believed her, which

answered my question about Lily's confession. I decided to play it as straight as possible with her, sensing she was a no-nonsense kind of woman.

"Olivia, we are sure that it took more than one person to kill Goodman. He was a big man to bring down, in more ways than one. I'd say your investment loss is a good motivation. I hardly doubt he'd turn any of you attractive ladies away for an affair if one of you wanted something from him, whether you liked him or not. I can say with certainty that at least one of you have had sexual relations with him. A love triangle is a pretty compelling motive, too."

Olivia's jaw dropped. "It was Lily, wasn't it?" she snapped.

I shrugged, "Was it?"

"Did she tell you that?" She shook her head in disbelief. "She's the one who applies the least discretion. I can't believe her!"

"I thought you'd know your friends better than that."

"Well, if she was having a love triangle with him, I didn't know. But, I do know that she wouldn't kill him. She's far too vain for that!"

"Why is that?" I questioned.

"Because she can have any man she wants, and I know for a fact that she loathed Goodman."

"Then why would she sleep with the man?"

"I told you! Because she doesn't have any scruples," she explained as if I were a dullard.

"Have you checked out Goodman's wife? She's been known to have a few affairs, too. Not that anyone could blame her. Maybe she and a current beau knocked him off. She stands to inherit a lot of money. Ours included, I might add."

And there it was, I was back full circle.

"She's surrounded by dead people," Alan said in wonderment. Olivia and I turned to look at him. He was still scrutinizing the woman on the couch. Olivia was by the woman's side in a flash.

"What? What do you mean?" She was frantic. "Idaho, Idaho, wake up." She began to shake the woman. She was hard to rouse. "What do you mean she's surrounded by dead people?" Olivia shouted at Alan.

"Ah…it's a figure of speech, eh? Like, she's dead to the world, you know," I explained as I shot narrow eyes of disapproval in Alan's direction. Alan mirrored my stare.

Suddenly, the woman sat straight up looking at all of us, her head wobbling. Her unfocused eyes finally came to rest on Alan. She gave a sleepy smile and said, "Hey cutie," then she fell back and promptly passed out again. Alan's cheeks flushed, and he began shuffling his feet.

"Oh, thank God," breathed Olivia. "I thought that she, well . . . Idaho is not a drinker, and she had a bit too much this evening."

I looked at Olivia questioningly.

"What! She drank on an empty stomach," shrugged Olivia.

Returning to our previous conversation, I asked, "Are you sure you all aren't covering up for each other? Perhaps one or a couple of you went to Goodman's house to confront him. I mean you certainly didn't seem to know that Lily had slept with the man. How do you unequivocally know that one of you in your group did not kill Ira Goodman?" I paused for effect, "Or are all of you guilty?"

"Look, Mr. Dubois," she began, "You are barking up the wrong tree here. We did not, either united or individually, kill Goodman." But there was that something's amiss instinct of mine again. I saw an ever so slight flicker of her eyes. Was she lying, or was there an inkling of doubt? She ran fidgety fingers through her hair and said, "We didn't talk about us being witches yet, although that's a relative term since we all have our days. You know, we might not be perfect women, and we all probably have a few skeletons in our closets, but Goodman's isn't one of them. We'd appreciate it if you would be able to report to us any hope of recovering our money. Until then, I don't know what more I can say to you."

"Getting your money back is not my primary concern. Although, I do hope the best for you and your friends in that regard. I'm more concerned about the skeletons you say that you and your friends have in your closets. Can you tell me about a few I might find in yours?"

She looked me straight in the eye and slowly swallowed, twice, possibly trying to decide to tell me the truth or a lie. "I have nothing to hide," she defended, settling on a lie.

Exhaustion finally got the best of me, and since it was impossible to talk with the drunken Idaho, Alan and I said our goodbyes. We headed back on to Highway 2 toward the Venture Inn to have dinner, take a swim, and get some shut-eye. Alan was quiet, and I figured he was angry with me. I can always tell because he folds his arms across his chest and looks at everything but me. "Long day, eh?" I prodded, but he gave no reply.

"Well, we may not have gotten a lot of information from these women, and they may or may not be witches, but each one of them has me bewitched," I chuckled, hoping to get a rise from him. Nothing.

"So, what is your take on these women? Do you have any insights?" He remained silent, so I continued. "All of them could have their own motives, but they all seem to support each other. I suppose they all could have had a hand in killing him. You know, now that I think about it, that seems like it could be a real possibility." The conversation remained one sided. "There's something definitely going on with Olivia, I've just got a hunch."

"See, there you go," Alan spat.

He can be a moody thing. "What are you talking about?" I asked calmly.

"You talk about hunches. Where do you think those hunches of yours come from?"

"I'm not sure," I admitted. "Okay, I'm guessing this is about the surrounded by dead people comment you came up with when you had Idaho under your microscope."

"Why don't you believe me when I talk about," he used his fingers for quotations, "the scary stuff?"

"It's not scary; it's nonsense." Okay, that was the wrong thing to say. I got the folded arms again. "Are you telling me that you saw dead people surrounding Idaho?"

"Yes," he was adamant.

unequivocally know that one of you in your group did not kill Ira Goodman?" I paused for effect, "Or are all of you guilty?"

"Look, Mr. Dubois," she began, "You are barking up the wrong tree here. We did not, either united or individually, kill Goodman." But there was that something's amiss instinct of mine again. I saw an ever so slight flicker of her eyes. Was she lying, or was there an inkling of doubt? She ran fidgety fingers through her hair and said, "We didn't talk about us being witches yet, although that's a relative term since we all have our days. You know, we might not be perfect women, and we all probably have a few skeletons in our closets, but Goodman's isn't one of them. We'd appreciate it if you would be able to report to us any hope of recovering our money. Until then, I don't know what more I can say to you."

"Getting your money back is not my primary concern. Although, I do hope the best for you and your friends in that regard. I'm more concerned about the skeletons you say that you and your friends have in your closets. Can you tell me about a few I might find in yours?"

She looked me straight in the eye and slowly swallowed, twice, possibly trying to decide to tell me the truth or a lie. "I have nothing to hide," she defended, settling on a lie.

Exhaustion finally got the best of me, and since it was impossible to talk with the drunken Idaho, Alan and I said our goodbyes. We headed back on to Highway 2 toward the Venture Inn to have dinner, take a swim, and get some shut-eye. Alan was quiet, and I figured he was angry with me. I can always tell because he folds his arms across his chest and looks at everything but me. "Long day, eh?" I prodded, but he gave no reply.

"Well, we may not have gotten a lot of information from these women, and they may or may not be witches, but each one of them has me bewitched," I chuckled, hoping to get a rise from him. Nothing.

"So, what is your take on these women? Do you have any insights?" He remained silent, so I continued. "All of them could have their own motives, but they all seem to support each other. I suppose they all could have had a hand in killing him. You know, now that I think about it, that seems like it could be a real possibility." The conversation remained one sided. "There's something definitely going on with Olivia, I've just got a hunch."

"See, there you go," Alan spat.

He can be a moody thing. "What are you talking about?" I asked calmly.

"You talk about hunches. Where do you think those hunches of yours come from?"

"I'm not sure," I admitted. "Okay, I'm guessing this is about the surrounded by dead people comment you came up with when you had Idaho under your microscope."

"Why don't you believe me when I talk about," he used his fingers for quotations, "the scary stuff?"

"It's not scary; it's nonsense." Okay, that was the wrong thing to say. I got the folded arms again. "Are you telling me that you saw dead people surrounding Idaho?"

"Yes," he was adamant.

"Okay," I said reluctantly. "Well, what do you make of it?" I asked as I pulled into the Venture Inn parking lot and turned off the ignition.

"I don't know. They seem to be clinging to her, asking her for things. I couldn't hear what they were saying, but some look like they are pleading. I don't know why there would be so many of them, unless she's connected to them in some way."

My heart lurched. I hadn't heard him talk like this since he was a child. Was this case too hard on him? Was I bringing out this instability by subjecting him to this investigation? When he was a boy, his mother and I sent him for counseling. He claimed he was hearing voices and seeing people who weren't there. That was a long time ago. The doctors said that it was probably due to his creative and over-active imagination. They said he'd grow out of it, and his mother and I thought he had. Until now. "Son, should we think about getting you medication? I think—"

"Been there, done that, remember?" He was trembling. "All I got was heart palpitations, high blood pressure, and night terrors. You and Mom have never believed that what I see is valid. Gram was the only one who'd listen."

"She's dead, Alan," I said softly.

"Yeah, I know! Duh! But I still see her often!" There was a long pause.

"Hmm, do you think you could ask your gram who killed Goodman? It would help to get this sorted out, and we could go home," I tried to humor him, in my sometimes-unknowing insensitive way.

He shot me a look of horror. "Do you think this is

funny?"

"Sorry, no—the medication—you were a child then. You know I wouldn't suggest—"

"I ask you again. How do you get your hunches?" Alan demanded. "You said you have a hunch about Olivia, and that she's hiding something. Where does that come from?"

"I don't know. I guess, well, let's see…with Olivia, there are certain things I note. Like her eye movements were jerky, she was fidgety, I felt there was something she was hiding. Her eyes seem haunted."

"How do eyes look haunted?"

"I don't know. It's like a feeling I got when I looked at her."

"A feeling! You mean it's not an exact science? Do you need medication? What is so different about what I see and your hunches? You can't explain it, can you?"

"Well, I guess not—."

"That is what I'm saying. I can't explain where my information comes from either. I am NOT a FREAK. Do you understand?"

I nodded. He certainly had a point. All intents and purposes, Alan was in control of his thinking, his cognitive skills, and all other functionalities. "Son, I didn't mean to offend you. I just want what's best for you. And more than anything I need to know you are okay. You are very important to me."

He got out of the car and slammed the door.

"I suppose this means that I don't have a swimming partner tonight," I hollered after him.

"Last one in the pool eats crow!" he yelled back.

No contest there. I think I'd already eaten my share.

Chapter 13 - Olivia Hope

I paced the floor waiting for Rocco Basham to arrive for our dinner date. Quite frankly, I was disturbed by how quickly Rocco had accepted my invitation since his good friend, Goodman, had just been murdered. But, I supposed, death may only be a speed-bump in the road of life to someone as vain and self-centered as Rocco. I cringed at the idea of having to spend a whole evening with him. He'd been after me for months to go out with him, but I had refused. I knew a lot of women who would jump at the chance to be seen with him. Most women swooned over his good looks with his dark complexion, long, dark hair, and mysteriously smoky eyes, not mention the seductive bad-boy pheromones he exuded. He was a defense attorney, who had recently stepped into the county DA position. He was also very rich, probably by the helping hand of Goodman. But to me, he seemed cold, calculating and sinister. I thought of his response to my phone call for a date, "I knew you couldn't resist this package for long," and then I added, sleazy arrogance, to that list of things I didn't like about the man.

I carefully chose my wardrobe. My first instinct was to wear a hoodie-sweatshirt to hide in, but I decided on a sexy, low-cut, lace blouse with a blazer I could take off if I really needed to get his attention. How else was I to loosen those lips to schmooze information about

Goodman? I drew the line on the pillow talk scenario that Lily suggested.

"Men really mellow after a little sex," counseled Lily. "Oh, come on Olivia," Lily had scolded. "When was the last time you had a little fun or sex—or even a date for that matter? You gotta use it before you lose it, sweetheart."

"Speaking of indiscriminate sex, I can't believe you slept with Goodman!" I had countered.

"Oh please, when Dubois asked if I was having an affair with Goodman, I made a reference to his peanut-sized penis. Should have seen the look I got from Dubois, it was priceless," she chuckled. "When I realized I had screwed up by making such a correct identification, I made up a story about a time I seduced him at a charity function but he was too drunk to perform. Ugh, even in a lie I couldn't imagine the deed. Hey, even I have more taste than that."

"Right," I wanted to believe her. "Before you go all Dr. Ruth on me, remind me why I'm going on this date and not you?"

"Because, honey, he's hot for your booty, not mine. Besides, I told you I don't date reptiles."

My mind slid right into an image of Rocco licking a red eyeball with a forked tongue, blink, blink—I shivered.

I looked at the clock. Rocco was almost an hour late—not a good impression for a first date. My phone rang, and I was hoping that it was Rocco canceling the evening. "Hi, babe," he said, as comfortable as if we were a couple. "I'm out front. Better hurry, we're already late. Oh, and watch those steps of yours, they look pretty slick."

"You are at my house?"

"Oh, got another call. Better hurry, babe," and he was gone.

"Strike two, buddy," I fumed as I slipped a coat on and stomped out the door. Several steps down my walk I slipped and fell. I lurched forward and half dove into a snow bank. Embarrassed, and pissed as hell, I looked up to see if he were coming to help me up. Still on his cell phone, he waved for me to hurry.

"You son-of-a-bitch," I mumbled, brushing snow off my clothing as I got into the car.

"Hey, babe," he greeted. "What did you say?"

"I said that snow's a bitch," I said, smiling sweetly.

"I told you it looked slick," he grinned back. "Don't say I didn't warn you. Have a good trip?" he snorted. His cell rattled a loud, obnoxious rap song. "Oh, that's my son." Into his phone, he boomed, "Hey, dude."

Jesus, the man had spawned. Rocco talked most of the way to one person or another enroute to the restaurant. I tuned out of his conversations to rehearse my questions to ask him. I'd practiced all day to sound nonchalant and not to ask too many pointed questions that would raise suspicions--that's if I had a chance to talk to him in between his phone calls.

Four calls later, we finally arrived at the MK Steakhouse. The steakhouse is a few miles out of town in an old, rustic cabin—rustic, the operative word, but classy in an old cowboy western way. The MK is probably the nicest restaurant around Libby and undoubtedly the best steaks in Lincoln County. It held its usual romantic ambiance with dim lighting, white tablecloths and red cloth napkins. Crystal drinking glasses adorned each table. Candles placed in the center of the tables offered very little lighting to the oppressive darkness of the restaurant. That was perfect, I thought, hoping no one would recognize me with him. But then he requested a table right by the fireplace and asked that I sit where the firelight could bounce off my, "lovely breasts. I mean your lovely hair," he chortled at his intended mistake. He probably thought he was suave. Then he ordered two gin and tonics—wink, wink—with two olives, for the both of us, not even bothering to ask if me if I liked gin and tonic, which I didn't. But I smiled graciously and said, "Make mine a double." His jaw dropped slightly and his eyes became dreamy as he seductively licked his lips and told the waitress to keep the drinks flowing. And then I heard—along with the rest of the patrons in the restaurant—the loud, familiar, rap ring tone. He told me to "hold that thought" while he answered his call. I replied with a sultry, "I certainly will." And I did—the vision of poking his eyes out with my olive skewer.

While we sipped our drinks, I counted at least seven more calls before the appetizers arrived. Each time he'd get up from the table. When he wasn't looking, I'd pour my drink into his almost empty glass. When he returned, he'd order another round for the "little lady."

His phone buzzed yet again. This time I reached over and grabbed it, answering, "Hello, I'm afraid Mr. Basham is unavailable now. May I take a message?" The caller hung up. "Huh, must not have been important," I said returning his phone to him.

"Probably the ex-wife," he smiled sheepishly. "She

was going to call me back to let me know when the funeral is for Ira."

Ah, ex-wife still taking care of business. Figures. But I took advantage of the perfect segue. "I'm sorry to hear about Goodman. I know he was a good friend to you," I comforted. I was surprised to see a genuine look of sadness cross his face as he nodded, but remained silent. I let the silence pass for a moment. Finally I asked, "The newspaper wasn't clear on the cause of death. Do they know for sure how he died?"

"No, the autopsy will be in tomorrow. We'll know more then," he said. He tipped his glass up and drained most of the contents. "Ira will be missed by many. He kept this community afloat; a lot of people owe him."

"Well, I kind of think he owed a few people, too," I bit my tongue to stop any further snarky comments.

"What do you mean?" Rocco asked.

"Well, our investment club had just given him a large sum of money and, in turn, he gave it to a construction company that he said had filed bankruptcy. He owed us an explanation and help in getting it back."

"Oh, that," Rocco said as if it were a trivial matter.

"So, you know about that?" I asked. "And you can help us get it back?" I was hopeful—but wouldn't hold my breath.

A slow smile spread across his face, "See, honey, there you go. There are some things that women just don't get about doing business. Nothing you can do about it. It happens, get over it."

Spoken just like a true Goodman clone. Fuming, but keeping my temper in check, I said, "Well, we're not going to roll over and give up. We've lost our life savings, Rocco. We're going after the contractor." None of us women could remember the name of the contractor Goodman said he'd hired, if he ever told us—we would know if we had received the signed papers by now, I silently fumed and once again chastised myself for putting blind trust in Goodman. But it occurred to me that Rocco might know the contractor's name. "You know that, um, guy from, oh, you know that guy from, was it Spokane, or …" I faltered, feigning a loss of memory.

"Oh, you mean RayCon?"

Bingo! "Yeah, that's it. We're going after him. Can I convince you to represent us?" I smiled coyly.

"No can do. Nothing to go after, babe, he's already filed bankruptcy!" snorted Rocco. "That money's long gone by now I'm sure. Nothing but a bee hive with no honey." Rocco gave me a piercing look that made me shiver, then said, "Goodman made a mistake working with that fly-by-night outfit. I guess even smart men can be taken in now and then. Best leave it alone." Rocco leaned in closer to me and breathed heavily, "Stick with me, babe, and you'll never need to worry about money. Come on over, hun, and give it a try. Put your hands in my pockets and play with my coins. Don't worry your pretty little head. Now that's something you won't hear from any other man," he said, slithering in his seat.

I certainly hoped not! I swallowed back a gag, steering far away from that subject. "Do you think the CTC is responsible for Goodman's death?"

"I don't know," he said, as sat back. "I guess I'll let Dubois muck around with the case for a while. He'll shake things up, and then I'll have to go clean up after him."

"I hear Dubois's pretty successful in his career, but it sounds like you don't have much confidence in him."

"Yeah, if you call success exploiting the good things people do."

"What do you mean?"

"If you remember the Gerard Gaits case, Dubois raked him over the coals and destroyed anything good he had done for the Environmental Health Association, the group that he strongly supported to clean up dump sites, and then built all those recycling plants. In the end, Dubois publicly humiliated him in the press."

My jaw dropped. I had remembered the case all right. "Excuse me, but Gaits turned out to be a serial killer. He also extorted money from the EHA. There was nothing respectful left about the man. He went to prison, where he belonged!"

"Well, with all the work he put into the EHA, he deserved something more."

"The man was a SERIAL killer!! He deserved nothing but prison! Dubois was just reporting the facts."

"I'm not saying he didn't belong in prison for murder. I'm saying I don't believe he should have been exploited for embezzlement."

"Oh. for god sake, Rocco. Are you condoning what Gaits did? Embezzlement is a crime!"

"Babe, life isn't always black and white," Rocco snarled. "That's business. Dubois is not from around here. He has no business poking around and stirring up shit on people."

"So, are you afraid he'll dig up some unsavory shit about your friend Goodman?" I couldn't help the disgust that accented my question.

"Goodman may have worked in some gray areas but he gave a lot to this community and I'll not have his name defiled. Besides, I think Dubois is gay."

"What! You think he's gay?" I blanched.

To that Rocco shrugged and swilled down the last of his cocktail. "He's French, Aren't they all?"

"Oh, isn't that rich," I laughed. "I happen to think he's a welcome breath of fresh air around here. I think we need more men like him fighting for a little justice in this community." Wow! I was defending the man who might be about to send me to prison. But I continued. "You think he's gay because he speaks with a French accent, and doesn't swear like a sailor, scratch his balls and fart?"

Rocco erupted in a roar of laughter, "Hey, that's no way for a lady to talk."

"Who said I was a lady?" I countered.

"I'm likin' you—a lot," grinned Rocco with a lusty sneer. Rocco's cell phone began to announce another call. I gladly let him take it. I noted that he was beginning to stagger as he walked away from the table, and once again I emptied my drink into his glass.

A waitress walked over to our table, "Smooth move," she said, catching me in the act. And then she set a frothy cream cocktail in front of me. "Here sweetheart," she said. "The MK Special, just for you. It's on the house." She looked in Rocco's direction, then turned back to me and lowered her voice, "You're too good for the likes of that shmuck. You look as if things aren't going so well."

I nodded and thought better than to say anything for

fear I'd mention something about wanting to kill Rocco.

"I hope you don't mind," continued the waitress, "but I've taken the liberty to call a cab for you. It'll be here in about ten minutes if you wish to take it. It's your choice, of course. I'll wrap up your meal with an extra-large steak and hand it to the driver." I really had enough of Rocco Basham, so I readily accepted the waitress's offer. It was the oddest—and most wonderful—gesture I had ever received from a stranger.

"Enjoy your drink," whispered the waitress.

I enjoyed every ounce of the thick creamy contents, resisting the urge to lick the glass clean. When the waitress nodded in my direction indicating that my ride had arrived, I quickly picked up my purse and jacket—leaving Rocco holding the phone, and in the words of Billy Joel's song, 'making love to his tonic and gin.'

Chapter 14 - Olivia Hope

Monday morning came quickly for me. In fact, I woke up with my head on my laptop and a major crick in my neck, with only a couple of hours sleep under my belt. Rocco had called several times wondering why I had abandoned him. If I was sick, why didn't I just go to his house. It was closer, and he had a big comfy bed with my name on it. So, I knew the waitress had told him I had turned ill and needed to leave, which was truer than he knew. But I didn't answer his slurred messages. I quite possibly would never speak to him again.

After I returned home from the date from hell, I'd immediately began surfing the internet and playing computer chess, which I often did when I needed time to think. I researched RayCon Construction. Eventually I found a construction company by that name out of San Francisco. Raymond Conley started the company and had hired Christopher Dumas eighteen months earlier. I read the scratchy notes I made before I had fallen asleep and hoped I was on the right track. A deep yawn escaped from me as I stood and stretched my back. I trudged to the coffee pot to make coffee. When I caught myself dumping coffee grounds into my cup rather than the pot, I decided it was best to head for the shower first to wake up.

Feeling somewhat refreshed after the shower, I attempted to make coffee again, only to find that I had indeed started the coffee, but had transferred the grounds from my cup to the garbage, not the pot. And then, peering at the grounds lying in the garbage, it dawned on me that was the last of the grounds. I stared at the clear substance in the carafe. "You're going to make me drink that instant crap, aren't you?" I screamed at the pot. And so, I dug through the cupboards mumbling, "I better have some damn instant somewhere." I found an old jar. There was some stuck on the bottom. I chipped at it and scooped out the lumps into my cup. "This day had better damn well improve."

After loading my cup with the instant brew, I looked at my watch and figured I had some time before leaving for work. What the hell, I thought, may as well make a few phone calls. I hadn't been able to track down a phone number for Dumas, so I called the number I had for Mr. Conley.

"Who the hell is this?" answered a gruff old man. It seemed I'd awaken Mr. Grumpy Pants, who berated me for not yet having his first cup of coffee. I told him I'd tried to have a decent cup myself, but had to settle for instant. He wasn't sympathetic. All the same, he didn't mind dishing out his ill feelings toward Christopher Dumas. I gleaned that RayCon Construction had been a family-owned business for several generations with a sound reputation. When the housing market took a dive, the company began to hemorrhage money. Christopher Dumas stepped in to help the family. He made promises that he'd financially support the company, make sure the families were taken care of, and employees would keep their jobs, while further promising to expand their work base to other states. However, it turned out that Dumas did nothing but "sit on his ass, smoke cigars and take long trips with the company's dwindling cash." Leaving them all to flap in the wind with no jobs, unable to even collect unemployment. The families had cashed in much of their investments, and some were facing personal bankruptcy. They were also facing lawsuits for unfinished projects.

When I asked for a phone number for Dumas, Raymond gave it to me but said, "Yeah, good luck with that. I've tried many times, and the operator says it's disconnected. I happened to find on the computer that he had bought a ticket to the Cayman Islands. Supposed to leave first week of January. And now I'm hearing from you that he may have filed bankruptcy on my company? Talk about a black fuckin' Monday."

That was odd. Raymond hadn't heard yet that the company had filed bankruptcy. I asked Raymond if he'd ever met a man by the name of Ira Goodman. He hadn't. I briefly explained the situation. Playing the pity card by telling him of our lost investments, I hoped if he had withheld any information from me, maybe he'd offer up something out of sympathy. He didn't. However, he did express sympathy—towards Goodman. "If he was mixed up with Dumas," Raymond said, "I pity the poor bastard. Give my regards to the Goodman family."

Not the outcome I was looking for.

As soon as I hung up, I tried the number Raymond had given me for Mr. Dumas. "Disconnected," was the answer. I tried a few variations of the number, hoping that maybe Raymond had written down the wrong number. Not so, road blocks all around.

I mulled this over while I fixed myself a sack lunch.

"Black Monday," I repeated to myself as I sliced thin chunks of steak from last night's uneaten dinner, stacked them on lettuce and sourdough bread, smeared horseradish dressing on top, cut it in half, wrapped it in cellophane, and threw it in a paper bag. Then I stopped to wonder if I should call the suicide hotline to put a watch on Raymond Conley. I'd heard about many contractors who committed suicide because of the failed market and bankruptcy. But wouldn't he at least try to track down Dumas first? But I realized, just as Raymond predicted, I too, had failed. A light bulb went on in my tired brain. Suddenly I had thought of someone who would probably have more success with finding Mr. Dumas—Rand Dubois.

Dumas could be a lead to Goodman, let him research this one. I reached over the counter and grabbed Dubois's business card and made a note to call him.

I was pressed for time by then, but I made another call to Goodman's office. I wanted to stop by and pick up the loan papers we women had signed and hadn't yet received copies. Surely the office assistant would have a copy. I was holding out the hope that Goodman's promise of deeds to a couple of properties as collateral was still part of the deal. However, as Black Monday might have it, the answering machine switched on and prompted me to, "please leave a number after the beep." I thought to leave a message, then decided to reach Tammy Jo, the office assistant, at home—that's one of the perks of living in a small town and knowing just about everyone.

So far, I was batting a thousand for waking people. A sleepy Tammy Jo came to the phone only after her roommate told her to get her ass out of bed.

Feeling a little guilty for the early call, especially if Tammy Jo was sick, I went directly to the point of my intrusion, "Hi Tammy Jo, sorry to bother you. But, I was wondering if you could get me the papers for the last loan we did with Goodman today?"

"You didn't get them yet?"

"No, we haven't, and it's pretty important that I get them as soon as possible so we know what we're dealing with."

"You haven't heard yet, have you?" croaked Tammy Jo.

"Heard what?" I asked, bewildered. Now what's happening, I thought.

"Goodman's dead, so I'm out of a job. I'm no longer an employee of Good Equities. Dubious was by over the weekend with a search warrant and went through everything with a fine-toothed comb. He was looking for clues I guess. It was kind of fun helping him too. Anyway, he released us to continue business today, but then Mr. Basham fired me. Said it was my fault for letting them in the door without him being there. He thinks he's above the law, that schmuck."

"Basham? As in Rocco Basham?"

"Yeah, he's Goodman's silent partner. Not many people know that. Maybe they're not supposed to know and that's why they call it silent, I don't know. But I'll be damned if I'll be silent anymore."

I was hit with a wave of panic as Tammy Jo was my best source to get the paperwork. After several minutes of the two of us trying to figure out how to get in the office, short of breaking and entering, I thought of something, "Did you get your final pay check yet?"

"No, I didn't as a matter of fact. This all happened so fast I didn't think about it. I'll call Basham and tell him to meet me there and I'll go in earlier. I'll see if I can find a hidden key or something. If not, I'll try a window. If I get caught, I'll just say I lost my key. And if Basham asks how I got in, I'll just say I forgot to leave my other key like he asked me," she said in a conspirator tone. She agreed to meet me at lunch.

As expected, Goodman's death was the talk of the school. The students were all a chatter as many of them knew or at least had classes with Goodman's son, Seth. As the day progressed, I overheard that Josh Pinkman, one of Seth's pimple-faced friends, wasn't in school either. The discussion started after I entered the teacher's lounge. Principal Gaylord commented that Josh was just goofy enough to be one of those Arian Nation bigots that could be part of the CTC.

"Yeah, he's a strange one all right," said Marion, the senior history teacher. "But Seth always seemed like such a nice kid. I could never figure out why he hung with such trash as that." That had been my thought as well. Josh had been in one of my health classes, and he'd been extremely disrespectful towards any student that didn't have blond hair and blue eyes. He'd call them Spicks, Chinks, darkies, gooks and such, even if they were dark-haired Germans. He'd even slapped me on the ass once and called me a sexy Puta. He'd spent a lot of time in Principal Gaylord's office. If anyone in this room knew Josh best, it would be the principal. I moved closer to the two of them in discussion.

"Do you really think that Josh is involved with the CTC?" I asked.

"I don't know for sure," said Marion. "But he's like the perfect candidate for the skin heads and it was those skin heads that started the CTC."

"Do you know anything about the CTC or people who have been involved with them?" I asked.

"You know, come to think of it, I think that one of Josh's uncles was one of those guys that went to jail after that one woman, Mary somebody, was murdered. But that was a while back. The people in this town would probably take matters into their own hands if the damn law didn't do something. I don't think he'd dare show his face for fear of a lynching."

"Certainly, Sheriff Bishop wouldn't let that kind of crap go on. He seems like a good man," I commented.

"I think many a good law man has been bought off or somehow silenced in this town," observed Principal Gaylord. "And I'm betting it's been Goodman behind it the whole time. I, for one, am not going to miss that man."

"You mean that Goodman was paying bribes to public officials?" I asked. "How do you know that?"

Marion nodded.

Principal Gaylord began to speak with a mouth full of cookie, "Remember when Julie Waver claimed she was gang-raped by those six football players?"

He popped the whole cookie in his mouth, brushing off crumbs from his suit jacket, so Marion picked up the story from there, "Julie said that it happened at an away game in Havre. She said she went down to get a soda out of the vending machine and the boys cornered her and drug her up to a room. She said they were drunk, and they all took their turn with her. The story was much more detailed and gruesome."

"And terrifying," I said.

"Wait, it gets worse," Marion went on. "Once they had their way with her, they walked her down the hall naked, with clothes in her hand, knocked on the door and ran. No one saw the boys who did it. Her roommate was on her cell and didn't bother to answer the door for about five minutes. So, there she stood for the whole world to see—naked, mortified, and bleeding—and believe me she had lots of lookers. I heard that most laughed and ridiculed, rather than help her."

The incident happened before I came to work at Libby Sr. High. I remembered pictures of Julie. She was an Ugly Betty look-alike. Long, stringy, dark hair, big black-rimmed glasses, braces on her teeth, and mostly dressed in dark, dowdy clothing. She had a cute figure, and I thought that when she got her braces off, got contacts, and dressed more stylish, she'd be a raving beauty. "Whatever happened to her?" I asked.

"She disappeared after the trial," Principal Gaylord answered, "She and her parents probably couldn't face anyone in town."

"Surely the boys were appropriately charged and punished. Why would she feel the need to leave?"

Gaylord and Marion exchanged glances. "They got off, Olivia," said Marion, with a mixture of pain and sadness in her eyes.

"How?" I was aghast.

Gaylord cleared his throat, "The boys said that she solicited them . . . for a lot of money. When she denied it, and her parents backed her up, the authorities came to the school and searched her locker. They found close to two-thousand in small bills stashed in there." My brows furrowed questioningly. Gaylord shrugged. "She claimed that someone had put it there. But no one believed her. End of story. The boys got a slap on the wrist, and were told about the evils of hiring prostitutes, wink, wink. Julie was charged with prostitution and did 'reform" juvie time in Helena. She and her family disappeared right after that."

"Jesus," was all I could say to that. "From what I heard, she was gangly, awkward, and painfully shy. Who the hell was the boys' attorney?"

"Rocco Basham."

I nodded as the pieces started to fall into place. "Son-of-a-bitch," I said under my breath. To Gaylord I asked, "So what did Goodman have to do with all of that?"

Gaylord shrugged, "He was the assistant football coach at the time."

My mouth went dry, and my stomach plummeted. "You think Goodman paid a bribe to Basham, and someone planted the money in her locker?"

Gaylord shrugged once more, "You be the judge."

I wondered how many other bribes and set-ups that Goodman had made since then. He probably owned the whole community by now. How many bribes has Sheriff Bishop taken I wondered. Maybe even Dubois! I had begun to have second thoughts about leaving Rocco at the restaurant. Clearly, one doesn't want to be on his bad side.

My cell vibrated, and the text I'd been waiting for

appeared. It was from Tammy Jo, "Papers ready-come quick-Basham's panties in twist-come b4 he duz."

I texted back, "B rt there." It was almost lunch and my next class was going to be cut short because of a pep rally. "Principal Gaylord, could you cover about fifteen minutes of my health class this period? I have some legal documents I need to pick up. The kids have their assignment, and it was just going to be a work hour anyway. They know what to do."

Principal Gaylord was a portly, fifty-something man. He wasn't the picture of health, and I was constantly trying to get him to eat right and exercise. He was a nice man, and I knew he adored me, so I didn't feel guilty about asking him to cover. Besides he might learn something healthy in those fifteen minutes.

He grinned ear-to-ear, "Are you kidding? Sure, I'll give them my lecture on why bran is important for their diet," he said, rubbing his belly and waved me goodbye.

"TMI," I hollered over my shoulder. "Teach 'em, don't scare 'em!"

I made it to Goodman's office in five minutes flat. "Hey TJ," I greeted.

Tammy Jo pressed the papers into my hands, and began pushing me out the door again. "Whoa, Tammy, what's going on?"

"Don't know, don't care," was her reply. "Go before Attila the Hun returns."

"What happened?"

"Basham was here when I arrived. I think he pulled an all-nighter with a worm in a tequila bottle. He smells like a distillery; his clothes are rumpled and I bet I could find my way to Bumbfuck, Texas, using the road maps in those bloodshot eyes."

"Gin, not tequila," I mumbled, "he was making love to his tonic and gin."

"TMI," crowed Tammy Jo, raising her hand in my face. "Whatever, he's grumpy as hell, and I don't need to be here when he comes back. I told Basham that I'd stay and help close things out, but he was rudely emphatic that I stay out of the way. But then he tells me I need to make out my own final check. Can you believe it?"

"Yeah, no surprise there," I said. "Make sure you charge Mr. Basham for a full day of work today, just for the inconvenience," I offered.

"I was going to be nice and clean up the place, but he can damn well do it himself."

"Who's going to run the office now? Him?" I wondered.

"I don't know, maybe just him. He was always hanging around anyway. The two of them were thick as thieves. And I always had to have the Kona Roast coffee ready by seven a.m. or, else—just for the Bash, or as I call him the Douche Bash," complained Tammy Jo. "Not going to miss that shit. There is something seriously wrong with that man."

I smiled to myself and couldn't agree more. But despite his being jilted at the restaurant and a hangover, I couldn't figure out why he'd be in such a state. Surely this wasn't the first time for either of those events.

"Hey, maybe you could give me a lift home?" asked Tammy Jo. "My brother dropped me off, and since I'm leaving earlier than expected, I don't want to walk home with all this stuff."

I helped her carry some boxes to the car. As we

pulled away from the curb, I saw Rocco pull into the parking lot. "Whew, just in the nick of time," cried Tammy Jo. She gave a little chuckle, "I used to have a crush on him, you know."

I laughed at that, "You? Ms. I got my shit together?"

"Yeah, well now that I think about it, I must have fallen in love with his money. He's worth millions, if not billions! Then I got to know him and realized you couldn't pay me enough to even go out with the jerk." She gave me a sideways, "Oh, sorry. He told me you guys have dated."

"Only once," I clarified. "Yeah, I guess desperate measures call for despicable acts."

"You, desperate? Hey, if you're that desperate, I could set you up with my Uncle Vinnie."

"Thanks, sweetie, but I can make my own mistakes, thank you very much." We pulled up in front of Tammy Jo's house and I helped her carry the boxes to the door. "I'm curious. How did Rocco come by all that money? Did Goodman help him make his fortunes?"

"Nah, Rocco is from old family money. And, if anything, Rocco made Goodman rich. Like I said, they were thick as thieves. I think Rocco idolized the man's brain since he doesn't have one of his own."

"That's a scary thought," I mused.

"You're telling me. But, even though Goodman was kind of weird, he was a sharp man, really had a head for business. I have to say, though, lately he just hadn't been himself."

"How's that?" I asked.

"He was becoming a recluse. He'd quit coming into

the office. He started taking lots of trips, but not telling anyone where he was going. He wasn't getting business done either. You know, like not getting your loan papers back to you. He was always very meticulous. He had insisted on doing that stuff himself. He lost some weight, and was distracted a lot. He even showed up to work one day wearing nothing but a t-shirt, briefs and slippers. Very unlike the expensive suits the man normally wore. Rocco and I thought maybe he was having an affair. But you don't look like death warmed over when you're on cloud nine. There was something else going on. I wondered if he was having health problems or something."

"Or, maybe headed for a nervous breakdown," I offered. "You mean Rocco didn't know either?"

"He said Goodman was just in a funk. I don't think he knew. And, although Rocco never said, I think it bothered him that Goodman hadn't confided in him. Oh well," Tammy Jo shrugged, "It's just office gossip, and it doesn't matter now anyway. I just need to focus on getting a new job. Thanks for the ride."

Driving back to school, I rolled our conversation over in my mind. Perhaps what was bothering Goodman was what killed him? What or who would be behind it? And how could I find out?

I couldn't wait any longer to see what the loan papers would tell me about the collateral we women now owned. Crossing my fingers, I ripped open the thick manila envelope. After searching through the document, I finally found what I was looking for. The collateral we held were deeds to a couple of property sites along the Kootenai River that should be prime real estate.

However, because this property had been a dump site for the asbestos laden Zonolite, I recognized these properties as part of the largest EPA superfund site in the nation's history. It was official, we owned a whole lot of nothing—Black Monday indeed.

Chapter 15 - Rand Dubois

I rather enjoy Mondays. It symbolizes a new week with new possibilities. And after a week with little to no success on solving the case, I needed a good dose of Monday. I also know you've got to be up early to get the worm, or is it the maggot? I wasn't eager to hunt either one, but I found maggots anyway—in a fermenting garbage can as its contents sprayed over my clean, pressed pant legs and my three hundred dollar, Eddie Bauer boots. I was dripping wet, with quickly freezing goo, and the rotting, sour smell of garbage. After many unsuccessful calls, Alan and I hit the street early to question Arch Holmgren, a garbage man by day, and a staunch member of the Chosen Trojan Children by night. At least he was at the time of the Mary Bell murder. Arch hadn't been implicated as one of the parties in the murder because he had an alibi. He was in jail. He's a card-carrying bigot and has never tried to hide the fact that he is affiliated with the Aryan Nation.

We caught Arch just as he was making his first trash pickup in the early morning darkness. I caught him in mid-pitch of a garbage can when I startled him, thus spilling the contents on yours truly. I began introductions with Arch, trying to keep a straight face as Alan stood behind him pointing, holding his nose, making crude faces, and silently laughing at me.

"What the hell!" Arch gasped holding his chest.

"Dude, what the hell are ya doin'? Bastard, you scared the hell out of me, JESUS." He didn't offer an apology for the foul shower I received.

"Dude, everything okay?" hollered the driver of the truck.

"Yeah, dude, hang on a minute," Arch called, then furrowed his brows.

"Sorry, sir," I grumbled, staring into his toothless, gaping mouth. I wondered which was worse, the smell of garbage or his foul breath. We completed our introductions. It was no surprise that he wasn't pleased to see us.

"I'm workin' here man. Wanna get me fired?"

"We just need to ask a few questions," I said.

"Yeah, figgered I'd hear from you," he admitted. "With that Richie Rich, Goodman, dying an' all. But, I'm clean, dude. I didn't do it. I read the paper. I know what yas gonna ask. And, I'm tellin' ya right now, I ain't got nothin' to do with the CTC no more."

"So, it's true. The CTC still exists?" asked Alan.

"Yeah, but they ain't the children of Satan that you think they is—it's those damn Jews that are the children of Satan you know. Those is the sons-a-bitches ya need to watch out for," Arch advised.

"You keep in touch with the CTC members?" I asked.

"Nah, most is young kids now. Hell, I ain't got no use for snot noses like that." Arch is only about twenty-five. What he failed to realize is, a few years earlier, he was one of those snot noses.

"Do you know those kids, Arch?" I asked.

"Some."

"Tell me the some you know, Arch."

Arch made a circular roll of his head and a quick crack of his neck with both hands, "They just kids. One's Bill Moran, Trenton Bormer, he's kind of wonky. And then there's one of Stormy Pinkman's kids." I raised my eyebrows in recognition of that name. "Yeah, you know her. Booth Pinkman's wife, one of them you nailed for Bell's murder. Don't know the kid's name though. And that's all I know."

"Is Goodman's son, Seth, one of the CTC?" I asked.

Arch shrugged. "Don't know."

"You still belong to the Aryan Nation though, Arch," it wasn't a question. I already knew the answer.

Arch gave me a nervous look.

"I know you and some of your friends borrowed money from Goodman," I said.

"Yeah, so?"

"So, you and your group have a beef with Goodman?" I pressed.

"No, we didn't. We only borrowed some money from him to build us a meetin' house," he explained. "We liked the dude, man."

"Did your Aryan Brothers need a sacrificial 'Richie Rich' to offer to whoever you pray to?"

I could see Arch's face pale, even under the greenish glow of the streetlight. Although it was cold, I could see perspiration build under Arch's nose. He wiped it away with a gloved hand, leaving something green hanging from his nose, like a piece of lettuce—at least I hoped it was. "Look, the last I heard, there's no law about hating Niggers, Chinks, and Spics, okay?"

"Goodman was a white philanthropist with lots of

money. Money has been the root cause of a lot of murders," I explained.

"We didn't kill him. I told you, we liked the dude. He's the only one who'd give us a loan, you know."

"Did you stay current on the loan?"

"Yeah, we did. Paid off now, too."

"I'm curious," queried Alan. "How do you guys get your funding? From bake sales, brotherhood yard sales, lemonade stands, swastika jewelry line, maybe sell an oozie or two?"

Arch frowned at Alan, and said, "We get money for dues and some donations, shit like that."

"Did Goodman give donations to you, too?" I asked.

"Nah," Arch shook his head. "He was all about us giving him money—high interest. But that's just business."

"Hey, you gonna work sometime today or, just stand around and shoot the shit man?" yelled the truck driver.

"Police business," I hollered back and held up my badge in the event the driver might be looking our way.

Arch moved toward the truck, "Sorry but I gotta work, guys. Can I go now?" We were done. I waved him on. But, then he turned and added, "Oh, and I ain't got nothing to do with those damn animal mutilations either."

"I didn't ask, but do you know who is? Should I be asking the snot-nosed CTC?" I hollered. He waved us off, jumped on the back of the moving garbage truck, and within seconds he was gone.

"What the hell is that smell?" asked one of the deputies who had the dubious honor of sitting next to me in our meeting. We settled into the conference room to debrief and plan our next strategy on the Goodman case. "Sorry. Didn't have the chance to change before the meeting," I apologized.

Frowning and sitting farther down the table, Sheriff Bishop said, "That's okay, we'll make this short. Mind telling us how you acquired this eau de toilette?"

Thankful for the opportunity to explain, I recounted the early morning get-together with Arch.

"Do you think Arch is telling the truth?"

"Sounds like he and his cohorts were on good terms with Goodman. I think he may know who's behind the mysterious mutilations though. I didn't ask but he made it a point to tell us that he wasn't involved. I'll follow up with those names as soon as I leave here. I'd like to get some more names from the Mary Bell case. Could be that some of the men back then have their kids leading the CTC now. Arch referred to 'those young, snot-nosed kids'."

"I'll get that file for you," offered Bishop. "Could be Goodman's son, Seth, is one of them at that. What about the women? Get anywhere with them?" asked Bishop.

"Yeah, Alan and I made a visit to Lily White. She's an interesting woman. She's a successful fundraiser and has acquaintances with a lot of celebrities."

"She's got quite a reputation. Was Goodman among her many conquests," he paused. "Oh, excuse me; did I say that out loud? I meant acquaintances." Bishop got hardy laughs with that.

Her reputation did precede her, "She said she had an affair with Goodman in the past. Said it was back when he looked like Alec Baldwin. My instincts tell me she's lying. Not about the affair, but perhaps the time frame." I heard a snort from Alan and looked in his direction. "Anything you want to add to that, Alan?"

"Instinct sir, how so?" he asked.

All eyes turned back to me. I could see where Alan was going with this. He was still pissed at me for not believing in his insights. I continued on, "First, she's a beautiful woman. I'm thinking any man, who wanted an encounter with her, wouldn't pass up the chance. Second, she seemed too flippant with the answer. I felt she was making it up as she went, and too ready to dismiss the present." Not a clear answer, but it was all I had.

"When I asked if she was a practicing witch, Lily said," I referred to my notes, "'Yes, I am a witch, at least once a month, or if I don't get my way. But I do not cast spells . . . I believe people make their own karma by voodooing themselves'."

Sheriff Bishop cackled at that, "So she knows about voodoo. But who do she voodoo?"

"Anything wearing pants, it sounds like," snickered a deputy, to more laughter.

"Any leads on the other women Mora talked about?" asked Bishop.

I nodded, "As a matter of fact Lily gave us the names and addresses of the other four women. Next, we visited with Pamela Phuchet. She's a single mom trying to run a Christmas tree farm by herself. She's a busy woman with two small boys. She claims she doesn't have time for an affair, and that she does not condone witches and that sort of thing. She said the world is too scary as it is without having to deal with 'The Blair Witch Project.'"

"I noticed she had the boys' baptism photos in a frame with a cross and the First Lutheran Church emblem on it," said Alan. "It looked like they were baptized when they were babies." He looked at me and said, "It was hanging on the wall by the kitchen table. It doesn't seem like she'd have that if she were into Wiccan stuff."

"Good observation," I said. "It could be a cover though. Thanks to Lily's call giving them the heads up for our visit."

"It's been hanging there for a while," Alan added. "I pulled it off the wall to look at it and a dark square marked its spot on the wall. So, I'm fairly certain it wasn't planted. I've read practicing witches and warlocks usually don't allow Christian artifacts in their space as it disrupts the aura, or something."

I continued with my brief, "We visited with Maggie Berns." I looked around the table. "I assume you all know that she's a childhood actress?" I got nods all around. I shook my head, berating myself for being the clueless one before our visit. "She claims not to be a practicing witch, but admitted to playing the part of a witch in a production of The Wizard of Oz in college. She, too, said that their involvement with Goodman was strictly financial and gave us some names of other investors. I followed up, and discovered most of these people were pleased with the investment process, although they didn't lose as much money as the women.

Some investors were a little disgusted with Goodman's business ethics. But, none of them seemed angry enough to incite murder."

"We interrupted Ms. Berns's evening as she had overnight company. I checked it out, and she's got a steady boyfriend. I'm thinking that she probably didn't have an affair with Goodman. Not that it matters if she has a boyfriend, but I don't see Goodman being her type. Lily, on the other hand," I shrugged, "Probably not as much discretion, as was stated by Olivia Hope, the next woman we interviewed."

For some reason my palms began to sweat talking about Ms. Hope. That was odd. When we met, I'd had a fleeting moment of deep familiarity. That felt nice. She had a gentle, calming nature with the dog. She was the same with the boy, when she put the cap back on his head. But something felt terribly amiss. I couldn't put it into words. Again, the red flags flew in my face. This woman had skeletons in her closet all right, and I vowed to find out what they were. But I had been running into roadblocks every step of the way in finding out anything about her.

I was speaking to everyone about our meeting mindlessly verbatim, when Bishop asked me, "Angry, what's she angry about?"

"Angry?" I asked mystified, as if I had just been awakened from a dream.

"Yeah, you said she's a nice gal and all, but she's angry about something. What's she angry about?"

I wasn't sure what I had said, but I'd come to the conscious realization that was it. She was angry. But what could it be? Although she didn't display anger at any time, I felt it as if it were a shield just under the skin.

"I . . .I" stammered as I spoke, "I think she probably has a lot to be angry for, since she's just lost a great deal of money," I said, not believing my own words. I didn't think money was a motivation for her. So, what would make her so deeply angry?

Alan did a double take in my direction, and to my pleasant surprise, he picked up the reporting from there. "Ms. Hope didn't offer a lot of information except to point a finger back at Mora Goodman and explained that she probably had motive as she was having an affair. Ms. Hope didn't know who, of course, but it kind of put us back to square one."

"Oh, and Idaho, as the women call her, I-d-a capital H-o-e," I added, trying to get my head back in the game, "was incapacitated to talk."

"Drunk," stated Alan.

"Drunk?" asked Bishop with a quizzical unibrow.

"On the couch, out like a light," said Alan.

"Evidently, she's not used to drinking, and on an empty stomach to boot," I added, as if she needed defending. "She's the daughter of a bricklayer in Bonners Ferry, Idaho. She won a few million dollars in a lottery and moved to Libby shortly after that. She seems to have a close friendship with Ms. Hope."

"Close friend," the deputy said, "as in live-in partner?"

"No!" I answered too quickly. Alan's eyes bugged out at me. I backed down, how did I know the relationship? "At least I don't think so," I said. "Idaho lives in a small house a few blocks from Ms. Hope's." Alan sat smirking at me.

Bishop reported that there were a few more animal disappearances—DUI's dished out, a drug bust, disturbance of the peace, but nothing relating to the Goodman case.

"What do we make of all this?" asked Bishop.

"Well," offered Alan, "I don't have the training and experience you all have. But, I'm thinking that the unsub or unsubs we're looking for, knew Goodman quite well. They either knew him for a long time, or had a current binding relationship with him. He is the dominant party in this relationship and called the shots. He pissed off someone, and it provoked them to act. Obviously, he got the short end of the deal. I think we need to continue looking at friends, family, and current business partners."

"Unsub? You watch too much TV boy," chuckled a deputy.

"He makes a damn good point though," said Bishop, nodding in Alan's direction.

Alan winked at the deputy. The subtle slam hadn't gone unnoticed by Alan, but he was cool when he said, "Think about it, Sheriff Bishop. We've been finding out that Goodman wasn't liked by a lot of people, women especially—and dogs. He was demeaning and dismissive. Maybe he crossed a line with a woman or women." Alan then withdrew a crumpled piece of paper from his pocket and ironed it out on the table with his hands. To my dismay, it was the drawing he had made while we were at the crime scene. There, in pen and ink, was the cartoon character drawing of the deceased tied in front of the fireplace and five daemons looking on. Now as I scrutinized the drawing a little closer, I could see that each one of the demon faces that looked over the body was a warped watery image of a she-devil. One dressed in sweats and Nike shoes, another dressed in a Roman toga with a Cleopatra haircut, and the next in a long coat with thick fur trim, cleavage heaved from a tight sweater and feet shoved into steep, spiked high heels. Then another tomboyish figure with rolled up t-shirt sleeves—and sexy, exaggerated female curves—loomed over the shoulder of a fifth one dressed in jeans and oversized shirt with long, blond hair, striking an incredible likeness of Olivia Hope. The hairs on my arms and on the back of my neck began to rise as I came to two realizations. One was that Alan could easily rival any hero cartoon artist and be making big bucks with his talent. The second thing was that Alan had drawn this before we knew anything about the five women. By God, had Alan really sensed something or was this just coincidence?

"Where the hell did you get that?" asked the deputy.

"I drew it when—" he must have caught the fleeting look of dismay on my face, "I drew it when I had some time on my hands," he finished.

I breathed a sigh of relief. Alan didn't say any more, and to my surprise, he didn't give me his usual scowl reserved for awkward moments like this, which were becoming much too frequent lately.

"I'm just trying to make a point," Alan said. "I think the women have something to do with this." He looked around at the staring faces, picked up the drawing and slipped it back into his pocket. "You know, I'm just saying—"

Sheriff Bishop said nothing to that and cleared his

throat, "Well now, let's sum this up." He referred to his notes. "The women are still suspect, though we don't have any facts to back that up," he emphasized. "However, they don't seem to be practicing in witchcraft. One of them had an affair—maybe. Our boy Arch and his Aryan Brothers aren't completely out of the picture, or at least the 'snot-nosed' CTC aren't. Other investors haven't lost money recently so they don't seem to be mad enough to commit murder. And concerned citizens calling in leave nothing for us to work with except more paperwork to fill out." Bishop frowned as he tapped his notes, "We don't have squat, gentlemen. We need—"

The conference door swung open, "Sir," said Linda, Bishop's office manager. "Just got the autopsy in on Ira Goodman."

"Your timing couldn't be better my Angel of Mercy," said Bishop. "Can you give us the highlights? We'll read the details later."

"Sure," Linda said, opening a manila envelope, then began sniffing. "What is that smell? Did you guys leave something rotten in the garbage?"

"It's just Rand," Bishop tipped his head in my direction. "He was dumpster diving for breakfast."

Linda frowned and handed me a doughnut. She began rifling through some papers as she said, "Rand, you do know we have a McDonald's now, right?"

Before I could think of a good comeback, my cell phone vibrated with an incoming text. My heart skipped a beat as I read it, and then Linda began to read the document.

"Okay, the actual cause of death is a fire poker

imbedded in the heart. There wasn't a lot of blood seepage because the heart had slowed down from the cold."

"Maybe Goodman wasn't dying fast enough," surmised Bishop. "The killer either waited, or came back to finish the job. Or maybe someone else, carrying a grudge, came along and took advantage of the situation and finished him off."

"Wow, it's hard to believe someone could do that," Linda shivered. "If a reasonable person found him, and had called the paramedics, instead of planting the object in his chest, he probably would have lived. That's very sad."

Bishop nodded as he took the papers from her.

"Says here," Bishop took over, "that he had frost bite but nothing that would have been life-threatening. It talks about a circular bruise in the palm of his right hand. Oh, look at this, this is interesting." Bishop pulled out a photo and laid it on the table. We all got up and peered over his shoulder as he picked it up. "What the hell am I looking at?"

Linda began to read the document again. "Well, evidently this is a photo of something that had been embedded in the cheek of Goodman's buttocks. The coroner thinks that he must have been laying on something, whatever this is, and it left a frozen imprint."

There were several photos from different angles of the imprint. It looked like a knife, or a spike, yet more like a cross. Not just an ordinary cross, but one with ornate scrolling, the exact pattern was hard to tell in the frozen skin. And both ends of the t of the item were curled down in a graceful, swirling spiral. The imprint of the item was four inches long. If it was a knife, it was too short to do much lethal damage.

"Is it a roach clip?" asked Alan.

"Could be," I said, wondering how much he knew about roach clips.

"Did we find anything like this when we did the crime scene?" asked Bishop.

"No," I said. "I've been over every inch of the evidence many times and nothing like this was in there. Look at this part," I leaned in closer to see. At the top of the t, it looked like a line of very faint tiny circles clustered together. "It looks like this could have been on a chain."

"Are you sure it's not a roach clip?" Alan asked again.

"Why, you got one like it?" inquired the deputy.

Alan at least had the decency to blush and answered, "No, no, but I've seen some that look like that." Turning to me he said, "And I've never used one either." Whether it was true or not, I simply patted him on the back.

"I think," said Bishop, "If this is something someone wanted, it may be valuable. Maybe Goodman was going to use it and tried to hide it under himself during the struggle."

"Or," I added. "It was dropped when he was wrestled to the floor and that someone came back and reclaimed it."

"Either way, folks, this just might be the key to our mystery," said Bishop.

"It could be a necklace," added Alan. "Once again leading us back to the women."

"So, where do we go from here?" asked Bishop.

"Well," I said holding up my phone. "I just got an invitation to attend an investment meeting tonight with our five women. I'll ask them if they've lost anything."

Chapter 16 - Olivia Hope

It was Monday evening and, we were once again circling the kitchen table full of superb comfort foods. Each brought her favorite dish, and each brought a desert—mostly chocolate. We started with a glass of wine and the chocolate.

We took turns debriefing our interview with Dubois. All cackled when I told them about Idaho waking from her drunken dreams to swoon over the young detective, Alan, only to flop back into drunk-snores before the prince could kiss the sleeping princess. To which Idaho declared that that was a lie, there was no swooning—snores a slight possibility, but said she really couldn't remember.

Discussion turned to Lily. Asked if it was true that she had an affair with Goodman, she explained, "...I needed to make up something when I'd stated the obvious about Goodman's diminutive manhood...Had to explain how I knew." I was certain none of us believed her.

Pamela took over from there. She told us how Alan had wound the boys up on Mountain Dew, and as payback, she put them to work loading Christmas trees on a flatbed truck. Giggling, she said she didn't have to call a work crew, and it saved her about a thousand dollars, considering time and labor.

Maggie picked up the story by grousing, "So it's your fault they were so late getting to my house. Byron and I fell asleep waiting for them, and then I wasn't able to rouse him the rest of the night—thank you very much." When the questions began flying about how much Byron knew about their escapades, she reassured us that she had said nothing to him about any of it. "He travels a lot. By the time he gets to my house he's exhausted. He slept through the whole interview. He never even knew they were there. Besides, I do interviews all the time, he wouldn't question it."

"So, Olivia, how was your date with Rocco?" clucked Lily. I told them every sordid detail. Chuckles and groans were the responses. Hoots, laughter and applause raised the roof when I got to the part about leaving him at the restaurant. The laughter died when I told them about my search online for RayCon Construction, and Christopher Dumas. Anger and disgust flared throughout the conversation when I recounted the story of Julie Waver, the young girl who was raped. Also, Basham's and Goodman's legal involvement with her plight and the unpunished horny pubescent boys. Chatter ceased completely when I handed out the copies of the loan papers to each of them and informed them that we were now slum lords of the largest superfund site in the nation.

"What do you think it'll cost to clean it up," asked a dubious Pamela.

"Millions," I confirmed.

Silence hung in the air. After a few moments, I said, "I think our best bet is to try and contact this Christopher Dumas." That's when I announced that I had invited

Dubois to our meeting.

"You did what?" asked a dumbfounded Idaho.

"Oh relax," I snapped. "I followed up on our bankrupt contractor, and this guy, Christopher Dumas, is the one who bankrupt them. I've tried to contact him but his phone has been disconnected. I figured we could tell Dubois, and let him do the investigating. He can get answers where we can't."

"Couldn't you have just told him over the phone?" whined Idaho.

"I've learned to keep my friends close, and my enemies closer," I said. "That way you always know what they are up to. Besides, maybe we can get some more information out of him," I smiled and popped a chocolate-covered cherry in my mouth.

"Yeah, but look at me, I'm wearing my shitty work pants and a holy long-john shirt. And look at my hair for Christ sake."

"Dressing for Alan, are we?" teased Pamela.

"Oh, honey," chimed in Lily, "You don't have to dress for a guy who has rattier hair than yours and poses for the press with a finger mining for earwax."

I caught the blush that spread across Idaho's cheeks. "Oh, no, no, no," I cautioned. "No. There is no sleeping with the enemy. Don't even think about getting involved with someone who'd sooner throw you in jail than in bed. Get a grip, girl."

"Well, I think life is too short, and love is too precious to waste," added Pamela. You should grab love when and wherever you can. Look at me. I met the love of my life when I was in junior high. We married right out of high school, gave birth to a couple of little monsters. Then he died. Just like that," she said, with the snap of her fingers. "Best years of my life."

"Oh pulleeze," crabbed Idaho. "You've already got me marrying the redheaded Q-tip?"

"Ah, well…life is too short—I'm just saying," sighed Pamela.

"Okay, first," said Idaho, "They are not the enemy! They're doing their job. And I'm not going anywhere with Alan, to jail, or otherwise. And may I remind you, we have no reason to be going to jail. And, his hair is curly—not ratty. Also for your information, I wouldn't like to have to explain my dirty clothes and tell them I'm a gravedigger. Not just yet anyway. That's just wrong and conjures up all sorts of suspicion since we're almost murder suspects. So, Olivia, help me find something of yours to wear."

"Me thinks thou doth protest too much," sang Lily.

I took pity on my friend and found a sweater, a scarf and a pair of black leggings. I had to admit, Idaho cleaned up well. In fact, she looked damn good. And if I wasn't mistaken, it was the first time I'd seen a hint of vulnerability in Idaho.

After the last chocolate truffle disappeared, it was time to start on the dinner. That was the moment that Detective Dubois and Alan arrived.

"Come in," I hollered at the sound of the knock. The door began to open and like a great wizard, Dubois entered the living room with a fanfare of swirling wind, and instead of a flurry of smoke, it was snow. Alan let the dog in and muscled the door closed against the wind.

"Well, look who just blew in?" noted Idaho.

"If it isn't Merlin the Great," cooed Lily, as she

brushed a little snow off the detective's mustache—I've never seen a man blush so.

Pamela jumped up to help him off with his coat. "That's a lot of snow you bring! What magic tricks have you got in mind, Merlin? Planning to make us disappear in a cloud of ice crystals?"

"Now, there is no way I would wish for any of you lovely women to disappear. In fact, it is a pleasure to see you all again," said Dubois. Alan lagged with the dog, talking softly to him as he petted, patted and calmed the frisky pup. Finally, Blue shook himself free of snow and icicles. He came to sniff and greet everyone, finally settling in front of the fireplace to thaw.

"Wow, you really do have a way with dogs," praised Maggie. "You should have seen how he had my dog eating out of his hand."

"Dogs know things and can tell us a lot, if we just listen," replied Alan.

"You better keep your mouth shut, Blue," I scolded. Then I realized that was probably not an appropriate joke considering our circumstance, then said, "Oh, did I say that out loud?" Luckily everyone laughed heartily. I invited everyone to grab a plate and chow down.

"Oh, no—," began the detective.

"Smells great," said Alan, grabbing a plate and dishing up a big spoon full of macaroni and cheese.

"Well, maybe just a smidgen," shrugged Dubois. His eyes widened as Alan's plate began to mount. "I used to be able to eat like that, but damn, now I need to keep these love handles to a manageable size, eh," he said giving his sides a pat.

"Oh, no need for that, Mr. Dubois," cooed Lily,

once again. "I can watch them for you," wink, wink. And there was that deep, red blush again. We all laughed, but not too hard because we all knew she would.

Pamela handed him a plate offering scalloped potatoes, ham, cheesy cream of broccoli soup, spinach artichoke dip and chips, and of course, decadent red velvet cake. "But, stay away from that sweet desert," she said, pointing at Lily. "That could give you a heart attack." Serious laughter followed that assessment.

Conversation was light. I watched as Dubois gazed carefully at each woman, whether she was speaking or not. He's sizing us up, I thought. He asked questions that weren't too personal, but may lead him to other hints about our lives, I surmised. Lily engaged us all in laughter about one subject or another. She really is charming. Pamela told stories about the boys. And Maggie made a publicity plug for the next play to premier right after the first of the year, and offered both Alan and Rand Dubois free tickets, front row seating. I was in awe at how easy and comfortable we all seemed to be. It was as if we'd been friends for years. I couldn't help staring at this man, whose hypnotic deep voice swept my imagination away to a more romantic land with his subtle French accent, imagining myself on the sunny beaches of the French Riviera, and warm ocean water lapping at my toes. I literally shook my head to bring myself back to reality and the conversations at hand—setting aside my glass of wine. Damn, I must be drunk. I took a deep breath, feeling warm and sleepy. Oh, he was a smooth one all right. I glanced away not wanting to be caught ogling. As I reached for another chocolate-covered cherry I caught a glimpse of Idaho and Alan with heads dipped together—their conversation quiet and serious. Alan's expression seemed pinched with frustration focusing on Idaho. But then, they began to laugh, and I saw Idaho show him her dirt-honed hands and nails. With that, I was back on alert.

"So, Mr. Dubois, how is the investigation going?" I asked finally, getting to why I invited him.

He turned to me and graced me with a warm, dashing smile. "Please, call me Rand." Then he cocked his head in a playful manor and said, "Ah, work, and we were having such a good time. Really, in this lovely room filled with family and friends, do you want to talk about murder?"

I returned his smile and said, "Well, Rand, maybe just the parts that might lead us to getting our money back."

"Well, if we find the killer, perhaps we'll find your money." He was still grinning at me like a school boy, and I couldn't help but laugh out loud. I could feel myself blush, and downed the rest of my wine.

"Perhaps I can help by giving you a name to follow up on," I toyed. Rand raised his own wine glass and nodded for me to continue. "His name is Christopher Dumas. He took over RayCon. They were losing money hand-over-fist in this economy."

"Ah, yes, RayCon," said Rand. "The family-owned business that Goodman was working with before it went bankrupt."

"Yep, that's the one," I confirmed. "Raymond Connly told me he hired Dumas because he had access to money and could keep the business afloat. He said he promised to take care of his family and possibly get him work in other areas outside of California. I've tried to reach Mr. Dumas and found that his phone has been disconnected. I don't have any other leads to check. I was thinking that, if you checked up on Christopher Dumas, you'd have better luck." I went on to tell him of my conversation with Mr. Connly. I told him how Mr. Dumas didn't just run the company into the ground, he kicked it in the ass, turning it into a quick nose dive, and then just disappeared.

"So, you've been doing some detective work of your own, eh?"

I nodded. "I have to say, I'm more than a little bothered by Mr. Connly's mood. He really didn't sound happy about the bankruptcy, which is understandable of course, but he really sounded depressed. I got the feeling he should be on suicide watch. How does one go about keeping an eye on him? Can you call someone to check on him?" Rand gazed at me quizzically. "I mean if I started butting into his personal life, I doubt that anyone would listen to me—I'm just a nobody. But you, you're a professional. You probably know people who know people." I was babbling, and a little embarrassed as everyone in the room had tuned into our conversation. "If you know what I mean . . ." I trailed off lamely.

Rand studied me for a moment longer. "I'll tell you what," he said. "I'll check out Christopher Dumas, and see what I can do for Mr. Connly, if you'll help me out with a little something."

"Sure, what do you need?" Did that sound a little too eager?

Rand reached for his coat, slipped a hand into a

pocket and pulled out a piece of paper. He spread it out on the coffee table, then stepped around the other side so everyone could gather closer to get a better look.

"What are we looking at," questioned Pamela.

"I was hoping you could tell me. Can any of you tell me what this shape means? Is it some kind of symbol, a cross, something used in Satanic rituals maybe, or Wiccan perhaps?"

"Is it a roach clip?" asked Lily.

"Ha!" crowed Alan and laughed, "That's what I said." Catching his father's disapproving eye, he shrugged shamelessly but sobered up.

"It looks like a cross or something like a key that is attached to a chain," said Maggie. "Is it a necklace?"

"Where did you get this?" asked Lily.

"This was in an autopsy photo."

"Oh, speaking of autopsy," said Pamela. "What was the cause of death?"

Rand focused on Pamela for a few seconds and then replied, "It was the fire poker that killed him."

I heard an audible sigh of relief from most of us. Not from me, however. I was still holding my breath, wondering if I could ever breathe again, because I had recognized the chain that held the cross and that damn key.

The sighs didn't go unnoticed by Rand. With his focus still on Pamela he asked, "You seem relieved. Why is that?"

"Ah, yeah. W-w-w-well, I mean no, it's just, you know, awful. Just awful!" stammered Pamela. Her face was beat red. Clearly, she was flustered and searching for something to say.

"Rand," chimed in Maggie, coming to her rescue, "before you came we were discussing horrible ways to die. I think what Pamela means is that she felt it would be better to die by fire poker than freezing to death. It's much quicker. Could you imagine how awful it would be to freeze slowly? From the toes and fingers? Up your arms and legs, until your heart can't beat anymore? Praying for someone to come and save you, only to die hours and hours later?" She shivered, aghast at such a thought. She was very convincing. I didn't think I could have sounded that convincing even if I were telling the truth. No wonder Maggie had so many acting awards in her closet.

"So anyway," piped in Lily waving a hand at the photo on the table. "What is this about?"

"It's a photo of an indentation from an object that had been embedded in Goodman's buttocks. He must have been laying on it while his body froze." Rand explained. He turned the paper so that they could look at it from another angle. A wide-eyed Idaho gave a chirping gasp and raised a hand to her mouth. I realized that Idaho now recognized the shape as well. I grabbed her shoulder and said, "Oh, sorry Idaho. I didn't mean to step on your toe." I gave Idaho a warning wink. "Are you okay?" Idaho dropped her hand from her mouth and gave a nervous quick nod. I gained another suspicious look from Rand.

"Have any of you ever seen this kind of branding before?" asked Alan. "Do you know if this is some kind of Satanic ritual sign?"

"Maybe it's one of those ornate keys you see in the old haunted house movies," said Pamela after closer examination. "What do you think, Maggie? Have you ever seen something like this in the movies?" The other three women were so cavalier about the whole thing, thank god. They were very persuasive. I hoped Rand was buying it. I relaxed a little.

"Nah," said Maggie. "To me, it looks like an ornamental top from those little garden fences you can get out of those dumb magazines I get all the time." Too close for comfort, I inwardly groaned, because that's exactly what it was. I had found the ornament buried in the garden. Thought it looked cool, and slipped my shed key on it. It normally hung by the back door for easy access on my way out, but it also posed as a funky wall ornament. My palms were sweating. and I rubbed them on my jeans. Jesus, never in my wildest imagination would I have ever thought it might one day implicate me in a murder. I reflexively looked toward the door and realized there was a sort of outline on the wall from where it usually hung. I jumped up, rubbing my hands together, "Okay, more wine anyone?" I walked into the kitchen diverting attention on me, and hoping that Dubois hadn't followed my gaze.

"You didn't find anything like this in your little bag of evidence?" asked Lily.

"No," Rand shook his head. "I've been through everything and nothing even suggests something like this."

"I know," said Pamela quivering with excitement, "I bet he was part of the CTC. Instead of getting horns implanted, like you see in those weirdo tattoos and piercing magazines. Maybe he got an implant or a brand of some kind that marks him as the grand poop-pa!" Of course, they all laughed at the witty pun. Even Rand managed a laugh out loud.

"Well on that note, sorry, Rand," I butted in. "Sorry, we weren't much help."

It was about then that Idaho stretched and launched a yawn. "Well, that was fun. Wow, look at the time. Sorry to be a party pooper, guys, but I've got an early meeting tomorrow." She immediately started picking up her dishes and carrying them to the sink.

"Yeah, me, too," murmured Pamela. And the other women followed Idaho's lead for clean-up.

I glanced in Rand's direction and watched as he slowly picked up the photo. He studied it a moment longer. He paused as he was about to put it back in his pocket and then thought better of it, and let it slide back on the table.

"You're wrong ladies," said Rand as he looked up and focused his smile on me. "You were a great help." I froze in my tracks. "We have an early morning meeting as well." Rand threw a set of car keys to Alan. "Could you go warm up the car, eh?"

Alan already had his coat on. "Thanks for the grub," he hollered. "You ladies are the meilleurs cuisiniers," He pivoted, bent low, swooped his stocking cap as if it were an exquisite top hat, and performed a graceful bow. "I bid you ladies adieu." Then slapped the cap over his ears and reached for the last chocolate chip cookie. He stopped only long enough to give a three-finger wave in Idaho's direction. Everyone in the room, noted that.

"What did he just call us?" asked a blushing Idaho.

"Ah, my son," said Rand. "Such joie de vivre. He

lives his life to the fullest. He said you ladies are the best cooks." He had his coat on then, too, and was ready to go. He turned to me and asked, "May I have a word with you before I go, eh?"

I walked him to the door. "Okay, shoot," I said. Rand grinned at that. "Oh, sorry, bad choice of words."

"No, no, quite funny," said Rand. "But, I was wondering if I could ask you a personal question?"

I took a deep breath. Here it comes, I thought. He wants to hear what I know of that damn key. I braced myself to tell yet another lie. "Okay, what?"

"What is your relationship with Rocco Basham?"

The question completely caught me off guard. "Are you spying on me, Mr. Dubois?"

He seemed too relaxed. He shrugged, and gave me a smug little smile, "It's this lousy job. I never get a break. So, tell me, what does a woman like you see in a man like him?"

I was furious now. "Information," I spat. "A woman like me sees information in a man like Basham. I want answers as to where our money went." I knew a few people at the restaurant had seen me with Rocco. He was sure to find out, so why did it bother me so much?

"Do you always use seduction to get information?"

"It depends on what I need and from whom."

"Why didn't you seduce me, eh?" Dubois grinned from ear-to-ear.

"I thought I had," I sneered back in his face.

"Well, I guess so, if wining and dining me along with my son and four other women tonight was your idea of seduction. You went to dinner with Mr. Basham, but then left him hanging in the wind before dinner was even served. And now, he's in danger of losing his job because of the likes of you. Was the information worth it? Did you get what you needed, Ms. Hope?"

No, not all that I wanted, I thought. Fuming, I growled, "Are you jealous, Mr. Dubois?"

"Hardly," snarled Dubois. "I don't pine for women who are liars. Do not forget for one moment that I am a detective, Ms. Hope. I suggest, if there is information you need, you come directly to me. And, if I need answers from you, you will be straight with me. I don't play games, Ms. Hope. And, I don't need someone like you screwing up possible evidence and my investigation. If you think you can get information by seduction, you better forget it, because you really suck at it," he turned his back on me and headed for the door.

I slapped my forehead with the palm of my hand. "Oh, that's right, I'm supposed to wait and ask my questions over pillow talk!" I said, feigning dramatic enlightenment.

Dubois, turned to face me again, "Now you're getting it. Fuck whoever you wish. That's a start. But you do not pull that shit while I'm on duty. Don't fuck with people's lives, and don't fuck with my case. Do we understand each other, Ms. Hope?"

He threw open the door, and his exit was as dramatic as his entrance, with wind and swirling snow. However, it seemed his exit carried him away on a dark horse. What the hell had bit him in the ass, I wondered. What did he mean when he said that Basham could lose his job over me? I slammed the door after him.

"What was that about?" asked Maggie.

"Oh, he's just got a bug up his butt," I groused. I

looked over at a wide-eyed Idaho, who was wringing her hands and pacing the floor. I flung myself on the couch. "But, I guess I can't blame him. I'm sure he wants to know why my shed key, that I loaned to Idaho, was doing stuck to Goodman's ass!"

"What the hell?" Maggie shot. The rest of the women began firing questions, too.

"I-well-I . . .I," stammered Idaho, holding up her palm for silence while continuing to pace the floor. "Olivia let me borrow her key because I was going to put some yard sale stuff in her shed and I lost the key and I didn't know where, and, I...I...I looked and looked, everywhere, and I thought I lost it in one of the garbage bags with my stuff, and I thought maybe it was in the garbage, or a closet, or maybe Olivia saw it and took it back and forgot to tell me, and with all that's been going on I forgot all about it." Idaho abruptly stopped her rambling and pacing, "On the bright side, we know where the key went." We stood gaping at her.

"The question is," I said, "Where is the key now?" Eyes were then on me. I could see the ramifications starting to register on their faces, of said "key" still missing.

"Holy-fuck-a-moly," breathed Pamela. "Whoever killed him has your key, Olivia."

"Oh, no," said an exasperated Maggie, "If they find that key we are up shit creek, ladies. We better get a story together and quick."

"Let's not get ahead of ourselves here," rationalized Idaho. "Let's think this through. First, they may never find the key. Second, if they do find it, it will be in the killer's possession, not mine or Olivia's, and they'd probably think it was a stolen key. Besides, it really doesn't have anything to do with the murder, it's just something that happened to be there. Third, who's to say they can trace it back to us?"

"I don't know, Idaho," I advised. "They have tracked killers down by simpler things than a key. Like a cigarette butt, or an earring, things like that. We're already on the suspicious side of their investigation. If they found the key, it would only take a few minutes to find where that key fits, and the owner."

"Not if you changed the lock," Idaho defended.

"Too suspicious," said Lily. "A new lock would scream 'I'm covering my ass.'"

"Fine, just replace the whole door," said Idaho. "Burn the old one. There's plenty more where that one came from. I bet I can find a used one at a yard sale or antique store."

"It's winter. People don't have yard sales in the middle of winter," said a dubious Maggie. "Besides, they could see fresh wood marks after replacing the door."

"I say we just lie through our bloody teeth," announced Pamela.

"Well, let's sleep on it and figure out what to do about it tomorrow," I said. "On the bright side, they don't have the key yet and finding it will be harder than finding the killer. Maybe once they have the killer, it will be forgotten. And, we know for sure now that Goodman died by fire poker, so we know we didn't kill him." I smiled at my friends, but I was exhausted and wanted to be alone for a good hard cry.

"Isn't it funny, Goodman is dead, yet he's still

making a mockery of us all," growled Lily.

"Well, you know," said Idaho drawing out the words, as if she had just heard the best gossip, "The funeral is Wednesday, right?" There were nods all around. "So, tomorrow is the last day of viewing the body. Mora doesn't want to have an open casket at the funeral, too invasive. Said she wants people to remember her vibrant, live husband. Since it's too cold and stormy, they won't be going to the cemetery until later. She wants the casket moved to the Catholic Church for the ceremony."

"Okay, what are you saying?" asked Pamela.

"So, because of budget cuts, I'm the one who has to transport the body."

"And so—just make your point," grumbled Maggie.

"Okay, okay," continued Idaho, "Think about it, you guys, I'll be alone with the body. I'm going to be the last person to see Goodman in his casket."

"What part of getting to the point don't you get?" growled Lily.

"I say we take our last revenge and send Goodman to the next world as a woman!" proclaimed Idaho.

"You mean, give him a sex change?" crowed Lily. The evil smile on her face told everyone that she was up for it.

"Oh, gross," said Pamela.

"No," exclaimed Idaho, "just some make-up, a wig maybe."

"Isn't it against the law to deface a body, or something like that?" I asked. "You really want to go to jail for turning Goodman into a transvestite?"

"Oh, come on," Idaho coaxed. "We're looking at

jail time anyway. The casket will be closed and sealed. We're the only ones to be the wiser."

"Too, risky," Pamela said shaking her head.

"Couldn't stand to touch that creep," added Maggie.

"I've seen enough of that limp dick. Too crazy, no can do," voted Lily.

"Out of the question," I finalized.

"Oh, fine!" Idaho conceded.

Silence hung in the air as several minutes passed. Each of us was alone with her thoughts, while we finished cleaning and packing up for the night.

Lily broke the quiet. "So, when are we going to do this.

Chapter 17 - Rand Dubois

"I'm getting too old for this shit," said Sheriff Bishop as he lowered his girth into one of the conference room chairs. I helped him move papers, charts, and books that I'd spread across the table.

"What's up?" I asked.

He sat back, stretched out his long legs, and folded his hands across his broad chest. "These two blond girls go to rob a bank," he starts. "They make a plan. On the day of their scheduled robbery they pull up at the bank. The one behind the wheel says, 'Okay, in and out in three minutes, you know the plan, right?' The other one says, 'Yeah, this is easy.' She goes in. Two minutes goes by, three minutes, four minutes, then eight minutes. Finally, after ten minutes, here comes the blond pulling a rope with a big-ass safe on the end. As the driver of the car jumps out to help put the safe in the trunk, here come two guards with their pants down around their ankles. As they speed away, the driver says, 'I thought you said you knew the plan?' The other one says, 'I did just as you said.' The driver says, 'No, you didn't. I said to tie up the guards and blow the safe!'" He laughed uproariously over his joke. I'm not fond of stereotyping. But, Bishop's laughter was infectious. Or maybe I just needed a light moment. I busted a gut, too, despite myself.

I asked, "Are you saying you're chasing dumb

criminals these days?"

"Pretty much," he nodded. "Some young punk stole that big Michelin Tire sign from Frank Gates's store. The kid asked his girlfriend to help him carry the sign out to a big tree-house in his back yard. I guess they struggled with it, so she called her dad to come and help."

"Now, that's funny," I laughed.

"Funnier yet, her dad just happens to be one of our local cops."

"Is she blond?"

"Yeah, as a matter of fact," huffed the sheriff. "Got some more mutilated animals, too: a cat, a small dog, and a goddamn iguana! A guy named Frenchie found them."

"All those found in the same area as the others?"

"Yup, well at least about fifteen-twenty yards from each other." He swung his legs down and his feet hit the floor hard. Smashed a paper cup that made a loud pop. It surprised the both of us. "Damn, cup fart." We heehawed again.

I said, "Hmm, who or what is doing the mutilations doesn't take time to bury the bodies. Do you think maybe it's some animal, like a wolf, maybe a coyote, doing the killing and not some deranged human?"

"Well, if it were an animal, I'd think we'd see some tracks in the snow. We never find tracks. I hope only humans are smart enough to cover tracks. Could be aliens," grumped Bishop.

"You are a funny guy this morning."

"I suppose, these storms blowing in and out could be erasing some evidence. Hell, who knows, maybe some of them are buried under a few layers of that snow. Hasn't happened for a week or two, but now, there are three found again. My veterinarian, has volunteered to do autopsies. Maybe that will show something. Frenchie has volunteered to keep watch of the area."

"Are you sure that's wise?" I asked. "I mean, that could be dangerous. If there are some kooks out there, he could get hurt."

Bishop started to laugh. "You obviously haven't met Frenchie. He's retired military. Some think he was, and maybe still is, an Irish terrorist. He can handle his own. Besides, he's pretty concerned about all of this. His hobby is patching up hurt and abused animals and returning them back to the wild. I can't think of anyone more perfect for the job."

"Huh, interesting," I said thoughtfully, "A military terrorist turned animal rights activist. I need to meet this guy."

"Where's Alan?" asked Bishop. He picked up some papers and held them at arm's length, adjusting his eyesight. He threw them back on the table.

"I sent him on errands." I looked at my watch and frowned. "He's been gone quite a while. He's supposed to bring some lunch before Goodman's funeral. It's Rosita's Mexican food. Want me to call him with an order for you?"

"Sure, how about some chicken enchiladas with green sauce."

I texted Alan, and gave him the order.

"So, what have you got going here?" He looked around the conference room at my mess and surmised, "Run out of space in your office?"

"I never had space in that so-called office," I growled. I'd already debriefed Bishop on the meeting with the women on Monday night. I told him about Olivia wanting me to follow up with Christopher Dumas. I had spent the good part of Tuesday digging for information and chasing my tail. "In my trials of tracking down Dumas, I keep running into brick walls, except that he showed up at RayCon and promised the sun and the moon, and then stole what was left of the company. Lots of pissed-off people. I found a bank account for him with a bogus address. He's got $643,000 in the account. That's not a crime, but it is suspicious, when everyone around him is losing money. I found an article implicating Dumas in a lawsuit." I shoved a printout of a newspaper article about him. "Here, read this."

"Sorry, don't' have my glasses. Read it to me." He sat back with his hands clasped behind his head, eyes closed. I picked up the paper and began to read, hitting the highlights.

San Francisco Bank Sues RayCon Construction & Developer Christopher Dumas

Christopher Dumas, one of San Francisco's most prominent infill developers, faces a 5.2 million lawsuit from a lender and a potential foreclosure after one of his companies defaulted on its loans.

Dumas had borrowed 1.9 million to buy land. Gold West Bank sued Dumas and his company in August after they failed to pay off loans when it defaulted in April,

The SF bank also says Dumas's company defaulted on 2.6 million in loans when it fell behind on payments on the Hillside Vineyard homes to the acclaimed James

Campbell Restaurant. This building earned platinum rating from the Green Building Council.

Dumas acknowledges he's behind on the Ravel Road loans but he says he's caught up on his payments for the Hillside Vineyard homes. "The loan has never been more than 30 days late," claimed Dumas. "This is just the way business goes sometimes. You all try to make too much of it."

Dumas claims his loan documents don't allow the bank to start a foreclosure against any of his properties. He said he plans to counter sue. "They (Gold West Bank) had been, up until now, the best bank to deal with," said Dumas.

A bank spokesman declined to comment. Daniel Blake, a SF lawyer would only say that the defaults are allowed with the loan documents.

Dumas, 52, has been a star in the circle of architects and designers who have rebuilt many of the troubled neighborhoods and commercial districts of San Francisco.

Dumas said he is very close to selling properties out of state and is focusing on revitalizing communities in other areas. Dumas said he is branching out to Oregon, Washington, Idaho, and most recently, Montana. He claims that he is excited to work with Ira Goodman, another developer who plans to work with the city of Libby, Montana, to revitalize the depressed town by helping build up the industrial and commercial area. And so on and so on—You can read the rest yourself," I finished, throwing the article on the table.

Alan entered the room with our lunch. "There you are," I scolded. "I thought I was going to have to send out a search party."

"Don't pay the ransom," he said. "Just checking some things out and then went to buy some stuff," he said, not making eye contact with me. I felt he was hiding something, but I let it slide. It was probably nothing.

"Oh, yeah," said Bishop, with drool dangerously close to escaping his smacking lips, as the sacks were opened. "Nothing like a little Rosita's. I'm springing for sodas, what do you all want?"

Returning with our sodas, Bishop plopped down in the chair and dug in. With a mouthful of enchilada, he said, "Sounds like what Olivia said is true. Dumas had pretty much run RayCon Construction into the ground. Maybe Goodman was upset about losing money and the bankruptcy. Maybe it was enough to challenge Dumas in some way, and Dumas paid him a surprise visit. He could have crossed Goodman, the men argued and maybe Dumas offed him? And then, he left the country."

"It's a possibility," I said. "My question then is why in the hell go through the trouble of nailing him down and later come back to stab him, or, 'off' him as you say?"

"It's an unplanned argument. Dumas gets the idea to treat it like a Satanic murder. God knows there's been enough in the local news about our little Satanic nest in town, and now our recent animal mutilations. It could be just wacky enough to keep suspicion off him. The neighbor said there was a pickup truck that came and went a couple of times between the time he was probably tied up and estimated time of death. It could have been Dumas." Bishop took a couple of bites of his enchilada and rolled his eyes in ecstasy.

"Well, we'll have to ask him once we find him. But, it's as if he's dropped off the face of the earth. I've asked Mr. Conley to send us a photo, if he can find one. Maybe someone around here knows him or at least remembers him. We still don't have any more word on Goodman's son, Seth, either. Also, one of his friends, Josh, has disappeared, too. I'm thinking they're together. I'm getting the feeling that this Satanic stuff surrounding the murder was an afterthought. Maybe someone came in and tied Goodman up, and then Seth came after the fact and finished his dad off. It's not a secret that the two of them had words before he died. Or, maybe Seth and Josh were angry, and things just got out of hand."

"How about the women?" asked Bishop. "How do they fit in?"

I thought about that a minute, not that I hadn't been thinking about it for days. "I'm trying not to focus on them too much just yet," I said. "If I can rule out all these other probabilities, then I'm going to put the squeeze on them. But, I have a hard time believing they could have done this. It's such a savage thing to do and I cannot see how any one of them, or even as a group could drive a fire poker into the man's chest. I've gotten to know these women just a little. I think that if they did it, one of them would have cracked by now. Pardon my stereotypes here, but Lily seems to be too 'girlie', I don't think she'd like to get her hands dirty. Maggie seems too smart, and something like this would be beneath her—not worth her time. Pamela has two small boys. I can't see her risking losing them. I've seen her tender side and her strength. It takes a coward to commit a murder like this. Idaho, hmm . . ." Alan's eyebrows shot up over a mouth full of taco. "What?" I questioned.

"Nophing," he managed to muffle. He put his taco down and waited.

"I think she's maybe had a hard life but, there's an innocent quality about her." Alan smiled at that and took another bite. I thought the boy looked smitten with her the other night, and now I was sure he had a full-blown crush on the girl.

"What about Olivia?" Alan asked.

"Now there's a complicated woman," I said. "The jury's still out on that one. I think she, too, may have had a hard life, but I can't seem to find out anything about her. She's tough, secretive. I think there must be some sordid history there. On one hand, she seemed to be concerned about Mr. Connly's mental health, and I can see she adores the little boy she allows to come to play with her dog. All of that shows a caring and nurturing attribute that doesn't match a cowardly killer. But there is a side to her that I can't help but feel is toxic. She gives me a cold look if I get to close to subjects she doesn't want to talk about." I shook my head, "I just can't put my finger on it. She's like an angel who's been to hell. And I'm not so sure she's back yet."

"And you think Mora Goodman, wife of dead husband, is probably not smart enough to carry off a murder like this," stated Bishop, interrupting my rambling.

"That's correct."

"Then we still don't have squat yet."

"Pretty much," I admitted.

We began clearing the table and taking out the trash

left from our lunch. I picked up my papers. Soon we all crowded into my vehicle and headed to the church for the funeral.

Attending the deceased's funeral is the worst part of this job. It usually turns out to be a very depressing day. But as a detective, I'm aware that quite often, the killer will show up. They show because they either feel a need to revel in their success, maybe revel in seeing family members grieve. Or, because they want to make sure the intended party is in the ground.

Before exiting the vehicle, Bishop asked, "Everyone know their spots?" indicating that each of us take a stance at some point in the building, albeit the building may only be a couple thousand square feet with only two exits. Nods were given all around. "Okay," said Bishop, "I'll stand in the back of the church and keep my eyes open for exciters." Meaning anyone leaving early, or looks suspicious edging toward the door, may be the killer.

We were somewhat late. Late meaning that probably most everyone that was coming to the funeral service were already there. As I looked around, many of the people I interviewed were in attendance. I saw city Councilman Roberts, who nodded in my direction with a half-smile. He was standing arm-in-arm with a lovely, middle-aged woman, who I recognized as the owner of one of the posher stores in town. She was talking to Sheriff Bishop's wife, who was just as beautiful, but much younger. I noted that the Sheriff and his Mrs. hadn't even acknowledged each other's presence, enhancing my earlier suspicions that not all was well on the marital front. My eyes wandered over to Mrs.

Hunter, wearing a bright red hat and a purple dress draped over her plump, short body. It made her look like a large grape as she rolled towards several other women who wore purple and similar red hats—banding together as only the Red Hat Society can.

Mora Goodman entered the church with her sons minus the youngest, Seth. We still had no clue where he was. We held hope that he would show for his father's funeral, and if so, we'd be there for him. They made their way to the front pews and were greeted by the District Attorney, Rocco Basham. I seethed at the thought of an argument we'd had when I'd gone to Goodman's office to talk to his secretary, who he'd just fired.

I had a sudden thought Perhaps Basham killed Goodman? I knew they were good friends, but it wouldn't be the first time a friend killed his buddy. What would be the motive, I wondered? I turned to voice my thoughts to Alan, only to see him snake into a throng of people and disappear into the crowd. That's when I saw the women. A striking Lily White, with a sleek black dress cut low down the front with a gleaming diamond necklace nested nicely in her cleavage. All eyes landed on her as she entered, men smiled, and their heads nodded in lustful approval while most women's heads shook with envious scrutiny. As I watched her capture the room, the name Cruella Deville came to mind, the nasty witch from 101 Dalmatians.

Maggie Berns was also in a black dress, not as sexy as Lily's but very nice. Her hair was down. She wore a black hat and dark sunglasses, making her look like the movie star she was.

Pamela Phuchet wore a gray pant suit that looked a little too big for her, but she, too, was catching a few men's eyes while their wives nudge them away to find seating. Pamela's two boys and a girl of about twelve followed behind her.

Olivia Hope filed in next, with her blonde hair floating around her shoulders, wearing a short, brown sweater dress that accented every curve, brown tights, or leggings, whatever they call them these days, and sensible boots that completed her outfit. I immediately thought of Victoria Secret once again and smiled. She smiled, too, when she caught my eye and nodded. I felt my face flush. She turned her back to me, and I was left to my scouting. Shortly thereafter, the group of women migrated to a pew towards the back of the church.

Idaho hadn't appeared yet, and I wondered if she was coming. But after about five minutes, I saw her streaming through a cluster of people. I was surprised to see she was accompanied by none other than my son. I almost hadn't recognized her. She wasn't wearing her normal jeans or overalls. She wore a flattering dark blue dress and her normal baseball cap was replaced by a blue newsboy type hat. Her hair was curled smartly around her face. She too, was a striking beauty in her own way. Her hand was slipped in the crook of Alan's elbow as he led her to where the other women had settled. Once she was seated, she patted his hand and smiled brightly while he beamed with delight. He acted the perfect gentleman. If it were other circumstances, I would be proud and happy for him. But, when he lays his heart out to a person of interest in a murder case, I feared the worst was about to happen to him. Why the hell can't he fall for a college girl?

I watched as Alan made his way back over to where I was standing. After he left Idaho, the other women began conversation with her. I could tell by Olivia's body language she wasn't too thrilled with her either.

Idaho sat, she put her palm up in front of Olivia's face as if to say, "Talk to the hand." Olivia finally gave up shaking her head. I knew why I wasn't thrilled with this relationship, but I couldn't help wonder why Olivia wouldn't be if they had nothing to hide.

Alan was still smiling when he joined me. I hated to burst his bubble, but I had to say something. "Son, it isn't a good idea to carry on with that girl."

"What?" he asked, barely hearing me with his head so high in the clouds.

"I said, it's not a good idea for you to be keeping company with Idaho."

"Why?" his defenses were up now.

"You know why. She's someone who may have committed a murder. You can NOT mix business with pleasure here."

"Dad, she only buries dead bodies. She's not the one who makes them dead."

"Do you know how comforting that sounds?" I fumed.

Alan shook his head. "Sarcasm, hah, funny, Dad. She's nice, she's smart. She's fun and funny and she likes me. She's not the murdering type, Dad. She has NOT committed any murders—"

"Oh, well, what is the murdering type? And, if you have the facts of this murder investigation, then you better start talking. What facts do you have that she and/or her friends did not kill Ira Goodman?" He said nothing, while I continued to stare at him. He looked mad and hurt. I was mad, too, but I had a harder time handling his hurt. "Son, we don't have all of the facts yet. I don't feel safe with you spending so much time with her. I don't want you getting hurt because of this." I still got nothing from him except pouting. "Listen, just wait until this case is over before you try to strike up a relationship. If she's all you say she is, it can wait."

More pouting.

"We are here today to honor the passing of a great man," began the priest, opening the funeral service.

Something short of dread was pulsing through me. I wasn't getting through to Alan.

"Let us pray," continued the priest.

Dear God, yes! Let us pray for sensibility, I thought. To Alan, I pleaded, "Just promise me you will cool things until this is all over, please." When I didn't get an answer, I reached over and gently squeezed his shoulder. He shrugged off my hand and stepped away.

Chapter 18 - Olivia Hope

"Idaho, what the hell are you doing?" I asked. "Are you and Alan dating now, or what?" Alan had just escorted Idaho to sit with us. I had a flash of panic when I saw their starry-eyed glaze. I wasn't sure if the panic was for Idaho getting hurt, or the rest of us getting caught in our secret little lies.

"Oh, good grief! Who are you, my mother?" spat Idaho.

"Well, obviously, someone needs to watch out for you," I growled.

"Talk to the hand, my friend," said Idaho, as she wagged her palm in my face.

I swatted at her hand, "You need to listen to me—"

"Olivia," whispered Pamela, cutting me off in mid-sentence. "Give her a break. Did you ever stop to think that it might not hurt to have someone like Alan as a friend, someone in our corner?"

"Yeah, who knows what kind of info Idaho might weasel out of him," suggested Lily.

"Enough with the pillow talk already," I admonished.

"Just saying," shrugged Lily.

"Well, I think we could use him about now," Maggie chimed in. "George Hammer just said to me, 'Bet you're pissed as hell about losing that money to Goodman.' Then he gave me one of those conspiratorial winks that made me squirm. If he suspects us, Dubois isn't far behind. If things are heating up, Idaho might have a good chance of wheedling info from him. We'd be ahead of the game."

"Hello, I'm right here," sassed Idaho. "Don't talk about me in front of me, okay? I'm not a piece of furniture. And Alan isn't a tattletale. He's a sweet guy and I'm not going to use him for anything. That's just rude," she sat back and pouted.

"We are here today to honor the passing of a great man," announced the priest. The funeral services had begun.

We settled back in our seats. Oh well, I thought. I guess they had a point. Maybe it's not so bad to have an ally in our corner. Idaho deserves a nice young man in her life, after all. But why couldn't she fall for college guy with a future? Damn, I *was* starting to sound like her mother. I squirmed in my seat to get comfortable. I viewed the attendees, while the priest waved his incense and spewed Latin phrases that I never could comprehend. I took the opportunity to look around, hoping that people had their eyes closed. Turned out I wasn't the only one scoping the crowd. Didn't people have respect for a good prayer anymore? I gave head nods to Fred Barlow, Arnold Grey, Alex Martin and whoever the old guy that was with them. They were investors from previous loan investments with Goodman. When I caught the old codger's gaze, he narrowed his eyes at me. I suddenly felt a pang of guilt under his scrutiny. Was he squinting because he couldn't see, or was he giving me a knowing look, peering deep into my dark, dirty soul? Stop with the paranoia, I told myself. But maybe he was looking for someone, too. Someone with a darker soul than mine who was responsible for this gathering. I could still feel his eyes boring into my back, but I shook it off and continued to look around.

I watched a sweet older woman wearing a beautiful and expensive blue pant suit. She was petite, pale and fragile-looking. A wisp of wind could blow her away. She put a wrinkled old hand into her purse and pulled out a hanky. She blew her nose and dabbed at her eyes. I couldn't help wonder what kind of a relationship Goodman would have had with her? Was she a relative, a business acquaintance, an investor, a lover? I snorted at that—Idaho gave me a hard nudge. I continued the perusal of the room. I recognized some parents of several of my students. Law enforcement stood sentinel. There were lots of people I didn't know, but had seen before. People I hadn't seen before I assumed were from out of town. It was amazing to see so many people gathered. There must have been at least four hundred or more—standing room only. Many looked like they were truly grieving the loss of a good friend. Goodman had his fingers in a lot of things, maybe in his own sleazy way he did some good, too. After all, he had bamboozled my friends and me.

I could still feel eyes on me. I took a quick peek. Sure enough, it was the old guy. I gave him a hard stare right back, spread my hands and mouthed, "What?" The old bloke broke into a shriveled grin, winked, and blew me a kiss. "Oh, man," I groaned.

"Shush," complained Idaho.

I poked a finger in the old man's direction. "That

geezer over there is making a pass at me—at a funeral!"

I gave an extra nudge to Idaho's ribs to encourage her to look at who it was. She turned her head, then nodded. He smiled when he saw her and waggled his eyebrows. The old coot was probably pushing ninety-five. His age-spotted face sported a long-hooked nose. He looked a lot like Ebenezer Scrooge. A top hat perched crookedly on his head as he suggestively stroked a wooden cane. I grimaced.

Idaho whipped her head back to me and said, "All right. Listen to me, there will be no bump-and-grind in the closets or the restrooms. Do you understand?" I poked my friend hard in the ribs. Both of us snorted, holding back muffled laughter as people turned to see what it was about. We quickly hung our heads and dabbed at our eyes with tissue feigning tears of sorrow.

Regaining my composure, I returned my gaze to the grieving family. There was an empty space by Mora. I presumed it was reserved for the unaccounted for, Seth. No surprise there, the newspapers said he was still nowhere to be found. I looked to the doorways to see if he was hiding around a pillar or curtain. But with so many cops standing around, he'd be a fool to show himself.

It seemed the sermon lasted forever as the priest droned on giving praise to God for giving them all such a well-respected, hard-working, generous and devoted family man. And one day we'd be blessed to be in his company once more. Obviously, the priest didn't know this man—but on the other hand, maybe we were all going to hell with Goodman. When the sermon was over, the priest asked if anyone had any last words to say about "...our dearly departed."

"Dear God, this is never going to end," I groaned. Idaho nudged once more. I grunted and whined, "What? Just shoot me now."

The old woman in the smart blue pant suit walked to the podium. She stood on tip-toes and tapped the microphone, which squawked loud enough to wake the dead—Goodman being the only candidate in question—to which I prayed that wouldn't happen. "Is this thing on?" the woman screeched into the microphone. After a couple of failed attempts to understand her speech, the priest lowered the mike closer to her lips. It was still a bit high, but she craned her shriveled turkey-neck up and began struggling with a pair of reading glasses. She smoothed out a piece of paper and began to read once again. Turned out, the woman was Goodman's sixth grade teacher. She talked about his tender heart as a young sweet boy. How he charmed the birds out of the trees. Then she expanded the inventory to include his strong innate talents and intelligence that were budding at that early age, and blah, blah, blah. The teacher took pride in, and credit for, teaching him the value of a dollar.

Some guy in a too-tight black, suit hollered, "Yeah, he earned his way through college as one of the best bookies this side of the Rockies." There were laughter and nods throughout the crowd.

The woman never missed a beat. Leaning closer to the microphone she retorted, "Of course, who do you think taught him?" That raised the grieving house of God into uproarious laughter.

I was laughing, too, and told Idaho, "Now we're

talkin.' That was the highlight of this whole damn farce."

After a few more speakers, who were much more morose than humorous, I zoned out and almost fell asleep until people stood and kneeled for prayer, and stood and kneeled for reflection, and then finally took their Communion. I pondered the idea that funerals and weddings were a lot alike. Lots of flowers and tears, usually prevalent at both. However, at weddings one wore white—at least the bride might, and funerals one wore black—at least the deceased might. Weddings you throw rice, funerals you through dirt. But, the nice thing about both is that there's usually a party after the ceremony. And, I was ready to get this party started.

Eventually Mora Goodman and sons were escorted from their seats into the lobby to greet the guests. The others were dismissed by rows and filed past the family to give their condolences. When I saw Rocco Basham standing with Mora in the greeting line, I executed a quick right to by-pass that disaster. I made a beeline to the rectory hall for the luncheon, music and wine, but not before I noticed how cozy the two were. Rocco's arm snuggled Mora in close, while he brushed quick little kisses to her cheek, whispering something periodically.

Lily, the socialite, stood in line and conversed with the crowd—mostly with the men—as they filtered past the family. Pamela and Maggie headed for the restroom, and Idaho followed me to the rectory hall. I heard the clack, clack, clack of wheels behind me. I moved to my right to let a young man wheel Goodman's casket past me and into the rectory hall. People were already loading their plates with food and grabbing drinks. Tables had been set in a u-shape around the hall, and the young man parked the casket at the center of the room. A couple of women followed behind the man with flowers, placing them near the casket. It was as if Goodman was made the center piece.

Idaho and I began dishing up our plates in the buffet line. I couldn't help but eye the casket along the way. "Isn't that just a little creepy?" I asked Idaho.

"What do you mean?" she questioned, while dishing up a generous amount of green salad.

"You know, the casket right here where we're eating? It's more than a little disturbing."

"Don't you think it would be rude to leave him out of his own party?" Idaho pointed out.

"He's dead, for crying out loud."

"You mean you're not into dancing with the dead?" Idaho teased. I leaned over for some bread and a green olive rolled off my plate landing in Idaho's wine glass. "Oh relax," said Idaho scooping it out and dropping it in my wine glass. "There is another funeral in about an hour so they had to bring him somewhere."

I frowned at my glass with the olive and took a drink. I winced and gagged. "Couldn't they just take him out back till we're done eating?" I grouched.

"What, and let the dogs get to him?"

"It's what he deserves."

"I was thinking of the dog's health."

"Oh, good point," I agreed.

Idaho and I were finishing our meal when Lily, Maggie and Pamela, with her boys and their older cousin Paige in tow, joined them. A couple of young guys walked in, one with a guitar and another with a harmonica, and a third with a box drum. They sat down and began to play and sing. It was a tune written specifically for Goodman. It was a nice melody but I had a hard time understanding the words. Evidently Mora Goodman understood them, as she clapped loudly, and sobbed loudly, when they finished. Rocco was still by her side, and I watched as he hugged Mora in close to him again.

I watched as Rocco tenderly pushed back a lock of Mora's hair from her forehead and placed another little peck on her cheek. That's when it hit me! Rocco must be with whom Mora was having the affair. I was about to say something to Idaho, when a group of people walked by looking for a place to sit and eat. Since we had finished eating, we stood to make room for them. As I looked around, it seemed there were more people now than at the service. Because of the crowd, Idaho and I were pushed a little closer to the casket and farther from the music. Some folks were dancing or swaying to some bluesy number. Now that we were standing, Rocco had caught my eye. He rose out of his seat and headed straight towards me. Some kids were getting restless and began running in and out of the crowd, almost tripping him as he came closer. I contemplated moving to the dance floor, but there was no one I knew to dance with—I even sought out Ebenezer Scrooge as an out, but he must have escaped with the investors. It was time to hit the restroom, but Rocco grabbed my elbow and swung me around.

"We need to talk," he growled.

"What's there to talk about?" I said as I watched

some kids playing hide and seek under tables and behind the curtains.

"You know dam well. You left me at the restaurant without a word."

"Excuse me, but I didn't think you were ever really there. That telephone never stopped ringing. I talked more to the waitress than I did to you." A couple of little girls playing tag screamed with delight when they made it to home base without getting caught—home base being Goodman's casket. Somewhere an argument arose with a little voice declaring that something wasn't fair.

"You know, while we're at it, you're awfully chummy with the widow, Mora. I'm thinking you should have taken her to dinner instead," I pointed out.

Rocco grabbed my wine glass and downed the rest of its contents and chewed on the olive. His face went beet red. "That is none of your business," he hissed. "And if you recall, you were the one who called me."

I ignored that, and said, "What is with you two? You two are cozier than last month's comforter in Home and Garden." Then I began to whisper a seductive little taunt, "Rocco and Mora up in a tree, k.i.s.s.i.n.g." He grabbed my upper arm tight.

A waiter saw Rocco had polish off my drink and immediately came to service—and the rescue. "Another wine, sir?" he asked.

"Yeah, and this time don't be so stingy with the olives."

The waiter frowned, then shrugged, mumbling, "To each his own."

I began to laugh, "Sorry, I should have said Mora and Moron up in a tree. Who the hell has olives served in their wine?"

"What?" He looked genuinely confused.

Still laughing I said, "Doesn't matter." Then said, "You're having an affair with Mora Goodman, your best friend's wife! Wow, with that information one can't help but wonder if you had motive to do her husband in." I was struck with the reality of it. Without thinking, I asked, "Did you?"

"Shut up. I had nothing to do with it," spat Rocco. "But you, on the other hand, I heard you've been asking way too many questions. Why are you so curious? Trying to save your own ass?"

"Don't try to turn tables on me, buster! I think I'm getting close to the truth about you." I began glancing sideways seeking out Idaho, or one of my other friends for help.

"You see here, I am warning you—," but he didn't get to finish because there was a bang and screeching of metal on metal.

As far as I could tell the kids playing tag had bumped into Goodman's casket—it was on the move. The wheels hadn't been locked down or maybe some mischievous child had unlocked them. It banged a couple of times off the wall like a bumper car, careened back and twisted right, then left. Flowers began to fly in all directions. It swayed to the right once more when one of the wheels broke off. The cart holding the casket twisted again, and the casket began to fall. Several men ran to catch it, but they were too late. The cart buckled and the casket hit the floor. The lid groaned under the weight breaking the hinges and then flopped open, pitching Goodman's body towards the crowd. The body rolled once, twice, then came to rest face up with his legs behind him, his left arm laying above his head and his right arm bent with his hand upon his chest, where a rogue flower landed within a very short distance from his fingers. His dead eyes had opened with the jolt and stared vacantly at the ceiling. He sported a wig with long blond hair that haloed around his head and whisker-stubbled face. His cheeks were bright with red rouge; his eyes were painted with eyeliner, lashes, and the works. His lips were colored a bright red, which matched his red lacquered fingernails. He wore a pink ball gown, sequins glittering under the lights casting sparkles around the rectory. His oversized feet were jammed into a pair of high-heeled, hot pink, fuzzy slippers. His big, sausage toes painted hot pink, poked out from the tips.

The rectory fell into dead silence. My friends finally reached my side. Everyone was looking at the casket and then at us.

"Awkward," sang Lily into my ear.

"You were wrong, Olivia," whispered Idaho. "This is the highlight of the funeral!"

"I thought you said that lid was locked," I hissed at my friend. "You said no one would find out about this! 'No one will be the wiser,' you said!"

"It was locked," insisted Idaho. "But who would have thought the Tasmanian devils would attack."

Maggie cocked her head to one side and said, "Looks a little like Marilyn Monroe doing tip-toe through the tulips. Don't you think?"

"Shit! That better have not been my kids," squeaked Pamela as she ran in search of her boys.

I could say nothing more. I stood staring at the heap

that lay at my feet. I was snapped out of my stupor when I heard Dubois's voice. "Are you ladies responsible for this?" He was clearly enraged.

"Nnnno!" I stammered. "I—well there were kids playing and—" I looked around at the children to see who may have been the instigator. I could see some people were aghast, some tittered, and some outright laughed. Mora Goodman stood screaming. Rocco went to her side and tried to console her.

"I'm not talking about the casket tipping; I'm talking about the tampering with the deceased. Are you responsible for this?" he pointed to Goodman's body.

"How are we responsible for Goodman being a crossdresser," Idaho asked, oh so innocently.

Dubois stomped his foot with total impatience. "Did you, or did you not, redress this body, eh?" he fumed.

Lily leaned over to take a closer look. She stood up and tapped her fore-finger against her lips and said, "No," she paused, stroking her chin, "No, definitely not."

"How am I to believe you?" shouted Dubois.

"Because," Lily said haughtily, "I would have gone with a lighter shade of lipstick, not that horrid fire engine red. It's all wrong for his skin tones."

"And look at that dress," added Maggie. "Mama Cass wouldn't have been caught dead in it."

Dubois put his hands up to cover his face in frustration. He took a deep breath and slowly pulled them down to his sides and looked directly at me. "How can you women be so cavalier? And why is it that every trail I follow in this investigation in some way, shape or form keeps bringing me back to the five of you? And this, this redressing smacks of passive-aggressive behavior. I get that you are all angry about losing your money. But this makes you all look very suspicious. Wasn't killing him enough?"

"Hey, buddy. You just wait a minute," Lily started, but I held up my hand to silence her.

Dubois didn't pause, he looked from one woman to the other and continued his rant. "Goddamn it, this is serious business! And don't think I haven't checked up on you women."

Dubois turned to Lily, "Lily White, you are a successful fundraiser, which has made you semi-rich. Your wealthy accountant husband mysteriously died of a heart attack after eating anchovies and a vat of pickled pig's feet. But the economy is down, and fundraising isn't what it once was. Maybe money is starting to run out, or maybe you just wanted more."

Dubois turned to Pamela. "Pamela, your husband also died. He died at a young age in a logging accident. Was it really an accident? I hope so. And I think it's probably true because I know that you are struggling to make ends meet, and there was no life insurance policy to take care of the funeral. Investing with Goodman made sense. But, he lost your very hard-earned money, and I bet you are really pissed about that!"

Next, Dubois pointed a finger at Maggie. "You just up and left Hollywood. You left an acting contract unfulfilled and an empty bank account for your ex-husband. You can't be making much as a local theater director and thespian high school teacher. I'm willing to bet Goodman lost your last bank roll."

"And Idaho," he said, turning to her next. "Your

one chance in life was winning the lottery. You probably saw all of your hopes and dreams go up in smoke with Goodman's bankrupt contractor."

He finally returned to me. "But Olivia, I have run into a brick wall with you. I know what your 'bio' says. But I'll be damned if anyone really knows who you are. You are like a ghost of some kind." He stood with hands on his hips, staring at me as I squirmed inside. He began speaking as if reading from a script. "Olivia Hope graduated from Boise State University with a teaching degree in health and fitness. Born and raised in Waybegone, Canada. A city I can't recall now but I know it's really far north, and you became a U.S. citizen about ten years ago. But you don't have any more of a Canadian dialect than Texas Pete! I've not heard even one 'eh' come out of your mouth. Growing up in Canada, you surely would have the Canadian speech patterns, but I hear none of it. In fact, I'd be willing to bet you don't even speak a bit of French! Who the hell are you?"

"You're from Canada?" quizzed Idaho.

"Shut up!" I snapped. My cheeks were burning red with fury, and my mouth was bone dry.

"All of you have a damn good reason to be mad as hell at Goodman. I'll give you that." said Dubois. "But all of you also have a damn good motive to kill him! And imagine my surprise!" he scoped us all then, "How surprised was I to find out your little investment acronym W.I.C.A. translates nicely to Wicca, as in a witch's pledge or some damn thing!" White spittle remained on his thin stretched lips.

Everyone was silent. I glanced at the other women

as they hung their heads like scolded school children. I, on the other hand, was hell-bent on holding my head high, even if it was in total rebellion, even if I felt like the dopey child I once was when, scolded by my parents. And, with that thought, tears welled up in my eyes, but I was stubborn enough to not let them flow.

Dubois pointed a deliberate finger in my face and exclaimed, "You! You must have some very scary skeletons in your closet. And God as my witness, I'll bring every one of them to light and parade them for all to see."

At that, I felt nothing but shame and humiliation. I felt like I'd let down someone important. I couldn't stand the thought. Was it my parents, my friends, myself, maybe all the above. And maybe even . . . Dubois?

In that moment, I vowed I would damn well find out who killed Ira Goodman. Even if I couldn't save myself, I would save my friends.

Chapter 19
Closed Casket Service Opens Closet on Ira Goodman

By Carol Cripes

Ira Goodman, Libby's well-respected and beloved philanthropist, was laid to rest yesterday at the Libby cemetery—but not before he took a dive from his coffin. Or, should that be closet. Goodman's body was not clothed in the, traditional, three-piece suit, but was clad in a pink sequined dress, blond wig, heavily applied make-up and red nail polish, resembling a poor mock-up of Marilyn Monroe.

Several rambunctious children, who were terrorizing the bereaved guests with a game of tag, skidded into the coffin, starting it in motion. After several moments of bumper-coffin frenzy, Goodman's coffin slipped from its not-so-secure pedestal and smacked to the floor, catapulting his body at the feet of his faithful mourners. Pirouetting from the casket, like a ballet dancer, a near-by funeral goer pointed to the dress stating, ". . . with an entrance like that he should have worn a tutu."

When Goodman's wife was questioned, she claimed the body must have been tampered with before the services. "I don't understand any of this," said

Goodman's widow, "This was supposed to be a closed-casket service. That is not what I dressed him in. I wanted people to remember him the way he was. This is . . . this is unacceptable!" It remains a mystery as to who might have been behind the re-dressing.

Ira Goodman had been found murdered at his home on Bull Lake last Thursday. Goodman's son Seth is still considered missing, and it is believed he may have fallen to foul-play as well, said his mother, Mora Goodman, "I just know he would have been here at the funeral if something hadn't happened to him. He loved his father. He just wouldn't stay away like this and not say goodbye,".

At first thought, there may have been some involvement by the Chosen Trojan Children (CTC) since the murder looked to be cult related. Up until now there has been no persons of interest responsible for Goodman's death. However, it seems there is a growing interest in a group of local women, who call their faction, Women's Investment Club Association (WICA). The acronym strikes a close resemblance to Wicca—from a history of witches and/or warlocks implicated in the religion that was influenced by pre-Christian beliefs and their practices of supernatural powers.

Could it have been these women who took Goodman's life after a business deal or romance gone bad? It's certainly a question that many may have on their minds. Jackie Banks, friend of the Goodman family, was the first to voice that thought at yesterday's funeral, "Do you suppose those WICA women could have killed him? After all," Banks stated, "he was found staked to the floor in the middle of a pentagram."

The women affiliated with the WICA investment club are Lily White, a fundraiser for Adam Blake Consulting, Pamela Phuchet, owner of Moosehead Tree Farms, Maggie Burns, the famous childhood actress from several television shows and movies and currently the drama teacher at the Libby High School, Olivia Hope, the Libby Sr. High School PE teacher, and Ida Hoe, employed by the City of Libby—it is noted that Ms. Hoe is assigned to work at the Libby cemetery. When questioned, all women refused comment. Pamela Phuchet, markedly upset when approached with questions, swung at the reporter and photographer with her purse.

Both Sherriff Bishop and Rand Dubois failed to comment on any of the day's activities. No arrests have been made at this time.

Rocco Basham-District Attorney
Faces DUI Allegations

By: Carol Cripes

Rolland "Rocco" Basham, Libby's District Attorney is suspended from his duties until further notice after an off-duty arrest last Sunday night on accusations of driving under the influence of intoxicants.

Basham, elected as District Attorney in last fall's election, was found passed out in his parked car at 9:08 p.m. Sunday night along River Road. A Lincoln County sheriff's deputy found him while responding to reports of an impaired driver. Basham was arrested after failing a field sobriety test. The deputy then administered a breath test, which he failed. Basham was transported to the sheriff's office, where he was processed and released the next morning with an order to appear in court.

Basham reported that he only had two drinks with a friend, while dining at the MK Steakhouse, and claims he must have been drugged. "Two drinks can't get you that drunk," stated Basham. "It's all a mistake. I'm sure someone slipped me something. I swear, it was only two drinks!"

Julie Becker, a waitress at the restaurant said she thought he seemed fine to her when he left. "He paid his bill and thanked me for the perfect dinner for him and his date, although, I didn't see anyone with him. And I didn't bother to ask about it because he was on his cell phone the whole time he was checking out." When reporters asked Basham why he felt he could drive home safely, he claimed he couldn't remember.

Nancy Higgins, spokesperson for the sheriff's office, declined to reveal Basham's blood-alcohol content at the time of his arrest. Some citizens are outraged and are asking for his position to be re-called.

Chapter 20 - Olivia Hope

"That bitch!" screeched Pamela, as she held the morning newspaper up, giving it a good shake. "I did not swing my purse at her! I was trying to get Gabe's attention. Then I got tangled up on Goodman's dress and tripped, just as Cripes stepped in front of me before I could connect with Gabe's scrawny little ass."

"Temper, temper," crooned Lily.

"This is not good, folks," I lamented, poring over the article yet again.

"Yeah, Ms. Cripes has pretty much been our accuser, prosecutor, and judge," said Idaho. "And I can't figure out if we're going to jail first or straight to hell."

My guess would have been hell. And as if things couldn't get any worse, I couldn't believe my face was on the front-page news, especially connected to such a high-profile story. I do not like publicity. After all these years, I'd been careful not to call public attention to myself. No, this was not good at all.

I glared at the news photo. It was taken as I stood before Dubois with his accusing finger in my face. His face was filled with anger. Idaho, was all cattywhompus reaching for the casket. She must have been trying to stop the bumper-casket frenzy. Maggie's face was filled with surprise, hands held high as if it were a hold up. Lily's gaze was thoughtful as she watched Goodman's body flying from the casket, probably wondering if they should have gone with a different shade of red lipstick. And then there was Pamela's off-kilter body captured in a pose that could have been a stumble—but just happened to look more like a leap—with her raised purse in full view as it arched its way towards the camera lens. Yep, there we were—all five of us, with our names in big, bold black letters. I groaned as my stomach took a roll. I couldn't look at the photo a moment longer and set the paper aside.

Lily moved from her chair to grab the newspaper as Pamela was saying something about planting a lawsuit on Cripes, and Maggie said she'd probably go with public humiliation. Then Idaho said she'd already wrapped up a bag of rotted fish and placed it in her car under the passenger seat.

"It's winter," scoffed Maggie. "The fish will freeze, and she won't smell it until spring."

"Na ah, she's got those fancy seat warmers and heat vents under there, too. Wait till she turns on the heater." Idaho looked pleased with herself.

"Oh my, there is a God," crowed Lily. "Look at this." She held up the paper. "Rocco Basham – District Attorney Faces DUI Allegations!"

"What?" I said, reaching to grab for the paper again, but Lily pulled it to the side out of my reach and began to read the article aloud. "Ha, this happened Sunday night. Olivia, that was your date night! What on earth did you slip him?"

"Just my drinks. But then, mine were doubles because he was trying to get me flat-ass drunk," I said. "Technically, I guess he only ordered two drinks for himself. God, no wonder he was so pissed when we talked."

"I say it's not your fault he thought he could drive," said Maggie. "He's responsible for himself. And if I remember right, he was pretty much an asshole to you. Sounds like karma to me."

I nodded, but I still felt a pang of guilt. I just wanted to loosen his tongue, not cause him to lose his job.

"Oh, did you see how cuddly he was with Mora at the funeral?" Idaho crooned.

"Yeah, I asked him about it," I said. "And I'm pretty positive that he and Mora are way more than friends."

"What does he see in that magpie?" Lily griped. "Olivia, you are ten times the woman Mora will ever be."

"But you're forgetting one thing," I said. "I DON'T WANT HIM!"

"But he looks so good on your arm," trilled Lily.

"Look," I said, changing the subject, because I was far too disgusted to reply. "We've got to step up our game. I know that Dubois is doing the best he can, but he has rules to follow. We, my friends, don't. We need to think outside the box and get creative, or our asses will be in jail and we won't be able to do a damn thing about it. It's time to get cracking!"

"And just what do you have in mind, Ms. Colombo," drawled Maggie.

"I don't know," I said. "Let's recap. We were angry with him when he didn't return out calls. We went to his house on the lake; we had words with him. He provoked us when we discovered that he had lost our money, which made us angrier. So, we took it upon ourselves to teach him a lesson by undressing him, tying him up and tacking him to the floor to chill in the cold—which, in hindsight, seems like a really stupid thing to do."

"I beg to differ," Maggie interrupted, "I call it therapy. I felt so much better afterwards."

"And, I'd call that karma, too," Pamela piped in.

"He certainly deserved it in my book—tacking him to the floor part, not the dying thing," said Lily.

"Maybe it was a little over the top," said Idaho. "Has anybody thought about what he would have done in retaliation if he hadn't died? We'd probably be up to our asses in lawyers right about now."

There was a long silence. "Still felt damn good," murmured Maggie. And that brought a round of high-fives, laughter, and an amen. When the conversation turned serious again, Lily said, "However, may I remind us all, we didn't kill him."

"Yeah, but we had a hand in setting the stage," I pointed out.

"Is it time to go to Dubois and tell him what we did?" suggested Pamela.

There was a resounding "NO" from the rest of the women.

Idaho piped in to say, "No way. Did you see the look on Dubois's face? He wants to eat us for lunch! At this point, I don't think we'd get a fair break at all." There was agreement all around.

"Okay," I started again. "Let's look at what we know. Seth, Goodman's son, is still missing. Mora thinks foul play is involved because she hasn't heard from him. Josh, his friend from school, is still missing as well. Maybe they walked in on whoever killed Goodman and then killed the boys, too."

"No," said Idaho thoughtfully. "There was no mention of other disruption in the house. Like blood or signs of a scuffle. That sort of thing."

"Or," I continued, "they could just be in hiding as we first thought. They may have killed him, but why would Seth kill his own father? He's generally been a really good kid." I had grabbed a piece of paper and began making some notes. "Then there is Mora and Rocco. Maybe Goodman found out his wife and best friend were having an affair, and Rocco took advantage of an opportunity to make things easier for them. Maybe the two of them bumped off Seth and Josh, too."

"I don't see him and Mora bumping off Seth though," said Pamela. "Mora's not my favorite person, but I could never see her doing anything to her children."

"Mora may not know Rocco killed Seth, though," said Idaho. I wrote down Mora and Rocco and circled Rocco's name.

I continued, "The construction company that Goodman worked with filed bankruptcy. Christopher Dumas was the acting super on the project and he's nowhere to be found. Is he dead? Or, did he take the money and run? What is the connection there? Did he have an agenda with Goodman and showed up after we were there?" I wondered aloud.

"Well, crap. Let's face it," growled Lily. "Goodman pissed off a lot of people, anybody could have killed him."

I held up my list, "Let's look at our list and brainstorm some clues."

"And what will that accomplish?" asked Pamela. "We'll only be in trouble for messing with evidence, or some dumb thing, and be in more trouble."

I began rifling through my drawers, looking for more paper. "I'm just getting us started. We'll brainstorm and define our priorities, quickest results and so on. Come on ladies, we need to start being more aggressive."

"Eww," groaned Pamela, "Once a teacher, always a teacher, with her little lists and graphs and distributed projects. I thought this was supposed to be outside the box stuff."

"Brainstorming is. It means getting every thought out on the table, or paper, just whatever comes to mind. No matter how insignificant or off the wall. Maybe we overlooked some things." I said, pulling out a pad of yellow paper. "Besides, have you got a better place to start?"

Pamela groaned again, swung her feet off the couch, and sat up. "But, what do we say when we start asking too many questions and Dubois finds out? Won't that make us look even more suspicious?"

"I think it's a good idea, Olivia," Maggie defended. "There are a lot of people who read the paper. Pretty much everyone by now probably thinks we're murderers. I'm just going to tell them flat out that we didn't do it, and I'm trying to clear our names. And furthermore, if Dubois doesn't like it, he can just suck it."

"And, I, for one, don't want to sit around and wait for the bomb to drop," said Lily. "I certainly won't look good in an orange jump suit."

"Okay, Idaho, maybe it's time to use your good friend, Alan, for help," Maggie suggested.

Idaho winced but said, "Okay, I'll think of something. But I'm not going to use him."

"I think someone's falling in love," Lily whispered loudly behind her hand, which started a group of awes and titters. A red-faced Idaho threw a pillow at her.

We finally began making suggestions as I started to write and prioritize. Idaho would prod Alan for information. Lily would use her charm to talk to some of the city councilmen to find out more about the city renovation project. Maggie knew a few men who had dealt with Goodman; she'd call for lunch dates. Pamela saw a good opportunity to connect with a few of Seth's friends. She was going to post part-time help for her Christmas tree orders at the high school, find out the rumors around school. I was going to follow-up with Ray-Con Construction to see if Dumas had surfaced yet. I'd question Mora, Rocco, and the woman who found Goodman's body. While I was there, maybe I could find a way to get into Goodman's lake house and look for something that Dubois didn't mention or the police missed. The B&E I kept to myself. If I was caught, that would just be on me. At least save these women from prior knowledge about that wrong. We were sifting through more questions and ideas when my cell phone rang. I excused myself from the group and took the call.

"Hi Olivia," greeted, Gregory Gaylord, the principal of the high school.

"Oh, hi Greg," I answered. That was odd. He had never called me at home before. "What's up?"

"Ah, well," he stammered. "I saw the newspaper

this morning. Ha, who hasn't," he said bestowing a nervous laugh. "I mean, you must be pretty upset with this whole adverse publicity thing."

"Yeah, not the way I like to start my day."

"Yeah," he paused, then said, "Well, I called to see how you're doing."

I could hear hesitation in his voice. "Thank you for your concern, Greg. But I get the feeling there's more to this conversation."

"Well, you know that I think this is a bunch of hooey, right? I mean you would never commit a murder like that! You're a nice, young lady. You're good with the students, and you're one of the best teachers I have. Buuut. . . there are those that only react to what they read in the newspaper." He spoke faster, his speech turning into one long sentence, not allowing me a word in edgewise. "But, there are others, who think that maybe you need a little time off, to think this over, and get some things sorted out. I'll still pay you and all, but I'm not firing you or anything like that. No, no, no, so you won't be without income, but I think that maybe you need a little time off. It's almost Thanksgiving anyway, so taking a few weeks would give you time, things will calm down, the murderer will be caught soon, you'll be back before Christmas, and by then, this whole thing will be forgotten. What do you say?"

I was stunned. I bit my tongue until I could choose the right words to respond. I always liked Mr. Gaylord, but I'd never pegged him for a spineless, little twit. After feeling torn between anger about being dismissed from my job and disappointment with my wimpy, little boss, I finally spoke, "Got a lot of calls from parents, did ya?"

"Uh, yeah, they're a little nervous about you being a . . . well, sending their kids to school when things are . . . um, so much in the air. It's just a little time, you know, a small amount of reprieve, Olivia, and soon this will be all over. Right?"

Did he add "right" to emphasize his support? Or, did he have his doubts about me, too. This angered me even more.

"Yeah, Greg, I'll see you very soon," and I clicked off my cell before I could say something I shouldn't. "You weak, little bastard!" I said, much too loudly. As I turned around, all the women were staring at me wide-eyed. I gave them a nice little smile and said, "Good news! I've just been given time to work on our project full-time."

"You got fired?" Pamela sputtered.

"Pretty much."

"Knew that was coming," said Maggie. I gave her a questioning look. She shrugged, "I got the same call from Greg before I left the house. He said I needed a little time off to get this straightened out. He wanted to give me fair notice that funds might be cut for the drama program, but he hoped it wouldn't happen. In other words, he couldn't guarantee that I'd be back after this is all over." There was silence among the women.

"Wow," said Pamela. "I've had a few Christmas tree orders cancelled this morning. I guess now I know why."

Idaho looked a little pale. "When I called in and said I'd be late, Margaret told me that his-all-mighty-honor, the Mayor, wants to speak to me when I get into work today. I'm beginning to feel the axe fall, too."

"Oh, relax ladies," sang Lily with a dismissal wave of her hand. "I believe there is no such thing as bad publicity. Look at Ted Kennedy, for example, once the Chappaquiddick hubbub died down, he was still just as popular! Once this blows over, this fickle, little town will be in awe of our heroism. We will become the women that all other women would like to be. Mark my words. They may even write a book about us. We'll all have more income and possibilities than ever before. You wait and see, we'll all be famous!"

That was easy for Lily to say. She had her nest egg, enough in fact that she could retire now and never need to worry about a penny ever again. My stomach cramped, and I thought I might lose my breakfast.

It was Pamela who put it into perspective, "Yeah, but it's a little hard to enjoy all that from a jail cell."

"Do you think I could get one of those jail jump suits in periwinkle?" asked Maggie.

Our wound-licking session was interrupted by a loud thump on the porch, and then scratching at the door. I pulled the door open to find the big black lab, Blue, carrying a rabbit in his mouth. He deposited it at my feet and stood back to look up at me. The dead rabbit was still warm.

"Hey," said Idaho, kneeling by the bounty. "Isn't this Frenchie's rabbit?"

"Indeed," I answered, dreading the thought of having to tell Frenchie about his little companion. Poor little rabbit wouldn't be reading the Wall Street Journal anymore. Blue nosed the rabbit closer to me and gave a little whine. Was it a trophy for me I wondered? Then I had a horrid thought, "Did you kill Frenchie's rabbit,

Blue?" I murmured, looking for signs of primal violence in the dog's eyes.

Blue sighed and plopped to the floor letting his head fall between his paws, lifting one eyebrow, and shifting to the other brow with a sorrowful whine. I tried to understand the clouded expression on his little, doggy face. Was it guilt, remorse, sadness? I reached over to ruffle my fingers through the dog's fur.

Wearily I said, "Well, my friend, you've come to the right place. Welcome to the house of suspects."

Chapter 21 - Rand Dubois

"That damn reporter," said Bishop, as he threw the newspaper down in front of me and slumped into a chair. "Did you read this drivel Cripes wrote?"

"Yes," I answered with a smile.

"What are you grinning about?"

"Relax. The whole thing is a farce." I too had been truly upset when I first read the article. I had no business flying off the handle like I did—especially in front of a reporter and the deceased's wife. However, after some thought, I realized it did shake things up a bit. Those damn women needed to face reality. I was still trying to figure out their angle.

"Damn straight it's a farce," grumbled Bishop. "Here she goes again, spewing statements she can't back up. We don't have enough to make an arrest with the WICAs. Do we?" he paused. I shook my head. "Yet, she makes us look like damn fools."

"Precisely my point. She hasn't got any more information than we do, and it makes her look like the fool. And when we get to the bottom of this murder, and her boss sees how far out on a limb she went, maybe she won't have a job. You said yourself that this isn't the first time she's over-stepped her position as a reporter by not checking her facts." I picked up the newspaper and set it down in front of him again. I said, "Read this again, only this time, take off your sheriff glasses and put on a pair of J.Q. Public specs."

He did, and read the article out loud. He was laughing heartily by the time he finished. "It was a pretty funny sight. Think those women redressed the poor bastard?"

"Yeah, I'm pretty sure, but again, no way to prove it. He lost their money. I get that they are pissed as hell. If we can prove it, I'm sure we could bring them in on some charges. I think maybe there's some law about defacing a corpse. But, Goodman's obviously not going to sue the city. Maybe Mora will make a stink. I guess we'll just have to wait and see. I'll call her later to see how far she wants to pursue it. I'm more concerned about catching a murderer."

Alan walked into the room with a couple cups of coffee. He handed one to me and then relinquished his over to Bishop, which Bishop accepted with gusto.

"Thank you, son," Bishop shifted his weight in his seat. "You must have ESP. You gave me exactly what I needed."

"If I had ESP, I'd have bought one more," Alan groused under his breath. Alan had had a bad night—up until all hours pacing and contemplating something to which I was not privy to. He had originally gone to get coffee for himself but I threw him some money for me as well. I slid my coffee over to him. But he waved it away, looking dejected? He slunk down into a chair next to Bishop. His red hair fell across his face, hiding any other expressions and his ever-growing mass of beard.

"What do you think the women will do when they see this damning article?" asked Bishop.

I shrugged. "Maybe it will rile them enough to

come tell me what they really know."

"I'll ask again; do you think they murdered Goodman?"

"My gut says no—but I need to look at the facts. I think they have some kind of involvement, and that's where Alan comes in."

Alan sat up straighter. "Me! What am I gonna do?"

"You are going to shadow your newfound friend."

He looked confused, but more animated than I'd seen him all morning. "I thought you told me to stay away from her?"

"I've been thinking." Feeling a little guilty, I still wasn't sure if I was setting him up for heartbreak. But we all gotta do what we gotta do—sometimes it ain't pretty. Take legal advantage where we can. I decided this was a learning experience for him. "Well, it certainly couldn't hurt to have an ear with those women. Maybe you can find out from Idaho what they are thinking. Are you up for the task?"

"Now that's a job I can handle," Alan beamed, but then his expression turned stern. "But I'm not a spy."

"Understood, son."

"Oh hey," said Bishop, "I heard from our good friend, Frenchie."

"Oh yeah, the Irish terrorist dude," Alan said and settled into his seat rubbing his palms. "What's up with him? Did he find any more mutilated animals?"

Bishop's return smile was predatory, "You are a man after my own heart. I love a good, gory story. And yes, he did. Or should I say your Olivia did." And there it was again, all things leading back to the women, or Olivia. My Olivia, he says? Why would he say that? And why does my heart skip a beat and my palms get all sweaty every time I think of that damn woman? I've never met a woman who could make me so damn angry one minute and make me smile the next. Why can't I bring myself to believe that she killed Goodman when all these damn clues lead back to her! I really needed to keep my distance.

"Hey, Rand," Sheriff Bishop snapped his fingers in front of my face. "Earth to Rand!"

"Oh, sorry," I replied, doing my best to clear my mind. "What were you saying?"

"Yeah, thought I lost you there for a minute. Anyway, it seems her dog brought home Frenchie's rabbit that went missing. He sent it to the vet to see if she could lift any clues. The rabbit was torn from stomach to sternum and his heart removed."

"How about its foot?" asked Alan.

"Funny you should ask; one foot was missing too."

"Ah," said Alan nodding his head. "The plot thickens. Someone is practicing Satanic acts and hopes he'll be lucky enough to get away with it."

"Why only one foot?" I asked. "Why not take all four?"

"Bad luck," answered Bishop and Alan in unison, as if I were a dummy.

"Well," I said. "I don't believe in lucky rabbit's feet, so let's just go talk to Frenchie and that vet."

"Still," said Alan. "Best to keep an eye out for people with fuzzy-footed key chains."

Bishop grinned and slapped him on the back. Both were out of the room before I could get my coat on.

Chapter 22 - Olivia Hope

I tossed and turned trying to forget all the crap that came my way that day. Counting sheep turned into counting the money we all lost, then how many times Mrs. Bixby said I should move to improve the neighborhood, and finally to count all the Irish curse words that Frenchie spewed upon finding his prize bunny slit open. Oh yeah, Frenchie took it damn hard. I didn't think it would be so tragic until he told me that the rabbit was an American Blue breed, a very rare breed.

"Duchy used to hop and play with the squirrels," Frenchie said. "He'd make chirpy noises, like he was trying to imitate the birds. And he'd fetch my slippers for me when he was tired and ready to go to bed." He laughed. "That was my cue to get ready. Once my slippers were on, he'd hop to the fire, because we would put one last log in the stove. Then he'd hop to the bathroom where I'd brush my teeth and then his. And then he'd use his litter box, and we'd head to bed. If I left the TV on too long, he'd hop over to the remote and turn the bloomin' thing off his self!" Frenchie laughed and then gave a long sigh. "He was such a smart bunny." He quickly brushed a tear from his cheek—which generated a few tears to course down my face as well. "I made him a little platform step by my mail box so that Duchy could fetch the New York Times for me in the morning." He clarified that the rabbit really didn't read the newspaper. But after listening to how smart Duchy was, I wasn't so sure.

Frenchie talked about other special times he'd had with the bunny. I knew he was trying to deal with his grief, so I sat and listened. He held the bunny like a baby and rocked and petted the poor little beast. It had been a beautiful creature, with it's incredibly soft bluish fur. Then Frenchie's grief turned to anger, as he hurled about a good number of curses and threats to whoever had done this. When he finally calmed down, he went pale as if he just realized something.

"What is it, Frenchie?" I asked.

"Oh dear, dear, dear. Duchy was a lonely sort. Oh, he loved me all right, but I wasn't his type, if you know what I mean." He gave me a wink. "I just purchased a female for Duchy so he could have a family. Now I don't know if I can bear to have another rabbit if I'm just going to lose the poor things. I don't know if my heart can take it."

"This isn't your fault," I tried to comfort. "You take good care of all of your animals. I can't think of a better home for her. I should think Duchy wouldn't have it any other way." Duchy had become as companionable as a beloved dog, which I was starting to identify with since I'd befriended Blue—the irresistible black Labrador that found Duchy. And the dog didn't even belong to me. I was thankful to learn that the dog had not killed the animal but was equally disturbed by the fact that some human could do such a thing to a poor little animal. Dear God, they cut out its heart, and cut off its foot? What the hell could that mean? I'd left Frenchie with his grief and a promise of a casserole. And I was left feeling empty and bewildered.

Not more than ten minutes after I had left Frenchie's, Mrs. Bixby arrived at my front door in a fury, "I told you! You need to move out of this neighborhood. Things were just fine until the likes of you moved in."

"Why, did Blue steal another one of your rugs?" I asked with an exasperated sigh.

"No, you little slut. I think you are up to your eyeballs in deep shit! I read the newspapers you know. You are a dangerous, young lady. And I. We. Don't want the likes of you living in our peaceful piece of the world."

"Oh, now you are speaking for the whole neighborhood?"

Mrs. Bixby began to cry, her eyes were wild and spittle dotted her lips. I could tell the woman was horribly distraught with her face beet red, and her shaking was uncontrollable. I began to feel a little sorry for the deranged woman.

"Goodness, Arleen, calm down. What has happened to put you in such a state?" I reached out to the woman, afraid she might be on the verge of a heart attack.

But Mrs. Bixby pulled away from me and reached into her pocket. "Don't. You. EVER. Call. Me. By. My. First. Name," she screamed. I kept an eye on her pocketed hand. I was afraid the woman was going to pull out a gun and shoot me. But to my stunned surprise the woman revealed a rock with a piece of paper wrapped around it. "You are a no-good hussy, and I can't stand living next to you. You need to leave!" She slapped the rock into my hand, swiped snot from her nose with a finger and turned to leave.

I unwrapped the paper rubber-banded around the rock. In bold black letters, it said, "I no what you dun. It's time to pay 4 yous sins."

"Mrs. Bixby," I called out. "What makes you think this was for me?" Knowing I wasn't the only one that didn't get along with Mrs. Bixby, it could have been any one of the other neighbors.

"I told you. I read the newspaper. You are a marked woman, you murderer!" Feeling a little vulnerable, I had to agree it probably was meant for me. But why throw it on Mrs. Bixby's porch and not mine. That didn't make any sense.

"Did you see who threw this on your porch?"

Mrs. Bixby stopped and slowly turned around. She was sobbing. "It wasn't my porch," she seethed. "It came through my living room window! It almost killed my little Trixie! And no, I didn't see who it was. I don't keep track of your friends."

"Oh, my God! Did you call the police?" I was more worried about the woman's safety and her cat than her outbursts.

Mrs. Bixby pulled her arms around herself and began a mournful whining bawl, "They said it was probably a childish prank. I don't think they care."

I truly wanted to reach out and give this poor, lonely, old woman a hug. Knowing it wouldn't be possible, the best I could do was to offer to pay for her window. To which she sobbed, "Damn right you will!" Then she ran a hobbled dance step slipping on the icy ground the rest of the way home. I could still hear the slamming door ring in my ears.

After the dampened visit with Mrs. Bixby, I set the rock aside and decided I may as well flail myself some more by calling Mora Goodman.

"Hi, Mora. This is Olivia Hope. I'm calling to find out if you've heard anything from Seth." I chose to ramble on a bit to sound like a concerned teacher rather than a suspected murderer of the poor woman's husband. "I didn't see him at the funeral. I'm so worried about him. And, oh my god, I read in the newspaper that you think something bad has happened to him. Do you really think that is true?"

Mora didn't speak for several long seconds.

"Mora, are you there?'

"Y . . . yes, I'm here." Then there was more silence.

"Have you heard from him?"

"Of course not!" Mora snapped. "Why do you think I told the reporter that I thought he met w . . . with foul play? He wasn't at the funeral. Not even in the background. He would have been there if he could." She began to cry. Dear God, I thought. If I need to have any more of these kinds of conversations today, I'm going to have a heart attack.

"Mora, I'm so sorry to have upset you. I just want you to know that I am very worried about him, too. I will do my best to find out what has happened to him. I have some clout to poke around; at least as much as a school teacher can get. But I promise you—"

"No, I have been told you have been fired. How can I trust a teacher who has been fired? I really don't think I need to be talking to you. My lawyer doesn't want me to talk to you, or anyone, for that matter. You just need to go away."

With that, the next thing I heard was the click of the receiver. So, news was out that I was fired. Great! I figured Mora's lawyer was probably Rocco. I was sure that he was all too eager to give Mora that information—more reason to call that bastard next.

I dialed his home phone, checking if he was home or at Mora's. No answer. I debated, but decided to leave a message. Since I hadn't heard from him, and knowing how mad he was at me—oh, and the fact that Dubois accused us of tampering with Goodman's body—I was sure he was waiting for my call. "Hey, Rocco, my friend. Olivia here, give me a call when you--" Rocco picked up.

Oh, crap, I thought. He sounded like he'd been asleep. Since I had to talk to him, I may as well try to be nice, "Rocco, I'm sooo sorry for disturbing you. I hope you weren't asleep."

"Well, if it isn't the murdering, body-defacing, career wrecker," Rocco groused.

"I didn't kill Goodman! And you can't pin Goodman's crossdressing on me, and I didn't ruin your career. You're a big boy. You need to pull on your big boy pants and take responsibility for your own actions." So much for nice.

"Slipping me drinks is really underhanded. And alcohol is considered a drug, you know. I could have you arrested for that."

Yeah, get in line, I thought. I could feel my blood start to boil. I needed to keep my cool. I took a deep breath, "I was calling to find out how you are—not to fight with you. I knew you were pretty upset about something yesterday."

"Ya think?" scoffed Rocco.

"I had no idea that you were being held up to such scrutiny until I saw the newspaper this morning."

Rocco was silent. I thought maybe he had hung up but then he said, "I just wanted to ask you yesterday, if you would come forward and say that supplying me with drinks was a mistake, that's all. It could save my career."

Now it was my turn to be silent. My blood was boiling even hotter. After how he treated me, there was no way in hell I was going to help him out there. I cleared my throat and said, as congenially as possible, "Rocco, I didn't make you drink those drinks. You were ordering a ton for me and I was just sharing."

"You are impossible! Throw me a bone, will ya?"

I needed the conversation to turn around, so I thought of just a little white lie to see how he'd react. "I thought I saw Seth yesterday."

"You saw Seth?" Rocco jumped on that one quickly enough. "Where did you see him? Did you call Mora to let her know? She is worried sick about him! Is he okay? Was he at the funeral? Did you talk to him?"

"Slow down Rocco, I said I thought I saw him. I was in the grocery store after the funeral. I thought it was him but he ducked down an aisle, and I didn't see him again." I hadn't seen him, of course, but I was proud of myself for the sneaky shift in conversation.

"Well, that doesn't help now, does it?" pouted Rocco. I wondered, Rocco seemed genuinely eager to find Seth. If Rocco was in love with Mora, it would make sense that he was looking out for her interests.

"Rocco?"

"Yeah?"

"Who do you really think killed Goodman?"

"You and your friends."

I puffed my cheeks and breathed out slowly, "We didn't kill him, Rocco. You know as well as I do that he had plenty of enemies." I kept my voice soft and thoughtful. "You could have killed him, too, you know. You and Mora having an affair, he walks in, things get ugly, you whack him with a fire poker."

"You are insane! He was my friend."

"Some friend you are, stealing his wife! But relax, Rocco, I really don't think you did kill him," another lie I realized, but it might calm him down. "But you are having an affair with Mora."

"What makes you say that we're having an affair? Think you're psychic or something?"

"Rocco, a woman knows these things. You don't have to be psychic to pick up on the starry-eyed looks, stolen, little kisses, hand grabbing and holding. You are having an affair." He simply sighed in response.

"Rocco, do you think Mora killed him?" I was waiting for a screaming match to begin or for him to hang up on me.

"I don't know. I've thought about that myself," he said softly.

I didn't see that one coming. Then I said aloud what I was thinking, "Wow! She must really be in love with you."

"We are in love. I've never felt this way about anyone. But you didn't let me finish. I don't think Mora could have killed Goodman, because she was in Italy."

"She could have had help. Like you for instance."

Rocco snorted, "I didn't kill him because I was with

Susan Baker that night."

"Oh, that is so you, Rocco. You're in love with Mora but you're sleeping with Susan Baker? Another married woman I might add. And trying to schmooze me, too? Unbelievable!"

"I didn't realize how much I loved Mora until after being with Susan. Mora came home, and we both decided we needed to be together."

"Bad timing, don't you think, Rocco? I mean so soon after her husband's death? Aren't you afraid you'll be a suspect?"

"Look, I've already lost my best friend. I'm looking at losing my job, probably losing, Mora too, if things don't start looking up. So, forgive me if I don't feel like I've got much more to lose. Hell, at this point, I don't know if I really give a shit about anything."

I could hear exhaustion and depression in the man's voice, "Well, if I were you, I'd keep that information to yourself, because that's kind of a huge motive for murder."

"I guess you should know!"

"Good night, Rocco."

Before I could hang up, Rocco said, "Wait! You wouldn't tell anyone about us, me and Mora I mean. Would you? I mean, if you do, this conversation never took place."

I hung up.

Maybe I really was evil, I thought as I finally drifted off to sleep.

I awoke with a start. The wind was blowing in from the north slapping at my bedroom window shutters. I wasn't sure if this was the winter storm blowing its way out of town, or another blowing in. It had warmed up to a balmy forty degrees. It was a definite improvement over the ten below from the past week.

I crawled out of bed, pulled my parka over my flannel nightshirt, and slipped on my boots. I nudged the dog out of bed—since he'd taken to sleeping with me during the cold snap—and we trotted outside. I fastened the shutter and returned to the front porch. I stood for a moment, collecting my thoughts.

"Something doesn't feel right," I said to Blue. He answered with a yawn and scratched at the door to go in. It was still dark—I guessed it must have been around five o'clock. I instinctively sniffed the air. What could it be, I thought? The warming of the weather, perhaps change of ozone? I couldn't see anything wrong, but still . . . somewhere in my world there had been a shift. I could feel it, just as easily as I could feel the cold on my face. Another gust of wind sent icy fingers up my legs and spine, but it wasn't the cold wind that made me shiver. It was a black limousine that passed by on the highway. I watched the flash of flickering yellow-green streetlights trailing across the long body and glinting across the windshield. I saw my life flash before my eyes—flicker—glint—flicker—glint . . . As the vehicle slowed, my panic accelerated. The car rounded the corner and was gone. My mouth became dry. I felt like vomiting. Even from several blocks away, I knew that car, and within it I knew exactly what storm had just blown in.

Five hours later, Idaho and I were on foot, headed for the County Library. We were on a mission to find all news articles regarding Goodman's death, hoping that the local reporters may have missed something others hadn't. We had just finished breakfast at the Surprise Cafe and crossed Mineral Avenue, when I caught sight of a limousine pulling away from the curb in front of Timberline Auto Center. A man wearing an expensive Armani business suit was getting into a black Lincoln town car that was parked in front. I froze and stepped back behind a light pole. The man drove the Lincoln over to the First National Bank parking lot. The hair stood up on the back of my neck. Idaho must have noticed the change in my mood, because she stopped to stare at me.

"Shit, shit and shit." I whispered.

Idaho eyed me for a moment longer and said, "What are you looking at?"

"Did you see that limousine that pulled out and that guy now driving that Lincoln town-car?"

"Yeah . . .I guess," Idaho hesitated.

"The guy driving it made the rounds by my house early this morning."

"And the problem is . . ."

"Deep fucking trouble."

"First of all, how do you know it's the same guy and sec—,"

"Oh, for crying out loud, Idaho, how many limousines and Lincoln town cars do you see driving around this town."

"—and second, why is it deep fucking trouble?" Idaho quizzed.

The man walked over to the bank ATM, conducted a transaction, and then headed back to the car. As I watched him walk, I noticed he had graying hair, but I knew that swagger. I conveniently slipped behind Idaho and began fussing with my already tied bootlace. When I peeked around Idaho's legs I caught a glimpse of that, oh so familiar, face. When I stood, I'd realized my cover was hustling down the sidewalk, right past the car. I turned and took the long way around the bank on the sidewalk side, standing in the shadows until the Lincoln passed out of sight.

When I rounded the corner, Idaho stood with hands on her hips, "What the hell are you doing, Olivia?" she paused, "Oh my God, I've never seen such a wild-eyed look."

I began to pace back and forth, running my fingers through my hair. "It's nothing, I mean, well it's not just nothing, it's something, probably really something. Shit, I don't know what I mean—."

Idaho put a hand on my arm. "Come on, calm down, we can get through this, whatever it is. You just need to talk to me. What's going on?"

I remained silent, pacing again, while shaking my head.

"Is it Goodman? Is all of this starting to take its toll on you? We can get through this, Olivia," Idaho tried to comfort. "We have nothing to feel guilty about. We'll figure this out. Would you just stop!"

I came to a quick halt, turned and stared back at Idaho, "We are guilty, and you know it as much as I do."

"Olivia, no—well, at least we didn't leave a fire poker in the man's chest!"

I came nose to nose with Idaho, "But we started the wheels in motion!"

"I'm a little confused here," Idaho replied. "I'm surprised at you, Olivia. You've been the level-headed, calm one. What's gotten into you? And what does this have to do with that damn Lincoln?"

I paced back and forth again, wringing my hands, my tongue flicking over my lips—nervous as a cat. Idaho continued to stare at me expectantly. I ran a hand down my face and groaned. Should I tell her? Should I just shut my mouth? Should I just run and hide? I mulled this over and continued to pace and hyperventilate. No, I decided, these women had a right to know for their own safety. And just before I was about to pass out, I took a deep breath, and exhaled, "Did I ever mention that I killed my husband?"

Chapter 23 - Olivia Hope

"Oh please! Pick up your jaw, would you? Someone's going to run over it." I scolded Idaho.

"Well, it's not every day my best friend nonchalantly announces she's a murderer!" Idaho looked around like she was looking for something. "Shit, I need to sit down. And you! You need to start talking! Let's go back to the cafe and get another coffee."

"No, that's too public. Someone will overhear us."

"Okay, we're just about to the library. We can—"

"No, it's too quiet, someone will hear. Let's go back to my car. That's safest."

"Safest?" scoffed Idaho. "Have you noticed your driving lately? And what makes you think I want to get in the car with a self-proclaimed murderer?"

"Oh, shut up! Do you want to hear my story or not?" I stomped toward the car, looking in all directions to make sure we weren't being watched. I was sure that the gray-haired man hadn't seen me yet—yet, being the operative word. All the while I wondered how much I should tell my friend. If I told her everything, I could be putting her in danger. But I realized, if I didn't tell her something, we all could still be in danger. Should I tell all the women? Should I just give highlights? Should I spill my guts? And then—should I tell Dubois?

By the time we were settled in the car, I'd decided to tell her everything and worry about the rest of the women later. If the tables were reversed, I'd want to know everything about Idaho. I didn't want my best friend, and maybe soon to be only friend, to feel betrayed. But what if I lost Idaho's friendship anyway? I needed to trust in someone, and I couldn't think of a better person. I started the car and pulled away from the curb. Without thinking, I reached under the driver's seat and pulled out my Glock.

"Jesus!" crowed Idaho. Surprised, I watched my friend cower into the corner of the passenger seat. "I—I just remembered I need to go home and wash my hair," she said with a squeak.

"Oh, for crying out loud," I said. "The safety is on. I'm not going to shoot you." I placed the gun on the seat between us and turned the car around on to Highway 37 and headed over the bridge out of town.

After several minutes of silence, Idaho moaned, "Oh, god! You really are from Canada, aren't you? Let me guess. You were actually raised by Yetis, you ran when you killed Gentle Ben, and now they've found you and want to take you back to breed with their kind."

"Don't be ridiculous," I snapped. "Big Foot wouldn't be driving a damn Lincoln. The man you saw getting in that vehicle wasn't that hairy. And, Gentle Ben wasn't that gentle."

"He could a waxed," Idaho mumbled. And I was thankful she didn't press me further until I was ready to speak.

I continued to watch if we had been followed. We hadn't. It was a week day with little to no traffic. I headed toward the Libby Dam. The dam is about fifteen miles from the city of Libby. It had been completed in the mid 1970's. Montana and Canada made a treaty that created a reservoir and a gorgeous lake that extends 48 miles to the Canadian border and another 42 miles into British Columbia. It's called Lake Koocanusa—named for the Kootenai River, Canada, and the U.S.A. It's popular with fishermen, hunters, campers, and of course, a myriad of water sportsmen, but not so much in the winter. I hoped for privacy, and that seemed the perfect place.

I pulled into the visitor parking lot. Although the visitor center is closed during the winter, they still plow the parking lot for maintenance vehicles. I left the motor running for the heat because suddenly I felt very cold. Finally, I was ready to forge on to tell my story while Idaho remained scrunched in the far corner. I rested my head on my hands that gripped the steering wheel.

"It was summer, and I was sixteen when I met Demetri Rizzo. I was waiting tables at the Sunny Side Up, a diner in Dilworth, Minnesota—the town where I was born and raised. It was a little town, with not a lot to do except dream about getting out. We used to call it Dildo, Minnesota." I heard Idaho snort. I looked over at her.

"What! You said Dildo."

In some stupid way, that helped me relax. I smiled, sat back and continued. "He flirted with me, and I fell in love—deeply and unconditionally. Demetri was a gorgeous, luscious, proverbial tall, dark and handsome Italian. Love at first sight. He was twenty something. Said he was visiting an aunt.

Idaho, I tell you, I lived a whole life-time in those two months. We talked, we laughed, danced, sang—he had the voice of Steve Perry from Journey. And, he sang me all those girly songs. I couldn't get enough of him. But, he had to go back to college. And I had to go back to high school, work at the hippy, dippy Sunny Side Up, and help my mom make stupid puppets."

"Eww, puppets—ventriloquists, all creepy," said Idaho.

"No, mom didn't make creepy stuff; she made fun, funny, and weird animals that she sold to stores and tourists—hundreds of them. If we'd had the internet back then, she would have made millions. She also made things that were like the precursor to the Muppets. She made more money than my dad did as a plumber. But, you know how teens are. They think everything is stupid and idiotic, especially if they are created by their parents. And I, the foolish teen that I was, told her she was "not right in the head."

Idaho laughed, "Have you told her how stupid you were?"

I bit my lip to keep it from quivering. Finally, I said, "No."

"Why NOT."

"Because she died," I said.

"Awww." Idaho paused, thinking about that, then said, "How did she die?"

I tried to speak but the saliva in my mouth thickened. I slurred, "Of a broken heart." Idaho put a hand on my shoulder and waited for me to collect myself. "Okay, let me finish."

Idaho nodded. "But wait, what about your dad? Did you tell him?"

"No."

"Why not?"

"Because he disappeared. I assumed, because mom died, he was grieving, and I was…absent." she squeezed my hand.

Idaho sighed deeply. "Okay, Demetri."

"Demetri Rizzo, yes. My parents didn't approve of him and forbade me to see him or even have contact with him. We made up an assumed name. It was Stephanie Clark. So, mom and dad didn't blink an eye when I got letters from Stephanie. He quoted sonnets, wrote poetry declaring our love, and told of a thousand ways that he could take care of me physically, mentally and financially. We remained in contact for eight months and twenty-four days—which just happened to be my seventeenth birthday. And that's when he climbed into my bedroom window and proposed. He said he had the JP lined up—all legal, of course, because he was almost a lawyer and I thought soon my parents would be proud of that fact—which made it okay for us to be man and wife. And so, I left with him." I looked over at Idaho. She remained stone-faced and quiet. I continued. "Go ahead and say it. Stupid, I know."

She shook her head. "A fairytale love story."

"Yeah, right." I paused for a long moment. "The caveat to this proposal was that I was never to speak to my parents again. I was young and thought I hated them—all we ever did anymore was argue and fight anyway. I was seventeen and thought about that for maybe ten seconds, and I was on board. I never had the chance to speak to them again." I couldn't say anything for a while. And Idaho didn't press. She left a reassuring hand on my shoulder.

I gathered my wits again. "We were married in a whirlwind ceremony. I had to lie and say I was eighteen. We were happy! Demetri delivered everything he promised. We lived in a luxurious penthouse. He didn't want me to work, I was deliriously in love and had no other ambitions. And then I got pregnant." Idaho gasped. She squeezed my shoulder and smiled at me. I shook my head no, and frowned. She looked bewildered.

"I didn't tell Demetri right away because everything was so perfect and I didn't want things to change. But then, a few more months went by, and I was beginning to show. When I told him, he was furious! He wanted me to get an abortion but I was too far along. That's when he started disappearing for long periods of time. I became lost and lonely. I wallowed in self-pity. One day, I finally pulled up the old boot straps, and decided I would do something to make, Demetri proud of me.

"I had just learned about eBay. I started making puppets and selling them. After three months of sewing, I had turned over almost $40K net. I learned to cook at the diner so I got the idea to package ready-made dinners that I had delivered locally. That took off like wild-fire. Canning became a hobby, too. The sugarless jams, jellies and salsa flew off the shelves. I was starting to feel good about myself.

"I was excited to tell Dimitri. I planned that, when he returned home from one of his business trips, I would "service" him as he requested upon his arrival—and then we would eat one of my fabulous meals, and I'd deliver my news. But I didn't get the chance. I had the baby early, before he got back. Although I was so in love with my beautiful baby girl, Emma, I once again became depressed. It was more the postpartum blues I think, and missing Demetri. I was having an episode when he finally arrived. He saw what a mess I was and started me on medication. Then, he hired a nanny to take care of the baby— he never called her by her name. When I was feeling better, I'd ask to see Emma. Demetri got mad and told me I wasn't fit to be a mother. Our arguments usually ended with him giving me a broken bone or two and heavier drugs. He was careful not to leave bruises on my face, though."

"Oh, Olivia, I'm so sorry," Idaho murmured.

"On the days I felt better, I'd sneak into Emma's room and play with her. She was beautiful, getting so big, and the sweetest smile. She called me momma very early, much to the chagrin of that stupid nanny, who didn't give her much attention. And I'd be in trouble if she found me in the room. I wasn't allowed out of the house, and nanny, Nurse Ratched, made sure I didn't leave."

"Oh, my god," Idaho's hand flew to her mouth and giggled. "The nurse in One Flew Over the Cuckoo's Nest."

I nodded, "At first, I didn't really care because I felt so shitty all the time. It was like I had a veil I couldn't shake off. I decided I wasn't going to take the medication anymore. When I said as much, Demetri strapped me to the bed and shot something in my arm. I wondered if he was trying to kill me. That's when I'd decided that Emma and I were leaving. I made the mistake of telling Demetri. I guess, in some demented part of my brain, I thought he deserved to know. Maybe even be happy about it. But that was when things got worse."

"Oh, dear god, Olivia, how could it have gotten worse?"

"He was home more, beat me more. and gave me more drugs. I was savvy by then. I'd pretend to swallow. But alas, he caught me flushing them down the toilet. So then, on one of my trips to the doctor for broken ribs, I asked the doctor for some vitamins. I hid them until I could substitute them with the other stuff Demetri was shoving down my throat. Voila, like magic I began to get stronger and think clearer. Oh, the beatings still came. I'd workout every moment I could and, literally, learned to roll with the punches, while acting a defenseless drugged-up girl. I figured the only way out of that hell hole was a fight and, by god, I was going to win. My attack was going to be a surprise when I was ready."

Idaho whistled. "Holy crap, I can't even imagine what you must have been through. You're sitting here now, so, I know you survived." Then softly she said, "I'm afraid to ask what happened to Emma."

I was silent. Then she asked, "You got anything to drink in this car?" I fished in the glove box and handed her a bottled water. "I was hoping for something stronger," she growled.

I gripped the steering wheel again, and continued my story, "The day finally came. My plan was set. I had $70k in the bank from my earnings. I'd grab Emma, go a couple of blocks, find a phone. Call a cab, rent a car, and head back to Minnesota. I scrounged around the house finding cash for cab fare. I even stole money out of Nurse Ratched's purse—which was satisfying, knowing that she was helping to subsidize my escape. I waited for her to go to her monthly nanny meeting. Demetri was god knows where. Luckily for me, the housekeeper was late coming in so I didn't need to sneak into the nursery. I got Emma ready to go. I packed some clothes in my oversized purse. I strapped her in the car seat, and we were ready. As a last-minute thought, I went into Demetri's study to call my parents to let them know I was coming home. If I hadn't done that, I may have just made it out of the house that day."

"Oh geeze, don't even go there, Olivia! He probably would have tracked you down anyway!" Idaho said.

I nodded, that may have been true. But, I think I might have had a better chance than what actually happened. "I was listening to the call ringing through, when I heard Demetri coming down the hall. I hung up. I knew, if Demetri saw me, a fight would happen and I didn't want Emma in the middle, so we quickly went into the closet. Thankfully, Emma was asleep. There was another man with him. They talked for a few minutes, and I couldn't quite hear him so I moved a little closer to the door for a peek. He looked a lot like Demetri, only with a longer nose. Demetri had never introduced me to his family.

"They said something about a shipment overseas leaving that evening. Just business stuff I thought, until I heard my name. Demetri said, 'Yeah, that fucking cunt is scheduled for tonight.' Then Long Nose said, 'Good, she's going to bring us lots of money with her looks. Her bruises healing up? Wu Kin don't like damaged goods you know.'"

"Change of plans I thought, the police station would

be my first stop."

Then Long-nose said, 'How about the baby?' And Demetri says, 'Fucking baby's going in the shipment next week with the other kids on a slow boat to China,' and then laughed like it was the funniest joke. 'That's great!' says Long-nose. 'I never would have guessed we'd get so much for the kid. Did you knock the cunt up for the baby bonus?' They laughed their asses off about that.

"Demetri says," I paused having a hard time getting the next words out. I couldn't breathe, as happens every time I think about that moment. I sat shaking my head until Idaho said something about not leaving her hanging.

I filled my lungs, "Demetri says, 'Sex with babies, who knew that was where the gold is, the cream of the crop!' And they roared with laughter again. That son-of-a-bitch was going to sell my Emma and me into the sex trade."

Idaho and I remained silent for a long time, until Idaho finally asked, "What happened next?"

"Emma woke up and started crying. I have never been so scared in my whole life. I saw Demetri reach for the door knob and in that moment, my anger, hatred and rage completely took over. I was ready for him, didn't even think. The door came open and I jumped for him. He went over backwards, and Long Nose drew a gun. I kicked that gun to the moon, I rounded and took his legs out from under him with my other leg, and came back with a heel kick to his nose. It put him out cold!"

"Wahoo!" Idaho yelled. "TKO, how about Demetri?"

'What the fuck?' he yells. 'You killed Anthony you fucking cunt!'

"And you are selling our daughter into sex slavery, you fucking asshole!" I yelled back. "Know what he did?"

Idaho shook her head.

"He shrugged. The fucker just shrugged. No remorse what-so-ever."

"Did you shoot him in the nuts?" asked Idaho with a hopeful look.

"No. Well, at least not right away. The monster in me hadn't kicked in yet." "Yes!" Idaho whooped again. "Okay, go on."

"We started sparring. I was trying to get close enough to knock his legs out from under him, but he kept backing up until I realized he was headed for the gun. It had landed over by Emma. In one swift motion, he grabbed the gun and the handle of Emma's car seat and threw her clear across the room. I couldn't see where she landed. And I heard no crying after that. The evil demon in me roared its ugly head, and I had no more control. I only saw red. I didn't care that he held a gun on me, I just went for him. He must have seen something in my eyes because he cowered back, and I remember him telling me I was one freaked-out bitch and I needed professional help. And I screamed, 'I am the professional.'

"I grabbed the gun out of his hand, and with no hesitation I put a bullet square between his eyes. He dropped to the floor like a lifeless puppet. With no hesitation. That's when I unloaded the rest of the bullets into him. Yes, the second shot was to his balls."

"Then what?"

"I don't know. I woke up in a hospital room tied to a bed."

"Did Nurse Ratched call the police?"

"No, in fact, I never knew what happened to her after that. I guess I called 911. I heard my own voice on the recording. I sounded eerily calm, asking the 911 operator to come and pick up some garbage."

Idaho laughed long and hard about that. "And Emma?" she finally asked.

"She was fine." I swallowed hard. "Things could have been very bad. There's more."

"More? God, Olivia. I'm liking the Yeti story better."

I nodded. "I remember the rage I felt. I guess my mind had snapped. The police reports say that, when they arrived, I was beating, kicking, and tearing at Demetri. I had literally beat him into a massive, bloody pulp. They had to tear me away from him. After a week in the hospital, I was finally able to tell the police everything. They didn't believe me."

"What? After all you had been through?" Idaho was incredulous.

"Evidently, there was so much blood and mayhem, they couldn't figure out what really happened. They didn't know if Demetri and I were in the trade together. Perhaps a soured deal. That, and they said the shot to Demetri's head was too perfect. Said I should have just kept the gun on him and called 911. I was charged with first degree murder. I argued about all the broken bones I'd been to the doctor for, and they said there was no record. And that's when I realized that Mafia wives have their own doctors."

"MAFIA! What the hell?" breathed Idaho. "Demetri was Mafia?"

"Yes, and I had no idea until that moment. I was so damn clueless. There were questions, interrogations, court hearings, and not once did I get to see my daughter. My head was on the chopping block. But I was okay with that, and I kept telling myself that at least I'd saved my baby's life. I was in prison for a while, until Malcolm Boyd, an FBI agent came to me. He said he'd been nosing around and piecing things together. He discovered Demetri, his brother, and his father were trafficking humans. When Demetri came to Dilworth, he had been on a shopping trip. Evidently, I wasn't the only woman he'd had plucked out of Minnesota that summer, and certainly not the only woman to be put up in the penthouse for the transition—in other words, grooming for prostitution. All the times he'd disappeared, he had been out shopping.

"Our marriage was a sham, too. Very long story short, Boyd said that was good because I could testify against him and his family. Boyd wanted to strike a deal. He would see about me going into the witness protection program. But I could never see Emma again."

"Oh! That is so damn cruel!" Idaho said.

"They kept Emma out of the news and any public statement. But, he said they would make an announcement that the baby had died from complications from that night. Boyd convinced me that that was the best way to protect Emma. The family would not continue to look for her. I didn't believe him at first. I was sure something had gone wrong. I made them let me hold her before I agreed to anything. When they brought her into the room, she smiled wide and held out her tiny little arms and wrapped them tight around my neck and said, 'Wuv vu, mamma.' And that was the last I saw of my baby girl." I began to cry softly.

"Damn. So, let me guess. You are in the witness protection program now, and that's why Dubois isn't able to find out anything about you?" Idaho's voice turned matter of fact, almost cold. I wondered was she too, having a hard time believing me?

"He keeps running into brick walls because my whole life was rewritten. I was sent to Boise, Idaho, for college classes so I could support myself. I'm not allowed to make puppets anymore because the Rizzos could track me down. I earned my teaching degree in health and fitness at Boise State University. Then I was sent here to Montana to start a new life."

"But I still don't know why they didn't let you keep Emma. That just doesn't make sense." Idaho's words stilted.

"Announcing that she had died would stop them from looking for her, Idaho. They will always continue to look for me until I'm dead and when/if they find me, they would kill her, too. I've resigned myself to leaving her in the care of people who don't always have to keep looking over their shoulders. They assured me she'd have a good family. The Rizzo's will kill anyone in my family. And I'm afraid for my friends, too." My voice was strained. I couldn't look at Idaho. Guilt overpowered me. Had I done the right thing by telling her?

"This all happened a long time ago. Don't you think

they would have moved on by now? Maybe you're just being a little paranoid."

"I hope I am." I said, but I instinctively knew better.

"When I was in protective custody, Antonio Rizzo, Demetri's brother, came to see me pretending to be one of my lawyers. When they let him in, he tried to strangle me. I kicked his ass, and almost tore off one of his ears before the guards got to him. If they hadn't come when they did, I would have killed him. I told you—the inner demons in me had been unleashed." I looked over at Idaho. She stared out the windshield.

"He vowed, if I ever got out, he'd hunt me down and kill me." I continued. "They threw him in jail, but I'm sure he wasn't there very long. The Rizzos have good lawyers."

"But why, out of the blue, would somebody show up now?" Idaho asked.

"My guess is that someone saw my photo in the newspaper and recognized me. I've been very careful to stay out of the media and definitely out of photos."

"So, this guy that's driving the Lincoln, you think is one of the Rizzos?"

I nodded. "Long Nose, himself, aka Anthony Rizzo."

We sat in silence. I could tell Idaho was trying to digest everything. I waited for more questions, but she said nothing. I was overwhelmed with a feeling of sadness, exhaustion was settling in.

Suddenly, she growled with such repulsion, I jumped a mile high. Her head swiveled toward me, eyes flaring, sinking her fingers into the dash as she yelled, "The fucker needs to go!"

Chapter 24 - Olivia Hope

There was a loud tap on the window. I jumped and instinctively brought up the Glock, poised for a shot.

"Holy shit, lady, are you nuts?" said a man wearing blue overalls and a parka that made him look like a grizzly bear. He began backing away from the car.

As soon as I realized it was a maintenance worker, I rolled down the window. I held up the gun and dropped out the clip, profusely apologizing to him, "I am so sorry, sir. It's just that someone has been stalking me, and I'm a little jumpy."

"Yeah, well. Okay, then." He took off his stocking cap, ran it over his sweaty brow. "This ain't the place to hide, lady, you gotta leave. I mean like now. We're bringing in some heavy equipment." As soon as he backed far enough away, he ran to where a pick-up truck was waiting for him. I could hear him exclaiming to a buddy about a crazy bitch pulling a gun on him.

"Should we get the poor guy some clean underwear?" asked Idaho.

"Nah, he's got a good story to tell his buds over a few brews," I said. "He'll be laughing all the way to town on his adrenalin high. All the same, I think it's time to get back." We drove in silence for a few moments.

"I'm wondering," I said, "Should I tell the other women about killing Dmitri and being in the witness protection program? I don't want them to be in danger by telling them, but I don't want to blindside them if something happens. They need to be able protect themselves if he's looking for me."

Idaho nodded slowly, "Tell them. No, wait. Don't tell them just yet. Let's see what happens in the next few days. We'll keep an eye on him. He won't be expecting us to come to him. Maybe we can take care of him first."

I still didn't like the look in Idaho's eyes and hoped a change in topic would snap her out of that darkness. "So, Idaho, how's it going with Alan? Had any good talks lately?" To my chagrin, her dark look remained, her eyes squinted and she began working her mouth from side-to-side. I began to get a bad feeling, "Okay, spill it, Idaho. What's going on?"

"Weeell . . ." she began. "I guess it's a day for confessions."

I held my breath, and waited.

"Okay, when I was in my drunken stupor at your house, did Alan say something about my being surrounded by dead people?"

I nodded, "Yeah, I do remember something about that now that you mention it. I was worried that you may have had alcohol poisoning. I thought his comment was kid slang for drinking too much."

"Well, evidently, he can see dead people."

"Whaaaat?" Concern for Idaho washed over me like a surfer's wave.

"Hold on, hold on. Let me tell my story now, okay? No interrupting until I'm done. Deal?"

I nodded and said nothing, only because I didn't know what to say.

"Sooo, he said that he's been able to see dead people ever since he can remember. At first, he thought they were just other people hanging around. His mom and dad figured that he had some imaginary friends, until they took him to a doctor, who gave him medication."

"Yeah, I should think so!"

"Zip it."

I shrugged.

"The medication didn't work. It made him sick, and he could still see the people. He saw how it frightened his parents. He began to withdraw and didn't talk to anyone, which resulted in his parents taking him to other doctors, trying new drugs, which produced the same effects as the first."

"He talked to his grandmother mostly. She was the only one who didn't think he was crazy. She said she could see these people, too. Said it wasn't something to be afraid of."

"Ah, so this mental illness runs in the family."

Idaho put up a hand to silence me, and then continued. "His grandmother explained to him that there is a thin veil between the living and the dead and that some people can see through that veil. Like some people have better sight than others who wear glasses, that kind of thing."

"Basically ESP."

"I guess. She said sometimes, when people die, they hang around for various reasons."

"Yeah. Is there a point to all this?" I wondered if she was going off the deep end, too. I frowned at her.

"I'm getting there." She cleared her throat, "So

anyway, his grandmother said she thought it was more of a responsibility to help these people to move on. But, it scared him. He practiced at not seeing them, and certainly not telling anyone if he did. He could only fool himself for a while. One day his mother overheard him talking to his grandmother. That's when she told him that his grandmother had died long before he was born. He was excited, and told his mom that seeing his grandmother proved that he could see dead people. He told her things that only his mother would know. But, that too, earned him more medication. He said, after a while, he thought his mother believed him. But Rand has always had a hard time with it. Rand thinks he's still crazy sometimes."

"Well, that makes two of us," I said. "You're not buying into this, are you?" Idaho shrugged.

"Okay, you are so not hanging out with this wacko any more, you hear me? Jesus, Idaho. You, above all people!"

"Just keep an open mind for a minute, okay? I'm just giving you the abbreviated version. There's a lot more to this, Olivia. I know how this all sounds. Please, just hear me out."

"Fine," I drawled.

"I had a hard time understanding at first, too. But I tell you, Olivia, he's really struggled with it. He said he needs to learn how to deal with it before it really does drive him crazy." Quite proudly she added, "And I think he's already beginning to get a handle on it. After he and I talked, we decided to put his insights to the test."

"What the—?" She held up a hand to silence me.

"He surmised, since I work at the cemetery, that is

why so many dead people hang around me. Only I can't see them, thank god."

"So, these dead people are hanging around you because . . . they don't like how you mow over their graves, take their flowers, maybe drop crumbs on their graves at lunch—," Idaho flashed me a scornful look. "Go on," I sighed.

"We went over to the cemetery. He saw Daryl Fenster. You know the guy. He was that army vet who was in a coma for a year or so before the family finally pulled the plug on him?"

I nodded.

"Well, Daryl had some money stashed away in a safe deposit box that no one knew about. He told, or showed, Alan—however that happens with the dead—where the key was and told him to tell his wife. She really needed that money."

"Oh, for Christ sake!"

Once more Idaho silenced me. "What part of keeping quiet don't you understand?"

I shrugged and she continued, "I went with him when he explained this to his wife. He had a hard time convincing her."

"Ya think?" I mumbled, producing another warning look.

"She asked me what I thought. I said I didn't know, but it wouldn't hurt to check it out. She asked us to come with her. I think it was more that she didn't want us out of her sight in case if she needed to call the authorities. But she didn't have to—it all checked out. She was so happy about the thirty thousand dollars in cash at the bank that she wasn't going to say anything to anyone.

Probably the IRS included. Anyway, we helped a few more people and so, now . . ." she trailed off.

I pulled the car over and stared at her.

"What?"

"You do know how trite this all sounds, right? You really can't believe all of . . ." I waved my hand like I could whisk it away, ". . . that! It's so cliché—seeing dead people, helping them do their bidding, and then helping them to cross over into the light. Cliché, cliché, cliché, right down to the goddamn name, Alan Dubois—aka, Alison Dubois—remember that TV character in the show Medium? He's playing you, Idaho!"

"Okay, stop. Alan is just Alan. Dubois is a common name, like Smith, Jones, and Johnson. It's just a coincidence. Look, I don't know how to explain what happens to him! He says it's not much different than having a hunch, gut feeling, or intuition, where does all that stuff come from any one of us? And may I remind you that truth is sometimes stranger than fiction? Who could make this stuff up?"

"Obviously, Alan can! Why are you telling me this anyway?"

"Because Olivia, there's more."

"Oh, of course, there is," I whined, throwing up my hands. I began driving again.

"Alan showed me a drawing he made. A very good drawing. He's an awesome artist, by the way—maybe too good."

"So?"

"So, it was a drawing he made of Goodman's crime scene. There were five beings—for lack of a better word—with caricature faces like demons or 'she devils' as Alan called them. But they had normal bodies. One wore Nikes and a running suit, another wore a t-shirt and jeans with a gun sticking out of the waistband, and another wore a fur coat, lowcut blouse with large cleavage and spiked high heels—with one heel neatly rooted in the palm of Goodman's hand, I might add." She stared at me now.

"So?"

"What were you wearing that night, Olivia?"

"I don't know," I sighed. I had to think about that for a minute. "I guess my black jacket, jeans, my knee-high boots and a scarf, I think."

"The paisley one?"

"Ah, yeah, I think so, why?"

"Bingo! Don't you get it? He had a drawing of the five of us looking over Goodman's body. We were the she-devils!"

"Don't be ridiculous! It's just a fa-reeking drawing, Idaho. He has probably seen us in those clothes a dozen times since then. He's been living and breathing this case for days and has had a lot of time to personify us because Rand is hell-bent on accusing us of murder. It's not so much a picture from beyond the grave as you seem to think—a coincidence, pure and simple."

"He made the drawing just moments after seeing Goodman's body."

I snorted loudly, "Oh, so Goodman talked to him, too? Did Alan ask him who killed him by chance?"

"He drew it before he met any of us, Olivia."

My mouth was dry. My tongue made a clicking sound as it stuck to the roof of my mouth when I said, "He's lying, Idaho."

"I don't think so."

"Yeah, he is." And then I had a moment of panic, "You didn't tell him anything, did you?"

She shook her head slowly. "No, of course not. I played it cool. He may have been waiting for a reaction but I was too numb to say anything. I complimented him on being a fantastic artist. When I finally worked up the courage to ask him what he made of it, he considered me carefully and said that to him it looked like the five of us women had something to do with his murder. I pointed at his drawing and said, 'Okay, first, of course, we would look like 'she devils.' Goodman knew how pissed we were with him for losing our money and if this is some scene from the grave then that's what Goodman would naturally picture us as. And second, my ass is not this big.' I told him point blank that he had better fix that. I said we didn't kill him and that, if he was getting vibes from Goodman he'd better go back to the grave and ask him who did."

"Then what?"

She looked flushed, "Then he flashed me this sexy smile and kissed me. He said, 'I didn't think so, and I'm darn sure I know a liar when I see one.' That's the last time we talked about it."

"Un-fucking believable," I said, "Sexy smile? Really? And then he kissed you. He actually said 'darn sure?' And that's it?"

"Yeah, that's it. Except, you know he's shown that picture to Rand."

"Okay, that's it, then," I said. "It doesn't matter what Rand thinks. So, he suspects. We were suspects from the beginning. We will never be convicted by a dead person because, well, quite frankly they have a hard time showing up for the trial. I don't think there is a jury in the world that would accept a drawing like that as evidence. It's just a tasteless cartoon. Seriously, nothing to worry about. Besides, we have enough on our plate without getting sidetracked on a stupid drawing. I need to keep my eyes open for Anthony Rizzo. I need to make sure it's him, and keep him from throwing another rock through Mrs. Bixby's window."

"Wait. What?" said Idaho. "You never said anything about a rock. What the hell happened?"

I explained the incident with Mrs. Bixby delivering the rock and the note that said, "I no what you dun. It's time to pay 4 yous sins."

"Are you sure it wasn't meant for her?" asked Idaho. "I'm thinking she doesn't have any bigger fan club than we do right now."

"Yeah, I'm sure it was meant for me, unless she killed her husband, too," I said, pulling the car back onto the road. "However, I suppose it's possible she bitched the man to death. Anyway, lo-and-behold, this morning I see a limo circling the neighborhood. It doesn't take a rocket scientist to add up those two facts."

"But why throw the rock through Bixby's window?"

"I don't know, bad shot— maybe blinded by all of Bixby's Christmas lights. Who knows," I said wearily.

My cell phone rang. "What!"

"Hello to you, too, Ms. Hope." It was Dubois. "Do you have a permit for that gun you carry?"

"Yes, I've got a permit for my Glock," I told Dubois. "I'm not an idiot."

"Well, apparently, you kind of are, because only an idiot scares the crap out of a maintenance man by pointing a gun in his face. Why in God's name are you carrying a gun anyway?"

"Well, in case you haven't read the newspapers, there is a killer on the loose, and I'm exercising my constitutional right by packing protection."

"Really, Olivia? I'm quite angry with you and your friends right now. I've been fielding calls about you all asking questions and rubbing people the wrong way. Could you just leave the investigation to us, or do I have to throw you all in jail?"

I started a snarky comment but a loud snow plow honked and swished by us traveling in the opposite direction.

"Are you driving while talking to me on the phone?" he was incredulous.

"You're the one who called me."

"You didn't need to answer!"

"If I knew it was you I wouldn't have."

"Pull over Olivia, and let's have a talk."

"Have you found Goodman's killer yet?"

"No, we haven't. Please, just—"

"Okay then, don't call me until you have something interesting to say. Besides I can't talk now, I'm driving," I hung up. "That man is driving me insane."

"You shouldn't be so mean to him, Olivia," said Idaho. "He's just doing his job."

"So, you're saying we should just sit and wait for us to be arrested for a murder we didn't commit?"

"No, I'm saying you could speak to him a little nicer. You catch more flies with honey, that kind of thing. Maybe he could be more help to us. Did you ever think of that?"

"Oh, whatever," I conceded.

We drove in silence the rest of the way home. I dropped Idaho off at her house. She wanted me to stay but I told her I needed to get some work done. I couldn't tell her I was about to do a little breaking and entering. If I was going to make my rounds to the Bull Lake house, it had to be as soon as possible.

I stuffed a few things in my backpack, readied my Glock and was set. I wanted to pay a visit to Jennifer Stevens, the woman who found Goodman. I needed to get there before dinner, but late enough for it to be good and dark by the time I entered Goodman's house. Besides, if I waited long enough, I'd have a better chance that Dubois wouldn't catch me there. It was still a little early, so I decided to make a few calls to the rest of the women to see why they were getting Rand's knickers in a twist.

Pamela didn't answer her phone, but I was sure she was busy with her Christmas tree orders. Maggie said her lunch date with City Councilman Aaron Miller was a bust. He told her that the city rejuvenation project was going to be Goodman's baby, and there had been no more word on it. He told her to check with Rocco Basham. Then, even though he's married with three kids, he proceeded to hit on her, and she resisted his advances. Evidently, he thought that was the real reason she had asked him to lunch. After she left him, he called Dubois and told him she was stirring up trouble and propositioning him with sexual favors for information. She figured he was covering his ass in the event she started talking about his philandering. We agreed we should have sent Lily in her place. Lily wouldn't rub any man the wrong way—she probably would have gotten more information and had a good time in the process. When I called Lily, she said she couldn't talk because she was "in a meeting" and would call later.

I fixed myself a sandwich and settled on the couch as I flipped through late afternoon TV. With my eyes glued on some infomercial about Kevlar backpacks for kids, I wondered what was becoming of this world we live in. Blindly reaching for my water, I spilled it across the coffee table. When I went to the kitchen for a towel, I happened to spot a man through my kitchen window dressed in all black walking down the road. It was about four-thirty. It was getting dark quickly. I watched as he walked by, slowly looking at all the houses as if he were casing each one. The man was tall and lean, much like I remembered Anthony Rizzo. He was wearing a ski mask. I couldn't see his face or hair. I had a gut feeling, whether he was Anthony or not, the guy was up to no good. I saw him turn at the end of the block. As he worked his way back, he began to lurk through the growing darkness around people's houses—weaving from one house to another. He was coming upon my house quickly.

I wondered if I should call Idaho or Rand. I ran to my purse and pulled out a business card. The card happened to be Policeman Dan's, the one who was so helpful with Mrs. Bixby when she called the police on me. I punched in his number and waited for him to pick up. I was impatient to get out of the house. I needed to move now. I started to slip out the back door to my car, when I heard Blue begin barking on the front porch. It was a strange bark that turned into a deep growl, which didn't make him sound happy at all. I jumped into my car, threw it into first gear, and sped out of the driveway. I watched the man run from the porch when Dan finally answered. I pulled over to see where the man was running.

I explained to Dan what was happening and told him to call me back when he caught the guy. I told him to be very, very careful as the man was probably armed and dangerous—to which I heard an audible snort from the cop. I couldn't very well tell him who I thought the guy was. I let it go, and told him to call me because I was leaving the house.

I arrived at Angel Island, crossed the bridge, and took the route around Halo Drive, which is the road that circles around the island. The island is half canal and half lake side. Bless the people of the island to give the roads such names as Halo Drive, Halo Court, South Halo Court, Cherub Drive and Heaven's Gate. Who knew such hell could reign on this piece of heaven?

I slowly drove by Goodman's house on the lake side. Dubois and son were there observing something on the side of the house. I put the pedal to the metal and searched for a place to park. I decided the best place would be the parking lot at The Halfway House, which was about a quarter of a mile from the turnoff to the island. There was a trailer park behind the tavern. A few cars parked there because people were busy buying Christmas trees from a guy, who sells Charlie Brown type trees cut from his property and tries to pass them off as "one of a kind." Others were parked for the burgers and brews at the tavern. My car fit in between two others that hid it nicely at the Christmas tree lot.

I walked back to the island along the highway and headed for Jennifer Steven's house.

The Steven's lived in a cute, little, green house with white trim. When I walked up and rang the doorbell, two little blond-haired boys answered. Jennifer was right behind them and invited me in. As I entered, I saw a girl of about twelve or thirteen sitting on a couch in the corner playing on an iPod. Another boy of about fifteen sat on the floor playing something on the Xbox.

"Sorry about the mess," Jennifer said. "The kids and I are trying to settle in here. We just came from El Paso, Texas. My husband is in the army, stationed in Germany now. They wouldn't let us go because my daughter has diabetes. Said we couldn't get the care she needs there. Like they don't have diabetes in Germany?"

I could tell she was upset. Listening to more of the story, she told me of how they had been jumping through unimaginable hoops trying to get their home orders changed. Since her husband's duty station wasn't El Paso, she could no longer stay there either. She and the kids had nowhere else to go except to come to Montana with family. "Just as you rang the doorbell, I hung up from some lame-ass woman telling me how our benefits are being cut as well!" Wearily, she said, "I'm so sorry, that is not what you came here for. I feel so out of control lately. I apologize for rambling on about my problems. Dear, lord, to a stranger at that."

"No worries," I said. "It was a nice diversion to listen to someone else's woes instead of my own."

"So, what brings you to my pity party?" she

laughed.

"I wanted to talk to you about the day you found Goodman."

"Oh yeah, then there's that. We couldn't have been here more than a week, and I find a murdered man. That went over like a lead balloon with my already stressed-to-the-max husband. It would be great to find out who did this so there can be some peace in my family."

"Hey, you're the girl in the picture with that ugly lady sleeping on the floor," said one of the younger boys.

"Yeah, that lady was uuuugly!" pipped the youngest one.

Jennifer looked at me apologetically, "Sorry, again. You're not really a total stranger to us. We read the newspaper. We know who you are."

"Hey Drew, that ugly lady was a man," said the girl on the couch, as she dropped her phone to the floor beside her. "And, he was dead—not asleep. What's for dinner mom? I'm hungry!"

"Well, daughter dear, how about some stinky beef and cheesy socks with a side of whoop-ass?"

I laughed. I liked this woman.

"Is there barbeque sauce for the socks?" the girl asked with her head buried in the refrigerator.

Jennifer shook her head, "Chicken's in the oven. It'll be ready in about ten minutes. Go to your room and do your homework. Dad's calling soon to make sure you all are done with it. I'll call you when dinner's ready."

Still laughing, I said, "Seems like you have everything under control to me."

"Are you sure? Because if you are here from the

insane asylum, I'd come with you without the straight jacket, no questioned asked. Just say the word, I'm yours."

"No," I said. "But if you are going, I'd need to request the room next to yours." We laughed together.

"Okay, let me guess what's happening," said Jennifer. "Your name and photo show up in the newspaper with all of you WICA women hanging over Goodman's dead body, and they all want to hang you for the murder, am I right?"

"Pretty much sums it up," I said.

"Well, pardon me for getting too puny here, but I'd say it's all a witch hunt. The local authorities want someone to hang this on so they can be done with it. God knows I've heard enough cover-up stories in this town, all to protect the likes of Basham, Goodman, and the previous Sherriff Gilmore and his ties to the Mafia." She was referring to the Mafia established in Eureka, trafficking drugs and who knows what else, across to Canada.

"I don't know. I think Bishop and Dubois are trying to do their job right. They're just not getting many leads, and I'm too antsy to sit around doing nothing. I need to help myself."

"I, for one, don't think you did it. It takes a hard-core killer to do what they did to that man. I don't see any of that in you or, the other women."

I blushed with guilt—not humility.

"Okay, what would you like to know about Goodman," Jennifer asked.

"Did you know him well?"

"No. I never liked the guy. He was such an

egotistical, bigoted snob. We've spent a few summers here. I always tried to steer clear of him."

"Can you tell me how you happened to find Goodman?"

"Yeah, I was out walking. When I started by his house, I noticed his car was in the driveway with the door wide open. I didn't think anything of it, until I got closer. Then I noticed he had a couple of bottles of wine sitting on the seat, and they looked frozen. I thought I'd do the neighborly thing and knock on the door to let him know. There was no answer, so I looked in the window. I saw a heap of something on the floor. I knocked again, and still no answer. I really couldn't make out what that pile on the floor was.

She gave a shiver. "Okay, now, this part I didn't tell the police. I went home and got my binoculars so I could see through the window better. That's when I realized it was him lying there. I went around the back and found the basement door unlocked."

The timer buzzed on Jennifer's oven, indicating the chicken was done. The kitchen smells were heavenly. She took take care of it, continuing the conversation.

"I ran upstairs to where he was. He was lying in front of the big fireplace with that big fire-poker sticking out of his chest. I barely recognized it was him. He was all blue and NAKED! I can't get that vision out of my head! Anyway, I panicked and ran home to call the police."

"Why didn't you tell the police about going in?"

She fidgeted, "Weeell," she drawled. "My first reaction was to help him, so I tried to pull the fire-poker out. Stupid, I know. Then I stopped suddenly realizing that I'd just put my fingerprints on the handle. In a panic, I wiped it down and ran home. After I called the police, I realized that I had just tampered with evidence. I don't know why I did that! I was so shook-up I couldn't bring myself to tell them. I've been filled with guilt this whole time. I just couldn't wind up being a suspect with everything else going on in my life. But I swear to God, I didn't kill him." She exhaled, "Wow! That feels good to get that off my chest. But if I need to, I'll come forward and tell them, I promise."

I knew how she felt. I nodded, "Your secret is safe with me. But, I don't think that's going to be an issue. Best left alone for now."

We continued to talk while she dished up dinner for the kids, giving me a plate as well. The children came in all talking at once, which left Jennifer and I to talk freely in the living room without them over-hearing us.

"I'm sorry I'm not much help to you," Jennifer said. "As I said, I really didn't know him that well, but he must have really pissed off someone."

"Did you ever see anyone hanging around over there?"

"No, just the normal comings and goings with his son and his friends. I never saw his wife over there. That Rocco Basham guy was there quite a bit during the summer, with one bimbo or another on his arm—usually wearing nothing but a thong bikini, as I overheard my fifteen-year-old son describe. It was never the same woman. But I haven't seen him out here since I've been back. But then I'm in Libby a lot while the kids are in school."

"Have you seen anything out of the ordinary,

maybe a different vehicle, a van, construction vehicles, utility service trucks, anything like that?"

"Now that you mention it, I did see a beat-up, old truck a few days ago. It looked out of place in Goodman's driveway. It was some kids. You know kids, sometimes to them the uglier the better."

"Was it before or after you found him?"

"It was before I found him. I didn't think much of it at the time because it had been parked there several times before. One day when I walked by, I heard an argument in full, hot-headed volume, and his son and some other kid stormed out of the house."

"What did the truck look like?" I asked. I knew some of the vehicles kids drove to school. If I could figure out whose truck, maybe I could find out who was there after we had been.

"It was a black Ford truck, probably early to late seventies. It was all rusted and covered in stupid bumper stickers like 'All I need is peace and quiet. If I got a piece, I'd be quiet.' And then there was the 'Well behaved women rarely make history, but they sure make me a good breakfast.' Then my all-time favorite PETA bumper sticker, and not the one that says, People for Ethical Treatment of Animals, but 'People Eating Tasty Animals'. What idiots!"

My stomach turned. I thought I knew who that truck belonged to. I wondered why Goodman's son Seth would continue to hang around with that creep, Josh Pinkman.

"So, just a wild guess here, do you have any thoughts on who killed him?" I asked.

"I really hate to speculate. I don't think his son did

it. I like that kid. Always polite. He came over and mowed the lawn a few times, and helped put up the basketball hoop for my kids. He was good with all the kids. I just can't see him doing such a thing. I don't know much about his wife Mora, except I saw how chummy she and that Rocco Basham were at the funeral. I think there's something going on between the two of them. Oh, maybe Basham did it! Wouldn't that be funny, him killing his best friend for his wife? There's one for the tabloids." Jennifer laughed. "Who do you think did it?"

"I'm not sure, but I'm doing my best to find out," I said.

Jennifer's phone rang and she explained it was her husband calling from Germany. I said a quick 'thank you' to her and we agreed to have coffee in town one day—I just hoped that coffee wouldn't be in the Deer Lodge state pen.

She apologized again for not being much help, but I had begged to differ. I had a lead on an ugly truck, and a possible way into Goodman's house without breaking a window.

Chapter 25 - Olivia Hope

The wind had kicked up on my way to Goodman's house. The swirling snow made it difficult to see. That was a plus for my cover. I stepped up on the porch and peered in the window—all was dark in the house. I shined my flashlight in the side window and caught a glimpse of the outline of the body on the floor. For some reason, that made me pause. I wondered if I could go through with my B&E. I finally decided, since I'd already seen Goodman's body naked and dressed in drag, nothing more could bother me. Still, I planned to leave this area of the house alone.

I followed a path around the back to where Jennifer said she had entered. As I suspected, the back door was locked by then. However, I found an unlocked opening to a wood chute that I fit into it nicely—but ended the tube ride to the basement landing on the cement floor, hurting my keister and bringing tears to my eyes. I was pulling out splinters when my cell rang, scaring the crap out of me.

"What," I groaned.

"Hello, this is Dan. I found your man."

"Who is he? What was he doing?" I asked anxiously.

"He's a cleaner."

"Cleaner." I repeated. So, that's what they call hit men these days. My hands began to shake.

"Yep, cleaner. At least that's what I call them. He's one of those environmentalists who can't stand to see garbage strewn about. He goes from neighborhood to neighborhood, picking it up and delivering it to the nearest house. He gave a bunch of shit to you, too."

"You mean shit, as in drug paraphernalia?"

"Nope, as in dog. A big bag of it is sitting on your front porch. And I see you still don't have your dog licensed yet."

"He's not my dog." I growled. I felt only a little relief in that it hadn't been Anthony poking around my door.

"He's a good dog to have around. He makes a hell of a good guard dog. But, I'm going to have to double your fine if I see him unlicensed again."

Ignoring his comment, I said, "Yeah, thanks for checking things out for me, I appreciate it. You've always been a good friend."

"So as one friend to another, let me give you a little advice," said Dan. "I think you're a little paranoid right now. I know there's a killer out there, and I don't think it's you. But I do think you and your friends need to just lay low for a while and keep calm. Keep that gun of yours in the safe. Let Bishop and Dubois do their job."

"Geez, isn't anything private anymore? Is that what all you cops do, sit around and exchange conversations about my activities?" I whined.

"Don't be narcissistic. We don't talk just about you."

"Okay. But, you aren't the one who's suspected of a heinous crime," I said. "How can I just sit and do nothing?"

"I'm just saying I think you need to go rent a bunch of movies and relax until this all blows over. It'll all work out, you'll see. You are safe to go home now. So, go home and don't do anything stupid. Okay?"

"Yeah, roger that," I said, as I clicked off and resumed the entering part of my break-in.

I slowly wound my way to the top floor to work my way down. As I prowled the house, I was struck by how big it was. There were several rooms upstairs that had not been furnished. Probably only five of the eight would-be bedrooms had a bed, maybe a dresser, and all closets were empty. At least it made my search of those rooms easy.

The third floor was much more interesting. It had a game room consisting of several tables, ping pong, air hockey, foosball and a pool table. There was a work-out room, a library, and a den. It took me longer to search these rooms but I found nothing of importance.

The second floor had a couple more unused bedrooms and an art gallery. In this gallery were photos of Goodman shaking hands and smiling with seemingly important people. None of the likes of Clinton or Sting like Lily had at her house, but I guessed they were important to him. Then there was a room totally dedicated to rows and rows of glass shelving filled with glass figurines. A whole damn roomful. It was dark in the room but, when I turned my flashlight on them, the whole room exploded into a ghostly blue hue. It was like some cold, ice-world. I was astounded, amazed and sufficiently appalled at some of what I saw. There were beautiful men, women and children, silhouettes, majestic animals, birds, rodents and waterscapes. Then there were the hideous sculptures of beheaded people. A couple of rows were filled with about a hundred young boys. Some were smiling, others running and laughing, and some were beheaded. It seemed as the progression of boys grew older, many that lay on their sides, were hollow-eyed and headless—seemingly giving this space to violence of the innocent. What could this mean? I realized then, what a demented soul Goodman must have been. This wasn't art, this was an altar of pure evil. And about that time, I heard footsteps running upstairs.

I quickly turned off my light and searched for a place to hide. Not an easy task when you're in a room filled with glass and your ass is magnified ten-fold by mirrors circling the room—reflecting into infinity, I might add. Stealthily as possible I ran back to the third floor and dove into a closet in the library, pulling the door shut quickly. The closet door still vibrated when the library door flew open.

My heart pounded so hard I couldn't hear a thing. I waited what seemed like ages while my eyes began to adjust in the dark. Someone was in the room with a flashlight. I heard a zipper slide, tugging, and the word "fuck" mumbled from beyond the door. I tried to breathe as quietly as possible. Suddenly I hiccupped. I instinctively slapped my hand across my mouth. But it was too late. My nervous hiccups continued with a fury. And once more the word "fuck" was reiterated. That time it was me.

The closet door flew open, and a light shined bright into my eyes. I hung my head and prepared to be immortalized with the other glass men, women and children on the second floor.

"What the fu…, Miss Hope! What are you doing here? You scared the crap out me!"

I shielded my eyes from the bright halogen light burning my retinas.

"Could you please dim the spotlight?" I asked, in between spasms of hiccups. The light quickly pulled to the side. I looked up to see Seth Goodman's handsome young face. "And I think the question is, what are you doing here?"

"Ah well, it's kinda my house."

"Yeah, okay. But where the heck you been? People are looking for you!"

"I…um…been kind of abducted."

"We've all been worried sick! Your mother is beside herself," I pushed.

"Look, Miss Hope, I need to hurry here. So, could you just shut up and leave or something?" he whispered.

"What's going on, Seth?" I whispered back.

He sat back on his haunches and looked at me. "What are you doing here?" he asked again.

"Crap," I conceded. "Looking for clues."

"Clues for what?"

He seemed genuinely mystified. "Ah, clues as to who killed your father?"

His butt rocked back and hit the floor. He rolled onto his back in front of me with fists bunched into his eye sockets and groaned. I crawled over to him and tried to console his grief.

"Do you know who killed your father?" I asked gently, but he continued to moan and snort, I couldn't tell if he was crying or coughing up a fur ball.

"Come on, sit up. We need to talk."

the hideous sculptures of beheaded people. A couple of rows were filled with about a hundred young boys. Some were smiling, others running and laughing, and some were beheaded. It seemed as the progression of boys grew older, many that lay on their sides, were hollow-eyed and headless—seemingly giving this space to violence of the innocent. What could this mean? I realized then, what a demented soul Goodman must have been. This wasn't art, this was an altar of pure evil. And about that time, I heard footsteps running upstairs.

I quickly turned off my light and searched for a place to hide. Not an easy task when you're in a room filled with glass and your ass is magnified ten-fold by mirrors circling the room—reflecting into infinity, I might add. Stealthily as possible I ran back to the third floor and dove into a closet in the library, pulling the door shut quickly. The closet door still vibrated when the library door flew open.

My heart pounded so hard I couldn't hear a thing. I waited what seemed like ages while my eyes began to adjust in the dark. Someone was in the room with a flashlight. I heard a zipper slide, tugging, and the word "fuck" mumbled from beyond the door. I tried to breathe as quietly as possible. Suddenly I hiccupped. I instinctively slapped my hand across my mouth. But it was too late. My nervous hiccups continued with a fury. And once more the word "fuck" was reiterated. That time it was me.

The closet door flew open, and a light shined bright into my eyes. I hung my head and prepared to be immortalized with the other glass men, women and children on the second floor.

"What the fu…, Miss Hope! What are you doing here? You scared the crap out me!"

I shielded my eyes from the bright halogen light burning my retinas.

"Could you please dim the spotlight?" I asked, in between spasms of hiccups. The light quickly pulled to the side. I looked up to see Seth Goodman's handsome young face. "And I think the question is, what are you doing here?"

"Ah well, it's kinda my house."

"Yeah, okay. But where the heck you been? People are looking for you!"

"I…um…been kind of abducted."

"We've all been worried sick! Your mother is beside herself," I pushed.

"Look, Miss Hope, I need to hurry here. So, could you just shut up and leave or something?" he whispered.

"What's going on, Seth?" I whispered back.

He sat back on his haunches and looked at me. "What are you doing here?" he asked again.

"Crap," I conceded. "Looking for clues."

"Clues for what?"

He seemed genuinely mystified. "Ah, clues as to who killed your father?"

His butt rocked back and hit the floor. He rolled onto his back in front of me with fists bunched into his eye sockets and groaned. I crawled over to him and tried to console his grief.

"Do you know who killed your father?" I asked gently, but he continued to moan and snort, I couldn't tell if he was crying or coughing up a fur ball.

"Come on, sit up. We need to talk."

He finally pulled himself up. "I tried to cut him free but Josh kicked me in the chest with his boot and I guess my head hit the fireplace—knocked me out. When I came to, I was sitting on the couch, and dad had a fire poker in his chest. They said I did it. But how could I, if I don't remember?" he said.

I began to get the picture. His friends, and I mean that loosely, had set him up. "Do you remember anything, Seth?"

"I remember that fire poker!" he was becoming more agitated.

"It's all right," I comforted. "We'll figure this out."

"What are you doing here?" he demanded.

"Same thing you are," I squeaked. "To find out who killed your father."

"I came to get money. Josh knows dad had a stack of cash. That's why I'm here."

"Do you think Josh killed your father? If he did, we can take care all of this right now."

"Why? What does it matter to you?"

"Well, have you read the news? I'm looking at a prison sentence here."

He shook his head as if to clear his brain. "What? You killed him?"

"NO!" I said. "But some of the authorities seem to think so because of us women doing loan business with him. I'm just trying to clear our names." I waited for that to sink in.

"Seth, I think you are being set up by Josh. I think you know Josh did this."

He didn't answer.

"Do you know why he'd do such a thing?"

He shrugged and chewed on his cheek, staring at the floor for so long I thought he'd gone into a fugue state. Then suddenly he jumped to his feet and said, "The why is a shit pile of wrongs and betrayal!"

He bunched his fists into to his eyes again. "I'm so tired." He sounded defeated. I could feel the exhaustion exuding from him. His voice was weak. "I can't do this anymore. This needs to be over." He grabbed my hand, "C'mon, I need to show you something."

He dragged me by the hand, running back down a flight of stairs to the glass-menagerie room. He knelt in the corner of the room. With a slight tug on the carpet, he pulled up a three-by-three-foot piece. Then he tugged on a handle imbedded in the floor and pulled up a hatch, revealing a hiding place below the floor boards. A huge silver case was exposed. Seth pulled it out and opened it. There were wads of money like I'd never seen. He pulled it out by the handfuls.

"What are you doing?" I asked.

"I'm saving my family's life! And keep your voice down." he whispered back.

"You didn't kill your father!" I said.

"Maybe I did," he mumbled. He reached back into the hideaway and dug a little deeper. He pulled out a small plastic thumb drive and handed it to me.

"What's this?"

He looked around the room and said, "You'll have to look at it at home—looks like they took all of dad's computers."

I nodded, "But what's on this?"

"See these glass pieces my dad collected?"

"Yeah, what's that all about?" I whispered.

"My dad believed that children, especially boys, were good and pure. Like glass, he said, until they reached a certain age. Then something takes hold of them like the devil, and they turn into little monsters. At least that's how he explained it to me. He said that he hadn't met a boy yet that didn't turn to filth by age thirteen. Look at that thumb-drive. Make your own conclusions."

We heard a voice downstairs. Seth looked around wildly. "I have to go," he said, flicking his tongue across his lips.

I grabbed his arm. "Is that Josh?" He nodded. "Then, no, stay here with me. Let's go talk to Dubois and Bishop. Tell them what you told me. They'll help you. I swear they will."

"Don't you see? If I don't go down now, they will kill my family and me. I can't stay."

"Where do you go? Where do they hang out?"

"I don't know. I'm always blindfolded when they take me."

"We can work this out. I've got my Glock. I'll make them come with us."

"No, they'll alert the others, and then they will kill my family."

"How many are there?"

He shrugged, "I don't know. I know of five of them but there are others and I think they are recruiting every day. These guys are sick fucks. I mean, they mutilate animals for fun. They say they are fueled by Satan, or some shit like that. They're crazy. Hey, if you see my mom, tell her I love her and I'm so sorry to worry her. I wish it didn't have to be this way. Tell her I love her very much. Promise me! Because, someone had to take care of this."

"Come with me now. Don't go." I whispered, holding up my Glock, cocking back the hammer.

It didn't seem to faze him. He must have figured I wouldn't shoot. He said, "If you want to help me, let me go!" With that, he grabbed his backpack and was out the door, leaving me with a lot of questions and a gaping hole in the floor.

I ran to the top of the stairs to see who was waiting for him. There were two of them. One I'd never seen before, but I recognized that mop of hair tied in dreadlocks, that cocky swagger and sagging pants. "There's my main bro," said Josh, slapping him on the back.

"Yeah, bro," Seth answered and smiled, returning the slap on the back. And then they were gone.

Looking down at the thumb drive in my hand, I returned to the glass room. I needed a close-up of Seth's cubby hole. The silver case was still open. I'd shined my light on it. Thick rolls of one hundred dollar bills were rolled up in rubber bands. I thought that it could settle at least half of what Goodman had taken from us. But then I decided it was probably dirty money, and I wanted nothing to do with it. Besides, how was I to explain how I got it? And then I reasoned that certainly Seth needed it more than I did. Yet, I sat staring at all that money for god knows how long.

I finally reached over and closed the case. A little yellow sticky note puffed up from the dark hole and came to rest beside the case. The scribble on it looked vaguely familiar. It said, "Here's your traveling money, compliments in part from WICA. Have a pleasant journey." It was signed RB. Of course, Rocco Basham!

"That son-of-a-bitch," I said to no one. So, Goodman was planning a getaway with our money! Where was he going? Why was he going? How many other people were funding his journey? Had he flipped his lid and knew we were going to drag him through the legal system? Somehow, I didn't think that would scare him away.

I heard a vehicle pull up. Before I had time to think, I slipped the note into my pocket, shoved the case farther into the hole and quickly put the floor and carpet back together. I ran to the window in time to see a snowplow parked in Goodman's driveway, and a man was peeing to the side of the drive.

As soon as he finished, I raced down stairs and out the back door. I came around the house and saw the snowplow heading to the right, so I headed left. I jogged to the bridge across the canal and skated my way back to the highway. I ran the quarter of a mile to The Halfway House. Just as I rounded the corner, I saw my car sitting in the middle of an empty parking lot with only one other vehicle parked beside it—none other than Rand Dubois and his sidekick—or I should say psychic—Alan.

"Shit," I breathed. I backed up and ran back to the highway. I followed an unplowed path through the woods. I tromped my way through the snow and then crossed over to the trailer park behind the Halfway House. Now what, I thought as I tried to brush my clothing clean of snow and ice balls that stubbornly hugged to my fur boots. I noticed that Richard Gelheart had closed his Christmas tree business for the night. I took a chance that it was his trailer parked by the trees. I knocked on the door and heard a voice say, "Go away, We're closed."

"Hi Richard. Is that you?"

"Who's askin?"

"Olivia Hope. I came out all this way to buy one of your trees. Sorry, I'm late. Can I please get one, since I'm already here?" I heard shuffling noises and finally the trailer door opened. I could smell something good frying. I unzipped my jacket and made sure some cleavage was showing by the time the door opened—thank you, Lily, for that tip. As expected, Richard leered about five seconds and swung the door wider.

"I need to flip my burgers. Come on in fer a drink," he growled.

"I'd like to pay for that tree over there," I said, pointing at one I hadn't even looked at yet.

"Come on in, you need to warm up those puppies before they freeze up on ya," he said, ogling my breasts. He handed me a shot of whiskey, which I downed in one gulp. And damn, didn't that taste good. We chatted for a bit more, and I downed another one. I hadn't realized how badly I'd been shaking until the third shot steadied my hand. I'd lost track of how many more shots I had. About that time, Richard decided I was drunk enough. I was ready to leave. He leaned in and went to make his move. He closed his eyes and kept leaning toward me with lips puckered. Just as he came forward, I opened the door, and he fell right past me onto the snow-covered parking lot. Once he peeled his lips from the ground, he mumbled something about that last step being a doozy.

I apologized profusely, and then I thanked him for

the drinks and left him fifty dollars for the tree. I trudged my way to the car with tree in tow, hoping not to see Dubois still lurking around my car. No such luck. He saw me coming, and the fearless duo got out of their vehicle to help me.

"What brings you to Goodman's neighborhood on this fine night?" Dubois asked.

"Gosh, I thought I was buying a Christmas tree—not visiting a graveyard."

"Funny, Miss Hope. Let me help you with that thing." He and Alan fought with the overgrown tree with not much success. Finally, Alan pulled out a hacksaw from a bag of tools and sawed at least a quarter of it off before it could be tied to the roof of my car.

"Good thing this tree is mostly bare on one side or we wouldn't be able to tie this down," he growled. "Who taught you how to pick out trees anyway? And why didn't you just buy one from Pamela, eh? Hope you didn't pay much for this damn thing."

I had been thinking the same thing but, of course, this evening's mission wasn't about buying a tree. "I like to support the little people occasionally. Besides, Pamela charges too much. But don't tell her I told you that."

"Your car has been parked here awhile. And the lot is closed. What have you been up to?" asked Alan, and damn if he didn't have a "knowing" look about him.

"I got here a little late and was visiting with Richard."

"You know him well?" snarled Dubois.

"He's a war veteran. I like to support the men and women who fight for our freedom," I said, hoping I had evaded the question well enough.

"Well, I figure you've had plenty to drink. Alan, you drive her car, and I'll follow you home in case you lose your precious tree," was Dubois's reply, and I didn't argue.

The first few miles were blissfully quiet, and my thoughts were of Seth. How could I help him? Should I tell Alan right now and have a search party for him? Or, should I keep my mouth shut and search for him myself? I was leaning towards the latter idea. For some reason, something didn't seem right about Seth's story. His last comment kept running through my mind, someone had to take care of this. What was the this he talked of? That's why I decided to sleep on it, since I was too inebriated to think straight. I started to nod off in the warmth of the car, and my head bobbed once or twice.

Alan's voice snapped me back around to the land of the living, "What exactly, were you looking for at Goodman's tonight?"

I had been careful to not let them see me on the island. And I was very sure there was no way they could have seen me after I dropped my car in the parking lot and walked back. Damn maybe the kid was psychic.

"I told you, I was there getting a Christmas tree."

"Hmm," he grunted.

I could tell he wasn't buying any of it.

"Way out in the middle of nowhere, you decide to come get a Christmas tree?"

"This is Montana, most Christmas trees are in the middle of nowhere. Besides, I try to make the rounds and go to different places each year. Spread the wealth, and all that." I didn't bother to tell him this was my first Christmas tree, ever.

To turn the conversation, I said, "Idaho had a chat with me about your so-called special abilities. Talked to Goodman lately? Is he feeling a little stiff these days?" Even in the dark I could see he blushed.

"It doesn't work that way," he said, shaking his head.

"Yeah, so I've heard. Is it by invitation only?"

He continued to shake his head. Then his face burst into a radiant smile. "Isn't she wonderful?" he said. "She's a special lady, that one."

"Yeah, she may buy into your crap, but I don't. And, if you hurt her in anyway, I'll personally blow out both of your knee caps."

His smile didn't disappear as he gave me a quick side glance, "Oh, that's just the booze talking. You're drunk."

"No, I'm not!"

"Are too."

"Am not."

"Are too."

"Am not!" It was maddening that I'd been reduced to childish arguing with this idiot. "You are so immature!"

"Am not!" he said,

"Are too!" I said. And so, it went for a few more rounds until we were both laughing.

Then he sobered, and said, "Listen, I'm going to tell you what I have told my father. The two of you don't have to believe me when I say I see dead people. The only thing that matters to me is what I see because, for me, it's real. For a long time, my family tried to change my abilities with drugs, which only made things worse and made me sick in the process. I'm learning to work with this, without making myself crazy and without drugs. And, I can help others along the way. What's the harm in that? I don't know why I have this ability. I didn't ask for it. I only know I have it. And whether Idaho believes me or not is not important either. But, what is important is that she accepts me for who I am. And that is as precious as gold to me."

We drove in silence after that. I let what he said sink in and I realized that his abilities really didn't matter to me one way or another. And it was time for me to quit worrying about Idaho, because even if he was a loony toon, he convinced me—maybe not so much in words as actions—that he was deeply in love with my dear friend.

When we pulled up to my house, he turned off the engine and handed me my keys, but he pulled them back as I reached for them and said, "I plan to continue to see Idaho after the investigation. It was important for me to tell her everything about me. And can you imagine, when I did, she didn't run screaming from the room or laugh at me! In fact, she supported me, offered suggestions, and helped me to think of ways to deal with it. I swear to you, Olivia, I never, ever, would intentionally do anything to hurt Idaho. I really care for her."

"I know," I said.

"Oh, you know," he laughed as he weaved and bobbed and teased me with my keys, while I grabbed and missed. "Are you psychic, too?"

"Maybe, but I think you highly value your knees and other body parts, as well. Give me those damn keys."

"So, do I have your blessing to continue to see your friend?" By then we were out of the car. He continued to hold the keys above my head just out of reach.

"And if I don't give consent?" as if he needed it.

He suddenly turned serious, still not relinquishing my keys, he said, "I'd continue to see her but it would mean a lot to me and her if you were okay with it, too."

I jumped and grabbed for my keys once more, and suddenly I was batting at them like a cat chasing a string, which made us both laugh hysterically again.

"Please, please," he began to taunt and then bargain, "We'll name our first born after you."

"You can't name a boy Olivia!" I howled with laughter.

"No, but it's a great name for a puppy, don't ya think?"

I jumped once more, colliding with him as I slipped on the ice. We both careened into a snow bank as we laughed even harder. Damn I was drunk.

"Okay, okay. I give," I said. "I give you my blessing."

Dubois arrived about then and saw us sliding around. He hopped out of his vehicle, "What are you two doing? What's going on here?" he raged.

"Oh, it's nothing," Alan hollered. "She's just not very, coordinated." He winked, handed me my keys and mouthed, "Thank you."

Dubois helped Alan up, brushing snow off him. He scornfully looked over his shoulder at me and said, "You're drunk!"

That brought another round of belly laughter from

Alan and me.

"I don't find it funny. It doesn't suit you," Dubois began to mumble as he and Alan helped me unload the tree from my car. Thankfully, Dubois received a phone call, and they had to leave right away. His parting words to me were, "Put that thing in a bucket of water for the night. You're already losing too many needles from it. And keep it away from the fireplace. That damn thing will go up like a Roman candle," he growled, yet again.

"I know how to take care of a Christmas tree, Mr. McGrump," I barked back.

"Really? You could have fooled me. Next time have Pamela pick out a tree for you. Trust me, it'll be worth it." Then he was gone.

Once more I wondered if I should have told him what I had done, and about my conversation with Seth. But, obviously, Dubois wasn't in a mood to stay and talk anyway. I'd reasoned, thinking it through first was best. Besides, considering Rand's mood, I think he would have thrown me in jail with no questions asked, and then we'd all be screwed.

He acted like he was pissed at me. Was it because he knew I was snooping around Goodman's? Did he see me tromp through the woods to Gelhart's? Was he pissed I was visiting him?

Oh, what do I care, I thought. I was way too tired and had plenty of other things on my mind than to worry about Rand Dubois. Not only that, I had a decrepit Christmas tree to attend to. And, then I had to decorate the damn thing.

Chapter 26 - Olivia Hope

After Dubois left, I stumbled into the house and fired up my computer. It hummed and whirred, while I took off my coat and boots. I heard an unexpected grinding—which had happened a few times. I crossed my fingers hoping that the machine wouldn't choose this moment to crap out on me.

I fixed myself a cup of herbal tea and pulled out the thumb-drive Seth had given me, and inserted it into the slot. Suddenly, the screen went blank. Good thing I did regular back-ups to save my lesson assignments. I thought about calling Idaho to use her computer but, when I looked at the clock, it was almost eleven. Then I'd have to tell her about what I'd done tonight. I wasn't ready to talk just yet.

As it was, the couch was calling my name, so I grabbed a blanket, and the tea and sprawled out. Blue took that as an invitation and hopped up beside me. I petted him softly for a long while letting my thoughts come and go in the dark. I was still a bit buzzed which added to my lethargy and soon I was fast asleep, or maybe I passed out—it was hard to say.

I woke with a jolt when the first light of day slid across my face. Lo and behold, the sun was coming up into a cloudless sky. I stumbled to the coffee maker and brewed a pot. Waiting impatiently, I promised myself a Keurig for Christmas.

Thoughts of the night before began to flood my foggy brain. My heart squeezed as I thought of Seth spending time with his abductors, Josh and his evil minions. Yet, I still had that feeling that not all was right with his story. When I saw them together, something about their actions seemed a little too familiar, too buddy-buddy, too at ease. I needed more information. And, perhaps, I could get that from Seth's thumb drive.

My finger nails drummed mindlessly on the granite counter, waiting for the coffee. It was starting to drive me crazy, so I left the coffee pot and took a quick shower. My plan was to drive to Sandpoint, Idaho, to get a new computer at Wal-Mart. I had time for the eighty-some mile drive, since it was only seven o'clock. I could certainly be back by noon. That was plenty of time to think things over—like what I was going to say to Dubois, and what would I do when he threw me in jail when he didn't like my confession.

The morning had started out with sunshine and blue skies, but by the time I reached Clark Fork, it was snowing again. The closer I got to Sandpoint, the more I wondered if I should have even been on the road. When I made it to Wal-Mart, the wind was blowing sideways and the white-out made for zero visibility. It didn't look like it would subside anytime soon. I took a couple of hours to sample a few computers, talk to a sales person, and finally make my purchase. When I returned to the parking lot, it looked like the storm had passed, and I followed a snowplow out of town. By the time I got back to Clark Fork, however, the snow beast returned with a vengeance, and I realized I'd better find a place to sit out the next storm. It was noon, but for as dark as it had become, it may as well have been midnight. I was hungry, and tired of fighting the drifting snow. The Cabinet Mountain Bar and Grill looked like a good place to hunker down.

I ordered a hamburger and water to drink. Still sporting half a hangover, I languidly listened to, and hummed a few choruses with, Garth Brooks on the jukebox. I slowly ate my hamburger and watched a soundless TV cooking show. I sang silently along with a few more tunes and learned how to make a flawless Beef Wellington. Time drifted like the snow.

At one thirty, watching the snow piling up, I was ready to crawl out of my skin. I ordered a Spanish coffee.

Two o'clock . . . Jimbo, somebody, bought another drink for me and tried to make small talk—until his wife called.

Three o'clock . . . I ordered a piece of apple pie and sang to myself, "Man, I feel like a woman," with Shania Twain, and learned to make Chicken Cordon Bleu.

Four twenty-eight, was when the lights went out. It became dark and silent. The married—and by then, inebriated—Jimbo, tried to convince me I needed to spend the night and he'd "be more than happy" to give me a ride to a motel as he started to drag me out of my chair.

Four twenty-eight and a half, bartender Duke called a cab for the married and inebriated Jimbo, and then handed him a few bills, telling him to take home a bouquet of flowers to his wife.

At four thirty, I happily bought bartender Duke, a bottle of his favorite whiskey.

Four forty-five, Duke told me a snow plow would be by to help plow a path for me to the Montana border.

By five-fifteen, I was slowly making my way homeward.

At six forty-two, I was greeted with a welcome tail-wagging from a hungry dog.

Six forty-three, I hauled from my porch a frozen bag of poo to the garbage can.

Six fifty, I washed my hands and fixed myself a sandwich and chocolate milk.

At seven o'clock, I cracked open a computer file that I had waited impatiently all day to view—and by seven-ten, I wished I had never seen it at all.

The first few files were photos of small boys ranging from four to about eight, maybe ten. It was hard to tell. They were laughing, playing ball, eating ice-cream, swimming, generally having fun. The next photos were of naked boys, playing, running, laughing, swimming, and taking a bath. And then there were the photos of those same poor, unknowing boys in sexually explicit ways, photos of boys with Goodman—many, many horrible, horrific photos and videos of pale, somber or crying boys. There were more files, but I couldn't bear to open them. I slammed the laptop lid down, as the room began to swim. I don't remember how I got to the bathroom. I only remember losing my dinner.

When I could finally bring myself to stand and clean up, I was shaking so badly that I had to hold on to the wall until I could get to the bottle of brandy in the kitchen cupboard. I didn't bother pouring it. I just kept taking little sips until my knees and hands quit shaking.

Only then did I pour a glass. I was aware of the irony that Goodman had been dead only weeks but was still driving me to drink. I took a long gulp from the glass. My tears began to fall as I thought of those beautiful, sweet, little boys. What was I going to do with this ghastly information?

Several moments later, I realized that I had been herded over to the couch by Blue. The dog laid his head in my lap and looked up at me, worried and expectantly. I patted his head, moved him over, and cried myself to sleep.

I slept fitfully, feeling the growing anger and hatred for Goodman even in my dreams.

Nine-thirty, I rose from the couch, walked to the computer, and yanked the thumb-drive from the lap-top. I couldn't stand to think of that dirty thing touching my computer. But what was I to do with it? Even now as I stood with it in my hand, I felt dirty, maybe even ashamed, for having seen some of it. I didn't want it to even be near me. But what should I do with it?

And then I had an idea, all the while my mind reeled as I busied myself. I wondered why Seth had given this to me. What did he think I was to learn about the murder?

I grabbed a zip-lock baggie and placed the thumb-drive in it.

Was Goodman molesting Seth? No, these were small boys. Josh killed him because—I couldn't think of a because. It didn't make sense.

I slipped on my boots.

Had he molested Seth, his own son, when he was younger? Had he molested Josh as well? Is that what this was about?

I threw my coat on.

Were Josh and Seth blackmailing Goodman? No, maybe Josh, but Seth knew where his dad kept the money; he could have taken it at any time.

I opened my door and walked down the porch steps.

Obviously, Josh was upset with something. You don't just stab someone with a fire poker just because. Does one?

I walked over to Mrs. Bixby's house.

Okay, so Josh was angry. Did he do it because he felt angry and violated? Depressed, maybe high on something?

I tip-toed up the steps to Mrs. Bixby's front porch.

Why kidnap Seth? If he knocked Seth out, why would he not just leave him there with his dad and run instead of waiting until Seth woke up? Maybe for the money? Again, the pieces didn't fit.

I began to dig in a large flower pot that Mrs. Bixby kept on her porch—okay chipped at the frozen dirt was more like it.

I remembered then that everything had been wiped down after the murder. Why would they do that? Who was smart enough to think of that? Was it Seth? Jennifer had wiped down the fire poker, but I figured someone else had already done that before she touched it. Why would Seth give me this thumb-drive if he were going to implicate himself? Was it remorse?

I checked the baggie to be sure it was closed tight.

Feeling the weight of the thumb-drive, I had a memory flash of the night we were at Goodman's. When we were leaving, I remembered trying to find something that would scare or make him think we had something on him. Make him as mad as we were at him. I remembered holding a breath mint container in my hand to resemble a thumb-drive. I remembered now, the horrified look on his face and his muffled swearing behind the duct tape. It made me smile. I fished the thumb-drive out of the baggie and held it in my hand the way I did the pack of gum that night. Then, with a renewed respect for the thumb-drive—but just barely—I thought, this is what he thought I had. This is what is going to bring him down. This is going to tell everyone who killed him.

I started to put the thumb-drive back into the baggie, when I heard voices.

"I don't know, you bastard," came a scream from inside Mrs. Bixby's house. "I told you I don't know."

I slid to the porch floor and crawled close enough to her picture window to see in. I heard a sickly thwack sound, and another scream, and crying. Careening my head around to the left I saw Mrs. Bixby, bleeding, and tied to a dining room chair, where a man slapped her once more with the butt of a gun. My heart lurched. I squinted my eyes once more to filter the light. Oh, my dear lord . . . could it be? I squinted harder, rubbed my eyes and looked again. It was unmistakably Anthony Rizzo.

At nine forty-three, I ran for my Glock.

Chapter 27 - Olivia Hope

I recovered the Glock. Moving with rote action, I did the lock and load. The next thing I knew, I was knocking on Mrs. Bixby's door. There was silence beyond the heavy door. I knocked again. Had he taken her somewhere? There was a slight movement of the curtain, and then Mrs. Bixby's frightened face peered through.

"It's her!" I heard her say with a strained voice mixed with worry.

I heard some scuffling, moans and yelps and finally Anthony Rizzo showed his face. As the door slid open, I had a burst of adrenaline that left me feeling elated, alive and fearless. My vision was keenly focused and steady as I looked down the barrel of my gun pointed into Anthony's surprised, wide eyes.

"Hello, Anthony. Nice of you to make my day," I greeted him, sounding like Clint Eastwood in Dirty Harry. I backed him up into the foyer and kicked the door shut behind me.

"Hands above your head," I said as I used the gun to back him up.

"Shoot him! Don't just stand there, shoooot him," Mrs. Bixby screamed.

I reflexively took a quick look toward her. Anthony had tied her to the chair again. My glance was only a split second, but that was just enough time for him to turn his gun on her. "Put your gun down. or she's dead."

"Ohoooo, no, no, noooo, don't shoot, no, no, no! You can't do this to me. She's the one you want, take her . . ." she continued to scream. Her tirade was so shrill and obnoxious that I shouted back at her.

"Shut up," Anthony and I yelled in unison. Anthony pulled back the hammer and pressed his gun into the back of her head. That shut her up.

We were at a stalemate. I knew he'd have no problem killing her.

I slowly lowered my gun down on to the floor.

"Slide it over here with your foot," he said.

Mrs. Bixby began another shrill wail. Anthony smacked her so hard with the butt of his gun that it knocked her over backward. I heard a sickly crack when she hit the floor. I was sure she'd be out for a while—if she ever woke up again. Blood pooled around her head. I felt responsible for this poor woman lying on the floor. I needed to kill that son-of-a-bitch, for her and a hundred other women, even if it meant I went down, too. One might ask how I was going to do that, since I'd just slid my only weapon over to an insane killer. But then, I had revenge on my side. And, I had the advantage of surprise, because I wasn't the same timid little girl he remembered. Maybe I'd become a little insane, too—all of that makes for hell of a motive.

He waved me over to sit in one of the dining room chairs. I stared at him, refusing to budge. He was the same Anthony all right, same chiseled, good looks, dark, wavy hair, dark eyes, and dark, suntanned skin. He wore an expensive, tailored, charcoal suit with a periwinkle shirt that accented his beautiful eyes. He was graying at the temples, and his skin looked healthy, like he'd been to the Bahamas or somewhere in the sun. He and Demetri had looked a lot alike. Anthony was older but his nose was bigger and longer, than Demetri's. If I'd met him in a restaurant, and he had possessed the same charisma and charm as his brother had, I probably would have fallen for him. But as my mother used to say, the devil is a good-looking man, too. Yes, a little older, but this was Anthony Rizzo, the devil in angels clothing. Yes, I remembered him, the same man who worked with Demetri to traffic drugs and humans—and would kill anyone who got in their way.

"What the hell are you doing here?" I asked.

"I saw you had your hand in yet another murder, another Good-man, no less." He clucked at his own pun. "You are too stupid to stay out of the newspapers. You know, flashing your face here and there."

"Yeah, I figured that's how you found out I was in Libby. But why are you here at Mrs. Bixby's house?"

"This is your house," he boomed. "Don't play stupid with me."

"What? What makes you think this is my house?"

"You always loved opulence, your flashy this and that. You're just idiot enough to light your house up like the Taj Mahal at Christmas. So much so, I needed sunglasses to get out of my car—in the dark! And your maid here, Mrs. Bixby—ha! I don't think she likes you so much."

"Mrs. Bixby my maid? You are a funny guy." I was thoroughly confused . . . and then it hit me. Anthony Rizzo was never the sharpest tool in the shed. I'd forgotten that. I began to laugh as the thought of him coming to Mrs. Bixby's house, and my maid, of all things. No wonder she was so willing to give me up. At that, I began to laugh until nervous tears ran down my cheeks. All the while he kept yelling for me to shut up, ". . . stop laughing…" and the more he yelled the harder I laughed.

"You so deserve what you are about to get."

When I finally caught my breath, I said, "Yeah, yeah, okay. But before you kill me, tell me why I deserve to be killed for protecting my child and a whole lot of women in a trafficking container headed for god knows what in some foreign country. How can you really believe that I am the bad guy here?"

"Women are whores!" he bellowed. "Like you. You were all over Demetri like a fly on shit. 'Oh, Demetri, I love you so much! Let's go fuck,'" he said in a little girly voice.

"I never said that. That's disgusting."

"Okay, let's see," he said, again with the girly voice, "Want to go tickle our fancies?"

Okay, I may have said that. "Well, in my defense, we were a young married couple in love. That's what people do when they are in love."

"Ha, Demetri wasn't in love with you. He had too many other women to train into the service. He kept you in the penthouse because you needed that extra training. He didn't give a rat's ass about you. Manny Carbone performed the marriage service. He wasn't ordained; he was the truck driver who delivered our goods." He laughed, "You thought you were really married?"

"Yeah, . . . Okay, well, now I know. But I want to know how you knew all of this. Wait, were you there?"

A chill ran up my spine and I shivered. "Gross! Watching us?"

He licked his lips and nodded with a smirk that gave me another reason to want to kill him.

He shook his head, "You see, women are only good for one thing—sex. You, bitch, brought down a whole shit storm of grief upon yourself the day you," he paused. "Well, let me count the atrocities. One, you killed my brother. Two, you sank our transport business, which cost us millions. Three, you brought the authorities to the family business and that shut us down—that really hurt. Four, I had to spend a whole month in prison after you wagged your tongue. Five, my father grieved every day and died without the revenge he deserved to get. You killed his youngest son, my baby brother. I promised him on his death bed that I would find you and take pleasure in making your death a slow and painful one. The list could go on, of course, but I'd rather get on with the business of making your last moments—shall we say, memorable?"

"Pffft, you spent one lousy month in jail? Really? That was all you spent in jail for ruining hundreds of young women's lives? Sending them into a fate worse than death?"

"Eh, technicalities. And you're right, it's not like we killed them—although some died I guess, not sure what happened—yeah, lost some big bucks there—and, that makes number six. Which, of course, is your fault, too. So, NO! We were giving them jobs. They were whores. They liked the business of sex."

"Yeah, they liked it so much that you had to kidnap, drug, rape and sell them! Do you really think you are a good man? And don't you think I haven't suffered? What about the baby Demetri killed, my baby, his baby, our baby?" At this point, I was hoping beyond hope that my Emma was still alive, at least that thought made it bearable to go down that line of reasoning.

"See how stupid you are. It's obvious! She came from a whore, she'd be a whore, too! Besides, do you know how much my people are willing to pay for children in the trade?"

The conversation was pointless. There was the proof that you can't reason with a lunatic.

I looked over at Mrs. Bixby. She was still out cold. I didn't know if that was a good or a bad thing. Seeing how peaceful she looked, I thought it could be the one thing that was keeping her alive. I figured her to be in her late fifties. Her nice figure, from a distance, made her look young. And she was a pretty woman, too. She always had her make-up on perfectly, her 1960's coif neatly in place. It was the permanent scowl she wore that made her look ugly, mean and old. I noticed her hair had a fresh look to it. She probably had just come from her weekly hair appointment before all of this came down, but now her platinum blond, back-combed hair was drenched in bright-red blood. She definitely wasn't going to be happy with me. She'd probably shoot me, herself.

"Look, Anthony. I'm the one you want to kill. Before we get the show started, could I check to see if Mrs. Bixby is still alive?"

"Bitch," said Anthony.

At first I thought he was talking to me, but when I looked up at him, he was looking at her. And in that split seconded, I made my move.

I feigned a slip-trip and fall that I could probably only perform once in my life. Thank god, it was a flawless performance. I flew over an ottoman and had enough momentum to tuck, roll, clutch the thing and bring it up to knock the gun out of Anthony's hand. I brought the stool down hard. The gun flew. I pulled the stool up again and shoved. Anthony fell to the floor. The gun had landed over by Mrs. Bixby.

Anthony was stronger and a little quicker. I had a hard time reaching for the gun while I sat on his sorry ass, pinning him to the floor. We scuffled some more. Then he threw me to the floor to sit on my sorry ass. But, we were closer to the gun. He had his hands on my throat. We struggled awhile until he clubbed me hard on the side of my head with something like a glass bowl. My vision faded for a moment and his grip let up just a bit until I could clasp my hands and brought them up through his arms breaking his hold on my neck. My arms spread wide, and when my right hand hit the floor, I wiggled the gun into my fingers, brought it up and fired straight up into Anthony's liver and through his heart.

"Bitch," Anthony whispered. That time he was speaking to me.

He slumped over, pinning me to the floor. My adrenalin spent, I was too weak to roll him off. I closed my eyes. I had no idea how long I laid there. I gathered my thoughts, figuring out what to do next. But it all was quite simple—get help for Mrs. Bixby, and convince Rand Dubois that I didn't make killing a habit.

I finally struggled out from under Anthony's body. When I stood, the room began to tilt. I looked over at

Mrs. Bixby, and my body followed my eyesight. I fell to the floor beside her. I checked her pulse; it was thready at best. Fueled by adrenalin once again, but still unstable. I searched for the phone and dialed the number that was becoming all too familiar.

"Rand Dubois, how can I help you," said the voice.

"Mr. Dubois, this is Olivia Hope," I wanted to sound calm and in control, but it came out breathy and scared.

"Olivia!"

I didn't answer.

"Well, what do you want now? Have you got a fire caused by a burning Christmas tree? Or, have you been drinking and need another ride home, eh?"

"No," I whispered. But his insult brought me around to reality, like a slap in the face. I suppose I should have been thankful.

"Well, what then, for god sake?"

"I need you to send an ambulance to Mrs. Bixby's house. And . . ." I was trying to get my breath as the room began spinning again. "And I need you to come. Come right now, please?"

"What the hell is going on, Olivia, what have you done? What happened?"

I licked my dry lips before I spoke. "One of my skeletons just fell out of the closet."

Chapter 28 - Olivia Hope

"Olivia, please stop talking in code and tell me what's going on? What skeleton," asked Dubois, the very irritated detective.

"Damnit, Dubois," said I, the equally irritated, but weak, Olivia. "Get an ambulance over here to Mrs. Bixby's ASAP. And get your ass over here so I can tell you about the man I just killed."

I listened to the annoying tick-tock of Mrs. Bixby's grandfather clock. Tick-tock, tick-tock, tick-tock. "Don't go anywhere," Dubois said. As if I had anywhere to run. "Don't talk to anyone until I get there," he added, as if I had anyone to talk to.

Tick-Tock.

I held Mrs. Bixby's hand, lightly stroking her forehead every so often, saying soothing words, urging her to wake up. Tick-tock, tick-tock, was the only response.

Tick-tock.

How long had it been since I called?

Tick-tock.

I heard a siren in the distance growing louder.

Tick-tock.

It felt like hours passing with each Tick...tock.

The ambulance finally arrived. Tick-tock. There was a knock at the door, and then the door flew open.

Tick-tock.

"About time you guys got here!" I said. My head was spinning again. A headache pounded my skull.

"Ah, only six minutes, so . . ." said an EMT, as he bent down beside Anthony's body. I heard someone quietly say, "Holy shit, what the hell happened here?"

"Over here boys, that one's a gonner," I heard myself say. But I hadn't realized there was already an EMT taking over my position with Mrs. Bixby.

With that, I stood and walked to the window. I was cold and shaking badly. I saw that Dubois had arrived and was talking, pointing and giving orders. There were men already staking out the perimeter of the house to hold gawkers back.

I felt such relief at seeing Dubois. I stumbled outside to meet him. But, nausea took its hold on me, and, by the time I got to the bottom of the steps, I began to vomit, on Dubois's shoes, and then everything went black—tick-tock.

"Get an EMT out here, NOW!" I heard someone shout. My next memory was me lying on Mrs. Bixby's couch with a very worried Dubois sitting beside me, his face hovering above mine. I reached out and caressed his face with the palm of my hand. Okay, maybe that was a dream, because when I finally opened my eyes, Mr. Dubois sat in a chair with his elbows resting on the arms, restless, tented fingers tapping together. He leaned forward and looked at me like I'd just crapped on his favorite carpet.

"Could you get Ms. Hope a cup of coffee, please," Dubois said to someone standing behind the couch.

"Yes, sir," said an obedient minion.

I heard the familiar gurgle coming from the kitchen. Damn, even Mrs. Bixby had a Keurig. "Could you put some creamer in it, too, please," I croaked toward the kitchen door.

A buff, good looking twenty-something year old handed me a heavenly cup of coffee. Mmm, French Roast with Italian Cream. Sweet. I said my thanks and, perhaps my gaze lingered a little too long, as Dubois cleared his throat, evidently several times, before I realized he was trying to get my attention.

"Sorry, head's a little fuzzy," I said, and winced when I felt the goose egg that took up a bit of real estate on the side of my head.

"Come sit at the table," Dubois said. "Here is some toast your boyfriend here made for you," he nodded toward the young EMT. "We need to keep you awake for a while; you've probably got a concussion. And, since we're going to be here for some time, you're gonna need something in your system. You've got a lot of explaining to do."

I stood and became woozy again. The EMT helped me to the table. They'd already taken Mrs. Bixby away. That calmed me some. Someone handed me an ice bag and gave instructions on intermittent placement. Then he explained that I was soon to have a monster headache—a little late for that news flash—but take no aspirin. I'd feel very sleepy, too, but don't sleep.

"Well, aren't' you Mr. Sunshine," I said as he slipped my jacket over my shoulders and slid a plate of toast with orange marmalade in my direction.

Dubois slipped off his jacket and hung it on the back of a chair beside mine. "I got a feeling this is going to be a long conversation so I'm going to get a cup of coffee, too. I'll be right back."

Mr. Sunshine, headed for the door and said he'd check on me later. At least he had the decency to send me a wink from across the room before he left. I tried to smile but it hurt, probably looked more like I'd snarled.

I was freezing and shaking, so I pulled on my jacket and slammed my cold hands into the pockets to warm them. I felt the thumb drive. I'd forgotten all about the thumb drive! What was I going to do with it now? I had to think of something, and quickly. If they took me to jail, I'd be in real trouble if they found that on me. If I didn't do time for murder, I'd spend plenty of time for possession of child pornography!

I heard the final hiss of the Keurig. I looked around the room but realized I wouldn't be able to get to the bookshelf and back in my chair before Dubois returned. Besides, who knew when I'd be able to get back to Mrs. Bixby's to retrieve it. So, without another thought, I wiped the thumb drive on my pants to rid finger prints, and slipped it into Dubois's coat pocket. There, I thought, let him figure out that mystery. My head pounded with each beat of my heart. I was resting my head in my hands when he returned. I lifted my eyes to look at him.

"Mmm, gotta get me one of those Keurig thingies. This is the best cup of coffee I've had since I've started on the Goodman case," said Dubois, reveling in the steaming aroma of the French Roast. He sobered up when he looked at me. "What are you looking at?"

"What?" I croaked.

"You look like you just swallowed a canary!"

"Well, what do you expect? I probably did, since there are a lot foul things going on around here."

"Ha, ha," he said humorlessly, and sat down across from me. "Start talking. Who was this Anthony guy and why did you murder him?"

"Hey, it was self-defense."

"That blood-soaked shirt you're wearing tells a different story. And why should I believe you?"

"Because, Anthony was a thug, a mafia man. A fucking kidnapping, human trafficking, raping, murdering, bastard," I sighed deeply, ". . . and my brother-in-law."

"Brother-in-law," he nodded. "Of course, and where's your husband?"

"Yeah, Demetri," I puffed my cheeks and exhaled, "He's dead. I killed him."

Dubois cocked an eyebrow.

"What? It was self-defense."

"Again, why should I believe you? I mean, you are a known liar, a drunk, a crazy, pistol-packing mama, a loan shark in your own right, you own a dog that's not licensed, you seem to have lousy taste in men and Christmas trees. For the love of god! You have a guy who delivers you dog poop, eh? And, oh yeah, now we're looking at your involvement with three murders!"

"Three? Are you talking about Goodman, too? I did not kill him, although maybe I should have because he'd have been in good company with Demetri and Anthony. And I just told you that I killed Demetri and Anthony in self-defense. Damn it, Demetri was the leader of that low-life pack of human trafficking devils."

"Wow, like I said, you really do know how to pick

'em. You better start at the beginning, but wait." He stood up again shaking his head. "I wonder if Mrs. Bixby has anything to spice up this coffee—."

He left the room and returned with a bottle of Cognac, poured some in his coffee and a glass, then slid the glass to me. I looked at the bottle, Remy Martin. "Wow, Mrs. Bixby, who knew?" I said, impressed. "Are you sure you want me, a known drunk, to partake in this alcoholic beverage?"

Dubois shrugged, "You look like you need a little something to help take the edge off. Might help with the headache, too."

It didn't, but I gladly took it just to keep my hands from shaking.

With that, I began telling the story I'd told Idaho only the day before. Had it only been a day? It seemed like centuries, and I never in a million years thought I'd have to tell Dubois my deepest, darkest secrets. He listened politely enough. He only asked questions for clarification. I left out the parts where I was so madly in love that I practically threw myself at Demetri.

When I started talking about feelings or drifting off track, Dubois would reel me back in with, "Yeah, right. Get to the point." I longed for Idaho's wit. But in Dubois's defense, he was working an investigation—that I invited him to. Oh, he had his tape recorder purring away, too. At least I didn't have to tell my story in front of a couple other cops in an interrogation room with bright lights, getting the good-cop-bad-cop run. And they certainly wouldn't have served me cognac.

I forged on. I couldn't figure out Dubois though. When I got to the parts about my daughter, he didn't bat an eye, and I thought what a cold, hard bastard. Didn't he understand the deep love a mother has for her child, that primal instinct to protect her young at whatever cost? He just sat there with arms folded across his chest and an unchanging expression.

I finally got to the part about me being in the witness protection program and how Anthony Rizzo saw my picture on the front page of that stupid, news article about Goodman. I lamented about Carol Cripes, a gossip-hungry reporter who can't get her facts right, and added that she was going to get her due one day because karma's an evil bitch. And why Dubois chose that moment to show he might be a little bit human, I'll never know.

"I know, right?" he said, siting forward. "That's what I keep telling Sheriff Bishop." He sat back shaking his head.

Huh.

I took another gulp of cognac.

I explained the events of the evening, and how it came to blows with poor Mrs. Bixby. I asked about her.

"She's going to be fine. They're going to keep her in the hospital for a while. Also, it's a crime scene yet again, thanks to you. Her sister's flying in tomorrow to pick her up. It seems her hair padded her fall. In fact, you probably have a concussion to rival hers," he chuckled.

I gave him the stink-eye. "What about all of that blood? I thought she was dying."

"Head wounds bleed a lot. They usually look worse than they are. It's the internal bleeding they want to keep an eye on. Now, please, continue."

I went on to tell him about the conversation I had with Anthony before we struggled. How he had made the promise to avenge me for his brother and father. And then I told him in detail about my smooth James Bond action with the footstool, which garnered the stoic look again. He wasn't as impressed as I was, and when I finished with the moment when I called the ambulance, I said, "So that's what happened."

He just sat there. Probably for a good five minutes. I fidgeted and pulled lint off my jacket. Tick-tock. Tick-tock. Tick-tock.

My head pounded, and it felt like the toast I ate was ready to come back for another round. I put my head in my hands and said, "Oh, for the love of god, would you please say something?"

"Why didn't you call 911 before you came back over here with your fancy gun?"

"I . . . I," I stammered and shrugged. "I was on the fly, I simply reacted and didn't really think of it in the moment." Then Dubois gave me the stink-eye. I flinched because, although I knew I should have called 911, I didn't. If I were to be honest, in a normal—if there ever is a normal emergency—I probably would have stopped to dial 911 first.

But this was Anthony Rizzo! I had dreamed for years about putting a bullet in him. I always thought it would be glorious. I just knew I'd feel that sweet feeling of righting a horrible wrong. But somehow, I felt worse about everything. In fact, I felt like I had just sunk to that bastard's level, and to make matters worse, I put Mrs. Bixby's life on the line as well—stupid, stupid move.

"Damn that fucking Anthony."

Dubois nodded and said, as if he'd read my mind, "Revenge is never as sweet as we think it will be." And then he looked at me with—what, sympathy? "Trust me, I know that sour taste."

Sherriff Bishop entered at that moment, and Dubois turned off the recorder.

"Thank you," Dubois said.

"What the hell for?" I asked.

"For finally telling me the truth," and then to Bishop, he said, "Lock her up."

Chapter 29 - Olivia Hope

"Wait! What?" I said, jumping up from my chair, knocking it over backwards. "Damnit, Dubois, you said you believed me! You just thanked me for telling you the truth. Why in god's name are you throwing me in jail? This was self-defense. I told you, I told you all of it!" I wailed on.

Sheriff Bishop stared at me wide-eyed, and then his eyes scoured the room full of blood—blood on the floor where Mrs. Bixby had lain, and Anthony. I watched his eyes trail back to the blood on my sweater and coat, and probably my face and hair, too. A horrible, sour look froze on his face.

"This little lady did all that?" he said, pointing at the floor, still trying to take it all in. And then he reached for his handcuffs and leveled his eyes on me once more. "It'd be my pleasure to take her in."

"Dubois, please," I said, as Bishop put the cuffs on, while reading me my rights. I started to sound whiney, like a little kid. I hated it—so much for valor and strength.

"I'll explain this later, Bishop," Dubois said. He turned to me and put his hands on my shoulders. "Stop sniveling and listen to me," he said.

It was then I realized I was crying, and it was only adding pressure to my already aching head.

"I'm taking you in to protect you for your own

damn good. Do you really think, after all you have told me, I'd let you just go back to your house and watch a movie and eat ice cream or whatever you do before bed? I'd be willing to bet that Anthony Rizzo was smart enough to have back-up."

I was beginning to see his point. Mafia usually don't travel alone. "I . . . I could go over to Idaho's house for the night."

"Oh, right. And put her in danger, too? If what you told me is true, I think Anthony has help. Hell, I'm not even comfortable standing next to you right now for fear there's a bullet with my name on it, too. We are taking you in and that's all there is to it."

To Bishop he said, "Quickly, get her in the car and make her lay down in the back. I'm going to take a couple of guys and canvas the area to see if anyone else is out there."

"Wait a minute," Dubois said, turning back to me. "Have you told anyone else about being in the witness protection program?"

I nodded.

"Let me guess. Idaho?"

I nodded again.

"Damn it," he said. "I'll have to bring her in, too. Well, at least you won't be lonely in that cell."

Dubois disappeared for a moment and returned with a pillow case. "Olivia, I'm going to put this over your head so that, if there is anyone out there gunning for you, they won't be sure who we are bringing out. Are you okay with that?"

I nodded, and he slipped the cover over my head, leaving just my face exposed. He asked Sheriff Bishop to give him his coat. Bishop is a big man with a big coat. Dubois wrapped it around my shoulders neatly tucking in my long hair, it was nice and warm. "Now, this is going to look like we've just taken someone into custody but from a distance, on-lookers won't know if you are male or female, do you understand?"

I felt helpless, but I said 'yes'.

To Sheriff Bishop he said, "Wait a few minutes at the back door when you get to the facility. I'll have Idaho delivered to you in just a few minutes."

"But why do you have to bring Idaho into this? This doesn't concern her," I said.

"Hey, you're the one who blabbed to her about the WitSec Program. This is for her protection, too." With that, he pulled out his cell phone and made the order to pick up Idaho and take her directly to the jail. Just like that. Do not pass go and do not collect $200 dollars. I'd bet the man plays a mean game of Monopoly.

To Bishop he said, "You and I will be the ONLY ones who know where they are going. Is that understood by you two?"

Bishop and I said yes, in unison.

"Good. Now Bishop, when Idaho arrives, I want you to take the two of them and lock them in the cell. Olivia will tell you all about what happened here tonight. Meanwhile, I'll check out the area and meet you in a couple of hours." He stepped behind me and checked my hand-cuffs, and then spun me around. He had a goofy kind of grin on his face.

"Oh, now who looks like they swallowed the canary," I said, parroting his earlier words.

He nodded. His smile didn't fade as he said, "That's

because I just did." He pulled the pillowcase over my face, and ordered Bishop to get me the hell out of there.

Although it was a short ride to the jail, I was terribly nauseated by the time we got there. Bishop didn't talk much except to make sure I kept my head down.

True to Dubois's word, another deputy pulled up beside us a minute after we arrived.

Bishop helped me out of the car. I heard the other doors open on the vehicle next to us. Bishop said he'd handle the "perps" from there. I heard a muffled, "Yes, sir." And the other vehicle drove away.

Bishop guided us through a door, down a long hallway, and into an elevator. I could feel we were going down but I couldn't tell how far. All I saw from under my hood was tips of fuzzy bunny slippers. I imagined that Idaho might be panicked, being taken into custody with a bag placed over her head. I was quite sure no one explained anything to her.

"Geez, Idaho. You have bunny slippers. And they're really pink!"

"Olivia? Is that you? What's happening?" Yeah, she was stressed.

"Quiet! Both of you," ordered Bishop.

Bishop guided us around a few more corners and then I heard electronic whirring as several doors clicked open and then shut behind us. We were secluded. Once we were in the cell and I heard the locks click, Bishop pulled off our hoods and then unlocked our hand-cuffs.

"Why the hand-cuffs, Bishop?" I asked, rubbing blood back into my wrists.

"Protocol," he shrugged.

Idaho blanched when she saw my blood-soaked clothing. "Oh, my god, what the hell did you do?"

"That's what I want to know," growled Bishop.

"Are you okay?" Idaho asked, while reaching out to me checking for wounds.

"Yes, I'm fine."

"Oh, thank god! Then what happened?"

"I shot and killed Anthony Rizzo."

"Yes!" And then we did a high five.

"And that's a good thing?" Bishop asked.

"Oh yeah," Idaho and I said in unison.

"Mind if I join in on your little party here?" Bishop sniffed. "And you better start from the beginning because, right now, I don't know whether to give you a medal of honor or book your asses."

I looked around the tiny quarters. The cell smelled of stale air and Pine-sol. In one corner, there was only one single bed with an army blanket and a tiny pillow. In the other corner was a tiny stainless steel sink and toilet. It was dank and dark. I shivered and said, "It stinks in here."

"Welcome to the esteemed Lincoln County hotel. Sit your asses down," barked Bishop.

Idaho and I obediently sat on the bed.

"I'm kinda hungry, could we order out for pizza?" asked Idaho.

"Yeah, right," said Bishop. "Right after the butler brings you your nighty-night tea." He reached under the bed and pulled out a metal tray, positioned it across the toilet seat and sat down. "Let's get this show started, shall we?"

And so, for the third time in two days I began my

story once again—with Idaho's help this time, interjecting things like, "Yeah, she was only 16..." Or, "Oh, and tell him how much money you made making those puppets . . ." and, "Oh, yeah, tell him about Nurse Ratched."

Bishop would roll his eyes and say, "Okay, ladies, let's get back on track." Bishop didn't have a recorder, but he took notes on a little spiral note pad—and swore when he ran out of paper.

Idaho was impressed when I described my move that brought Anthony down. Sheriff Bishop, not so much.

By the time I finished my debriefing with the Sheriff, I was physically and mentally spent. I was thankful when Dubois arrived and brought changes of clothes for both Idaho and myself. I was a little unnerved to think of Dubois picking out my lacy underwear, but I was too tired to really care. He threw each of us a sack of towels and wash cloths, soap, toothbrushes, tooth paste, the works. He planned well. Alan followed behind him, carrying a fold up cot and a couple of sleeping bags. Idaho brushed a kiss on his cheek when he set it down. He beamed without embarrassment.

I looked to Dubois and tilted my head toward Alan, "He knows? I thought we weren't to tell anyone else?" I chided.

"He knows all he needs to know."

"Ah, weaseled it out of you, huh."

He shrugged and mumbled something about Alan being worried about Idaho.

Alan and Idaho had their heads bent together,

whispering, and so did Sheriff Bishop and Dubois. Finally, Dubois gave a curt nod in my direction and said, "Okay, listen up you two. Here's what's going to happen next. You finish the night out here. But I have no idea how long you're going to have to stay. I need to make some phone calls and run red-tape, which could take a while. Any meals you get will be delivered by me or Sheriff Bishop. If you see or hear anyone but the two of us down here, and that includes Alan, you immediately push this button."

Dubois handed me a small beeper-like thing.

"Oh, that's like those beepers you get at restaurants," said Idaho.

"Yeah, and don't get any ideas about beating someone to death with your tin cup," said Dubois, pointedly, at me. "No heroics, do you hear me? You are in some serious shit, here and we all need to be vigilant. Got it?" His voice echoed down the hall as if to emphasize the danger. He didn't have to. I knew it all too well.

"Do I get my gun back?" I asked in a small voice.

He glared at me for a long moment, and with a scowl, he finally said, "Here's my gun. Yours is in evidence. I trust you won't shoot me or Bishop—or Idaho?"

I nodded meekly.

"Okay, you two get some sleep. I'll bring breakfast."

"And a newspaper?" I asked.

"Oh, whatever," he said.

"I'll go check on Mrs. Bixby," said Bishop. "Got a feeling she's gonna be a little pissed when she wakes up.

Maybe I can do some reconnaissance before the local newsies get to her." We all watched him walk down the hall until the darkness devoured him.

"So, did you find an accomplice out there?" I asked, breaking the silence.

Dubois nodded.

My heart stopped. "You did? What did he have to say?"

"Nothing."

"What do you mean?"

"Well, let's just say he won't be saying much of anything ever again."

"You mean you—"

"Not my finest hour," he said. "Now, I need to know who your WitSec contact is. Do you have that information?"

When I entered the Witness Security Program (WitSec) I was presented with a contact agent in the event I was ever in trouble. I'm also supposed to check in with him at least once a quarter to give him a report of what's going on with my life. I now had something damning to report and feared that I may be relocated once more. I had the information all right. I've known it by heart since the beginning of my new life. I gave Dubois the name, contact number and code word as a deep sorrow filled my heart.

As a matter of protection when something like this happens, WitSec will relocate their charge and, once again, I'd have to start a new life. I wondered, where will I go next? Who will I be? What will I do? I'll never see Idaho or my other friends again. Or my students. And what will happen to, Blue? My stomach churned. I watched Dubois and Alan leave in a blur of my silent tears.

"Well," said Idaho rubbing her hands together. "This is quite the sleepover. Pretty exciting. Isn't it?" Her expression changed when she looked at me. "Oh, Olivia. I can't imagine what you went through tonight."

I began to cry silently again. I felt like I was crashing, I began to shake violently. Idaho grabbed the army blanket, wrapped me up, and held me in her arms while cooing that everything was going to be all right—I was safe. But her words only made me sob harder, because I knew better.

Chapter 30
Shoot Out at the Bixby Corral

By: Carol Cripes, Staff Reporter

A shoot-out ensued at Arlene Bixby's home last evening as Sheriff Bishop and his posse chased, shot and killed a young Indian man, who the sheriff claimed was an alleged sniper. The victim was 23-year-old Aadi Abhoy, the son of Abhijit and Abha Abhoy, who relocated to Eureka, Montana, from east India fifteen years ago. Aadi Abhoy, a graduate from Eureka High School, served three years in Afghanistan as a front-line foot soldier, in the Armed Forces, fighting for our country. He was honored and loved by many.

The 911 call came in at 10:48 p.m. The caller asked for an ambulance and specifically asked for Rand Dubois, a private consultant to Sheriff Bishop, to come to the scene. When the ambulance arrived, they found Olivia Hope, a next-door neighbor, hovering over the unconscious Mrs. Bixby. Another unidentified man found in the home was shot and killed. Sources say that Hope broke into the home, and that she is the shooter of the dead man found in Bixby's home.

"We entered the home of Arlene Bixby and found she had been held against her will. We have no identity yet of the man who was shot. That's all I can say for

now," said Sheriff Bishop.

Olivia Hope is one of the suspects in the Ira Goodman case, the local philanthropist who was violently murdered several weeks ago. Neighbors agree that Hope and Bixby had their feuds in the past.

"I never talked to that Hope woman, but Arlene Bixby always said she was nothing but trouble," said neighbor Marlene Drake. "And now I believe her. How could she do such a thing to poor Mrs. Bixby—over what, a missing throw rug?"

Jack Garm, another neighbor, commented, "I haven't felt comfortable living in this neighborhood ever since that article came out about Ms. Hope's involvement with the Goodman murder. Gives me the heebie-jeebies—her living next to us. About time they lock her up. Seems like Sherriff Bishop's not doing his job lately."

It is unclear if Hope broke into the home and held Mrs. Bixby against her will, quarreled with her, and finally clubbed Bixby unconscious with her gun. The visiting, unidentified man may have tried to stop Hope when she shot him. With the sound of the shot, it is speculated that Abhoy came to check it out, and was there to help, when Bishop's posse shot and killed him.

The parents of young Abhoy were devastated by the news. "Aadi was always a sweet boy. He loved his role in the Army, and wanted to continue to protect this great country until medical issues occurred, which forced him out of the service," said Abhijit, Aadi's father.

Hope has been taken into custody and is unavailable for comment.

Bixby was admitted to the St. John's Hospital in

Libby with severe head wounds resulting in a concussion. She is in serious condition.

Services for Aadi Abhoy will be announced as soon as the final investigation reports are filed. In the meantime, you can send cards and donations to Holy Angels Catholic Church in Eureka, at 728 Alder St., 59917.

Chapter 31 - Rand Dubois

I knew something was amiss with Olivia Hope. Too many secrets, nothing seemed to mesh with her. Her past too squeaky clean, her moves evasive, her smiles disarming, her banter cunning, and her answers to questions, too vague—or downright lies. Yet, in some ways, she had a simple honesty about her, and depth—for a lack of a better word. Quite an enigma. I saw an undeniable compassion for others and a furious fight for life. I saw a world of hurt, agonizing pain, intelligence, strength and infuriating stubbornness—to a fault. So, learning that she was in the WitSec program was no surprise, and it's why I believed her story. Finally, she had told me the truth, and I was resolute to do my best to help her. But, how do you protect someone who's so stubborn and doesn't think they need your help? I wondered if I could keep her locked up long enough to finish the Goodman case without her meddling.

With all her intrigue, I knew she was involved somehow with the Goodman murder, too. I really didn't believe that she and her friends killed Goodman, but my gut told me they were involved. But, how did that fit into the scheme of things? Were the two men and/or killings connected? Was Goodman working for the mafia? Nothing had surfaced as far as that was concerned, except for Olivia's comment that "he'd have been in good company with Demetri and Anthony," the two mafia brothers. Or, did she just know things about him that entwined with Anthony Rizzo? I needed to dig deeper.

I couldn't sleep as these things continued to swirl in my brain. I was waiting for the butt-crack of dawn to make my phone call to Olivia's WitSec contact.

"Oh, to hell with the sunrise," I said to the pre-dawn, and dialed the number for Saul Jackson, Olivia's contact. It was about 6 a.m. on the east coast and I caught the man while he made his morning jog and, apparently, before his morning coffee. He was less than congenial and said that, if I wanted answers to anything, Olivia would need to call him. In the meantime, he would run a check on me. So, as politely as I could, without sleep and coffee, I said I'd have Olivia on the phone in a couple of hours. I'd let her sleep. What a nice guy I am.

I was getting my coffee from the vending machine when Alan and Sheriff Bishop showed up. Bishop slapped the morning newspaper in my hand.

"How can that woman deface my department and me with one lousy sentence," bemoaned Bishop. "I've been fielding calls about this for twenty minutes already, and it's not even 5 a.m. yet." He dourly moved on to his office as I began reading.

"Ah, Cripes," I sighed, "She's at it again. Someone needs to bind that tongue of hers." I read, while sipping my vending machine cappuccino, as Alan and I walked back to my desk.

"She really needs to get her facts right," I said. "She could sink Bishop in the next election with her venomous words. He doesn't deserve that. He is hard-working, and really cares about this community. This community needs him. We need to find a way to make her disappear."

Alan bobbed his head in agreement and said, "Want me to get some breakfast burritos for Idaho? Oh, and Olivia?" he asked.

"Sure," I said, with my nose buried in the newspaper. "Get some for all of us and save the receipt for reimbursement." It was true, Aadi Abhoy was a young military man, but what Cripes didn't know—or failed to report—is that he had had run-ins with the law before. She didn't report that his medical leave from the Army was emotional and mental in nature. He was even on the Isis watch list as he may have had terrorist connections. And how Anthony Rizzo connected with him, we may never know.

I replayed the night's horrible event in my head. There wasn't a posse of Bishop's men who chased Aadi Abhoy, only two deputies that followed footprints into the woods. They spotted him and called for me. We tracked him down to the river. When I saw him, I identified myself and ordered him to drop his weapon. He raised his rifle and aimed a laser beam at the center of my chest. I ducked, while firing a warning shot just in front of him. He'd been close enough to the river that the shot pierced the snow-covered ice where he stood, the ice broke, and he flipped over backwards into the ice-cold river. His heavy clothing pulled him underwater. Bishop's men found him minutes later down river, drowned. As I told Olivia, it wasn't my finest hour. Yes, he was only 23 years-old, only several years younger than Alan. The young man's parents were torn apart. I understood their devastation. This was a matter that would continue to haunt me.

Alan arrived with the burritos. Alan, Bishop and I gathered in the conference room to eat and debrief. I was to follow up with Olivia's contact and get that red-tape started and then make time for a nap. Bishop had a meeting with one of the parents from the high school, something concerning Goodman. And then he was going to interview Mrs. Bixby, as she was awake and ready to sing like a bird. We figured she could either be helpful with good information, or hurt us with more false accusations, knowing that Carol Cripes was suddenly Bixby's best friend—which led us to more discussion about Cripes's articles.

"What all did you say to her, Bishop?" I asked.

"Hey, you read exactly what I said, no less and no more. At least she got that right. I guess I should have been more specific as to who was holding Bixby hostage though."

"Why don't you go and just talk sense to her," said the naive son of mine. "I'm sure she'd understand how harmful her words can be. Want me to talk to her?"

Sheriff Bishop took a deep breath and flashed a wide smile, "Son," he said, "You are one very bright, young man."

Oh, here it goes, I thought, another buddy-buddy moment.

"You know, there are people in this world who you can talk to, who seem like the nicest, well-meaning people, talking truths, and rights, and God bless America. They look at you with feeling and understanding and they say 'Yes, yeah, sure, you betcha,' and then they turn around and use your well-meaning intentions, words and goodwill to bury you six feet deep.

"Well, son," Bishop continued. "One of those people is our Ms. Cripes. She has a way of taking our words, no matter what we say or do, mind you, and paints them on paper to look like we, your dad and me, are the devil incarnate. What she doesn't know, she makes up. And if you chose to talk to her for us, she'd take that opportunity, albeit in the name of 'Goodwill and the people's right to know' throwing in some sensationalism, to write our death warrants with your dick."

When I looked at Alan, his eyes were as big as saucers. And so were mine.

"All righty then," nodded Alan.

With that said, Alan reported he was spending a few hours at the library and then had to run a few errands. Errands, what errands? And off he went before I could ask.

"So, Bishop," I said, "Are you and the Mrs. going to have children some day? Because, you'd make a damn good dad."

"Don't get me started," he grumbled, as he exited stage left.

I picked up a couple of the burritos, coffee, orange juice and the newspaper and headed to the dungeon of Lincoln County.

I needn't worry that the two women were starving. They were still sound asleep. I woke them up and let myself into the cell.

"Oh, the breakfast burrito!" said a sleepy Idaho, and

reached out to receive it. I handed Olivia her breakfast and the newspaper.

"Hey! Someone cut a hole out of the front page," complained Olivia, her face framed in the open gap.

I shrugged, "Mice, what can I say. Bishop didn't pay the exterminator bill this month."

"But what if I missed the funnies?"

"Trust me, there was nothing funny in today's paper."

"Ah, Cripes," Olivia nodded. "What did she have to say?"

"As I said, there's nothing you need to read about yet."

I ignored her glare and said, "When you finish with your breakfast, I'm going to take you over to the showers, and then we'll find a secure spot for you to call Mr. Saul Surly-to-rise—he wasn't much interested in talking to me."

She put the paper down and sighed, "There's nothing else in the paper, Dubois. You managed to sensor a whole newspaper with one snip!"

"Well, small town, and it is the Cabinet Mountain News, so . . ."

"Yeah, Olivia, you wouldn't even get that much if Cripes didn't live vicariously through you," snorted Idaho.

"Glad I could provide you all with fabulous entertainment," mumbled Olivia, with a mouth full of burrito.

Once Olivia finished her meal, I lead her to the showers.

"Dubois, could you let Pamela, Lily and Maggie

know that things aren't as bad as Cripes might have portrayed? Please? They will be very upset and probably hound you anyway."

"Damn, call me Rand. Sounds like you're talking to my father. And I'm way ahead of you, kiddo. I'd planned to call them right after you talk to Mr. Happy."

"Thank you," she sighed.

We walked the rest of the way to a secluded room with a telephone. She paused for a long moment, then finally lifted the receiver and dialed the number.

"Hey, Saul, What's up? . . . Yeah, it's colder than a well-digger's bottom here. How's the wife and kids? . . ." Olivia giggled sweetly saying, "How cute. I bet you were proud of her."

After listening to more of the casual chit-chat, I motioned for her to get to the point. She frowned and held up her hand, waving me off.

Finally, after a few more familiar exchanges, she casually said, "Oh, you know the usual, boy meets girl. Girl finds out boy is a rat, girl kills rat . . . What? I did not club my neighbor!"

She looked at me sharply and mouthed silently, "What did you tell him?"

I shrugged, and she turned her back on me.

"No . . . no . . . and no!" There was a long pause, while she listened and then explained. "I did not do any of that. Okay, listen, a very horrible man named Ira Goodman was murdered. I did not, nor did my friends, kill him. We had given him money to invest our funds to supplement our retirement earnings. I guess because of that, detective, Rand Dubois," she said my name like it was a bad thing. "Thinks we had the perfect motive for killing him. All I've been trying to do is prove our innocence. There was a scene at Goodman's funeral service where he fell out of his casket—"

She paused, listening again, and then silently mouthing to me, "What the hell did you tell him?"

"What? Why does everyone think we dressed him in drag. . .. Yeah, well, just because he landed at our feet simply does not prove anything. Anyway, a stupid reporter snapped a picture and wrote a scathing article about my friends and me, and that's when Anthony saw my photo in the newspaper and came after me. He said he was avenging Demetri and his father's death. He thought that Mrs. Bixby was my maid, if you can imagine. The idiot got the wrong house. He tied up Mrs. Bixby, and he is the one who clubbed her, not me. And I have a concussion, too, if you care to know. . . Where did you hear that bullshit? . . . Oh, Cripes," she nodded. He must have read her the highlights of the article.

"Well, don't believe everything you read. That woman is journalistically challenged.

"What's that? Yeah, I knew that was coming, do you know where I'll be moved to? . . . Wow, does it have to be that soon?" she said quietly, slumping into a chair.

I felt a wave of pity for her. She would need to relocate once again.

". . . Yeah, he's okay. Hmm, a real teddy bear, but don't cross him or he'll throw you in his cell . . . Be nice to him, Saul . . . Okay, I'll tell him," she looked in my direction and winked. "Good-bye, Saul. Give those kids a hug and kiss for me, will you?" She was all smiles when she said that, and then hung up.

"Wait, I wanted to talk to him," I complained.

"He said he'd call you later. He's at his daughter's basketball game. Take me back now, please," she said sadly.

We said nothing more as I walked her to the shower and back to her cell. Idaho was asleep on her cot, softly snoring.

As I started to walk away, Olivia said, "Cripes did a real number on that last article—over the top even for her."

I nodded.

"I can take care of myself, Rand. I can handle anything Cripes throws my way."

"I know. I'm sorry, I just thought you had enough to deal with right now without reading a whole lot of bullshit. And, too, I should have known that Saul would have seen the article to ask you about it—my bad."

She nodded slowly. "Thanks for trying to watch out for me, Rand," she said softly. "But, please don't ever sensor my newspaper again." And with that, she lay down on her bed, curling into a fetal position, her cheeks glistening, wet with tears.

When I got back to my desk, I made the calls to Olivia's friends, doing damage control, putting out the fire that Cripes had set.

When I finally heard from Saul, he asked a few questions verifying the story from the newspaper, and what Olivia told him. I added a few more facts, and he seemed satisfied. He didn't say much to me, except that he and a colleague were catching an early flight and would arrive at the Spokane airport in the morning. He assured me we'd discuss things in detail when they arrived.

Chapter 32 - Rand Dubois

Saul Jackson and Agent Anna Romano arrived about 4:00 p.m. the next day. Saul looked like an older Harry Potter, with an untamable cowlick and the big, dark-rimmed glasses to boot. Ms. Romano looked like Angelina Jolie without the full lips. She wore her long, brown hair straight back in a ponytail that swung back and forth to distraction while she walked. She wore one of those tight pencil skirts and a cashmere sweater that nicely hugged her full bosom. Sheriff Bishop couldn't keep his bugged-out eyes off her—okay, maybe her pony tail wasn't the only distraction. I couldn't blame him; I was admiring, too. However, he followed her like a puppy, staring, and then he'd run up and fetch the door for her, quite disturbing—especially since there were three more doors to go.

We finally reached a comfortable conference room, where Alan had drinks and cookies ready. We settled in with cups of coffee, talked about the flight and drive into town from the Spokane airport, the weather, and where we would all go to dinner—suggested by Bishop.

Bishop and I briefed the two of them on the latest activities leading up to the death of Anthony Rizzo. As the minutes rolled by, Saul seemed to relax and was more congenial. Perhaps it was because Romano was like a drill sergeant, doing all the talking and demanding answers. Soon, I felt as if I was being interrogated. She drilled holes through my brain with her eyes, asking me again and again, why I couldn't save the young man I shot.

"I told you, he wouldn't stop when I identified myself. He put a beam on me, so I fired a warning shot. I didn't shoot him. He just happened to be standing on a chunk of ice that broke, and he fell into the river."

"Why didn't you pull him out?"

"He was wearing a heavy parka and boots, and the current was strong. He was sucked down into the water. Good God, his wet clothing alone must have weighed at least eighty/ninety pounds. He finally washed up down river about fifteen minutes later."

"We also told you the boy had mental issues," said Bishop. "He was kicked out of the U.S. Army. We're not sure how Mr. Rizzo found him, but it's my guess he was looking for a sharp shooter to help him kill Olivia. For Christ sake, he was even on the Isis watch list."

"Oh, and that makes it okay to shoot him," stated, not questioned, Romano.

"I didn't shoot him," I said once more, "And I think what Sheriff Bishop was trying to point out is that we are not the ones who brought this on Mr. Abhoy. He lived a very sketchy life, Ms. Romano. Mr. Rizzo, is the one who hired him to help kill someone."

"Says, you, Mr. Dubois, but we shall see about that."

And so, it went for two grueling hours, as Sheriff Bishop twirled pens, doodled and squirmed in his seat. Finally, he stood, rubbing his hands together and announced it was time for dinner.

As we waited for everyone to use the restroom, I

mumbled 'thanks' to Bishop.

"Not a problem," he said. "I knew she was coming after me next, and I don't have much of an ass left to chew on." I observed he didn't open any more doors for Ms. Romano on the way out.

We arrived at the MK Steak House and had barely slid into our seats before Saul said, "I need a drink. Anyone else need a drink? Because I need a drink."

Romano said she'd like a red wine, and I ordered a Coke because I was driving.

"Are we done for the day and not going to talk shop?" asked Bishop

Romano and I nodded.

"I'll drink to that," said Saul.

"Then, I'll have a whiskey sour," said Bishop. With a side glance at Romano, he added, "Make it a double."

We did talk shop, however. Because, after all, what do you talk about with a couple of people you just met, brought together for the same purpose. However, the conversation was more relaxed. Thank god for alcohol.

Saul filled in a few details to corroborate Olivia's life story. Agent Romano was all business, stating facts, as if she made it her life's mission to study the Rizzo family.

We tried to change the subject several times so that we could enjoy our meal until, finally, Saul said, "Hey, I thought we weren't going to talk shop." After that, it wasn't hard as Romano kept checking her phone messages and going out for a smoke.

After dinner, we dropped Romano and Saul at their vehicle, but not before Romano announced she wouldn't be in until the afternoon the next day as she was going to

Eureka to interview Aadi Abhoy's parents. "To find out the truth about the boy," she said.

"Good," I said with gritted teeth. "Let me know what other news you might find out. But you should know that Mrs. Abhoy is a member of the NRA. She has a sniper rifle of her own, and she's real pissed about losing her boy."

"Not a problem, Mr. Dubois. I'm sure she and I will get along famously. I'm invited for tea at ten."

"Please keep in mind I have a victim to protect, Olivia Hope. Remember her? She's in my jail eating up the taxpayer's money. So, once you're done with your little tea party, find out how much protection she's going to need so we can either get her back home, or send her to some other safe place, eh?"

"You read my mind, Dubois. When I return, I'll want to question Ms. Hope. Have her ready for me." Then she walked away—flip, flop, flip went her ponytail.

Bishop and I stood side-by-side as we watched. Bishop harrumphed, "Any bets that she's not married?"

"Oh, hell no."

"What, you think she is?"

I shook my head, "I don't think there's a bet."

The next morning Bishop said he'd do the breakfast run for Olivia and Idaho. Alan said he was getting up for a morning swim. Feeling tired and sore from tromping through the snow and woods to rescue Abhoy's body, I decided to sleep in. I awoke around nine, showered, watched some news and ordered breakfast in. I did the Sudoku, word jumble and the crossword puzzle in the Spokesman's Review. I stopped at McDonald's for lunch and, by 1:00 pm, I was feeling revived and rested, I was ready to take on the world once more.

Or was I . . .

A woman in tight-sequined Miss Me jeans, a fitted blue flannel shirt, cowboy hat, and sequined, turquois cowboy boots, leaned with one foot perched up against the door. As I got closer, I realized it was our very own Agent Romano. She looked, well . . . kind of luscious—and smelled of heavenly lavender.

Surprisingly, she smiled and said seductively, "Howdy, pardoner." And I thought, 'is this the same woman I met yesterday? Maybe she's schizoid or something.'

"Howdy?" I said cautiously. "I guess you better come into my office before you leave black marks all over that door."

"Ah, the janitor will clean it off. You do have janitors in these parts, don't you?"

There it was. Agent Romano was back.

"What's with the cowboy duds? Did the airport lose your luggage?"

She waved me off. "I found this quaint little weed and feed store selling seeds, fertilizer, candy, gerbils, and western clothing. Oh, and they have tanning beds in the dressing rooms. I thought, with this outfit," she did a twirly thing, "I'd fit in with the locals."

"Oh," she said as an afterthought, reaching into a big bag. "Want one? Because I've got two." To my amazement, she pulled out a pair of kittens.

"No thanks," I said tentatively. "Ah, I've already had my lunch?"

"No silly."

At least she laughed at that.

"I bought one for Rotty."

"Rotty?"

"Yes, Rotty the Rottweiler."

"Um, feeding cats to dogs is illegal around here."

At that, she really laughed and shook her head, "I met a little boy who was crying because they lost their cat, which Rotty was very attached to. I felt so bad that I got the name of the boy from the cashier, and I'm going to drop him off later."

"You will stop the car first, eh?"

"Why, Mr. Dubois, you must think I'm a monster!"

I shrugged, "All right, so you do have a soft side after all. But if you are dropping one off for Rotty, what are you doing with the second one?"

"Oh, that one's just a snack."

I nodded my head, very slowly.

"So, what did you find out about Aadi Abhoy?"

She returned the kittens to her bag making sure they were comfortable and leaned back in the chair. "Well, his mother was very sweet. It's true, she's pretty upset about the loss of her son. That's to be expected. She said she saw emails back and forth between him and Mr. Rizzo. From what she said it was clear he hired him to do a job. She just didn't know at the time the job was murder, of course. She said her son was a loner, so there was probably no one else he worked with or told. They found the hit money rolled up in a duffle bag. So, looks like a cut and dried case. You shouldn't have too much of a problem with the courts."

"Gee, thanks for the vote of confidence."

"You're welcome," she smiled sweetly—the smile

of a wily fox.

"But tell me something that I didn't already know," I said.

"Well, I bet you didn't know about this." She bent over and pulled a plastic bag out of her purse and handed it to me along with a pair of rubber gloves. "This is a diary of sorts that Mrs. Abhoy found after you were there. She didn't tell you about it because she didn't think it was going to matter, since he was already dead."

"What does it say about, Olivia?"

"Oh, he was all in with Rizzo. But he'd planned to help Rizzo take her, and then he was going to kill Rizzo. He'd deal with her himself. He was going to make her a rape slave, torture her, and use her to bring in others."

My jaw dropped.

"Oh, there's more. You really need to look at that diary."

I pulled on the gloves she handed me and opened the bag.

"I have to use the lady's room, I'll be right back," she said, and left me with two crying kittens.

I began reading the diary while the kittens mewed the theme song to Dexter. Soon I found myself steeped in an episode of Criminal Minds. There were other women he had captured, raped and murdered. There were names of at least five women—from Germany, to New York, to Seattle and places in between.

I was in mid-read when Sheriff Bishop dropped by.

"What's that you're reading? Anything good?"

I looked up, startled. I must have looked ill. "Hey, are you all right? You're white as a god-damn ghost!"

"Findings from Romano's excursion to the Abhoy

home today. You are NOT going to believe this," I said, as I threw him a pair of examination gloves from my desk.

He waved me off, "Just give me the highlights, Rand. I ain't got time to read today."

"No abbreviations today, buddy. You need to read every word, very closely."

Annoyed, he donned the gloves and began reading. I watched him, while my mind reeled with revulsion. Soon, he too, began to turn white.

At some point, Romano re-entered the room. When Bishop finally realized, we weren't alone, he looked up and almost fell out of his chair when he saw her.

"Romano, that you?" he asked hesitantly.

"Bearing gifts, I might add," she said, pointing to the disheveled book.

It took a few minutes for Bishop to take it all in. I wasn't sure if it was the book or the transformation of Romano. He cleared his throat and squeaked a bit when he started, "Whadaya make of this Rand?"

"I'm thinking we did a lot of people a favor by taking-out young Mr. Abhoy the other night."

"I ah, ah," he stammered, and then sharply turned to Romano. "And what the hell is up with that giddy-up stuff you're wearing?"

"What? I'm a local gal now."

"Well, you have yourself a nice rodeo, because I've got a shit-storm to deal with now!"

"Nancy, get me the number for the national crime agency," he called out, as he left my office.

"All right, all right, all right," said Romano rubbing her hands together. "You heard the man, let's get this rodeo started! Bring in our little Ms. WitSec gal and see what she has to say for herself."

It took about an hour to get some of the logistics figured for the interviewing audio and video set up. There was discussion about security at the doors as I brought Olivia in. I asked what may happen to her after this, but Romano didn't know. Conversation with this new Romano was hassle-free, enjoyable even. She could be funny; I enjoyed her sense of humor. We laughed and kidded each other, while moving tables and chairs. It was nice to see her relaxed as we worked together. I was thinking I could use a partner like her.

We were finally ready, and all people were on deck for security. I walked down to the lower cells to retrieve Olivia. The minute I saw her I felt guilty. She looked pale, and fragile when I brought her into the light. Her hair was mussed, her clothes askew, and her eyes were swollen—I assumed from crying. I felt like shit, and I wondered if I had forgotten something she needed. I tried to talk to her, but she remained listless and unresponsive on the journey up to the conference room. As soon as we walked in she stiffened.

"YOU!" Olivia screamed, and before I knew it, she bolted across the table at Agent Romano. Romano jumped up wide-eyed and held up her hands in defense but Oliva had her hands around her throat in a nanosecond, choking the holy shit out of her.

Chapter 33 - Rand Dubois

I raced behind the table and grabbed Olivia, "Olivia, stop! What has gotten into to you? Stop! Stop!"

Damn, she was strong! I had a hell of a time prying her fingers off Romano's throat. Romano was turning blue, and her eyes were starting to flutter closed.

"FOR GOD SAKE, OLIVIA, DON'T KILL HER!"

Oliva dropped her hands, and scurried back. She opened the door to run, but one of Bishop's deputies detained her in the hall—I'm sure it wasn't an easy task.

In the meantime, I called for a paramedic and began to attend to Romano. Bruises were forming on her neck as she gulped air. The EMT arrived and checked her over. In a few moments, she was breathing fine, although her voice was raspy. She refused to go to the hospital. She drank water, coughed, sputtered, and finally told the medics to 'get out' in her demanding way. They had no problem with that, but encouraged her to go to the hospital for a further check to make sure her esophagus wasn't injured. Then she told me to get out, too, as she was going to, 'freshen up'.

I returned to the hallway and found that a deputy had taken Olivia to another room.

When I walked into the room, she began to yell at me. "What the hell?" she yelled. AT ME!

Shocked, I yelled back, "Why did you try to kill Special Agent Romano?"

"No, no, no, no no, Rand! She's one of them!"

"What do you mean one of them?" She continued to glare at me. "What?" I was truly confused. What was she talking about?

"Rand! She is Nurse Ratched!"

"Nurse Ratched?" There was a pause as she sat, shaking her head. I asked, "Are you on drugs? Did somebody slip you something?"

She looked up at me as if I had just won the Dumb Ass of the Year award.

"Rand! Sh-she, she, she works for the Rizzos! She's the nurse I told you watched my baby!"

The cogs and gears in my brain began to dial and click into place. I began to realize why I had just won that Dumb Ass award. A deep and burning sensation began to broil in my gut, and I suddenly wanted to choke the shit out of Romano myself. A quick think back, I remembered running security checks on her. Had this woman found out what was happening and killed the real agent that was supposed to be here? I jumped from my chair and ran to the conference room. Before I went in, I phoned and asked the FBI to send a photo of Special Agent Romano, giving a quick explanation of what was happening and asked them to verify ASAP.

When I entered the conference room, I was relieved to see Romano was still there. I needed an explanation from her, even if the outcome came from the barrel of my gun.

I had my gun trained on her as I entered the room.

She didn't seem surprised, and sucked in a hiss saying, "Yeah, I didn't think she'd take it too well, seeing me again, and all."

"Ya think? After all, you worked for the Rizzo's," I said.

"Rand, listen to me, and put that damn gun away."

"Give me a damn good reason why I should. Better yet, maybe I'll put this damn thing away and strangle you myself."

She sighed and said, "Sometimes my job as an agent is to work undercover. I have a nursing degree—I'm an RN and an FBI Agent—and I've been hired by the Rizzos for years off-and-on. It's the FBI's way of keeping an eye on them. The Rizzos don't know I'm FBI, though. I worked for them to take care of Olivia's baby. Were you not wondering why I knew so much about the family?"

I had.

"Rand, come on. Put the fucking gun down. I don't want to ruin my new Miss Me Jeans. They cost a small fortune, and I can't use them as a tax write-off, so put the gun down."

"Why didn't you tell me before we got this far?"

"Because there is nothing specific about ruining Miss Me Jeans in the tax code."

I wasn't amused.

She sighed again, "I have trust issues. I didn't know how well I could trust you."

"Okay, so maybe you are an agent. But, you also work for the Rizzos. How do I know you aren't here on their behalf to kill Olivia? As Sarah Palin says, you can put lipstick on a pig, but it's still a pig."

"Oh, come on! Would I have turned that diary over to you today if I was working for the Rizzos to kill Olivia?"

"I hear you talking, but all I hear is oink, oink. You could have turned it in to keep yourself and the Rizzos out of the limelight, posing as an agent—like you did. Derailing us, by sending our focus in a different direction while you completed your mission—to kill Olivia."

"Would I still be here if I was working for Rizzos in that regard? I could have run off and you'd never find me. Well, except when you called my office on Monday, after I got back to work."

"Oink, oink. Olivia's still alive. The mission is to kill."

"I don't want to kill Olivia! If you let me explain, I think you will see that things are going to be fine."

"Right. Now I'm going to ask you again. Where the hell is Saul today? Is he working for you or, did you do something with him, like tie him up and throw him in a closet? Or shoot him? Where is he?"

She shrugged wearily, "Poor Saul had too much to drink last night. You saw how he gulped down that scotch. He's nursing a headache, and said he'd be here to sit with Olivia during the interview this afternoon. He should be here any time."

Sheriff Bishop entered the room about that time and saw my gun still trained on Romano.

"Whoa, wait, what? What the hell have I missed?" asked Bishop.

"Miss Piggy here may be trying to kill Olivia. I haven't quite decided, and I'm not letting her out of my sight until I know for sure."

Romano shrugged, "Got a deck of cards, Bishop? This could take a while."

My cell buzzed, and I saw it was the FBI returning my call. I handed my gun to Sheriff Bishop and told him not to let her out of his sight. I stepped out of the room and took the call.

"Yeah, this is Agent Dom. Regarding your question about Special Agent Romano? I just texted you a photo of her. I'll wait for you to take a quick check."

I put him on hold while I checked my phone. The photo was a typical ID you'd see on a badge. It was her.

"Okay, looks like the woman we have. You guys sure she's legit? Says she works for the Rizzos undercover occasionally?" I said.

"Yeah, she's legit. In fact, she's there on behalf of the Rizzo family—undercover for us of course—just to clarify. She's a nurse, and they call her to come fix up people sometimes, if you know what I mean."

I asked, "So, why didn't anyone tell me this before she got here?"

"She didn't tell you?"

"No, quite conveniently, she didn't!"

"Yeah, she likes to control things. Keeps her cards close to the vest—and what a vest I might add."

"And is Saul part of the Rizzo family, too?" I asked.

"Nah, they don't know anything about him. He's one of us. Mrs. Rizzo, Anthony's mother, asked Romano to bring her boy's body back. We sent Saul to help Olivia relocate, since he was Olivia's contact with the WitSec Program. It's all good, man."

I started back to the interview room when I ran into Saul. He didn't look so good. "Hey, man," I said. "I wondered what happened to you."

"Yeah, drank too much. I should know better on an

empty stomach. But I couldn't help myself last night, you know? That Romano woman, she scares the crap out of me."

"Yeah, you and me both, buddy," I said. "Hey, Olivia is in that room at the end of the hall. Tell her everything is all right. That Romano is FBI and on her side. She'll listen to you. Tell her I have verified it. I just hope she believes me. Then bring her in to this interview room."

I entered the interview room and retrieved my gun from Sheriff Bishop. "She checks out. She's okay," I said.

"Okay, Romano, so you're not here to kill Olivia. But, I need to know what exactly your relationship is with the Rizzo family."

She stared at me for a long moment and finally asked, "Why do you care so much about Olivia Hope, huh? She viciously killed Dimitri and shot Anthony. You suspect her of killing Ira Goodman, and she tried to kill me. She's a crazy bitch. Why do you care?"

"Well, for starters, I don't think she killed Ira Goodman, and I've got a funny feeling that she's going to help me find who did. The way I see it, she killed two men out of self-defense. It's all a matter of perspective. I think that girl has a strong desire to live, and I can't fault her for that. And YOU! How did you expect Olivia to react when she entered that room? You could have saved us all from that drama a few minutes ago, if you'd just told us who you were from the beginning.

"Huh."

"Huh," I replied.

Saul and Olivia entered the room. I stood to make

sure Olivia was okay, and that she was going to be on good behavior. She said she was fine, but still looked pale and refused to sit. I sat in a chair beside her, hoping it would relax her, yet I was ready for any move she might make towards Romano. Saul stood on the other side of her, resting his hand on her shoulder—for comfort or control, I wasn't sure which.

"Hey, Saul," Romano said, "Feeling better? They were just asking me if you got tied up somewhere." She threw me a wink from across the room.

"Let's get started," I said, "Tell us about your relationship with the Rizzo family."

"Fine. But, Olivia, you need to sit for this interview."

"You do not tell me what to do, Romano. I suggest you start talking."

Romano gave me a pointed look. I shrugged, "You heard her."

Sighing, Roman began, "Okay, when I heard about the news of Anthony Rizzo's death, I checked in with Mrs. Rizzo, his mother."

"No," said Olivia. "I want to hear how you know the Rizzos. Start from the beginning. You know, 'Once upon a time in the land of hell,' when you first joined those monsters."

Again, Romano looked to me, with a pinched face. Again, I shrugged. There was silence for a good minute, and I don't think Olivia's eyes blinked once while they bored holes through Romano.

"It was a cold day in December. I was born in Fargo, North Dakota, in 19--"

I slammed my fist on the table, "Fast forward,

Romano!"

Romano threw up her hands, "Okay, okay . . . just calm down." She began to mumble, "Um, let's see . . . pre-school, grade school, Jr. High, high school--" I tapped the table. "Well, you wanted me to start at the beginning."

"If you don't knock it off, you will be sitting behind bars for obstruction of justice. And once your fancy, city lawyers get you out, I'm sure you and your little Miss Me jeans won't last long in this redneck country. They know how to roast a mean, wild boar, oink, oink."

"I'm not mean, wild, nor a pig--"

"Prove it," Olivia and I said in unison.

Romano swallowed hard, "When I graduated from college with my nursing degree, I answered an ad in the newspaper for a part-time, live-in nurse for a nice rich family, the Rizzos. I had no idea at the time they were mafia. They paid me very well. So much so, that I decided to fulfill my lifelong dream of becoming an FBI agent. I applied, got in, did well and was about to graduate from the academy, when I got called on the carpet."

"You mean to tell us that you never suspected mafia ties when you were fixing all those bullet holes in their friends?" asked Bishop.

Then Romano did something I thought she would be incapable of, she blushed. "I was young and innocent, and too focused on my studies to really pay attention. Oh, did I mention I was getting paid well?" I heard Olivia give a snort. Romano looked up at her and smiled, it was a sad little smile. "I know, Olivia, that you were young and innocent at one time, too. Me and you, we've come a long way, baby."

To my amazement, Olivia let go a long sigh and sat down beside me.

Romano continued, "From the first interview with the Rizzos, they explained that their Italian family mistrusted hospitals and local doctors. Besides, a lot of rich people hire private doctors. That is why they wanted an in-house nurse. Okay, I bought into that. And I became smitten with the family's two cute sons. However, I wore thick glasses before I got my contacts. And no thanks to Mama Rizzo, who made me wear my hair in a bun under a nurse's cap, a dowdy nurse's dress, and thick, orthopedic shoes, the brothers never paid much attention to me."

"You said you got called on the carpet. What did you do?" I asked.

"Yeah, I was ready to graduate when the director called me in. They interrogated me about my affiliation with the mafia family. I was probably as surprised about that fact as Olivia was when she first found out." I saw Olivia nod out of the corner of my eye. "I was confused and endured a loooong interrogation, before they believed me. Then, I suggested that I was in a good position to do undercover work for them. Long story short, after graduation and a lot more undercover training, I was an official FBI undercover family employee."

"Why didn't you help me when I was with Demetri? I was alone and scared and you limited my time with my own baby!"

Romano pinched the bridge of her nose and rubbed her temples before answering. "We had no idea where you stood with the Rizzos. We knew that Demetri made a few visits to see you, and then you two came back home, married! You seemed so much in love with Demetri. And then when the baby came, you started using drugs..."

"I was..." Olivia started, but Romano cut her off in midsentence.

"Being drugged. I know. I didn't know it at first. But it's when I started keeping you away from the baby."

"Emma," Olivia looked furious. "The baby has a name, EMMA!"

Romano's eyes softened. She reached over, gently patted Olivia's arm, and said quietly, "I know. Emma. I love her, too, Olivia." Olivia glanced away. I noticed her eyes becoming watery.

Romano settled back in her chair, "I thought you had postpartum depression, and when I realized drugs were missing, I assumed you were stealing from my cabinet. So, I put in a nanny cam. It was not you stealing. It was Demetri, who was drugging you. Obviously, I couldn't confront Demetri myself, so the bureau decided to start an investigation on him to find something on him and get you and Emma out of there without my cover being blown. It didn't take long after we bugged his office to find out about the human trafficking he and Anthony were into."

Oliva shivered, "D-d-did you hear him when he said he'd take Emma, too?"

"Not until later. Let's just say we heard enough, that we knew you were in danger, and he was going to sell you, and all the other girls and boys they took out of

Minnesota." Romano, turned pale and paused a minute. "In fact, the day you decided to leave was the day that I had a meeting with my director. We decided to follow him taking you to the ship that night. However, as you know, you brought him down first. When I arrived back at the penthouse, you were standing over Demetri, covered in blood and still ripping at him. Paramedics were right behind me. I let them take you. And Anthony was also taken."

"Emma! What happened to Emma?" I asked.

"I took Emma. I knew if Anthony came back, the first thing he would do is scarf Emma away somewhere. I told the family that she had been hurt in the fight, and that I ran her to the hospital, where we announced later that she died. We had a funeral and everything. I certainly didn't want to worry you about a fake funeral, so I never told you."

Olivia remained silent, staring at the table, pulling on the sleeve of her jacket.

"Olivia, when we first got to the scene, you were standing over Demetri with a crazed smile on your face like you had just accomplished a climb up Mount Kilimanjaro and were ready to plant your flag. We thought you had lost your mind. We weren't sure what happened, and what drove you to mutilate your husband. At first, FBI wanted to put you in a mental hospital. They still felt that you may have been part of the business. I didn't know about that at first, which is why they put you in prison. When I found out what was going on, and showed them the tapes and videos. I sent Agent Boyd to talk to you.

"You are a strong woman. I knew you would snap

out of what happened, and you did quickly. I am the one who put you in the witness protection program. But, I was also the one who suggested that Emma remain with another family. At the time, I really felt that was the best for her. And for that, I can understand why you probably hate me."

Olivia nodded.

"So, here's the good news out of all of this," Romano did a little drum roll on the table. "Look at me, Olivia." Olivia raised her eyes, as Romano said, "You are free."

"What are you talking about?" Oliva asked, skeptical.

"I've been observing this family for a long time. I know them better than my own family. Here's the deal. First, I'm going home to tell them that this situation was a case of mistaken identity. So, there is no need to relocate you again." Romano smiled, and Olivia looked terrified.

"How is that going to stop the rest of the family coming back and checking it out for themselves?" I asked. "Certainly, his mother isn't going to sit still for that answer."

"You'd be surprised. Oh sure, his mother was quite upset about losing her last child. But, she knew he was a good-for-nothing son. She mourned for all of those who were hurt or killed by her sons. When I told her Anthony was dead, she cried. But when she dried her tears, she said to me, 'At last we are done with all of this violence and hatred. There will be no more killing.' She is not going to pursue things any further."

"What about the rest of the family coming after

me?" Olivia asked anxiously. They're just as bloodthirsty as Demetri and Anthony."

"I'm confident that's not going to happen, and I'll tell you why. Anyone who knew Anthony realized he was a loose cannon. He was the last one to carry on the vendetta. The rest of the family really doesn't care. And, I don't think he'll be missed by anybody."

"But Demetri was in line to take over the family business. They were all pretty upset that I killed him," Olivia reminded Romano.

"Yes, true. Demetri and Anthony were the only two children the Rizzos had. Before Demetri's death, he was being groomed to take over the family business. He had been smart, and he had charisma. But he really blew it when he started the human trafficking without the consent of his father. As far as the rest of the family is concerned, Demetri made the mistake of a lifetime, thinking that his father was just a rotting old fool.

"Also, Jimmy Rizzo, the next oldest cousin, was always jealous of Demetri and Anthony. Now that Anthony is out of the way, Jimmy is happy as a clam because he's taking over. He's not going to want to keep this can of worms open. As far as he is concerned, you did them all a favor by getting rid of Demetri and Anthony. The bureau, on the other hand, is going to have to keep an eye on him because he's got bigger fish to fry than to come after one young woman. You are no longer a threat."

Olivia looked doubtful, and the room was silent.

"Look," Romano said, "If I hear of anything at all, I'll call you immediately and send you to the next safe house. We won't let anything happen to you. I promise.

And besides, if you are convicted of this Goodman's murder, you will be in jail anyway, and that might be the safest place for you."

Olivia, chuckled over that. "What about Mrs. Bixby? She saw and heard my conversation with Anthony. She knows it wasn't a case of mistaken identity."

"I just came from seeing her," Sheriff Bishop said. "I'm thinking she doesn't remember much at all. She had quite a severe hit on the head. Even if she does remember later, I don't think anyone would believe her. Everyone knows she's a little off her rocker."

Olivia pinched the bridge of her nose and looked to me, "Can I go home now?"

Chapter 34 - Olivia Hope

It took a while to process the paperwork to let Idaho and me go home. Dubois ordered in Burger Express for a late lunch, and we all feasted on burgers, fries, and shakes. Idaho and I chatted, and rehashed our adventure vacationing in the County Hotel. To her, it was an event of a lifetime, and she bubbled with excitement.

"And to think you were just about to be relocated," squealed Idaho. "I would have gone with you, you know."

"Not sure that would have been allowed," I said.

"Nuhuh, I know too much about you now. They'd have to let me go with you."

"What about the new love in your life? Somehow I don't think Alan would be excited about that."

She shook her head, "You are my first priority, sister. I've never had one, and now that I got one, I'm not letting you go."

"But, what if I were relocated to a remote cabin in Alaska, or bumfuck Kentucky? What then?"

"Hey, every little village needs a grave digger," beamed Idaho.

I laughed aloud. "You are a true friend. I don't deserve you."

"Okay, you giggly girls," interrupted Rand, "It's time to take you home. Are you ready?"

When I stood, I became a little woozy. I teetered a

bit, and Rand caught me. "You okay?" He looked worried.

Even though I got the green light on my concussion to go home, my head was killing me; the residue of pain was reaching crescendo proportions. I felt nauseated. I just wanted to go home to a warm bath and bed. "Yeah," I said. "Just exhausted, it's been a long couple of days."

We dropped Idaho at her house first. Rand and I drove the next couple of blocks in silence. It was dusk, and the tree shadows stretched into long ghoul-like monsters. The cloudless, moonlit evening reflected off the snow and engulfed everything in a blueish hue. It was pretty and eerie at the same time. Thinking about all the things Agent Romano said made sense, so why was I feeling so skittish? I tried to shrug it off.

When we got to my house, I sat for a minute looking around, taking in the site of the police tape draped around Mrs. Bixby's house. The wind puffed clumps of snow off the trees. As the clumps hit the car, I jumped.

"Hey, it's just snow. Are you all right?"

"I'm fine, a little jumpy yet, I guess."

"Fair enough. I think Romano is right, you know. I don't think you need to worry any more about the Rizzo family. If it helps, I'll keep an eye on you, too."

"Mmm, love the thought of big brother watching me. No thanks, I got my big girl panties on. I'll be okay." I saw movement behind Mrs. Bixby's house. Did I just see someone on the back deck? My eyes strained to see more. I relaxed and smiled when I saw a deer bound around to the front. It stopped and stared at us for a moment, then ran across the road. I was just being paranoid.

"Rand?"

"Yeah?"

"Would you like to have dinner with me? I mean, after you finish with the Goodman case. And, if you don't arrest me as his killer—wrongfully, I might add." I turned in the seat to look at him; he paled, and looked a lot like the deer in the headlights we just saw.

"I . . . we . . . I ah . . . well. . ." he stammered.

I patted his arm, "Relax, Rand, It's just dinner! Besides, I owe you."

He sniffed and shook his head. After a long moment, he turned in his seat, "So, you're buying then?"

I nodded, and asked, "Oh, and can I have my gun back?"

"How about after that dinner?" he countered.

"Are you afraid I'm going to shoot you?"

"Um, you know, your track record with your last few dates didn't really end well, sooo . . ."

I punched his arm.

"Seriously," he said. "Let's just wait until this Goodman mess is all over, and we'll see."

I nodded, slipped out of the car, and watched him drive away. As I turned to step onto the porch, I caught movement again, out of the corner of my eye. I froze—and then bolted up the steps. It's just the wind I told myself, as I fumbled for the key to my door.

I slammed the dead bolt into place and leaned against the door. I dropped to my knees and crawled to the window that faced Mrs. Bixby's house. After about fifteen minutes of eyestrain, I conceded that my paranoia was taking over my life. I prayed it would pass quickly before it became a habit. I stood and returned to the kitchen, turned on the light, found the brandy—at least what I had not polished off earlier. I took a good long swig and waited for my body to quit shaking. I took another, and another. Feeling better, warmer, and exhausted, the bottle of brandy and I headed for the bathroom for a long soak in the tub.

I filled the tub with bubbles, took another long gulp of brandy, leaned back and relaxed. That was the last I remembered until I heard a thud, glass tinkle and a thump. I had fallen asleep. At first, I wasn't sure if I really heard it, or if it was my paranoia once again. The tub water was cold anyway, so I got out and put on my sweats and t-shirt. When I went into the living room, cold air was wafting through a broken window. A rock wrapped in paper lay by the fireplace. I unwrapped the paper; it said, We no what you did bich and now you gona pai. But Anthony was dead! I tried to reason as my panic swelled.

I heard a dog yelp. That gave me more alarm than the note did. I called for Blue, but he didn't come, and I heard no more. I dropped to the floor and crawled to get my cell phone. Then the living room window completely shattered apart, and a tall figure crawled in, taking only a couple of steps to kick my hand away to intercept it. Two other figures followed through the window. Tall figure number one lifted me up by the hair, flung me on the couch, and pinned me in the chest with a cold wet boot, waving a gun in my face. I couldn't breathe. The light wasn't on, but the moonlight, even brighter then, lit the room enough so that I could almost make out a face. I recognized him.

"Josh? That you?" I squeaked.

"What?"

I said it again.

"What?"

"Take your damn boot off her, you moron," came a voice behind Josh. He did, and I made a loud gasp.

"What the hell do you guys think you're doing?" I croaked.

Josh wagged something else in front of my face. I stared at it, but perhaps the concussion, or the brandy, didn't allow my eyes to adjust.

"This key mean anything to you?"

Oh, lord. The key frozen to Goodman's ass, the one that made the mysterious indentation Rand asked us about—the key to my shed. But, why would they be so anxious about it? "Should it?" I asked.

He backhanded me across the face, hard. "I am out of fucking patience!"

"Why? You just got here."

He backhanded me again. "You smart-ass, bitch. Tell me what's behind the door that this key unlocks. Is it the money?"

"What money?"

Then he kicked me in the head with his boot. That time the pain from my battered face and concussion began taking me down a long dark tunnel. And, did I hear him say something about Pamela, my friend, Pamela? He smashed my face again, just because.

I spit blood out of my mouth and repeated, "Pamela?"

"That's right. We got her for clapatol."

I was confused, "What is clapatol?"

"Banks use it, dummy. Don't play stupid with me teacher. So, if you want to see your friend again, you need to give us the money, you bitches took." I took another hit to the face, and kick to the head.

Oh, collateral, said my brain. "What money?" I slurred.

"That's behind that key!" screamed Josh.

My brain was fading in and out. I vaguely remember starting to laugh and thinking how this was all so stupid. I got another backhand. Why did they want my old table and chairs from the shed? And, why would they hold Pamela hostage for them?

"Hey, man, she keeps yamerin' about the shed," said a voice coming from the direction of my broken window.

Once again, I was pulled by my hair up off the couch, dragged out the back door, and on to the shed. Josh put the key in my hand. I could barely see the lock, and not that it wouldn't have taken much just to give the door a good kick, it opened.

"All fucking right. 'Bout time you cooperate."

Once inside the shed, Josh slammed me into one of my Adirondack chairs. Someone found some duct tape and taped my wrists, then my ankles.

They began searching the shed, only to find chairs, a folding table, a lawn mower, paint cans, tires, rakes, shovels, a kerosene lantern, and lots of dust. One of them lit the lantern, and threatened me with fire, when they didn't turn up any treasures.

"I will only ask once more. Where is the money?" He punched me hard in the face.

I had no clue what he was talking about. I needed to

keep him talking and figure a way out. I thought hard before I answered. I remembered the money that Seth had pulled out of the floorboards at the lake house. Could that be the money?

When I didn't answer right away, Josh said, "We know you have money, cuz that's why you went to Goodman's house. Cuz you knew he had lots of money. You took the money. It was our money—my money!"

"You mean the money that Seth had at the lake house? The money you were looking for the night you killed Seth's dad? That money?"

One of the boys behind Josh gasped. "How does she know, dude?"

"Shut up!" hissed Josh. He backhanded me again. "You, bitch, killed him. And everyone in town knows it. It's in all the news. I would never have killed him."

I heard snickering behind Josh. "Hehe. Yeah, he was in love with Seth's dad."

"SHUT UP!" Josh bellowed.

"Hey, it's okay, relax. We don't care if you're a gay boy," said the other boy.

That's when I realized that Josh must have been one of boys that Goodman had molested. That fucking child molester, Goodman!

"Josh, did Seth's dad molest you?" He paled. He shrunk back like a little boy. If I wasn't mistaken, I could have sworn he wiped a tear away. I suddenly felt sorry for him, losing his boyhood innocence to the likes of Goodman, the perverts and ill-witted assholes of the world who took that away.

"Josh, I can get you help. What Ira did to you was wrong. It wasn't your fault. I promise I can help you. It's understandable that you would want to kill the man who hurt you like that."

"I didn't kill him! I wouldn't. We were going away together." Josh shouted. "Seth was the one that stabbed him."

One of the guys began teasing Josh, "Nah, he wouldn't do that. Josh was in luuuve with him," then more chuckles.

"Shut up!" Josh screamed again.

"Josh, it's okay," I said. "A jury will be very lenient with you. They will understand."

"Josh luuved, him. He loved to have sex with him. He was Seth's dad's little bitch." The two other guys kept up the sing-song teasing.

"Shut up!" This time Josh turned the gun on one of the guys.

"Hey, dude! It's okay. If it weren't for Seth's old man, you might be in jail, too, for stealin' and likin' little boys, too. He saved you man! It's all good."

In a tearful rage, Josh cocked the gun.

"Josh, don't do this," I tried to get his attention. "I promise. I'll make sure you get help!"

He pulled the trigger. The boy dropped like a sack of potatoes.

He turned on me, burying the muzzle into my temple. He came close, and looked deep into my eyes. "I did NOT kill Ira!"

Something in his eyes made me pause. I believed him. Pieces started falling into place. I remembered Seth's strange behavior the night I talked to him at the lake house. Of course, he killed his father. It all suddenly made sense.

"You killed Zip, dude! You fucking killed him!" The young kid was in shock and began to cry. He'd wet himself, too, when Josh turned the gun on him.

"Josh! No!" I heard my scream, "You didn't kill Ira, don't kill anyone else. We can sort this all out! Where is Seth? Let's go get Seth. Let me help you!" I pleaded.

He turned the gun back on me and looked at me for a long moment. And then, he lowered the gun and nodded.

We heard a thump against the door. Josh turned the gun on me again and pulled the trigger. I dove to the side and took the bullet to my shoulder. He shot again, but missed, as the door flew open.

The next few moments became a blur. There was a crash. Blue, that beautiful, black Labrador, knocked Josh into the boy who held the kerosene lantern, dousing fuel everywhere, on Josh and on the other boy. Everything covered by kerosene exploded into flames.

Josh turned on the dog and kicked it hard. Blue yelped and howled. He bolted through the door before Josh could turn his gun on him. I could hear Blue barking and yowling all the way down the block.

Suddenly, the young kid began screaming and dashing about as flames engulfed his sleeves and pant legs. Josh was on fire, too. Panic-stricken, they began running like human torches. As the shed burned, the air thinned, and I went down that long tunnel again, only this time I could no longer breathe; and the darkness engulfed me like a giant wave.

Chapter 35 - Rand Dubois

"Wow, I didn't see that one coming!" I said to no one. "Imagine that, Olivia asked me to dinner!" I was still contemplating a fantasy of more than just dinner with the beautiful Victoria-Secret angel—envisioning Olivia in nothing but a pair of wings—as I pulled into the parking lot of government offices. I marveled at how quickly I had agreed to her invite. When, only a few minutes before, I had explained to Romano that I wasn't over my wife's death, and waiting for me to accept a "rendezvous" with her would be a bad idea, since she'd probably be retired with grandchildren by then. That was right before I said goodbye to her.

Smiling to my studdly self, and thinking it was a fine day to be alive, I realized that maybe I could join the living again. Even Alan kept telling me it was time to get on with my life. He said five years of mourning was enough. I just hoped I wouldn't become one of those guys who rejects women because they don't live up to his dead wife.

I looked at my watch. I still had a few things to catch up on. I needed to get my head back in the game. Softly whistling Rod Stewart's Do ya Think I'm Sexy, I slid into my chair and sifted through phone messages. Most calls lately were false leads on the Goodman case. I grumbled, wondering if we'd ever get a break.

Lily White left a message, asking if Pamela Phuchet

was with Idaho and Olivia. Why would she think that? I thought. I punched in Lily's number.

"Hey, Lily, Rand here," I said, when she answered. "Why do you think Pamela was with Idaho and Olivia?"

"Because no one has seen her since the day before yesterday. Her mom called me this morning, and said that she had the boys, but that Pamela hasn't even called to check on them."

"Maybe she's trying to take a break from them. Every mom needs a break now and then."

"Well, her mother said that they weren't even supposed to spend the night. It's not like Pamela to not call. Those boys are her life. I've been to her house but she's not there. There are a couple of newspapers in the paper box and, when I checked the gym, they said she hasn't been there in the last few days either. I'm worried. That's not like her, Rand."

"Hmm, that doesn't sound good. I'll round up Alan, and we'll check things out." I asked her a few more questions regarding Pamela and hung up.

I sailed a file to the other side of my desk, and a poof of air brought another message flying in the air to land on my keyboard. Curious, I found four more messages, all of which were from Raymond Connly of RayCon Construction. The last message left was marked Call ASAP. Interesting. I struggled out of my jacket, and threw it to a chair while I dialed the number. Missing the chair, my coat hit the floor. Something flew out of the pocket and skidded across the floor. I bent over to pick it up, when Connly answered the phone. As soon as I identified myself, he began talking, almost breaking my eardrum.

"It's him!" Connly bellowed.

"Him, who?" I was confused. I fingered the item that had fallen out of my pocket. It was a thumb drive. Where in the hell did that come from? I threw it on my desk and focused on what Connly was blathering on about.

"It's him. I just saw a photo of Ira Goodman. It's him!"

"Ah yes, okay, so it's a picture of Goodman. Is there some significance to that photo?" I was beginning to think Connly had been tipping a few.

"He's a dead ringer for—pun intended with that asshole, Christopher Dumas."

"What?" That didn't make sense.

"I went to the local newspaper office, and they gave me a photo of Dumas. I'll fax you the photo now."

I gave him the fax number, and he promptly hung up. A few moments later, the fax machine began beeping away. I stood by the slow-chugging machine drumming my impatient fingers on the counter. Two photos finally birthed, dropping onto the desk. One was a photo revealing a picture of Ira Goodman, the one the news people used with every article printed about his death. The other was a photo of a man digging a shovel into a pile of dirt with what looked like some business professionals surrounding him. Perhaps city councilmen, maybe even Connelly with him, too. I compared the two men. At first look there seemed to be some differences. While Goodman had dark hair, Dumas had a clump of longer blond hair peeking out from under a hard hat and was wearing safety glasses. I strained my eyes to see any resemblances.

I sat back in my chair, "Damn, can this day get any weirder?"

"Weird how?" asked Sheriff Bishop, as he plopped down in the chair beside me.

"Huh, our friend Raymond Connly, from RayCon Construction, seems to think that Christopher Dumas and Ira Goodman are one in the same man. Doesn't make sense. Did Goodman own RayCon? The company that went bankrupt? Why on earth would he change his name?"

"Maybe he felt it was a conflict of interest—to own a construction company that he used for investments."

"Yeah, change one wrong for another. But look at this," I said. I used a magnifying glass to compare the photos. I got a close-up of Dumas, and Goodman side-by-side, looking for identifying marks like moles on the face, maybe a broken nose. Suddenly, there it was.

Bishop leaned in close and gave a slow, long whistle. "Lookie that, they both have the same chipped tooth. Eyes are the same. If you look close enough, the nose is the same. Look at the eyebrows, too. They sure look one-in-the-same."

I sat back in my chair thinking, mindlessly tapping the thumb drive on my desk. "Yeah, but why? I don't get it. Why would he assume another identity?"

"What do ya got there, sport?" Bishop asked.

"What?"

"The thumb drive you're using to tap out that Rod Stewart song I heard you whistlin'?"

"Oh, I just found it. It fell out of my pocket, not sure what it is." I shrugged, "Let's have a look."

I plugged the thumb drive into my computer and

clicked on a file. Photos of young boys, in bathing suits, boys swimming, and then, naked boys, boys in different sexual positions, with grown men.

"Where the hell did you get this?" Bishop all but screamed. "Holy Christ!"

I was dumbfounded. What was this? Where did it come from? I racked my brain, running my fingers through my hair. "Just when I thought this day couldn't get any screwier, it goes viral."

"Holy shit, look at this!" screeched Bishop. "That's fucking Goodman! Having sex with boys! Who the hell is the other guy?" Bishop pulled the mouse out of my hand and started scrolling.

I suddenly thought I knew where this thumb drive had come from. That little shit, Olivia. She must have slipped it into my pocket the night she killed Rizzo, when I interviewed her. That is what she had been doing at the Halfway House out at Bull Lake. She'd been through Goodman's house! That little sneak.

"Hey, look at this." Bishop had clicked on a video. At first, it was a hand covering the lens and then a picture of someone's butt as he walked away. Voices were muffled in the background and then, screams and chaos. Bishop stood wide-eyed staring at the screen. When the video ended, he ran a hand over his face and began to smile, and clapped me hard on the back. "We just solved us a murder, my man! We need to find those boys, pronto."

"Yeah, and we need to find Pamela, quicker." I said, because I had a funny feeling things were going to get nastier.

"Find Pamela? Pamela Phuchet?"

"I'll explain in the car. I need to round up Alan."

I figured, since Idaho was home now, that's where I'd find Alan. If only finding Pamela would be as easy. I was right. Alan was with Idaho. They were drinking beers when I arrived. I didn't want to alarm Idaho about what was going on yet, but pressed Alan to hurry, while I waited impatiently. It gave me time, however, to gather my thoughts before we set out search parties.

Suddenly, there was a dog barking wildly and running down the road. Soon the damn dog was on Idaho's front porch jumping on the door, about to rip it off the hinges.

"What the hell is going on?" Idaho said, as the rest of us peered out the window.

"Dad, that's Blue, Olivia's dog."

Blue was clearly in a rage. I was half afraid to open the door. I began to open it slowly, but the dog backed off and turned to run back down the road. I came out on the porch, and the dog began to run away. He suddenly stopped and ran back to me. I spoke calmly to get him to settle down. But when he reached me, he grabbed my coat sleeve with his teeth and tried to drag me with him.

"Hey, guys," I yelled, "Something's up. I think we need to follow him." That started the parade of the four of us running after the dog.

We didn't have to go far to see where he was leading us. Flames licked the sky from behind Olivia's house. From the side, I could see her shed was on fire. I heard screams coming from the back yard. Bishop pulled out his phone, while still running, and dialed 911. By the time I reached the back of the house, there were two bodies flapping in the snow. They looked like flaming snow angels, melting wings faster than they could fly. We all began throwing snow on the figures lying there. I prayed that one of them wasn't Olivia. The dog quickly darted passed me, banging open the door to the shed. The door bounced back several times with the dog's weight. He was inside, tugging on something. I dove through the door after him and found Olivia lying on the floor, taped to a chair and the sleeve of her sweatshirt had just caught on fire. She was covered in blood. Without another thought, I grabbed her in my arms, chair and all, and hauled her out and away from the burning building. I quickly rolled her in the snow making sure the flames were out, and then cut her loose from the chair. She was barely breathing. She probably was suffering from smoke inhalation. I did a quick check to see if there were other burned areas. As I rolled her over, that's when I saw her bloody face. She had been battered, and she'd been shot. I almost lost my dinner. I wet my sleeve in the melted snow and began to wipe her face. She regained consciousness, but only for a moment.

"Rand," she whispered hoarsely, as I strained to hear her. "Find Pamela. They have Pamela." And then, she was gone.

"NO!" I screamed. She was no longer breathing. "Stay with me!" I shook her and gave her mouth-to-mouth breaths. I gave her chest compressions, "Come on! Damn it! Don't leave me now. You owe me a fucking dinner!" I have no idea how long that went on, but eventually, the ambulance arrived and the paramedics peeled me away from her.

Chapter 36 - Olivia Hope

I stood beside Rand—well, more like slightly above and beside him—as he gave someone CPR. Idaho knelt beside him, she was crying. An ambulance pulled up. Two men ran over to the body.

I turned to walk away. I felt so light and free—free of pain. I felt calm, and something else I couldn't put my finger on...at peace? I watched Rand curiously and wondered what happened. I heard him say something about me owing him a dinner. I began to float away from him. Then suddenly, Alan stood before me.

"No, no, no. You get back there!" he said, but he sounded so far away.

"Back where?" He pointed in the direction of Rand and Idaho. I abruptly had the feeling that something wasn't right.

"You are not leaving us! Idaho needs you. Maybe even my dad."

"Oh, that's right. You think you see dead people. You think I'm dead? What are you smoking? If that's true, I wouldn't be standing in front of you and we wouldn't be having this conversation."

Alan pursed his lips and gave me a sour look, "Funny. Now go!"

At that moment, I began to fall, as if someone dropped me from an airplane—suddenly I did a full-body slam to the ground. Disorienting pain filled my body. My lungs gasped for air that seemed non-existent. I must have fallen, I thought. My lungs burned, my head ached, and the pain was unbearable. I rolled to the side and vomited, on Rand's boots—again. I vaguely remember thinking that I probably owed him a new pair of boots, too. Someone jabbed something into my arm. I felt something flowing through my body, I relaxed, and blackness engulfed me.

Chapter 37 - Rand Dubois

I rode in the ambulance to the hospital with Olivia. Another ambulance arrived about the same time and took the two boys to the hospital, all the while fire trucks arrived with wailing sirens. Bishop followed with Alan in my car. Paramedics whisked Olivia out the back doors and wheeled her straight into the emergency room. My stomach clenched as I watched long enough to see the incredible damage to Oliva's face in the bright light. It was worse than I imagined. Those son-of-a-bitches beat her to death's door. Nevertheless, by god, she fought back, and was finally breathing on her own.

I left the doctors to do their work and went to find Sheriff Bishop and Alan. They were over by the boys' gurneys. Bishop shook his head, indicating they were both dead. The bodies had burned beyond recognition. Bishop was pale as a ghost, and Alan was a sickly shade of green. Bishop grabbed my arm and escorted Alan and me back to the car.

"We gotta find Pamela and Seth," said Bishop. "Before Billy Hemgren (aka Woot) passed away, he told me they had taken Pamela to an abandoned cabin. If I could understand his garbled speech, I thought I heard him say that Josh shot Seth. I put together bits and pieces of sounds. I think he said the cabin was up Gains Road, and then he became delirious, saying something about watching for moose. At least we have moonlight to help us find it." We loaded up and were on the road.

We didn't drive far to the turnoff to Gains Road, but it seemed too long on the snowy back roads—must have been nine or ten miles and not a cabin in sight.

Finally, Alan called from the back seat, "Wait, back up. See that post? That might be another road." We pulled up beside it. It didn't look like a road but a bedraggled post leaned way to the right and the letters MO peaked from under a fresh pile of snow. Alan hopped out and brushed off the sign. The letters, M-O-O-S-E were shabbily carved into the weathered wood.

"Found our moose," hollered Alan.

"Good eye, son!" I called back. He hopped back in. The road was so narrow that it had been hard to tell if it was a road. It looked as if the boys had the smarts enough to brush away about thirty feet of tire tracks by the main road, but we quickly found their trail and drove for another long while. A cabin finally appeared. A ramshackle building that was beginning to lean precariously. A good windstorm would push it over, if a tree didn't fall on it first.

We didn't know if there were more of these boys that we'd need to deal with. We bailed out of the car, our guns drawn, and headed in, calling out to identify ourselves and that we were coming in. Behind the cabin door, we found Pamela bound and gagged. Embers were all that was left of a fire burning in a wood stove. The walls of the cabin were chalked full of holes and gaps. If the temperatures had dipped to near five below as had been predicted, she very likely would have frozen to death before morning.

There was no sign of Seth. Bishop and Alan began

looking for him, while I took the gag out of Pamela's mouth and cut the ropes that bound her to an exposed pipe. She began coughing, gulping air, and crying. She threw her arms around me and clung hard to my neck. She was a strong woman. Once she calmed down, she immediately began firing orders.

"We have to find Seth. I think they shot him. They took him outside. I heard them arguing about money that Seth's dad had. Seth kept saying that they already got the last of it, but they didn't believe him. There was a gunshot, and Josh said something like, 'There you, shit, that's a present from your dad,' and then they left in the pickup. I don't know where they went, but they said something about Olivia and that she must have it. We must help Olivia! I think they might kill her, too. We need to hurry." She said shaking and crying again.

"Shh, it's okay," I tried to comfort. I noticed she had a couple of black eyes and bruises on her neck. "We've got Olivia. She's fine." I didn't tell her that I prayed she remained that way. "And we've got two of the boys, too."

Her eyes became big, "There were tttthree of them." She was shaking badly.

"There was Wwwoot, Zip, and Josh. Don't know their real names. Who did you get?"

"Woot and Josh"

She relaxed a little. "Thank God you have Josh. He's the scariest, and he's mean. I think the other two are just followers."

"Is Josh the one who put those bruises on your face?"

She nodded.

"Found him!" Bishop hollered. I heard shuffling. Bishop and Alan appeared at the door.

"Is he—" I started to ask, but Bishop shook his head. Which started a fresh round of tears from Pamela.

"I can't get cell service," said Bishop. "So, Alan and I will stay here with the body, and you take Pamela to the hospital. As soon as you get cell service, call for my deputies and another ambulance."

Pamela and I bounced around on the old backroad as I drove as fast as I could.

"Are you okay, Pamela?" I asked of the sunken-eyed, pale, and bruised woman beside me.

She nodded, "I am now. What a fucking nightmare."

I couldn't argue with that. "Why did they kidnap you? Can you tell me what happened?"

"I'd put an ad out at the high school for students to help me with my Christmas tree orders. I needed the help and figured they could get a little extra Christmas money. The three of them showed up at my house day before yesterday. At first, I thought they were there to help me with the Christmas trees, but then, they started asking me about money. I had no idea what they were talking about. They said they saw us in the newspaper and that they knew we killed Goodman, and that we took his money. Rand, we didn't kill Goodman. I swear to you on a stack of bibles. I have no fucking clue as to what money they were after!"

"It's okay," I assured her. "We know you women didn't kill him."

She sighed wearily. "Are my boys okay? Are they safe?"

I smiled, "They are safe, and your mother will be very happy to know that you are, too."

We sat in silence for a while.

Assured that she was calmer, I told her about finding Noose, Woot, Zip and Josh at Olivia's and the details of how it all ended. I let her know also that Olivia was the one who alerted us to her kidnapping, demanding that we go find her.

"That's Olivia," she said, dabbing at watery tears pooling in her eyes, "On her death bed and she's still worrying about her friends."

When I finally had cell service, I notified the deputies. The ambulance passed by us on the highway. I left Pamela in the emergency room with a nurse and made my way to Olivia's room. I stood by her bed, holding her hand, watching her sleep. Slowly her swollen eyes fluttered open. "Hey, young lady, how are you feeling?"

"Like shit," she slurred weakly, with the effects of the drugs. "Thank you, for saving my life."

"Don't thank me. Blue is the one who alerted us to the fire, and he was the one that began pulling you from the fire."

"That's my dog," she said as a slow smile spread across her face. "Did you find Pamela?"

"Yes, she's fine. Scared to death. I just brought her in to have the doctors give her the once over. I'm taking her to her mother's tonight."

She nodded. "Did you get Noose and Woot?"

"Yes, but they didn't survive the fire."

"Josh shot Zip," she said with a strained sob. "He was teasing Josh about being Goodman's lover, and then, Josh said that Seth killed his dad. But how do we prove that now?"

"You don't! Bishop and I do. And we did."

"How?" she managed to look genuinely surprised.

"The thumb drive."

"What thumb drive?" said Olivia, feigning innocence.

"The one you planted in my coat pocket."

She nodded, ever so slightly. And then, I realized that she may have not seen all the files on the thumb drive. "Let's not play this game of innocence and lies, okay?"

She said nothing. Her face was so bruised I couldn't even tell if she blushed.

"You must have missed the video that Seth recorded. We saw him stabbing his dad with the fire poker. I don't think the other boys knew he was filming. After things calmed down, Seth said to the camera, 'I'm sorry, mom. He had to be stopped.' We think he knew his dad was abusing boys, and perhaps that's why he did it."

"How horrible," Olivia whispered, and tears pooled in her eyes.

Her eyes fluttered shut again. Her face was horribly bruised. She had a big bandage surrounding her head, and arm in a cast and sling. The doctor had told me that she was lucky to have only a cracked cheekbone, but there was renewed concern about the concussion. They were treating her other arm for third degree burns. My heart squeezed thinking that we almost didn't get to her in time. Out of reflex, I bent and placed a soft kiss on her forehead, then tiptoed toward the door.

"Rand?" Olivia croaked.

"Yeah?"

"Would you do me a favor?"

"Yeah, sure, anything."

"Buy a dog license for Blue? I'll pay you when I get home."

"Yes, I will. However, I think that dog deserves a free one from the city for his bravery. And I think you owe him a steak dinner, too."

She nodded slowly, as her eyes fluttered shut once more. "And a pretty, blue collar," she said, as her voice trailed off toward a drug-induced slumber.

"You are still talking about Blue, right?"

She waved me away with a flick of a couple of fingers and a slight smile. "Matching ones."

I smiled knowing she was going to be all right.

I thought that was a good ending to a horrific night. We got the bad guys and saved the beautiful ladies. But, it was too late to walk off into the sunset, as it had set eight hours earlier. I found Alan in the waiting room. He was alone and pacing the floor.

"How's Olivia?"

"Just fine," I said. "Let's get some shut eye, eh?." Alan hesitated, stroking a thickening beard, and continued to pace.

"Sheriff Bishop told me about finding the photos and the video of Seth stabbing his father. His dad was a child molester!"

"Yeah, it was pretty horrible."

"He did some awful things to those boys. He was a monster of the worst kind; and I hold Ira Goodman responsible for those boys' death tonight. I don't condone them taking Olivia and hurting her and all of that. But Goodman fed into their lost souls and used them to do horrible things." As Alan paced and talked, he kept rubbing his stomach like it was bothering him.

"What is it, son?" I asked. I figured he'd need to de-stress after seeing the burned bodies. Hell, so did I.

"Could you humor me for one second?"

"Sure, I can understand where you're coming from."

"Can you, dad?"

I was confused, "Of course, I can. It's not every day we see burned bodies and slay dragons!"

He looked at me dubiously. He walked over to me—shoulders back, spine erect. "Sir, I'd like you to accompany me to Ira Goodman's lake home to investigate a hunch I have about a buried body."

After a few, probably long, seconds, I asked, "A what?"

"Sir, I have reason to believe there is a body buried on the grounds of the Goodman lake home."

"What in God's name are you talking about, and can't this wait until morning?"

"Let me ask you this, sir. If I had been missing for months, and someone found my body, would you want to wait until the morning light to know I'd been found?"

Incredibly, my whole body convulsed, "Of course not! What is this about?"

"If you want to know, then you need to come with me, sir, and I'll explain on the way."

So, we loaded up, and headed out to Bull Lake.

Alan began explaining as we walked to the car.

"Remember when we were first at Goodman's place and we were watching those guys trying to get Goodman's body out of the house as he dangled there for a while until the rope broke? And then, I saw that little boy out in the snow in shorts and a t-shirt, but I didn't find him?"

"Okay, yes. I remember you saw the boy. But Alan, the boy was alive. What makes you think someone killed him, eh? Just because you didn't find him, doesn't mean he's been murdered since."

"Dad, I don't think the boy was alive. I think it was his ghost I saw."

"Ah, here we are again. Back to this."

"Ah yes, this, this little mental problem you think I have. But I'm telling you, dad, I believe that he was murdered, probably last summer sometime, and I think that Goodman buried him somewhere around the tool shed, or maybe even in the tool shed. Believe me, dad, I hope this is one time that you are right, and I'm wrong. All I ask is that you try to understand what I do."

"Fair enough, son. I just want you to know that no matter what, I'm in your corner. Okay?"

"Thanks, dad. I appreciate that."

We said nothing more the rest of the way.

When we pulled up in front of Goodman's home, Alan turned to me and said, "We'll need a shovel and some bolt cutters. I think I saw a padlock on the shed door. Oh, and a flashlight."

Alan obviously had been thinking about this for a while. I pulled the shovel, flashlight, and cutters out of the trunk, and then we headed to the back yard. Alan shoveled snow out of our way as we trudged on to the shed.

"Let's check out the inside of the tool shed first."

"Good thinking," I said.

Good thing we brought the cutters because the lock was a heavy-duty brand. I struggled getting a good grip and then squeezed. The lock didn't give much. Alan took a couple of turns as well before it finally broke apart. The shed was small, holding a lawn mower, shelving with tools and gas cans, shovels, rakes and assorted nails and screws. Alan moved the lawn mower outside, and I set aside the shovels and rakes.

"This is pretty small. There's no body in here, Alan."

"Look at the floor. This is an older shed. These floor boards look new, not even stained with gas and oil, like our shed is."

"Maybe the floor rotted out and he replaced it this past summer."

"Yeah, and placed the body under it."

Allen picked up a pry bar and began pulling on the boards. Once the boards were up, we peered into a shallow hole that appeared to be filled with a layer of cement.

"This is fairly fresh cement," I said, as I chipped a piece off.

"Funny, this little shed is set on dirt. It's not like this was poured as a foundation," Alan said, as he stood. He brushed his hands together, and wiped them on his pants. He picked up a sledge hammer, and said, "Okay, here we go, moment of truth."

He pounded, and pounded, and pounded away. I don't think I'd ever seen him so serious and determined. After a good half-hour, the cement was broken and we had it cleared away. He then began digging up the dirt. He dug down a few feet and hit something. He bent down and brushed the dirt with his hand, wiggling his fingers around. I heard him suddenly groan. He stood, went outside, and vomited. I bent down to peer into the hole and saw an exposed hand of a small child. My knees went weak, and I couldn't breathe, I joined Alan outside. Alan began to weep silently. I hugged him tightly. "I so wanted to be wrong, dad."

Chapter 38

WICA Flies Free for Ira Goodman Murder

By Carol Cripes

Members of the Women's Investment Club (aka, WICA) are off the gallows for the murder of Ira Goodman. Goodman, a financial guru revered by many, had been found dead in his lake home last month. He had been staked to the floor with a fire poker imbedded in his chest. The women were under suspicion as they had business trades with Goodman that went bad in a construction bankruptcy. It was reported that they had become angry, "casting spells of doom."

New evidence appeared late yesterday afternoon when authorities announced that they recovered a video of Goodman's youngest son, Seth, impaling his father with the poker.

"We are not sure what motivated the young Goodman boy to kill his father. And, frankly, we may never know for sure," commented Sheriff Bishop, at yesterday's press meeting. "Things had been tumultuous between father and son for some time, so it seems Seth, along with several friends, took matters into their own *hands."*

However, other sources say that there is no video of Seth and his young friends tying Goodman down. There was no mention of the WICA women taking their own responsibility leading up to the murder leaving some questions unanswered.

"Could those WICA women have taken their little brooms and magically swept their part of the murder under the rug?" asked Mary Edwards, president of the Red Hat Society. Sheriff Bishop had no comment.

The plot thickened last evening when a whirlwind of events ensued. WICA member Pamela Phuchet, who was reported missing since Wednesday, was found bound and gagged in an abandoned cabin along Moose Road. The cabin had been the hideout for Seth and his friends since the death of his father. The boys assumed that the WICA women withheld money from them that Goodman had promised to the boys. Things took a turn for the worse when an argument riled the boys, resulting in the shooting death of Seth Goodman.

After the shooting, the boys found their way to Olivia Hope's home in Libby, hoping to find their riches with her. They bound her, dragged her into her shed, and began to beat her for information. Arguments among the boys arose, and Billy Hemgren, was shot dead by Josh Pinkman.

Sheriff Bishop said, "The boys had lit a kerosene lantern. During arguments, Olivia's dog came to her rescue by knocking the shed door open, dousing kerosene and lighting the boys on fire. The fire spread quickly, completely burning the shed to the ground. Both boys died from severe burns.

In the meantime, Olivia's dog ran to the neighbor's home, alerting them to the excitement. Moments later Rand Dubois pulled an unconscious Olivia from the flames. Olivia is recovering in St. John's Hospital from minor burns, smoke inhalation, a gunshot to the shoulder, and a concussion.

However, it turns out Ira Goodman may not have been such a "good man" after all. The body of a five-year-old Spokane boy, missing since last August, was found buried in his lake house tool shed.

"The child had been sexually molested and strangled to death," said Lincoln County Coroner, Maxwell Hunt. "It's not clear if Goodman had murdered the child, but it is thought that the boy may have died during a sexual act."

Sources say that Goodman was affiliated with a ring of child pornography agents. More evidence containing videos of several unidentified men and Goodman with other children was found. Investigations are underway to connect all parties involved with this ring and bring them to justice.

"This all sickens me," said Mary Edwards. "This leads to a major question left unasked. Just how many more molesters are out there, waiting to prey on our children?"

If any other children were victims of this ring of child pornographers and molesters, authorities are asking them to, please, come forward. Authorities assure privacy for information. However, no offer of help for these victims has been announced.

Chapter 39 - Rand Dubois

"That news hack!" Bishop said, as he dropped a copy of the Cabinet Mountain News on my desk.

"Ah, great. Cripes is, once again, wielding her mighty poison pen," I replied. I picked up the newspaper, read the article, and flipped it aside when I finished.

"She makes me seem like a dolt, and she definitely has it in for those little ladies."

"Huh, maybe she's bored and needs to dig up dirt to sell, eh?"

"Yeah, and frightening the public to boot! The phone has been ringing off the hook this morning. I have both my assistants answering phone calls trying to calm the masses. Shit, they haven't even had their first cup of coffee!" Bishop shook his head, "They deserve a raise for putting up with this shit."

"Do we have any new molestation victim's come forward?" I asked.

"Won't know until the calls slow down and see who's called about what."

"I figure there'll probably be a few, but I sure hope not many. Is Elizabeth ready for counseling these children?" We hired Elizabeth Hardy, a well-known and highly-respected child psychologist out of Spokane, Washington, to help us interview and offer counseling services to the victims. I worked with her before. She is a sweet, calming, grandmotherly type. She works miracles with abused kids. Some are working for her now, after they've grown up. A regular Mother Teresa.

"Yeah, good woman. She wasted no time in getting here to help."

We sat in silence for a couple of minutes, sipping our coffee and eating the box of doughnuts Bishop brought in.

Bishop's mouth was half-full when, he munched, "You think Cripes has a point about the women though? I mean do you think they had a part in the murder somehow, even now that we know Seth actually stabbed his dad?"

"I guess we'll never really know the whole story, but I got a feeling that maybe they were there first. And if they did tack him to the floor, what could we arrest them for? Roping, bagging and tagging?"

Bishop laughed, "How about, compelling, spelling and cursing?"

That was so bad I bust a gut, "Terrible witch humor."

"Yeah, I think the real witch is that Cripes woman," grumbled Bishop.

"If they did do those things to Goodman, it might have been nasty pranking gone awry, and it could have turned deadly." I said. "They're probably lucky Seth was the one to seal the deal."

"Think we should pursue considering what led up to the stabbing?"

"Depends on if you have the time and money to spend. If we found out they were part of it, they might get accessory to murder charges," I paused, and took a big gulp of coffee. "Do you think they deserve that, Bishop?"

He sat and thought for a long time before he said, "I think they are all normally law-abiding citizens. I think they are lovely women. Nowhere near the likes of a scumbag like Goodman and company. I don't think anything good would come out of pursuing the matter, and wasting the people's taxes, time, and money on it."

I let loose a long breath I hadn't realized I was holding. Yes, I was relieved, because I didn't want to touch it with a ten-foot pole. And quite frankly, now that I knew what a barbaric animal Goodman turned out to be, I was damn glad he was lying in the cold hard ground. As far as I was concerned, those women and Seth did society a major favor by making him go away, not that I condone murder, but it certainly was what he deserved. That is nothing I would ever voice aloud, however, so what I said was, "Yes, I for one, am anxious to put this case to bed."

"But, on the other hand," said Bishop—my breath caught in my throat again. "If we get information or confessions, I'm going to have to uphold the law."

"Understood, my friend," was all I could say to that.

Bishop brushed his hands together, whisked away donut crumbs from his uniform, took a sip of coffee, and lean forward. "Okay, now I need to finish off my report. I've got to know. How did you and Alan find that little Belmont boy last night? Whatever possessed you to go back out to the lake and start poking around in the middle of the night, looking for someone we never even knew about?"

I knew this was going to be hard to explain.

However, it has always been my philosophy that you tell the truth, and don't hedge your bets—just let the beast out of the box. You need to put your rams head through it, and plow away. Come clean and deal with the consequences. I had other clichés' rolling around in my head—but now I had to get to it, and let the fat lady sing.

"Rand, hey, you still with me?" Bishop was waving a hand in front of my face, pulling me back out of my head.

I sighed. "I need to get Alan in here because he can tell this story best. It's an incredible story. I'll go get him." I jumped from my seat and went to find him.

The best way was to let Alan explain. I promised to support him every step of the way. When Alan and I returned to the conference room, Bishop was clicking a pen in double time with one hand and eating another donut with the other. Crumbs were piling up on his yellow note pad. He seemed as nervous as I was. We sat down and were ready to start when, Pamela Phuchet walked in.

"Hey, Pamela," we all said in unison.

"Hey yourselves," she said, sliding into the room as if she owned the place, carrying a bag of something.

"How are you doing, little lady?" asked Bishop.

"Um, better than you, it seems." That stopped Bishop in mid-bite, and his cheeks turned a crimson red. Pamela pulled the donut from his hand, and replaced it with the bag. Alan and I must have looked as if she had pulled a gun from his hand as she said, "Relax, guys, this one needs to knock off the donuts and eat something healthy." She turned to Bishop, "I knew you'd be scarfing these things down," she looked at the donuts as if they were vile rodents. "So, I made you one of my power breakfast burritos."

Bishop looked like a little boy, who just had his sucker taken away. "Ah, ththth thank you?"

Bishop's face was so red by then I thought he was about to have a heart attack.

"All righty then," she sang. "Oh, and I booked a four o'clock appointment for you at the gym. Dr. Rusk will be there too, to ah," she stole a quick glance at Alan and me and lowered her voice, "to brief you on a few things before we get you started." She patted his shoulder, "I expect you to be prompt. Bon appetit," she smirked, and then, she was gone.

Bishop had bitten into the burrito and groaned in ecstasy, "This isn't half bad."

Alan and I sat, bug-eyed, staring at him.,

Bishop stopped chewing, and with cheeks bulging, asked, "What?"

"What the hell was that?" I asked.

"Goddamn women." Bishop put the burrito down, and finished chewing. "All right. I drove Pamela to her mother's house last night. The doctors had given her a sedative. She was kind of in and out of sleepy consciousness. I tried keeping her awake because I didn't want to have to carry her into the house. So, I started talking to her. Keeping her focused on something. And well, I happened to tell her that my wife has decided she likes a younger man, and she's leaving me."

"Bishop, I am so sorry to hear that," I said

"Bummer, man," said Alan.

"Yeah well, anyway. I said it because I didn't think

she'd remember it—she was in an out, you know. But, damn, women never seem to forget anything. Pamela told me that the way she got through her husband's death was to eat right and get fit. She offered me free personal training for saving her life. So, she, ah, she wants to save my life. So here we are, you looking at me like I'm some damned alien, eatin' a damn power burrito."

The room was silent, until he slapped the table with his hand.

"Damn it, get to telling me how you found that boy!"

Alan and I jumped in our seats. I nodded toward Alan.

"Um okay, so," Alan cleared his throat, "I need to start from the beginning sir, so please bear with me. To understand, I need to tell you a bit of my history."

"If this is going to be too damn long, son, I'm gonna need another cup of coffee and a donut." He reached to the side to grab a donut but they were gone. "Damn that woman." He poured a cup of coffee. Alan and I followed suit.

"Well, sir, I was born with a gift," Alan began. "To coin a worn-out phrase, I see dead people."

Bishop sat back in his chair, folding his arms over his chest, looking dubious and a little weary. "Go on, son."

Alan explained when he was a kid he'd wake in the night to see people in his room. He could see them talking but he couldn't hear them. His mother and I feared he was plagued with night terrors and so, under doctor's orders, we medicated him. The medication only made him sick, and did nothing to make the visions go away. Since the meds weren't working, his mother and I sent him to a psychologist. Once again, he was on medication that made him sicker. He told how the only person who could console him was his grandmother. She often talked him through his anxieties. In the meantime, he learned not to say anything to his mother and me because we "just didn't get him."

For years, he tried to ignore the people. However, no matter what he did, no matter how hard he tried to ignore them, nothing worked—in fact, it seemed to get worse. They haunted him day and night. His grandmother explained he needed to face it head on—said it was a gift that he needed to embrace. His grandmother continued to comfort and teach. It wasn't until he came with me to work the Goodman case that the pieces started to fall into place for him. It began when he first met Idaho—dead people surrounded her. She is a gravedigger, after all.

He explained his gift to her. She didn't believe him at first but said they should do some experiments. So, he faced his visitors, one by one, and slowly began to hear their voices. One decedent had told him to visit his wife and tell her about money he had stashed in a safety deposit box. Another one told him where to find his daughter's favorite doll she lost in the barn—and so on. He had many more experiences to share, but Bishop said that he had got the picture.

"So, you see," said Alan. When I paid attention to these people and helped them, they could move on."

"And where do they go?" quizzed Bishop.

Alan shrugged, "I'd like to say into the proverbial light, but, I usually just don't hear from them again."

"So, this is the unexplained errands you have been taking care of?"

Alan nodded.

"Your grandmother sounds like a wonderful woman. I'd like to meet her."

I cleared my throat, "She died before Alan was born. She eked out a living as a fortune teller. Nice, sweet woman, but we, ah, thought she was a little wacko. Yet Alan has described her to a T even though my wife and I never said much about her."

"Yes, of course, I knew that," said Bishop, with a wave of his hand. He smacked the table with a hand. "Damn it, no, I didn't! Okay, so tell me about finding the boy."

"When you and your deputies were trying to get Goodman's body out of the window on the second floor, dad and I stood watching as the body swung and swung and swung."

"Yeah, yeah, yeah, I remember," Bishop said dismissively, with a slight smile that cracked one side of his mouth.

"Well, while dad and I continued to watch, I saw a little boy watching from the yard. He wore a red t-shirt and blue shorts and no shoes. He didn't have a coat on either. I told dad about him."

I nodded to Bishop. "He described the boy to me then, which was exactly what he was wearing when we found him."

"When I stepped out the door to find him, he stood staring at Goodman. He saw me, waved, and walked away towards the shed. I ran to follow him, but he just disappeared. I searched, but never found him."

"Goddamn," said Bishop.

"So, as time went on, and Alan honed his gift," I began, but Alan placed his hand on my arm.

"Dad please, I need to tell this."

"It continued to bother me that the boy seemed to disappear in thin air," he said. "There had been no footprints, so I knew that something was terribly wrong. After I helped all these other people, it came to me that maybe Brian Belmont was telling me where he was buried. I figured he had to have been buried either by the shed or in it."

"So, when he came to me with his hunch," I said, as I winked at Alan, "We checked it out, and found the body." I placed my hand on Alan's shoulder. He was now as pale as he had been last night.

"I was really hoping to be wrong, sir," whispered Alan.

When I looked at Bishop, he was grimacing like someone had punched him in the face. "I can't even imagine what you have been going through, son!" he said finally.

"Having those dreams, thinkin' you're crazy. Hell, your mom and dad thinkin' you're crazy. By god, son, you do have a gift. And damn it, I gotta put you on the payroll, boy!"

Alan remained silent and pale.

I sighed in relief. The hard part of telling Bishop about how we found Brian Belmont was over. I was pleased with his reaction, he questioned but did not condemn. On the other hand, I was ashamed of my part in my son's painful upbringing and my condemnations. My sigh of relief was more for the fact my son was finally getting some peace in his life. He can now embrace this thing he calls a gift and live his life like a normal young man—which is all I ever wanted for him. I am well-aware of how selfish that sounds. And, yes, I need to learn to embrace the gift, too—just as soon as I can quit calling it a curse.

Chapter 40
Olivia Hope - One week later

Finally, I was getting out of that hospital. I was damn tired of being poked, prodded, and having to do deep breathing with sore lungs. And then, awakened in the middle of the night for blood pressure checks and poked again with antibiotics and pain meds. My neck, back, and butt ached from lying in bed all day.

"How are you feeling this morning?" asked Dr. Jenkins. "I see you wasted no time in getting dressed."

I rotated my shoulders and cracked my neck. "I need to go for a good, long run. Get these kinks worked out," I said.

"Whoa, whoa, whoa, slow down, little filly. Stop kickn' at those gates too soon," said my wise, old doctor. "Your lungs have taken a beating, and you need to be nice to them and your shoulder. Slow and steady, as they say. No runs until I say so."

After the fire, and the beating, I developed a lung infection. I'd been heavily drugged. All I knew was that my lungs hurt, and every breath was painful. I felt tons better. It was being in the hospital that made me miserable.

"I just feel so cooped up. I've got hospital fever or something."

Dr. Jenkins gave me a quizzical look and started to

reach in his pocket.

"Oh, wait. no, no, no. I don't have a fever," I said, waving the palms of my hands in front of me, fearing he would pull out a thermometer and not let me leave. "That was a joke; you know, cabin-fever, hospital-fever."

He chuckled, "You are a funny one. Not to worry." Dr. Jenkins pulled out a business card from his pocket. "Here's my card. My home phone number is on the back."

"Ah, Dr. Jenkins, aren't you married?"

He gave a good belly laugh, "Oh, you do flatter me. No, in fact my wife would like you to call her. She's been following you women in the news. She inherited some money and wants to play around with some of her new funds."

"Ah, well, in case you didn't hear, we haven't done so well ... we lost—"

"I think it's more like she wants to play around with your little WICA group."

"Sir?" I asked, confused.

"Seems you ladies have become somewhat of heroes. She thinks your band of sisters have all the fun. The way you dressed up Goodman for his funeral and all, I laughed my ass off. Couldn't have happened to a better guy." And then, he winked, "You're building quite a fan club. She wants in on the action."

I pocketed the card. I didn't know what to say to that.

"Want me to call you a cab?"

"No, thanks," I said. "Idaho and Alan are on their way to pick me up."

The good doctor warned me again to take it easy. No running until he gave his okay, which probably was a good idea since it was still below zero. Freezing my lungs didn't sound like a good idea.

I didn't have to wait long before Alan and Idaho arrived.

"Hey," said Alan, "how's our favorite prize fighter?"

"Oh, Olivia!" Idaho gasped. "You look horrible!"

"Ah, thank you?"

"Olivia, why didn't you put the make-up on I brought for you. Here let me go get it." She began going through my bags to find foundation, blush and other colors to cover my face, but I waved her away.

My face was still swollen, but at least the fluid that surrounded my left eye had subsided enough to allow me to see through a slit. The bruises that surfaced were a gruesome green, black, and blue. A couple of stitches and some dried blood made for a nice bride of Frankenstein look. It was perfect for what I had planned for that day. The time I spent in the hospital gave me a chance to think. An idea had come to mind as to how to get our money back. It might be a long shot, but I had to try, and these unsightly wounds might help me achieve it.

"Idaho, stop. I'm just going home, and it hurts too much to put that stuff on my face anyway." She cupped my face in her hands. I was touched by her nurturing gesture but winced at her painful look. "That bad, huh?"

She shook her head and said, "Well, you might have a bit of a scar, if that's any consolation. Badge of honor and all that."

Alan and Idaho drove me directly to my house. Idaho began fussing about my living room, bringing pillows and blankets to the couch. Making sure I had enough in the fridge to eat, and pills to help me sleep.

"Wow, she makes a great nurse," I said to Alan.

He grinned and said, "I couldn't agree more."

"So, Alan, you know when Rand was giving me CPR? Did you and me, you know, have a conversation?" I remembered a dream. I was standing in front of him, feeling light and peaceful. I felt as if I could float away. Then Alan told me to go back—to my body, I guessed. I remembered falling to earth, and pain and blackness. It all seemed so real. I couldn't stop thinking about it.

"Really?" he answered, sourly. "You really have to ask?"

I shrugged.

"Do you mean, did you actually die?"

I shrugged again. "It was just a dream, right?"

He puffed out his cheeks, "No, it wasn't. And, yeah, you were at death's door. I simply coaxed you back."

"Ah, then I guess I owe you a big thank you."

"Look, I didn't tell Idaho how close we came to losing you. She was beyond upset, seeing you so badly beaten. You know, not everyone is as lucky as you. You got a second lease on life, so use it wisely."

"Hmm, I figure I have at least eight more lives left."

"You are a bitch, not a cat," Alan teased.

"Hey," Idaho said, "What are you two jacking your jaws about over there?"

"Olivia thinks you make a great nurse."

"Eww, no! I can barely keep my breakfast down just looking at you, Olivia." Idaho flashed me an apologetic look. "Sorry, sweetie, nothing personal. I just can't stand the sight of blood and bruises."

"Besides," she continued, "I'm going green, remember? I'm going to have a farm one day. And speaking of which, I need to get to work so I can earn a living to stake my plot."

"Yay! You got your job back." I was happy for her. Something was finally getting back to normal.

"Yeah. But, it's contingent upon attending a law class about the perils of defacing bodies, or some dumb thing." Idaho gave me a little wink, and said, "Not sure why that's so important."

Alan and Idaho left me with a promise that I'd take care of myself and get lots of rest. She said she'd fix dinner for me, and that she would be back at my house at 6 p.m. sharp.

"One more thing," said Alan. "You need to talk to Mora—something about a promise you made to Seth?"

"What? How do you know—"

There was that sour look again.

"Oh, so you talked to him after …"

He shrugged.

Shit, Mora was the last person I wanted to see right then. But Alan was right, a promise is a promise. However, something told me that these bruises wouldn't get me any sympathy with her.

Chapter 41 - Olivia Hope

The visit with Mora went better than I expected. That is, if you consider her not calling the cops on me for trespassing and harassment.

"What the hell are you doing here?" Mora had spat.

"I, ah, just felt I needed to talk to you for a minute," I stammered.

"Well, if you've come to apologize for making a mockery of my dead husband, you can forget it."

"We didn't mock him," which was kind of true because he looked good for a painted-up man-lady. "And really, Mora, after all his horrible pedophile philandering, why would you care?"

She snorted. "Come on, let's go around back so I can have a cigarette." We sat on her back-porch swing in the cold, while she lit up. She pulled in a long breath from the cigarette, then exhaled little smoke rings. Her hands shook.

"I meant forget about apologizing," she paused for a couple of heartbeats. "Because he deserved much worse. You're right, he was the scum of the earth. And now, my baby boy is gone because of him, too." Tears sprang to her eyes, she didn't try to wipe them away. "I didn't know Ira was abusing him. I didn't know about any of those other poor children. He was gone all the time. I figured he'd had many affairs, but with children? Dear god, that is just unconscionable."

"Did you ever suspect he had been molesting Seth? At any time did Seth become despondent or different somehow?" I asked. I couldn't imagine that she didn't notice something.

"No, no. I didn't. Seth traveled a lot with Ira when he was young. When he started school, he'd only travel during the summer. He loved his dad, and Ira related to him better than the two older boys. If Ira had told Seth to keep his mouth shut, he would have done it. He would have done anything for his father." Mora paused for a few moments. "I guess it's starting to make sense to me now though."

"What's that?" I asked, as gently as I could.

"I guess Seth was around ten years old or so when he stopped going with his dad on trips. He wanted to, but Ira said that he was getting to be too much of a handful. Seth resented it, then he turned very quiet, but seemed to have gotten over it after he made a few friends from school. As years passed, he was constantly arguing with his dad. It was horrible. When Ira came home from sales trips, Seth would make himself scarce, staying at friends' houses. I figured it was because he still resented Ira, maybe still felt abandoned. I resented Ira's absence, too. I certainly couldn't blame Seth for his actions. I thought they'd work through it, but they never did." She snorted again, "I don't think anyone could work through what Seth had experienced. I should have asked more questions, paid more attention. You must think I'm a terrible mother."

I shook my head. I wasn't there to judge. "Don't be too hard on yourself. People like Ira are masters at hiding secrets. They know how to manipulate people.

You can question things all you want, but the bottom line is that Ira is the one to blame. Don't blame yourself."

"Why, exactly, are you here to see me?"

"Actually, I'm here to talk to you about Seth. I talked to him before," I swallowed hard, "Before he…"

"Before he died, just say it," Mora croaked.

"Before he died," I said. "I tried to talk him into turning himself in, that he would get help, that things would work out, but he refused. He told me to tell you that he loved you very much."

Mora hitched a little chirping sound as more tears welled in her eyes.

"He said he was sorry. Sorry for everything. He wanted you to know that, and made me promise to tell you."

"He was such a nice, loving boy. A gentle soul. He just fell in with a bad crowed."

I felt her pain. "He was that and more, Mora. However, I think the only reason he was with those other boys was through Ira's connection to Josh and the others. They weren't friends of Seth's. They just happened to be the same age. Seth was smart, too. He would have gone on and done wonderful things with his life. I am sure of it, Mora."

Mora's bottom lip began to quiver, "Thank you for saying that," she whispered. She took a couple more, deep drags and snubbed out her cigarette in a big pie pan overflowing with butts. "I'm cold. I'm going in now." She got up and paused at the door, "Thank you for coming to tell me that. It couldn't have been easy for you. And by the way, you look like shit."

I chuckled at that, and nodded.

"Well, I'm sorry those boys did that to you. You didn't deserve that." And she shut the door behind her. I could hear her sobs as I left the porch.

I stopped for a double mocha latte, and wished I had something stronger to put in it to calm my nerves. Finally, the caffeine kicked in. It was time to gather up my confidence and make my next visit—to Rocco Basham.

I rang Rocco's doorbell. The door flew open wide, "What the hell are you doing here?"

"Wow, like I haven't heard that already today. I'm glad I'm such a welcomed guest."

"You look like shit."

"Yeah, I get that a lot lately."

"What do you want?"

"Relax, Rocco, take a chill pill. I just want to talk. Maybe even make an apology. Can I come in? It's cold out here."

He stood in the doorway for a few seconds but finally relented. "Oh, all right. Even I can't turn away a whipped bitch." He, begrudgingly, stepped to the side and let me pass. "I'd ask what the other guy looks like, but wait! You killed him."

"Didn't kill him. You need to read more." A waft of body odor hit me and almost knocked me over. "Whew, and shower more."

I sat in a chair next to his fireplace, which felt soothing in his cozy living room. Rocco wore sweats, a wife beater t-shirt and a ratty robe that hung on him. He looked as if he'd been living in them for a while. He'd lost weight, too. I scanned the room. He had good taste in décor and quite an art collection. Then I saw a couple of balls of yarn and knitting needles stuck in what looked like the start of a mohair sweater.

"What are those?" I pointed. "Rocco, are you a knitter?" I began to laugh at the dichotomy!

"Yeah, it's mine. I knit, okay? I knit when I'm stressed! It helps to calm me. I have a lot of stress right now. In case you don't remember, I just lost my best friend--"

"And you were sleeping with your best friend's wife. Oh, and no job! Yeah, lots of stresses, I get it."

"Get to the apology part, I'm getting bored, and it's almost time for my nap."

"I have to know something first. Are you involved with Goodman's sexcapades?"

"No! God no! Why would you even ask?"

"Because I'm not into doing business with disgusting deviants as in the likes of Goodman. He was your best friend. Did you know about his ill-begotten behaviors?"

"I knew nothing about it. I had nothing to do with his . . . his personal sexual conquests. He was more of a business friend, not a confidant. He was getting kind of wacky and weird. He told me he was going to leave Mora, go hide some place. I was all for that. I wanted him gone, and out of Mora's life."

"I guess that explains the note I found."

"What note, what are you talking about?"

"Well, here's the thing, Rocco. You see, I found a pile of money—money that Goodman took from us and then said he was bankrupt. As it happens, the pile almost rose to the ceiling." I exaggerated. I was trying to make a point. "There were thousands, maybe even millions of dollars, in CASH! And a note attached." I paused, but Rocco only glared at me.

"The note said, 'Here's your traveling money, compliments in part from WICA. Have a pleasant journey.' And imagine my surprise when it was signed by RB."

"A lot of people have the initials RB."

"It's your hand writing."

"I don't believe you."

"And I can prove it in a court of law. You knew Goodman was committing fraud."

I handed him the copy I had made. He wadded it up and threw it across the room. "Get to the apology part before I call the police for harassment."

"I'm getting there, hear me out. You see, while I was in the hospital, I had time to think and do some research. You come from old money, meaning lots of money you didn't personally earn. The deal was that you had to have a REAL job until you were forty years of age, or you would never see the old money. Am I right?"

"How did you—"

I held up my palm, "Doesn't matter how, what matters is that it is a fact, counselor."

"Apology, now!"

"Okay, I'm sorry."

"For what?"

"I'm sorry I got you drunk on the night of our date. You kept leaving the table, and I kept filling up your glass with my drink, and then you would order me another one. Even though you are a grown man, you could have stopped drinking at any time, but you kept guzzling, and I kept filling."

"So, what does that have to do with my old money?"

"Here's the deal. I want you to buy the worthless property we hold as the collateral that your best friend left us with. I want all of the money that we gave to Goodman in good faith, plus twenty percent interest."

"You are off your fucking rocker! How about this, I sue you for trying to poison me, leading up to ruining my life."

"But you won't, and here's why. I will go to your boss and tell him what happened. It was a prank gone awry. You'll get your job back, and your inheritance."

"Why on earth would I want that worthless piece of real estate?"

"Because, you're probably the only person in this town that has the money to clean up the property. Clean it up, and it will be prime, river-front real estate. Once it's clean, you can resell it for far more than what you are going to give us. Or, do something nice for the community like build a park or a resort. The community will love you. You'll be their hero instead of an old frumpy knitter."

"You are insane!"

"Probably, but it's a good plan. Oh, and by the way, I want real estate papers signed before I talk to your boss." I could see the wheels turning in his little, pea brain behind his angry red face.

"Get out of my house."

"Your choice. But don't forget, I still have that original note that will implicate you as an accessory to Goodman's fraudulent business deals. You only have until tomorrow morning before my offer is off the table." I hadn't planned on giving him an ultimatum like that, but I was angry, too. I slammed the door good and hard as I left.

Rocco was right about one thing though. A good long nap was in order.

Chapter 42

Rocco Basham Returns to Position of District Attorney

By Stephanie Freeman, staff reporter

Nancy Higgins, spokesperson for the Lincoln County Sheriff's Office, reported that Rocco Basham has returned to his position of District Attorney. Basham was on leave of absence during an investigation concerning his misconduct leading to a DUI charge. When last interviewed Basham told reporters, "Two drinks can't get you that drunk. It's all a mistake. I'm sure someone slipped me something. I swear it was only two drinks!" It seems he was telling the truth.

"It was a prank that got out of hand," said Olivia Hope who stepped forward to explain that she was the one to slip him, "a little more than two drinks."

"We were at dinner, and he was on his cell phone the whole time," stated Hope. "He would take a call and walk away. I saw his glass was empty so I'd fill it up with my drink. He'd come back to the table, finish his drink, see that my glass was empty and order me another one, take another call and I'd fill his glass again. I don't think he was aware he was drinking so much, he's under

a lot of stress you know, with the murder of his good friend, Ira Goodman. I don't know how much he drank, but it was a lot. It was funny at first, but then I knew the date wasn't working out, so I hopped a cab and left. I'm sure it had been a while before he realized I was gone."

When asked why Hope hadn't come forward sooner, she explained that she has been a little busy lately herself. You may recall that Hope was the victim of a horrible beating by three teens who later died in a fire at Hope's home. She spent several days in the hospital recuperating. Hope said, "I hadn't heard about Basham's investigation until I returned home from the hospital. I promptly notified authorities. I couldn't let a bad prank lose him his job. That's just not right."

"I am thankful Ms. Hope came forward to explain this mess," said Basham. "I probably should have rescheduled the date since I was too preoccupied with my many responsibilities. I should have put my phone away, and paid attention to her. It was rude...Let this be a lesson to one and all," continued Basham, "Put your phone down and pay attention to your date, because you may miss a wonderful opportunity, or worse."

Since this was Basham's first offence and that he does not have a history of heavy drinking, he paid the fine and returned to work this week.

On another topic, Basham announced that he is buying the river-front property that was heavily contaminated by WR Grace Zonolite Mine. Interestingly, the property was collateral to Hope's WICA group after an investment went bad when Ira Goodman's contracting company filed bankruptcy.

"I felt badly for the women and thought I should do

something to help them out. And since I have the heart and means, I thought it would be a good idea to buy the property from them so they don't have to deal with the clean-up. Plus, I would like to give a little something back to the community."

Basham is contracting the EPA to clean up the site and is drawing up plans for a recreation area, and possibly a casino.

Small Town Woman Makes the Big Time

By Stephanie Freeman

Cabinet View News will be losing one of their reporters. Carol Cripes has accepted a position at The Enquirer, a nationally known entertainment newspaper.

Cripes grew up in Libby and graduated from Libby High School. Because her father is a Blackfoot Indian, she received a full scholarship to attend Chief Dull Knife College, in Lame Deer, Montana, where she graduated with a communication degree. She went on to Montana State University to finish her college career with a dual degree in journalism.

Shortly after graduation, Cripes, went to work for Cabinet View News and has worked for the newspaper for over two years. She will be leaving her reporting position immediately.

Landing the job with The Enquirer came as a big surprise to her as she had not actually applied for employment with them. The excited Cripes said, "I guess someone saw my talent and skills and decided they needed me. Can you imagine! It has always been a secret dream of mine to be a paparazzi and/or work for The Enquirer. I must have a guardian angel out there."

Cabinet View News wishes her well, and the best of luck

Chapter 43 - Olivia Hope

It had only been a few weeks since my WICA friends and I had been together, but it seemed like a lifetime. I called a meeting, and they had just arrived. All chattering and giggling like school girls. Blue, after greeting all the women, yawned and curled up by the fire on his new, cozy dog bed—blue, of course, the one I let him pick out. We laid out pastries and coffee, filled our plates, and settled in to get the meeting started—albeit, more about celebrating good friends.

High energy and excitement filled the room. Pamela had finally sold all her Christmas trees, and in fact, it was a major boom from other years. She wasn't sure if it was the fact that she had done a bit more advertising, or that our group had become well-known because of our recent news coverages.

Lily landed a contract for a major fundraising event in Portland, Oregon, working closely with a "rich, hunky Tom Selleck look-a-like." They are raising money for the Human Trafficking Hunters—a program started to raise money for public awareness, education and protection. I was to be one of their guest speakers.

Idaho was back to work, and because of the increased deaths lately, she was very busy—and she got a raise. It seems that she and Alan made a few good friends in the past few weeks, who had in turn, called the mayor and raved about their "helpfulness." The mayor didn't exactly know what help they lent to the community, but he was pleased to be praised for "hiring the best" employees—and well, it's election year.

Maggie didn't get her drama teaching job back with the school, but the city decided to help fund her idea for a community theater. She is hiring some of her Hollywood friends to help her. It's rumored Kevin Bacon may make a return visit to Libby for a part in one of her plays. It would be his first trip since The River Wild had been filmed on the Kootenai River. "Why not invite Tom Cruise," cooed Lily, "He doesn't need to be in your play, he can just come." Maggie threw a pillow at her in response.

I would return to teaching health and PE. Well, as soon as my bruises faded. Principal Gaylord also wants me to teach self-defense classes to the girls as well as the teachers. Evidently, he heard about my smooth moves incapacitating Anthony. I'm attending an in-depth self-defense "train the trainer" class so as not to disappoint.

Conversations rolled along peacefully. I listened, contentedly reveling in their happy rhythms, thinking how lucky I was to have these wonderful women in my life—until perky little Pamela piped up, "Olivia, you promised to tell us more about being in the WitSec Program."

"Yes, we've been waiting on pins and needles for you to tell us all about it," squealed Lily. "Tell us what happened, and don't miss any of the juicy details."

"Well, in that case," I said, "I'll need a little something stronger in my coffee." I went to the cupboard, pulled out a new bottle of brandy, and gave myself a liberal dose—several others helped themselves as well. Someone exclaimed, "It's Saturday, and we don't have anything to do today anyway, do we ladies?"

That's when Lily pulled out several bottles of expensive champagne, and announced, "I came prepared." All eyebrows raised. "Well, it's a celebration, that's for sure."

We sank into our seats, curled up on the floor and couch and chair and settled in. With libations in hand, I, once again, began my story from the very beginning—with Idaho's help, of course. I told them about my courtship with Demetri. "How romantic," someone murmured. Lily made me describe in detail "Dreamy Demetri." I told of our brief marriage and my baby Emma—I paused for a tissue.

"Oh, my god," Idaho drawled. "You have to tell them about nurse Ratched!" And so, I told them of the woman with the slicked back bun, ugly black sweater, and nasty, thick soled shoes, with a pinched face and nastier attitude. I described the woman I grew to hate, to hoots and hollers from my friends, making them laugh until tears rolled.

That gave me the courage to plunge forward to describe my baby, her sweet baby breath, and her tiny hands in mine. They sat quietly riveted. while I talked about hiding in the closet. Their eyes widened, and they sucked in deep breaths when I spoke of confronting Demetri. Pamela hollered with a loud "boo-yah" when I shot him between the eyes. "That was too good for him!" one of them said. I told them of my temporary insanity and the release of anger that followed. And how I continued to beat his lifeless body. The women asked questions, sympathized, empathized, and supported me the whole way to the end of that grizzly tale—the one that landed me in prison and into the WitSec Program.

When the time came to explain about the details of the death of Anthony, they offered hurrahs and more support for the underdogs of the world. We all spoke of our sympathy for Mrs. Bixby, the accidental victim. I left the rest of the story for Idaho to tell about our stay in the county jail. She told of our burrito breakfasts, and how we passed the time making up rap songs, singing old kids songs, and playing poker games with Sheriff Bishop—and what a sore loser he was. All the while I wondered where I would be once again, sent to who knows where under the WitSec program.

I then told them about the agents from Washington D.C., who came to interview me and how I went off the rails again and began to choke the woman agent—"

"What!!?" they all gasped.

Idaho stood and did a little drum roll, "Wait for it . . ." and then pointed back to me, and poured herself another champagne.

"Turns out it was nurse Ratched, aka, Agent Romano!" More hoots around.

"Unbelievable!" crowed Pamela.

"What the hell?" said Maggie. "I need to write a screenplay about this."

"You should write a book!" said Pamela. "Wait. That wouldn't work. Are you still in the WitSec Program?"

With that, I told them what Agent Romano had told us. About Romano working for Rizzos as an undercover FBI agent, how she told me I was no longer a threat to the family because the ones who cared were all dead and how the other family members were glad they were. They wouldn't care any longer, "Unless I made a movie or wrote a book," I added.

Huh, I thought. I had kept theses secrets for most of my adult life. It roiled in my belly turning me into an, angry, paranoid, and distrustful person. But the moment I had opened up to Idaho, I'd felt a pressure release. After I told it again to Rand and Sheriff Bishop, and yet again to Agent Romano, I was exhausted. I felt I never wanted to speak of it again. I dreaded facing my friends with this horror. But after telling them, I felt stronger. I enjoyed watching them live vicariously through me. It helped to laugh, perhaps in inappropriate places. But it made some of those moments more tolerable, instead of horrific. There were lots of questions and comments from my friends. All of them curious and all supportive. I guess it was okay to laugh about some things now. I suppose psychologists would call that healing. Whatever, I felt more bonded than ever to these women I now call my sisters.

"So, Olivia Hope," said Maggie. "I take it that isn't your real name?"

I shook my head. "It's Rachel Hansen."

"Oh, yah, yah. Very Nordic!" said Pamela in her best Norwegian inflection. "Makes more sense than being Canadian."

"How did you come up with the name of Olivia Hope?" asked Idaho.

I took a sip of champagne, "When I was sitting in Demetri's closet waiting for him to leave, and then he didn't, I began to hyperventilate. To calm myself I closed my eyes, visualized Emma, older, playing on a playground with friends, laughing, having fun, being a normal kid. I kept breathing rhythmically and saying to myself, 'I'll live, I'll live, I'll live. I swore I would, to save her life, make a better life for her. 'I'll live' became my mantra in that closet, I said it over, and over, and over. When I burst out of that closet, in my mind I shouted, 'I'll live to give you hope, baby girl.' So, when all was said and done, and I had to choose a new name, it just popped out like I'd had the name my whole life, Olivia Hope.'"

Everyone stared at me. I shrugged, "And that is how I became, Oliva Hope." They continued to stare. I added quietly, "And that is how, and why, I allowed my baby, Emma, to go live with a normal, loving family—to live without fear."

Many heartbeats later, Idaho raised her glass and shouted. "Here's to fucking living with hope! Bravo, Olivia Hope!" That started a round of toasts, cheers, tears…and more drinks. Of course, hugs were involved, too.

"Okay, enough sap," I said, jumping to my feet. "It's my pleasure to present to you the return of your invested money, compliments of Basham's purchase of our worthless collateral. The lost has been found." I grabbed the envelopes from my desk and began handing out the checks.

Idaho had hers opened first. "What is this? Did you divide this up correctly? I have way more than I put in."

"That's because it's paid back to you with interest." The women knew the property was sold to Basham, but I had kept the interest a secret.

"This has got to be at least twenty percent interest!"

said Pamela.

"How on earth did you finagle this?" asked Lily.

"Call it payback for pain and suffering."

"I still can't believe you worked a deal with Rocco," Lily said. "Did you sleep with him after all?"

"Nope. I just found his weak spot and held it till the little weasel cried uncle," I said. "Let's hear it for taking care of business."

"I didn't know the weasel had weak spots," Pamela chirped.

"Speaking of business," Idaho said. "Did you see that article in the paper about Carol Cripes moving on up, or at least out, as the case maybe?"

"Oh yeah," Pamela laughed. "What a lucky break for us."

"Luck had nothing to do with it." Idaho gave Maggie a conspiratorial grin.

"Oh, no, Idaho, we all have Alan to thank for that," Maggie winked. "He came to me and said 'da bitch, she gots to go.' He was the one with the idea. He asked if I had connections to move her out of town. I said, yeah, I know a guy who knows a guy, who owes me a favor or two. All I did was make a phone call. And the rest was fate. It's a win-win. She gets the job of her dreams, and we get some peace."

"I'm thinking you just about saved the whole town, and everyone in it, from that fire-breathing, news monger," said Pamela. "Hollywood biotchs,' watch your backs 'cause you're about to get the 'cripes' beat out of you."

There was boisterous laughter, and more champagne popping.

When the mayhem calmed, Maggie said, "Okay, back to business here. This is serious, people. Remember our conversation about what we would have done with our money?" there were nods all around.

"Yeah," I said. "But you all probably don't want any of my investing ideas anymore. Maybe we should disband WICA?"

"Hear me out first, Olivia. When you were in the hospital, we had a meeting, and we made some executive decisions."

I figured it would come to this. I hadn't handled our money well. I couldn't blame them if they never trusted me again. I let their dreams down and I'd almost lost their money. I was ready to resign. They could take their money and begin building their dreams. I nodded in understanding, ready to take my licks.

"We want to continue investing, but…" said Pamela.

"We can't take no for an answer," said Lily.

"We don't want you to leave, but we decided that this idea is the best thing for all of us right now, and for you as well," Idaho said, stepping closer to me, taking my hand in hers.

"It was a unanimous decision," said Maggie.

Whew, this was harder to take than I thought. I started to speak, to beat them to the punch, to let them know that their decision was okay by me. I wanted to say it first to make this easier for them. But I found I couldn't get it past the huge lump in my throat.

"We don't want you to leave Libby, so we've decided we are going to pool some of our money and invest in your new restaurant," finished Maggie.

"Remember, you can't say no," reiterated Idaho.

The women became so animated that their words rushed out and over me like a waterfall. Each one talking at the same time, rolling over one another's comments.

"You said you wanted to have a tiki bar and restaurant."

"…Libby's not in the Florida Keys, but..."

"…good sandy beach down by the river…"

"…Prime real estate…"

"…town needs a good restaurant"

"…architect lined up and everything..."

And so, it continued…

"Olivia! Olivia, are you okay? What is it? Somebody, get her a drink of water!"

"…is she having a heart attack?"

I didn't know what my face portrayed, but theirs were filled with great concern. The lump in my throat grew exponentially. I couldn't breathe. I had been rendered totally speechless

Chapter 44

Epilog Several weeks later Rand Dubois

I looked odd, I thought, noticing my reflection in the window. Aside from the warped glass that portrayed an abnormally large forehead, I didn't think I looked half bad. I leaned in for a closer look. But, what was so different about me? I suddenly realized, under all the hair covering my upper lip, I was smiling. I was smiling for Christ sake. When was the last time I really smiled?

Olivia had called. Our conversation was light, with a hint of flirtation. I liked that—a lot. She was going to make good on her dinner invitation. She was in fine spirits, and I had a date! Scrutinizing my face, I decided perhaps it was time to shave off this mass of fur I called a moustache, so Olivia could see that smile, too.

Still leaning far into my reflection, Sheriff Bishop blurted, "What ya see out there?" Startled, I jumped, and my chair rolled out from under me. I hit the floor hard, coffee landing in my crotch—we began to hoot. He reached out to help me up. "Sorry about that, didn't mean to make you piss your pants."

I brushed coffee from my slacks and righted the chair, muttering, "No worries my friend, no worries, eh. What brings you in today? I thought you had a meeting this afternoon?"

His face turned grim. "Yeah, meeting with my divorce lawyer."

"Oh man, I'm sorry. I'm sure it's tough. You two have been married for about ten years, right?"

He nodded. "She was my best friend. I lost my wife, best friend and house, all in one fell swoop, to a damn marketing genius. I guess he just proved how good he is, persuading my wife to run off with him like that. It's a lonely world right now, Rand."

I patted him on the back. "Not too lonely, I hope. Pamela pledged to keep you busy in the gym, and I might be spending a lot more time in town. We can hang-out more—that is, if all goes well tonight."

"What's happening tonight?"

"I got a date."

"With Olivia, I hope."

I nodded.

"I'm happy for you. It's about time. I was starting to wonder if you were going to be joining a monastery, or something. That's good. You deserve a good woman."

"Thanks, but it's just a date. No big deal."

"Right," scowled Bishop.

"I was just off to go get a haircut and a shave."

"Hm, just a date, no big deal, huh. You're shaving off your handlebar masterpiece? Who won, by the way."

"Yours truly, took first place," I bowed. "My prize is a new razor. While the Doernbecher Children's Hospital is six thousand dollars richer."

"Hey, dad," said Alan, poking his head in the door on his way by.

"What the…?"

Alan kept on trucking.

"Whoa, whoa, whoa, young man. Where do you think you're going? Get in here, and let me have a look at you."

Alan popped into my office and slid into a chair. I'm sure my mouth gaped open like a dummy. All his red, thick curls that splayed over his shoulders and halfway down his back were—gone! He'd traded in his beanie cap for a curly Tom Cruise cut. And, he was wearing a suit and tie! He looked very handsome and…and… professional. He was no longer a boy. A man sat before me steepling his hands, exuding confidence as if he just accepted his next Mission Impossible.

"You… you, look great! What's going on?"

"I have a job interview in Missoula today."

"Interview?" I was astounded.

He nodded and grinned. "I submitted a resume to be a sketch artist for the Missoula County Court. I got an interview. While I'm there, I'm registering for criminal justice classes with a minor in art."

"Congratulations, son," said Bishop shaking his hand. "I knew you'd make the right choice."

My breath hitched in my chest, "Right choice? Criminal justice?" I blanched. "What on earth made you choose that?" My mind reeled as I thought of my fragile son exposed to all the unsightly things he would surely witness. Facing all the horrible dredges of the world. I was sure his poor mother was rolling over in her grave.

Bishop closed in on me, with a hand on my shoulder, he whispered, "Time to cut the apron strings,

Dubois. He's becoming his own man. Let him make his way."

"This is what I want. You're the one who told me I needed to go back to college, and figure out what I need to do with my life. I've made a decision, dad."

"Yes, but—"

"Relax, dad. I can handle it. Sheriff Bishop and I talked about this. He thinks I have the skills to be a great detective, like you. I want to be of service to the living, and help the dead."

Bishop nodded.

I was stunned.

"Dad, when I unearthed that little boy, Brian, I had to reach way down to the depths of my soul to put all of this into perspective. I could have flown out of my mind and drove myself crazy with the what and whys of shit like that. But when I surfaced again, I brought back a sense of calm purpose to my life. When I talked to the parents of that boy, I felt the peace and closure they finally got from a horrific violent crime. You were the one to show me that helping people get through times like that is rewarding work. There is a lot of pain with it, but you just need to put it in a safe place to deal with it as you can—another thing you taught me. I've helped a lot of people in the last few weeks with my gift. That has been rewarding for me, too."

"So, I'm going to go back to school, take some classes, hopefully get the sketch artist job, and make pizzas until I graduate."

"But, you'll be alone. By yourself."

"No, dad. You'll be alone, but you'll be all right. Besides, Idaho is going to take some classes, too. So, she'll be with me in Missoula occasionally."

"See," interrupted Bishop. "A good woman by his side. The young man will be just fine."

I suddenly understood the meaning of empty nest syndrome. And I didn't like it. Not one bit.

"Oh, my! Rand, is that you? What happened to your mustache?" asked Olivia.

"Like my smile?"

"Yeah, it's really different. You, ah... I mean, you were handsome before, albeit in an old-fashioned sort of way with the handlebar moustache and all. But now, you look, um—younger. You turned your barber quartet image into a sort of Russel Crowe'ish... sexy."

She said the word, sexy, soft and breathy, which made me all tingly inside. I think I stood a little taller, but struggled to keep the old flag pole under control. As a distraction, I said, "So, we're headed for The River Bend?"

"Yep," she said with a flip of her long, beautiful, blond hair as I helped her slip into a cozy, white parka—which covered up a slinky, lacey sweater thingy. "It's steak night." Zip, went the coat and I followed her to the car.

The steaks were cooked to perfection, and the company was sublime. Only a half hour into easy small talk, and we were scheduled for a skiing date for the following weekend. So far, so good.

I watched her speak. Her face was beautiful. Her skin was creamy, and she smelled like gardenias, with a hint of lavender.

She stopped talking, "What are you looking at? Do

I have something caught in my teeth?"

I shook my head, "No, I was noticing how nicely the bruises disappeared. Lucky that you have no lasting scars, either."

"Except on my skull." Her hand brushed the side of her head.

"How have you healed mentally?"

She shrugged, "I'm down to only one nightmare a night. I suppose that's something. I have some great friends, who check on me several times a day—everyday. I'm fine really. I take great comfort in knowing I don't have to run anymore, and that all loose ends are tied up in a nice neat package."

"Yeah, I guess. There is one thing. I still don't know why Goodman would buy a construction company under a fake name. None of that makes any sense."

"Oh that," said Olivia, as matter of fact. "It makes perfect sense."

I dropped my fork, "No, it doesn't!"

"Yes, it does. I think Goodman bought the company so that he could launder his money. I bet he was saving to run off to the Cayman Islands."

"What? What do you mean he was running off to the Caymans?"

"Sure, I was talking to his secretary. She told me that he was beginning to act weird. I think he was losing it."

"She never said anything like that to me!"

"You have to ask the right questions."

I shook my head and frowned, "Well, weird, how?"

"He always wore a suit and tie, always professional, right? That was his brand. She told me he showed up to the office one day in just some t-shirt and undershorts."

"Oh, there's a visual."

Olivia giggled—it was a sweet sound, "I know, right? Anyway, she said he was disoriented and agitated. Basham had to come get him and take him home. I wonder if, maybe, he started losing it after he murdered that poor child. Perhaps, in his own sick mind, he figured he'd cut out of Dodge before he got caught, disappear, change his name, and move far away. I'll bet you'll find a hefty bank account in the Grand Caymans in the name of Christopher Dumas."

"He could have done that without buying up a failing construction company, though."

"Rand, he was losing it. He wasn't in his right mind. Crazy people do crazy things. Check out the bank account. Just sayin'."

I grunted. She had a good point. "You're pretty good at this stuff. Ever think about going into law enforcement?"

"Na. Too dangerous. I'd probably accidently shoot someone." She winked. "Hey, Idaho told me that she's going to start taking some agriculture classes online from U of M."

"Hmm, so I've been told. She'll be corrupting my son by staying with him on weekends, and during her labs," I groused.

She giggled again—and it made me smile. She said, "How do you really feel about it?"

"My boy is growing up. Bishop says I need to let him go. I had my reservations at first, but after seeing him so cleaned up today and sound so mature and all, I think it's time."

"They're good together. I've never seen Idaho so happy. And, I'm confident he'll take good care of her. He's head over heels for her. The dweeb even asked for my blessing to keep seeing her after Goodman's case was closed." She put her hand on my arm, and the tingles came back in spades. "You raised a good man, Dubois."

The waitress brought us another glass of wine. "I'm having a good time," I said.

Olivia nodded, "Rand, there is something that's been weighing on my mind that I've been needing to talk to you about."

I froze, dear god, I hoped she wasn't about to confess to being at Goodman's house the night of the murder. I sure as hell didn't want to have to throw her back in jail. Not now! I had to head her off at the pass. "Listen, don't fret about things that happened in the past. Goodman wasn't a nice man, and I'm sure he got what was coming to him. Just drop it, leave it alone. I don't want to talk about it anymore."

She sighed heavily. "Do you think those poor boys got what was coming to them, too? I don't think so. None of them had a chance for a normal life, as long as Goodman was alive. I'm not sorry about his death, but I sure wish I could have saved them. Especially Seth, he was a sweet soul, who had a monster for a father."

"Between you and me, and I'm sure this is going to sound cold and cruel, but I'm thinking it's not such a bad thing that those boys died. Certainly, not the way they died, but I see it as they are now set free. I've been around the block a few times, Olivia. I've seen abuses beyond belief. I don't know that some people can be saved after what they had been through."

"You don't think people can change? I wanted to be able to help them, Rand. Maybe I could have made a difference with them."

"I really don't know for sure if people can change or not. I don't think anyone really knows. But I can tell you this, Olivia, I saw that life had been cruel to them, they had been abused to the point of no return, they were damaged, and they would continue to damage others the same way for the rest of their lives. Look what they did to you! Sure, I also thought that Seth was a good kid, but he'd been abused time and time again. You didn't see the cold look on his face in video as he plunged the fire poker into his father's chest. I think the anger he had was not the fact that his father had abused another boy, but more that he betrayed Seth. We'll never know for sure, of course, but he was headed for jail. His tender soul would have been crushed under the boot of another prison monster. And what about Josh? Josh would have killed you for sure. Premeditated murder—and he almost succeeded. Even if you had the money he thought you did, and you gave it to him, he would have still killed you. I've spent my life tracking down people like him who never change. Ever watch Dexter? Can you take the serial killer out of the boy? I don't think so. Olivia, some people just need to be locked up, or die."

She was silent for a good long time. "Goodman needed to die, that's for sure."

"Yeah," I said. "He did. And Goodman was abused as a boy, too. So, don't dwell on the past. And don't do anything stupid that would land you in jail by confessing to a prank gone bad."

She smiled at me and put her hand on my arm again, "Oh, honey, why would I confess to something as stupid as that?"

I deserved that. I was a little more than embarrassed, but I breathed easier all the same.

"As I started to say a minute ago, I have something I need to talk to you about."

"Okay, shoot—oh, wait, bad choice of words. How about, what's on your mind?" She looked so solemn. "Hey, what's wrong?"

"Nothing is wrong. I just want to ask a favor. Remember I told you about my daughter?"

"Yes, and I'm so sorry you had to leave her." I put my hand on her arm this time—got the tingles again. "It had to have been the hardest thing in the world to do. But, under the circumstances, I think you did the right thing."

"Thank you, Rand, really. But I've never been able to get over it. So, this is my favor. Now that I don't have to run anymore, I want to find her."

I pulled my hand back. "Are you sure that's a good idea? I mean, she's got a good life now, I'm sure. What is she, about eleven?"

"Twelve years, three months, sixteen days and," she looked at her watch. "Ten hours and twenty-six minutes."

"Impressive. But, do you think that this is really good for you?"

"Rand, I don't want to interrupt her life. I just want to know that she is well, and happy. I really want to know who her parents are. I'd like to just see her. I don't even have to talk to her. I want to see her smile… please,

Rand? Can you find her for me?"

How could I resist those beautiful baby blues?

I nodded, "Sure, kiddo, sure."

With tears welling in her eyes, she jumped from her chair and planted a long, lingering smackaroo on the old kisser. And then she slipped off to the restroom. My smile spread as wide as the room. I thought, I could get used to that.

When she returned to the table, we turned to lighter subjects. "Have you returned to work yet?"

"Yeah, I have. But it's not the same. It feels weird. I don't feel like I fit there anymore. It feels hollow somehow."

"Perhaps it's the after effects of the adrenalin rush that you've been living with for the last few weeks, even years. You've been through a lot. Maybe a little post traumatic syndrome?"

"Could be some of that, but I don't think I ever really enjoyed teaching that much. I've totally loved the kids and all, but I was just kind of thrown into this job because of the WitSec Program."

"Is there any other profession you might be interested in?"

She nodded thoughtfully. "You know, I've never been able to stand the cold winters in this country. Minnesota was bad, Chicago was worse. I would've liked to settled in the Florida Keys. I wanted a tiki bar. But WitSec sent me here." She paused for a long moment. My heart began to sink a little. Was she thinking of leaving? "I've had my heart set on white beaches, warm green ocean water, and drinks with little umbrellas. So, I've been planning some things."

Shit, I thought...

"My friends presented me with an option. At first I was against it, but after I thought about it, I might be able to work with it. They want to invest in my tiki bar. They have set aside some money to get me started. We've all been researching property. I'm meeting with an architect from Seattle next week who has done a lot of work in Florida and Mexico. I'm really starting to get excited about the idea."

My heart sank.

"Rand, are you okay?"

"Yeah, great, that's great news," I said, trying to snap out of my sudden funk. I'm sure my smile had faded to a grimace. I probably looked like I was having a heart attack. Wishing I could hide from what my face was giving away, I longed for the cover of my moustache. I couldn't believe I was having so many feelings for this woman, and now she was talking about moving away. Far away.

"Well," she sighed. "Want to hear the name I picked? You'll be the first to hear it."

I tried to swallow the lump in my throat with a sip of wine. "Sure, what is the name of your new restaurant?"

"I want to name it... drum roll please..." I did the drumming on the table and opened my palms to her.

"Montana Tiki."

I blinked a few times.

"Well, what do you think?"

"There's a bit of dichotomy with that title."

"I know, right! That's what makes it so great. I was thinking about it. I don't have to leave all my friends to move to an overrated beach in the south of Florida. I can bring the beach here to Montana."

"Here, in Libby?"

"Or Kalispell, or Missoula. Like I say, we're hunting for property. But I'd really like to keep it in or around Libby if possible. You know, bring in more tourists. But think about it, everyone gets so depressed around here in the winter months when it's so dark and gloomy, and not many can travel to Florida or Mexico. I can offer an oasis in the middle of the tundra! I'd like to have an indoor wave pool with a bar that opens to it. Make it all tropical like, and then in the summer I can slide open some big doors to be right on a real beach. Doesn't that sound like paradise in Montana?"

My heart was beginning to beat again. "It sounds like a dream come true," I said, smiling real big, again. And I thought, I don't need no stinkin' moustache. I reached over to give her a congratulatory kiss, and spilled her wine in her lap.

Chapter 45
Epilog, Olivia Hope

I stood in the restroom wiping off my sweater and pants. I smiled, recalling the look Rand had on his face when he spilled the wine in my lap. Poor guy was nervous, that's for sure. I was thinking how thankful I was to Rand when he said "yes" to finding my daughter. Most of my nightmares had been about someone finding out she was alive. Maybe Demetri's family would take her away, maybe they would shoot her, or worse, sell her into prostitution. I had to get some peace. I felt a whole lot better knowing that Rand was there for me. I thought, I could get used to that.

I freshened my lipstick and was fluffing my hair when a woman walked in behind me. "Well, hello, Olivia Hope," she said as if I was a long-lost friend.

"Hi, and you are…?"

"Evelyn Marcs. I work for Sotheby Realtors." She pulled a business card from her purse and handed it to me. "I heard you were looking for some property to build a restaurant."

"I'm all ears," I said.

"I believe I have what you're looking for. It's at Bull Lake. As you may know, Bull Lake has a growing population. The population count is even more than Libby now. This property is in the best location for a restaurant like yours. It's on the highway to catch tourist traffic, plenty of land to build and for parking. It faces the best view on the whole lake!" She sounded almost more excited as I was at the thought. But, of course, I probably couldn't afford what she was selling. It sounded too good to be true.

"Sounds pretty spendy," I said.

Eyes twinkling, she said, "That's the best part. It just came up, and I thought of you immediately. It's a steal for ten dollars. Are you in?"

"You mean ten hundred thousand?"

"Nope," she said shaking her head. "Ten bucks."

I was suddenly disgusted with this twit standing in front of me. "Listen, I'm not picking up what you're puttin' down, lady. Whatever con game you're trying to run isn't going to work on me. Stop wasting my time. Go find some other sucker." I turned back to the mirror, shaking my head—silently cursing her.

She cleared her throat. "A tragedy happened there. A death in the family. The wife just wants to dump the property. I don't think she liked him much. Bad memories and all." She huffed, "Who could blame her." I looked at her reflection in the mirror. Her smile hadn't faltered. "Oh, and isn't it a shame that big beautiful house that sat on the lake burned to the ground?"

My eyes narrowed, "What house…?"

"Why, Ira Goodman's house, of course. The bad man's house. I think they said it was arson or something. Just happened this morning. Didn't you hear?" she paused, smiling as the realization began to hit me. "What better place to build your restaurant, for a deal of the century. And the cherry on top, the house—well, I

452

should say the property with a big fireplace surrounded by ash and snow—is all part of the deal."

Still skeptical, I asked, "And just what do you get out of it? Why don't you scarf it up? Make a big profit?"

"A deal like that would be against the law if I bought it before it was on the market. Oh, it's not like I'm not getting something from the sale. The seller is seeing to it that I'm compensated well. Did I mention, the stipulation for the sale by the seller is to offer it to you first?"

"What... are you saying?" I was stunned.

She winked, "Karma's a bitch. Don't you think?"

After the initial shock, I began to envision my restaurant built on Goodman's property. I began to laugh, "Oh, the irony."

She held out her hand for a hand shake, "I thought you'd see the opportunity."

I said, "You know, you could have lead with that first."

"Nah, the look on your face right now—priceless. This was much more fun," said Evelyn Marcs. "I'll see you tomorrow for the signing."

By the time I got back to the table, Rand had received a message that he needed to return to Bishop's office—seems there had been a fire earlier. He was needed to help question a possible arsonist. I told him about my visit to the restroom.

We sat in silence all the way back to my house, with goofy smiles on our faces.

"So," said Rand. "Do you think I should throw the book at this arsonist? Or congratulate him on a job well done?"

"Just don't be too hard on the guy," I said. "I got a feeling he was compensated well for it. Something tells me, he probably won't be doing it again any time soon."

"It sure was a beautiful house."

"Rand, it was a house of horrors! I can't think of a better way to cleanse it."

Rand nodded.

"Hey, I think you need to come to my house tomorrow night so I can prepare a dinner entrée for you that I'll be serving—in my new restaurant." I smiled.

"That will be built on your ten-dollar piece of property," Rand winked. We laughed. It felt really, really, good.

"It's a date," said Rand. He reached into his pocket, and handed me an envelope with my name on it.

"What's this?" I asked.

He shrugged, "I'm not sure, but Agent Romano asked me to give it to you when things calmed down. I just wished things would have calmed down sooner."

I sat wondering what on earth Romano would want to give me. "Mind if I don't open this just yet?"

"Not at all. It's yours. It's none of my business anyway." He reached over and kissed me softly, sweetly. I smiled big, thinking, we have another date.

Once in the house, I called Idaho over to help me celebrate. We skyped the other women, and we all drank a toast to new, and happy, lives—filled with adventure and excitement. Blessed be my friends.

The envelope remained unopened.

I was awakened the next morning by a tap-tap-tap sound. I pulled on my clothes and stepped on to the porch, where I saw a woman in Mrs. Bixby's yard pounding a stake into the ground. She hung a sign on the post.

"Hey," I yelled, making my way over to her. I could see it was a 'for sale' sign. "What's up with this?"

The woman introduced herself as Mrs. White, a realtor from Spokane, and Mrs. Bixby's sister. "Arlene has decided that this town is too small for the both of you."

"Well, that's just stupid," I argued. "She doesn't have to move! I'll move!"

"No, no, dear. Although, that is a sweet gesture. Listen, my sister hasn't been the easiest to get along with since Mr. Bixby died. I've been trying to get her to move to Spokane with me for a long time now. I think this—well, this last episode between the two of you—finally convinced her. I'm tickled pink, sweetheart. She's going to be just fine."

I felt water coming to my eyes, "It's weird," I said. "But, I think I'm going to miss her."

She smiled sweetly, and patted my arm, "What a delusional young lady you are. Why, she won't miss you at all, dear." She turned and climbed the steps onto Mrs. Bixby's porch. Mrs. Bixby peered at me from the dining room window. I lifted my hand and waved good-bye. Mrs. Bixby waved me the middle finger.

The envelope remained unopened.

I went to the grocery store, and the post office, and I stopped for a mani-pedi. When I returned home, Blue greeted me at the door. He was excited to see me, giving me wags and kisses, until he finally calmed down enough to sniff the grocery bags. Swish, swish went his tail knocking the envelope off the coffee table and onto my feet. Blue lifted it in his teeth, looking at me like, "Are you going to open this already?"

I took it from him and tore the envelop open. It was a short note from Romano. My breath caught in my throat. I sat down hard on the couch. The room spun, and I began to sob. When I could finally contain myself, I lifted my cell, and punch in a number."

"Hello?"

I tried to speak but nothing came out.

"Hello, hello? Damn solicitors." The phone went dead.

I got myself together again and redialed.

"Hello!" came an angry voice.

"Don't hang-up!" I said. "It's me, Rachel." I silently cried, "…I know, yes, I know. I've missed you so much, too, daddy."

###

Special Thanks To:

Karyl Landeau
Dawn Holbrook
Gina Mazzotta

Karyl, you are not just a fantastic writer, you're also an exceptional editor. When I handed you my manuscript, you had it back to me within just a couple of weeks. Way ahead of schedule. You had it thoroughly edited, and had excellent suggestions along the way. You have an eagle eye, and amazing attention to detail. You possess a true gift. I highly recommend your work.

Dawn, thank you for helping me to gather my "darlings" to send them to their proper and peaceful burials. I have learned so much from you.

Gina, thank you for your feedback and special insights. Thank you for taking the time out of your busy schedule to critique my work. Also, I have you to thank for keeping me on the financial straight and narrow.

Thank you all for your editing, corrections, comments, reviewing and support. I couldn't succeed without you.

Thank You, Readers!

Thank you so much for taking the time to read Frozen Assets. Please, please, leave me a review. The more I hear from you, the better I can continue to delight and entertain you. I look forward to hearing from you. Please email me at anita@amillerwriter.com.

About the Author

Anita Miller lives in a small town along the Columbia river near Portland, Oregon. She also has roots in Libby, Montana. She is a member of the AWAI. When she isn't writing—or preparing taxes, you will find her traveling, hiking, biking, golfing or walking with her husband and golden retriever, Alvin.

Made in the USA
San Bernardino, CA
24 December 2018